Praise for Chequered Justice

"A chilling tale set on the twin tracks of motor racing and justice, exposing the hazardous pit stops of one against the systemic pitfalls of the other, in which truth becomes the loser."
Michael Mansfield QC - Barrister for the Birmingham Six miscarriage of justice appeal

"As bold and innovative as its author, *Chequered Justice* gives the reader a breath-taking guided tour of race-track suspense, lifts the lid off lethal insurance brokers, exposes the bent nature of law enforcement, and dives into the depths of emotional whirlwinds, I loved it"
Howard Marks - aka Mr Nice

"A fantastic read whether you're a racing fan or not - a proper page turner... highly recommended!"
Ed Foster, Associate Editor, MotorSport Magazine

"...a compulsive read... could well have a future on television or ...even a movie."
Leslie Phillips OBE

"Ex-racer John Bartlett's first novel charts the nightmare of wannabe racer Will Middleton as an insurance-indemnity scheme rebounds on him. Sinister high powers seem to be plotting against our hero, as the tale often veers into 'faction'..."
Haymarket Publishing - Autosport

"...*Chequered Justice*... a chilling Kafka-esque tale that sees the hero, who begins with a confidence in his own innocence and an absolute faith in the fairness of the British justice system, frustrated and defeated at every turn... The dust jacket for *Chequered Justice* claims the story is "inspired by true events". If even a 10th of this book is true, we should all feel very afraid indeed."
The KM Newspaper Group

"I would recommend this book for the plot ... be concerned about the corruption that is portrayed in *Chequered Justice,* be assured it really does go on!"
Inside Time

D0452802

First published in Great Britain in 2010 by
The Book Guild Limited, Brighton, BN1 1UF

Paperback edition published by Amazing Journeys Limited

Paperback typesetting in Baskerville by Nick Ebdon Limited

An environmentally friendly book printed and bound in
England by www.printondemand-worldwide.com

A catalogue record for this book is available from
The British Library

Paperback format ISBN 978-0-9569104-0-0
Hardback format ISBN 978-1-84624-524- 4
Kindle eBook format ISBN 978-0-9569104-1-7

*To my wife Mary, my sons George and Jonathan,
my friend JS (aka Piglet) and the four per cent
who spoke the truth but were denied justice!*

Childhood is measured out by sounds and smells and sights, before the dark hour of reason grows.

John Betjeman

Author's Note

From December 1988 to March 1997 a series of strange events overtook our lives, bizarre happenings that would later be dismissed officially as a string of coincidences, flukes and regrettable errors. These errors were destined to dramatically derail my life and that of my family, changing our perception of the justice system forever. For reasons that may become apparent (despite living in a country with supposed free speech), I am not permitted to publish my full and factual account of the proceedings, but I am allowed to write a novel or a fiction based on them ... what follows therefore, is a novel based purely on personal experience.

John Bartlett

Acknowledgements

My sincere thanks go to those who stood by us when our world collapsed, particularly Alan Madge, Terry and Liesbeth Bennett, Dirk Schoysman, Simon Payne, Paul and Sue Rush, D&H, Dr Roger Eve and Jonathan and Amanda Stevens.

My thanks also to all the test readers who helped to correct my various dyslexic drafts of *Chequered Justice*, especially Hilary Wilkes, Pauline Cutts, Steve Treherne and the ladies of the Tonbridge reading group: Liz Dawes, Gabriele Wight, Denise Cosedge, Yvette Nagle and Joan Shipley.

But my greatest thanks go to my wife Mary, for standing by me when my world plunged into darkness and who saved me at my blackest moment; a very special lady who was strong enough to have put up with my dreaming and, despite all my failings, has loved me in a way no one else ever would.

Prologue

Childhood never ends. The games just get bigger.

Old English proverb

Cavendish Place, Brighton, England. Spring 1962

Stretching off to the horizon, the dark green waters of the Channel glistened in the afternoon sun. A few flecks of cream crested the swell and overhead the ever-present gulls circled tirelessly. A small boy made his way up the slight incline towards the Claremont Hotel. He was wearing short grey trousers, a red school blazer and a matching cap which was perched on tousled golden hair. Both socks hung at half mast, their garters purloined for the creation of some highly secret weapon. His skin was freckled from the sun and his knees were scuffed.

It was Friday, the end of yet another long school week. As usual, it had ended with Will joining a small group of trembling boys outside the headmaster's study on the first-floor landing. Mr Wickham, the head, was a stickler for discipline and had an enthusiasm for boxing. In a world of rigorous rules, infringements of any kind usually resulted in a thrashing either in the school boxing ring or bent over a desk in the study.

That week Will's infringements had been as numerous as ever: bad reading, inexcusable spelling, illegible hand writing, terrible mathematics homework and a generally appalling attention span. According to Mr Wickham, punishment for violation of discipline was the only true route to scholarship and he dispensed that punishment with relish to all the boys in his care. It would be many years before dyslexia, from which Will suffered, would be formally acknowledged. Will was just seven years of age; destined

1

to live out the rest of his school life at the back of a classroom, lost in his dreams, six strokes of the cane or three rounds in the boxing ring the typical end to most weeks. Will quickly learnt that authority was not always fair.

He defiantly pulled free from the firm hand that was attempting to lead him and stood transfixed before the sports roadster that was reversing in front of his father's hotel. His frustrated minder was the fifth in the line of nannies, and in keeping with the tradition already set by the last four had just handed in her notice.

The door of the car swung open and a distinguished-looking man with a trim moustache and long sideburns emerged and made his way up the steps of the hotel. He wore an open-necked shirt and his thick collar-length hair was swept back from his face.

'Mister,' Will called, motioning towards the car, 'what car's this?' The man turned but did not get the opportunity to reply. The firm hand of the minder administered a thunderous slap to the back of the child's head.

'Who's that man?' Will enquired, through clenched teeth.

'That's Mr Hill. He's a famous racing driver,' hissed the frustrated nanny. 'He's staying at your father's hotel.'

Will had heard of Graham Hill. He was the man who had just won a big race at Goodwood. In his father's *Daily Sketch* he'd seen the pictures of the huge crash that had almost claimed the life of another famous driver, Stirling Moss. It was the start of the swinging sixties, the classic era of Formula One, the time of world-class drivers like John Surtees, Jack Brabham, Dan Gurney and Jim Clark, when legends were being created. To the boy it sounded exciting, with characters straight out of his Boys' World Annual. He decided there and then that he too would be a racing driver.

Before the nanny could stop him, Will stuck the stubby thumb of his free hand against his freckled nose, poked out his tongue and waggled the remaining outstretched fingers mischievously. The guest, head cocked, did not immediately respond. Then, slowly, he raised his thumb to his own nose and, his face breaking into a broad grin, returned the salute.

The nanny gave a self-conscious nod of apology to the future

Formula One, Indy and Le Mans Champion, and dragged the boy off to administer further retribution.

The guest smiled at the boy who, now under firm control, grinned back. 'I'm going to be a famous racing driver when I grow up!' the boy announced. The nanny shrugged dismissively, 'I doubt you'll survive long enough to get a licence Master Middleton!'

Sandown International Race Track, Melbourne, Australia. 20th November 1988 (26 years later)

The sun beat down relentlessly on the packed spectator enclosure. The rev counter flicked as the Hilton-sponsored DFV-powered Tiga accelerated hard out of the esses and down the back straight, effortlessly scorching to 180 mph as it approached the end of the straight. The 200-metre board flashed past in a microsecond. Cocooned within the thin fibreglass shell, swathed in fireproof Nomex, Will twitched his right foot across to the brake pedal, viciously punching 180 lbs of pressure to explode the pads onto the discs. His right hand snatched third gear as Jochen Mass the race leader in the Works Sauber Mercedes shot past, turbos popping, flames billowing.

Suddenly the Tiga twitched violently and without warning slewed sideways across the track, sending up a rooster tail of dirt. Will's race was over. Inside the ferocious heat of the cockpit he removed his damp helmet, peeled off his fireproof balaclava and three-layer Nomex gloves, and eased himself into the bright Australian sun. For Will Middleton, the last race of the 1988 World Championship had ended with suspension failure.

He was frustrated but hardly surprised. After all he was an underdog in a runner-up team driving an unreliable car, there for one purpose only, the glory of taking part. It contrasted so sharply with his previous results that year in the National Championship: four wins and five lap records; the best season of his career.

This was Thatcher's 1980s, the era of the young corporate whiz-kid, the yuppie; the time when individual bonuses easily topped a quarter of a million pounds. Companies had been growing exponentially and hostile takeovers abounded. The euphoria had been infectious and it was an incredible time for an up-and-coming racing driver to secure corporate sponsors. Merger mania and leveraged buyouts had generated phenomenal sums as companies raised massive amounts of capital by selling junk bonds with a high risk of loss but also an irresistibly high rate of return for those willing to gamble.

With total disregard of risk, and looking only to satisfy shareholders' hunger for bigger and bigger dividends, the pension and insurance industries had gobbled up their share of junk bonds, the billions of pounds generating further hostile takeovers as the bubble continued to grow. It had been the banner time for the stock market, everyone apparently winning. But if everyone had been winning, it meant nobody was losing ... so money had been generated from nothing. No one had wanted to consider the obvious, that the bubble might soon burst; logic had spiralled into a black hole of delusion.

Will and Beth had been home almost a week when Ned, Will's broker, arrived at the Old Granary. The bell in the hall rang and Beth opened the door. 'Good morning, Ned,' she said, as she took his coat. 'Will's in the lounge. He's not in a very good state.'

'How did all this happen?' Ned asked with a genuine look of concern.'

'He's done something to his back falling off a damn race horse! We were in Malaysia having a few days' break before returning home after the Australian race.'

Will was wrapped in a blanket, heavily sedated and lying as flat as possible on an old grey recliner. Glancing up, he grimaced as a fresh spasm of pain lanced through him – his lower body felt as though it had been set in a rigid cast. The day was damp and overcast which seemed to only exacerbate the pain. A fire crackled in the grate. In the corner of the room a computer hummed, its screensaver bouncing a multicoloured cube endlessly around the confines of the small silver screen.

Will grinned at Ned but didn't attempt to rise. 'I wasn't even moving when I fell off the bloody thing!' he said, reliving the agonising moment in his mind, with all the locals dashing around the accident scene. It happened in a moment, but those seconds were to run endlessly through his thoughts, like a series of still frames in a movie. Coming directly to the point, he added, 'I suppose I'm insured?'

Ned sat down, flipped open his briefcase and began shuffling pages of small print.

'Oh yes. Comprehensively. It's just that, well...' Ned looked past Will and for a moment he seemed distracted. 'You know, "back injuries".'

'You don't say!' Will replied dryly with a lift of one eyebrow.

Ned shrugged. 'Sometimes insurers like this just don't like paying out, and currently the industry is not in good shape.' For more than fifteen years, Ned had worked extensively in the shadowy world of the exclusion zone, before finally setting up his own brokerage in the sleepy town of Arundel. 'This type of accident policy was devised back in the boom period,' he went on. 'Thatcher's recession was never anticipated and risk to the underwriters was considered to be very small. If I submit a claim that's when we'll find out how good your cover is.'

The door of the lounge swung open and Beth deposited a pot of coffee and plate of shortbread biscuits on the table. Will drew in another uncomfortable breath. 'Ned, I don't have much choice, I can hardly walk, never mind drive a racing car. I'm likely to be out of it for weeks, if not months. I'll have to put in a claim.'

'I'll get onto it first thing tomorrow,' replied Ned, 'but be prepared for delays. The staff in the claims departments are little more than paper pushers, it's their job to review applications and if possible reject them there and then. It may take a lot longer than you think.' He added ominously. 'They're a bit of law unto themselves.'

It took a further six months before Will was, incorrectly, cleared to race again, but that mistake was just the beginning of the nightmare to come.

It was the end of the 80s and the country's buoyant economy had already turned; the era of the yuppie had come to an end. The Maxwell pension fund reported hundreds of millions of pounds missing and other similar funds were said to be on the verge of collapse. Endowment policies, designed to pay off mortgages and provide lump sums for retirement were found to have been mis-sold and worthless. Likewise, the junk bonds wolfed down by the insurance and financial industries were living up to their name.

The entire British financial system was sliding beneath a sea of debt and appeared set to take everyone down with it. More than fifty thousand businesses a week were now going bust and the insurance industry, with its fingers in many of these financial pies, was even being sued by its own underwriters. Claims were running into hundreds of billions of pounds. In short, this was the start of a massive increase in claims and a dramatic drop in profits, a time of huge redundancies and record unemployment.

Underwriters and shareholders had to be accounted to, very powerful people were due to take hits. Inevitably those making claims would suffer, but it was a sacrifice the industry was willing to make.

1

October 1992

The Wapping presses never ceased. The press hall occupied an area the size of a football field, housing sixteen massive machines; the noise, heat and smell were oppressive, particularly in summer. The presses were living, breathing monsters, consuming millions of kilowatts of power each day, existing on sensational stories and the misery of others; stories of sex, sleaze, murder, politics and political spin. There was a never ending supply; today was just another edition.

It was the night shift, a balmy October evening, the busiest time; more than three million copies of Britain's favourite tabloid had to be printed, cut, collated and distributed before dawn. By midnight, front pages would be sent by courier to every 24-hour TV news channel, allowing each to present a quick review of the next day's headlines to an audience greedy for gossip, desperate for sensation and fresh scandal.

The printer's routine had not changed in the past fifteen years. As he'd done countless times before, he flicked a switch on his console. Overhead a conveyer whirred, diverting a finished tabloid from the main belt, a few seconds later it rattled down a chute into his booth. He opened a page at random; it was page 3, it usually was page 3! He scrutinised the colours, the alignment and the curvaceous body of some nubile eighteen-year-old with brand new silicon breasts. He felt guilty and quickly scanned the page for something else, something short: '*WPA Bank pays racing driver £4000 for bouncing cheque*'. Huh, he thought, how many of his cheques had his bank bounced, and each time charging him for the privilege. He scanned the short article, checking for print density and quality, ignoring the content.

Lee Burton was twenty-eight, short, trim and ambitious. It was 9.30 am, a little early, but he wanted to be prepared. He slipped on his jacket, straightened his tie, and collected the claimant file and the newspaper he'd purchased that morning. Stepping into the lift, he was whisked up to the executive floor. An hour previously he'd sent a memo to his boss, the head of claims, but within minutes it had been relayed to Alexander P. Finnigan, the Chairman and Chief Executive of the WPA Group.

Nobody liked it when Alex Finnigan (Fin behind his back) got involved, but following the BBC exposé, there was little choice. Fin's reply had bounced back almost instantaneously:

Meeting, my office at 9.45 today. Tell Burton to bring the article and the claimant's file. I need hard evidence that Middleton was working during the currency of the claim; send in surveillance, we will need to attract the interest of the police.

Fin had been chairman of the WPA Group for more than twenty years. At almost seventy, the ravages of a stressful city life were written into every pore of his being. He sat in his darkened office hunched behind his cluttered desk, his face wrinkled like an old leather bag. Behind him, resting on ornate Corinthian columns, perched two globes, one celestial, and the other terrestrial. On the wall hung a portrait of his father, the former chairman.

A visit to Fin's office was not generally considered a pleasurable experience, but following his discovery, Lee relished the thought of making his triumphant entry. He had been working in the banking division of WPA for more than eighteen months but this was his first break. He had been responsible for agreeing the out of court settlement, but after reading that the claimant was a racing driver, out of curiosity he'd punched the claimant's name into WPA's main database. What he found was intriguing. The claimant was supposed to be out of work, and according to the computer he was claiming on a WPA PPI policy, yet the newspaper said he was racing endurance cars.

A secretary showed Lee in and shut the door firmly. Fin worked

8

in the shadows; nobody outranked him. He liked solitude and closed doors, it gave him a sense of security. Myopic eyes and an overbearing glare were augmented by a pair of heavy horn-rimmed spectacles. 'Sit.' He spat the word without lifting his eyes from his desk, as though to a dog. There was no offer of coffee, no good morning and certainly no word of congratulation. So much for the triumphant entry, Lee thought, beginning to feel a little less confident.

'You have the article?' Lee handed over the tabloid, the heading reflected in Fin's thick lenses: '*WPA Bank pays racing driver £4000 for bouncing cheque*'. Fin, his nose only inches from the story, appeared almost to sniff the words from the page.

The WPA Bank yesterday agreed to pay racing driver Will Middleton damages of £4000 for incorrectly bouncing a cheque valued at just £18.00. Will, who lives in a half million pound manor house, complained to the bank when the cheque, payable to his local corner shop, was mistakenly bounced. When a second cheque was also bounced in error within days Will, who races sports prototypes in the World Endurance Championship, threatened legal action. WPA, who claimed it was due to a computer error, settled out of court.

In the brief time since receiving Lee's memo Fin had done his research. The claimant was out of work and WPA's payment protection division was being shafted for the monthly mortgage payments. They were also picking up the monthly finance on the family's car; the claimant seemed to have too many convenient WPA PPI policies. He was clearly insolvent, no savings and all bank accounts were heavily overdrawn. A quick check showed he'd also had an on/off claim running with WPA's sister company for a back injury. Fin scanned a confidential internal report on the back injury, mumbling to himself as he inhaled the words, 'He's broken his back!' If that was true, the claimant was potentially eligible to claim a hefty lump sum. Fin turned back to the newspaper article. *If his back is broken, and he's out of work, claiming to be redundant, how is he racing at all?* A vicious grin touched his lips. He put the paper down and fixed Lee with a glare, then repositioned his horn-rims for a look of self-importance.

'You signed off on this settlement?' it was a rhetorical question; Fin already knew Lee had authorised the settlement. He went

9

on, 'This claimant is seriously in debt, hanging on by his fingernails. He was close to bankruptcy, he needed a shove, the heat turning up, not a handout! There was no way he could have sued us.'

'But he *was* suing us...' Lee responded, 'with a WPA Legal Cost policy.'

Fin's complexion changed from its usual pallor to a fetching crimson, his lips quivered. 'He was suing us using one of *our* legal costs policies?' he seethed, his words catching in his own saliva.

Lee took a deep breath. 'There was no other option, it was checkmate Sir. Either we settled, or we went to court paying both his and our legal fees. Combined costs would have been four times the settlement figure and we would have lost the case anyway. We have no defence for bouncing his cheques; at the time his account was in credit.'

Fin swept away Lee's reply angrily. 'Cases are not won or lost on evidence alone. More that some lawyers are smart, others not. This unknown racing driver is having a laugh at our expense. He's claiming for both injury and redundancy ... how? He doesn't know his back is broken, only that he has an injury of some kind. Our policies contain wonderfully nebulous words, it's called small print. Use it!'

'But he has a claims negotiator, and they suspect something; they are asking for the report,' Lee insisted.

'An ambulance chaser who thinks he's a lawyer,' Fin replied with a curt wave of his hand, fixing Lee with a cold stare. 'You're confident this Will Middleton is the bastard who set off the BBC Consumer Alert fiasco?'

Lee nodded. 'Absolutely, we know for a fact; he warned us in a letter that he'd written to the programme, there's a copy in the claim file.'

For a long time Fin said nothing. To Lee the darkened room chilled, the walls appearing to close in; even the books, files and very fabric held their breath, waiting for Fin's response.

Over the years Fin had woven his network like strands of an invisible silk web; strands that extended in all directions throughout big business, manufacturing, retail, pharmaceuticals, the City, the legal system, police, and even a few judges; decent people who could easily be persuaded. Hands could be shaken, backs scratched, words dropped in the ears of willing officials at Lodge dinners.

Fin began softly, as if the room might be bugged, 'Do not release the specialist's report, it's ours. Bury it and find reasons to delay the redundancy payments, turn up the heat and stop paying his bloody car finance.' His voice rose. 'I want that car repossessed, I want him watched, I want to know everything. I want all the dirt, every skeleton, all the background, his family, where his kids go to school, the lot. If he scratches his fucking ass, I want to know!'

2

A police officer who carries out an investigation, invariably and properly, forms a view as to the guilt of the suspect. Having done so, without any kind of improper motive, he may be inclined to shut his mind to other evidence telling against the guilt of the suspect or to overestimate the strength of the evidence he has assembled.

(Sir Cyril Phillips, Professor of Oriental History and architect of the Crown Prosecution Service. Reproduced from *The Case for The Crown* by Joshua Rozenberg)

January 1993

The house was large and the surveillance had been difficult, at least that's what he'd told Fin. The private detective worked from a small terraced house in Kent and had spent almost three months on the case, hiding in the shadows, rummaging through the rubbish and talking to the locals. He'd even tracked the target's wife each day as she took the kids to school in their bright blue Mitsubishi. It had been a long and profitable job, but costs didn't matter. WPA had deep pockets and their instructions had been clear. 'Get the evidence!'

His close watch team, no more than shadowy shapes unseen by the target, had been called in as a last resort after two months of stake-outs by no fewer than three other surveillance operations, each resulting in assertions that the target appeared completely genuine. It was not what Fin had wanted to hear. WPA was a worldwide organisation, the principal provider of payment protection, the target was simply a claimant and a troublemaker.

The target had appeared a little shorter than the detective had been led to believe during Fin's briefing which was odd. The target's hair was darker, which was also odd but of minor relevance. What was important was that the spooks had secured the evidence that the others had been unable to unearth. Clearly

12

they'd uncovered a nice little fraud. The target was obviously fit despite claiming both injury and redundancy payments from WPA. The report the detective had produced confirmed that the target was out every day exercising horses and mucking out the adjoining stables. For a small additional fee the detective could provide Fin with video evidence of the crime. It was conclusive proof that the target couldn't be injured.

On the 18th of January 1993 the detective faxed his report to Fin's office at WPA and within days edited highlights, prepared by Fin, went to an appropriate contact within the Metropolitan Police. Days later a raid would take place, followed by a trial to determine the guilt or innocence of the target. But well before that, an inconvenient discrepancy would be found in Fin's report.

Climping, Sussex, approximately 9 months later

Will shivered; it was a cold, dark, unfriendly October night. He wrapped his jacket around him tightly and checked his watch; it was 6.15 pm. His two sons were with the sitter and his wife was working late; he knew he wouldn't be disturbed for at least another hour. He opened the fridge, selected a bottle, discarded the cork and placed the bottle to his lips, downing a quarter of the wine in a single swallow.

In the garage, he collected the garden hose and stuck one end into the exhaust pipe of the Mitsubishi, running the other end through a crack in the rear passenger window. He got into the car, took another deep swallow from the bottle and started the engine.

He felt miserable, yet strangely relaxed, suddenly much calmer, as if all the fears of the past months, the accusations of the private detective, the police taunts and hints, the raid and suspicions, had just been lifted. Soon he would be dead and the physical world with all its pain, would cease to exist. Everything that had been Will Middleton, his thoughts, hopes, dreams, the love of his wife Beth and his children, would simply fade away.

The faces of the detectives flared up in his mind like whispering demons, their sneers and words had haunted him for months: *'You're going down Will, you'll see... Admit it Will ... you're just making it harder on yourself.' 'Perhaps we should take a look at your*

13

wife's involvement then... If we arrest her as well...' 'One might have to consider the custody of your children. Why put them through all that Will? All we want is an admission. Save everyone a lot of heartache!'

Will had expected the case to be dropped the instant the private detective's mistake had been discovered, his faith in British justice being so strong, but for some reason these officers had decided to run with it and they wanted a result. It was as if he'd slipped through a gap in reality into a nightmare. Suddenly he was the criminal; hearsay, gossip and rumour abounded, endorsed by the very system he had grown up trusting and had always believed in.

Will knew he'd done nothing wrong, but the investigation had been the final straw financially, and had already destroyed the new race team, despite the result at Zolder. More than any of that, his family, totally innocent bystanders, were being threatened, dragged down with him. Perhaps with his death they would avoid the humiliation that would otherwise follow.

His eyes streamed as he wrote his goodbyes to Beth. His writing was scribbled, spidery, barely legible. He loved her so much, oh how he'd loved her; could she ever understand, he thought. He felt so very sad, but he couldn't go on any longer. It seemed that for some reason he'd been singled out as a scapegoat, but to bring him down these officers were prepared to implicate Beth, and even to take away their two sons.

He prayed to God to forgive him and inhaled deeply. Holding in his breath, he exhaled slowly. He wanted to die, to drift slowly to sleep, to see his father again. He gulped another quarter of the wine.

The engine continued humming but nothing seemed to be happening, he just felt slightly drunk. He stumbled to the back of the car. The hose had fallen out and lay coiled in a loop on the ground. He quickly stuffed it back into the exhaust and returned to the driving seat.

At last it was working, he was dying. The agony would soon be over. The pipe behind his head emitted strange bubbling sounds and the windscreen misted over, rivulets of silver condensing, then streaking down like rain. Sparkles of white light flared around him as the noxious fumes permeated his lungs. In his mind, his wife's smiling face appeared and he felt his heart pound. The air was moist with exhaust; the stench of death thickening with each minute, every breath gagging in his throat. He took a last gulp of wine and emptied the bottle.

Suddenly the passenger door opened and Beth jumped in, a big smile on her face. 'Hello, darling! Where are we going?' Her gaze swept around to the hose poking through the rear window. 'Oh my God! Will!'

Will had planned a private suicide, just turn the key and drift off to another, less hostile world, but for some unaccountable reason Beth had decided to finish work more than an hour early that night. He leaned against her shoulder, broke down and wept as they hugged and cried together. He felt embarrassed, like a naughty schoolboy caught raiding the fridge. Later that evening the family doctor prescribed anti-depressants. Together Beth and Will vowed to fight on, to get through the ordeal as a family.

The trial, set for 11 months' time, had proved to be the death knell for the fledgling race team. Over the weeks that followed, all that remained of the ill-fated Trans-Atlantic project was gathered up and meticulously packed away, like discarded toys that had lost their appeal.

Everything was going to have to go and that included the Sierra 4x4 estate car. Will cast an eye over the impressive Trans-Atlantic graphics and the still shiny metallic paintwork. It was worth little more than scrap, he told himself, having been seriously damaged, its back end destroyed when a local farmer accidentally slammed his Land Rover into the parked car one rainy day just a few weeks earlier.

A loving hand touched his shoulder. 'Come on darling, dinner's ready.' Will looked over at the two primary assets of the team, a pair of Lola Indy racing cars, proceeds of the Zolder race. They had just been returned from workshops in Weybridge where they had sat in storage since Trans-Atlantic's last race just two months earlier. 'It's all going to have to go,' he said in a mournful voice, glancing back to Beth. 'You never know, if we're lucky it might just about clear the team's debts.'

Will went over to the scarlet, day-glo Lola T86 Buicks. One of them still bore his name on its carbon bodywork. They looked as beautiful today as when they'd been collected almost a year earlier, like a pair of Formula One cars that had overdosed on steroids. He lifted the rear body panel and for a moment examined the 3-litre Buick V6 turbo engine, capable of producing more than 800 horsepower on full boost.

Will replaced the engine cover and threw a dust sheet over each car in turn, then tapped a four-digit code into the security pad at the front of the garage. A motor whirred into life and the twin-roller shutter doors descended, curtains closing on a final act.

3

Where there is a will to condemn, there is evidence.

(Jung Chang, *Wild Swans*)

Beth smiled, her hand tightened encouragingly around mine. She was always kind. We had originally met at our local judo club some eighteen years earlier. I had been keen on the sport since childhood but only taken it up seriously since my eighteenth birthday, following the recommendation of my best mate Des. 'It's the most amazing way of picking up the birds,' he explained.

Des was a first Dan black belt and ran a club in Worthing. 'The dads bring their innocent daughters to me to learn the art of self-defence. I teach them the basics,' he said with a roguish grin that required no further elaboration.

When it came to meeting girls I was not as accomplished as my mate. In fact I was shy and naive, having been brought up in a family that felt it was 'not nice' to discuss the complexities of the opposite sex. Unfortunately this outdated attitude did not prepare me for life, as I found to my acute embarrassment on my first trip abroad with a group of friends.

We'd travelled to Benidorm on a cheapie lads' holiday of booze, sun and, hopefully, bikini-clad girls, the four of us crammed into a room the size of a matchbox. The small en-suite bathroom was equipped with all the usual amenities, including what I had been told was a footbath.

Returning from the beach, I decided to avail myself of this luxury. There I stood innocently rinsing the grains of sand from between my toes when one of my mates appeared in the doorway. To my confusion, he proceeded to collapse amid hysterical laughter, while pleading for his mates to bring the camera. To my embarrassment, the resultant image was destined to do the rounds, popping up at every conceivable opportunity.

Regrettably Benidorm was a week of rejections, embarrassment

17

and acute hangovers coupled with a savage awakening of my digestive system. But I was left with a burning determination to investigate the hidden delights of the opposite sex.

The local Judo Club provided the ideal opportunity and within twelve months of Des's tuition I had secured my brown belt along with a Masters Degree in ground techniques. When not helping out there, Des and I would tour the south coast judo circuit in search of local talent. It was on one such sortie that we stopped off again at our local club.

A new girl was being enthusiastically introduced to the gentle art by one of the blue belts. The poor girl was barely able to remain on her feet for more than a few seconds before being unceremoniously dumped with a thud onto her rather attractive rump, followed by her eager partner who had appeared to have become an expert on ground holds.

'Her name's Beth and that's her younger sister Barbara.' Des pointed to a blue-belted girl in her early teens. 'Their father died years ago. They live with their mum and two other sisters in Littlehampton. Beth's the best one though, Littlehampton Carnival princess! But I wouldn't bother wasting your time with her, you don't stand a chance. Stuck up little thing. I know. I've tried.'

She was a little brunette who would make any of the guys stop in their tracks for another look. I wasn't surprised Des had been given the cold shoulder. She was unlike most of the girls that frequented the clubs. Not at all stuck up, just shy and reserved, and Des was far from subtle. I watched from a discreet distance. Despite her petite frame she fought like a tigress and there was a glint of fiery determination in her eyes that would not be extinguished, despite the somewhat unorthodox lesson being administered.

It was 9.30 pm and with the mat packed away I finally plucked up enough courage to make my move. Not a particularly striking move, but it worked.

'We're walking downtown to the Chinese, if you fancy something to eat?' I inquired as casually as I could. The Hong Kong Garden was only a five-minute walk downtown, our usual haunt following the weekly three-hour workout. The food was plentiful and, for a restaurant, the beer was cheap.

Beth turned to her sister for support. 'We could do,' she replied shyly.

It was 10 pm by the time we arrived and the Hong Kong Garden was packed. John Lennon was playing in the background. A cute teenage waitress showed us to one of the few remaining tables at the far back, nearest the kitchen. 'Beers all round?' Des asked.

'Just water for me, please,' Beth replied softly. 'And a coke for you Barb?' she said, turning to her sister.

I smiled at Beth. 'Only water, don't you fancy a beer or coke?'

'No thanks, I only drink water.'

I could read Des's thoughts. *Never get anywhere with a girl that doesn't drink!*

A few minutes passed and the waitress returned carrying a tray of ice-cold beers. She actually smiled at Des as he ordered his chicken curry and house fried rice. 'I'll have the same,' I said, 'but with a couple of pancake rolls.' I turned to Beth, who was still studying the menu. 'What are you having?'

'We're not very hungry,' she said, turning to Barbara for acknowledgement. 'We'll just share an egg foo-yung please, but no mushrooms and no rice.'

'I'll have to remember that for our next date,' I said, smiling, 'you dislike mushrooms and only drink water!'

She cast an uneasy look at her sister but said nothing. I gave Des a knowing glance, a glance that said *I've got a date!*

'How is it you say "I love you" in Chinese?' asked Des, admiring the retreating waitress's narrow waist and slim legs.

'Wu ai lin,' I replied, without thinking.

'Can you speak Chinese?' Beth asked, clearly impressed.

Des cast me a knowing grin that quickly turned to a snigger.

'Er, no not really...' I spluttered, unconvincingly. 'I just know how to say that.'

'What ... "I love you", in Chinese! Why would you learn how to say that?' she asked curiously.

'He used to have a Chinese girlfriend,' Des said helpfully, taking a long swallow from a tall glass of beer. 'She liked him to say it during moments of...'

'That was a long time ago!' I interrupted, my trainer heel colliding hard with Des's shin.

'Shit, that hurt!' he exclaimed. 'What the hell was that for?'

Beth flushed slightly as the answer to her question became clear.

Des flagged down the teenage waitress and requested her phone number. The request was firmly refused, and he settled for another round of drinks. 'Just halves for me from now on,' I said to Des, causing his eyebrows to rise. Beth ordered a second glass of tap water.

The food arrived, Lennon continued singing and Des drinking. By the time Lennon had moved on to singing *Woman* all the food had gone, Des was barely coherent and the teenage waitress was hiding in the kitchen, actively avoiding him. Des declined the suggestion of coffee and Beth surprised us by moving on from glasses of cold water to cups of hot water.

I sat next to my future wife Beth, listening to John Lennon's poignant lyrics – lyrics that I was utterly unaware would have such significance in my life.

4

The phone erupted on the bedside table. I'd slept late, it was 9 am. I answered, trying to sound alert and awake. 'Hi, Will, it's Toby. There's a problem. The police want to interview you again.'

Toby Jackson was in his mid thirties, recently married and a partner in a firm of solicitors based in Southampton. As the family's solicitor he'd handled everything from drafting wills to the purchase of our home, the Old Granary, so it was to Toby that I'd turned immediately following the police raid. I sat up, suddenly fully alert, like a child awakened from a bad dream. 'What? Now what are they after?'

'They've been taking a look at this Prize Indemnity scheme that you and your co-driver were involved in. They want to see you at Chichester, tomorrow. I'm sorry Will... I think they are going to charge you again.'

My heart sank. I felt sick. Why? Now what was I supposed to have done? I'd been expecting the current charges to be dropped, not extra ones added.

'Toby, tomorrow's my youngest's sixth birthday. Can't they do it another day?'

There was a long pause. 'Barnet's been taken off the case.'

'What?'

'The CPS are evidently not happy with what he's prepared, I think they're trying to bolster it up by bringing in extra charges. There's a new guy been drafted in to head up the case, a Detective Sergeant Probert. I don't know much about him but he's apparently not your typical form-filling target watcher. They say he gets results; "old school". He's just returned from Florida. He's been out seeing Mr Mamet.'

'Oh, great! David Mamet hates my guts. He thinks I stitched

21

him up over the Brands Hatch and Zolder races. Toby, you advised us on the Prize Indemnity at Brands and Zolder. Are you quite sure everything was okay?'

There was a pause. Toby cleared his throat, then continued, 'I provided the legal advice. As far as I could see all the contracts were correct and legally sound...' The phone crackled and for a moment Toby's voice was lost in the static. Unbeknown to us, a few hundred metres away a man parked in a lay-by adjusted his earpiece and checked his recorder.

'Sorry Toby, there's something wrong with the phone line, can you speak up?'

'We'll talk about it tomorrow. Probert wants you at Kingsham Road police station in Chichester for 11 am. Don't worry; it just looks to me as though they're trying to brace up a crumbling case.'

'Toby, this really is getting beyond a joke, it's like being made to act out some bizarre part in a bloody film plot. I should write a book about all this one day.'

5

If a police officer approaches an inquiry with a pre-conceived notion, he is liable to see only those facts that fit his pre-conceptions. Such an attitude can result in a lost conviction or, even worse, an unjust conviction.

(John E. Heymer, Royal Fusiliers, retired, Monmouthshire Constabulary Scenes of Crime Officer)

It was the first Friday of the month, 4th March 1994; our youngest's sixth birthday. The day was warm and sunny. Beth drove me to Chichester to buy treats for Jonathan's party. I'd arranged to meet Toby outside the local magistrates' court for 10 am. He appeared promptly, dressed smartly in a businesslike dark grey suit with a white shirt and blue tie. We walked the mile or so to the Kingsham Road police station. Buses rumbled down the dusty street, spewing clouds of diesel over the busy shoppers. Women laden with shopping dragged reluctant, bawling offspring to yet another store.

As we approached the police station, Toby slowed and turned to me. 'Will, there's something very curious going on. Why suddenly, more than twelve months into the investigation over your injury, have they decided to drag up the Prize Indemnity again? And why interview just you? The Prize Indemnity was run by Trans-Atlantic wasn't it?'

'Yes.'

'And Rob Allan and Terry Thompson were the directors of that company?'

'That's right.'

'Have you ever been a director of Trans-Atlantic?'

'No, not a director, but I was involved with Rob in getting the company set up.'

'I assume it was Trans-Atlantic that paid the Prize Indemnity premium?'

'Yes. In fact it was Terry Thompson who invested around ten

thousand pounds into the team and those funds went directly to pay the Prize Indemnity premium.'

'Fraud is defined as an "*intentional* deception made for *personal* gain". The Prize Indemnity was based on an undisputed race result and there was no *personal* gain.' Toby shook his head. 'If for some reason they arrest you, I can't see how they can avoid arresting Thompson and Allan as well. Will, they're going for you in a very big way. I recommend that you decline to comment any further. Just answer "no comment" to any questions until we find out what the hell's going on.'

We entered the red brick Victorian building and were greeted very formally by a pair of officers. Toby shook hands and performed the introductions. He proffered a card. 'Good morning. Toby Jackson of George Evans and Crowthorp, I represent Mr Middleton.'

The detectives were both in their late 30s and spoke with East End accents. I studied the close-cropped heads, the dark suits, the broad shoulders and protruding beer bellies. They looked more like bouncers than detectives. They flashed some ID.

'Are you Will Middleton of The Old Granary, Climping Street, Climping, West Sussex?' Probert, the larger of the two, asked formally.

'Yes, I am,' I replied.

'Will Middleton,' he continued, 'I am arresting you for obtaining by deception the sum of £160,000 from the Track Star Insurance Company.'

'What?' I exclaimed. 'Obtaining what?'

'I must advise you that you are not obliged to say anything, but anything you do say will be taken down and may be used in evidence against you. You have the right to consult with a solicitor. If you do not have a solicitor present, one will be appointed for you.'

I turned to Toby, the only one present with a legal background, but he was busy studying his shoelaces. My heart throbbed and my legs felt like jelly. I struggled to hold down my rising apprehension. If they were now going to overlay the other trumped-up charges with the complexities of Prize Indemnity, would any jury ever see through such a tangled web?

The two officers escorted me down the corridor and into an interview room equipped with table, chairs and recording equipment. The floor was tiled and the walls peeling. The only light came from an unshielded lamp that hung from the centre of the ceiling. There are times when you instinctively know, however innocent, that fate is about to release a very large bucket of shit on your head. The knowing smirk on the accompanying detective's face was telling me that time had arrived for me. Whatever they had in store, it was going to stink.

Detective Probert switched on the tape recorder and the small spools of the machine turned slowly, absorbing the sounds of the tiny room. He appeared to have second thoughts and reached across the table to flick off the record button; the tape weaved into a tiny noose as the spools stopped abruptly. 'Before we begin let me ask you a question, off the record. Can you think of any reason why you might be targeted?'

I glanced over at Toby, but Probert just pushed on. 'Does anyone hold a grudge against you?'

It was a curious question. I'd learnt the hard way at least once that nothing is ever off the record. The need to reveal my thoughts had to be resisted, but was he referring to my suspicions over the investigation? Or my worries over past business acquaintances; both Rob and Mamet had axes to grind. For years I'd worked in a highly predatory environment and there had also been a fair share of litigation. I'd battled it out in the civil courts and usually won. Over the years I'd picked up more enemies than a wild dog has fleas.

In the past I'd always supported the local police and I didn't like the idea of stonewalling an investigation, yet since the Metropolitan Police raid I'd developed a profound distrust of what was going on and was unsure about confiding in these two detectives, new to the case. But who else was there to speak to? I glanced at Toby for inspiration but he was busy counting ceiling tiles. I suddenly felt very alone; the room seemed to chill further. Their attitude hardened. I'd been advised to say nothing; I'd do as I'd been instructed. 'No comment.'

'We're trying to give you an opportunity to help yourself,' Probert replied.

'No comment.'

'Fair enough.' He cast a knowing look at his colleague and flicked the recorder back on.

Probert took a deep breath. 'We would like to start by asking you a few questions. The interview will be recorded. When we have finished the interview, one tape will be sealed and will remain as a back-up. If you or your solicitor require a copy, one will be made available for you. I must remind you that you do not have to say anything. Is that clear?'

'Yes.'

'When we have finished this interview we intend carrying out a second search of your home The Old Granary.'

I turned to my solicitor. 'Toby, all the defence documents are at home and it's my son's birthday party today.'

The detective interrupted. 'We will naturally ensure we do not examine documents that carry legal privilege.' Picking up a sheet of paper, Probert glanced in my direction and sighed deeply. 'Been a little industrious in the past year,' he said, adopting a more cynical tone.

I shrugged, 'I don't understand.'

'Well, I am going to show you some documents. The first is exhibit 3002, a photocopy of a Trans World invoice, for the purchase of one Porsche Spyder racing car.' Probert slid the document across the table. Toby's eyes quickly scanned it. 'Do you recognise this document?'

'No comment.' I replied.

Detective Probert flashed an anxious look at his colleague. They were clearly disappointed, but he pushed on. 'If we look at the date of this invoice, you will see that it has been typed in the British format; day, month, year, not the American format; month, day, year. Mr Middleton, did you produce this document?'

'No comment.'

Probert closed his eyes. 'Mr Middleton, are you intending answering no comment to all my questions?'

An intriguing question, I thought: if I answered yes, presumably the interview would terminate, and we wouldn't know what the hell they were trying to get at; if I replied 'no comment', they would have to continue and show us their hand.

'No comment.'

I don't recall quite how long the interview lasted before the officers finally gave up and turned off the recorder. Until my solicitor's phone call of the previous day, everyone had expected the charges to be dropped, not new ones to be added. I had cooperated fully earlier on with the investigation and had spent two days with the former officer, DC Barnet, giving taped interviews, but he had now been removed from the case. The two new detectives seemed intent on trying to find some way of rekindling the investigation.

I was placed in the back of a police car and driven the short distance back home to Climping. By the time we arrived, the celebrations for Jonathan's sixth birthday were in full swing. Beth had her hands full, with more than twelve boys and girls greedily stuffing their faces, occasionally escaping from their chairs to run screaming round the table.

The two detectives busied themselves working their way through the house, but the second search of our home proved as unsuccessful as the first. The wardrobes and bedside cabinets had revealed no bizarre personal habits, always so useful in persuading an otherwise respectable middle-class suspect to comply. There were some more papers to collect, a few more bank statements and my passport, but nothing more.

With the search completed, the two officers walked slowly towards me. Detective Probert's eyes narrowed and he smiled. 'Now we'll take a look in the out-buildings, Will,' he said knowingly.

I tried to work out why all this was happening. I tried reading the body language of the officers. It was something I'd always been good at – reading behind the looks of the men in power, and I usually managed to second-guess the thinking of the marketing men and company directors. It had often given me the edge when trying to secure a new sponsor, but trying to understand the motive behind what these officers were doing was totally beyond me.

We stepped outside and they immediately made their way to the garage.

'Why are you doing this?' I asked.

'Because we can,' was the abrupt reply.

'What judge is ever going to believe all this nonsense? You know about the riding accident and you know the reason I was unemployed.' My voice was cold, clipped with barely controlled anger. They stopped, turned and looked at me, sarcastic smirks on their faces.

'Oh, I think *our* judge will understand,' the other detective pronounced the emphasis, relaying both the warning and threat of the trial to come.

'But you know I've done nothing wrong. I can prove I'm

innocent. You seem so determined to prove me guilty you're not even looking at the facts.' There was little point in raising my voice, they appeared to enjoy confrontation, and they knew they were getting to me.

The response from Detective Probert was low and venomous. They were clearly still annoyed about my refusal to comply at the taped interview and having found nothing of interest during the search. 'Innocence is for a jury to decide. It's my job to interpret the facts, not yours. You might "appear" to be very guilty, proof is not what's important. Doubt's what's important. You'd be surprised at how it works. You will be treated very sceptically; we on the other hand, will be treated very politely. Listen to me, Will...' he growled, the stench of stale coffee hitting my face, his finger pointing accusingly, 'you're going down; I want you to get used to that. Think about it, that way it won't be quite such a shock for you when it happens.' He glanced over at his colleague, grinning, 'A bit like being made to act out some bizarre part in a film plot, don't you think?' He turned back to face me, 'You could write a book about all this one day ... when you get out.'

I tried to think where I'd heard that phrase before. Then I remembered my phone call of the previous day with Toby. The shock of what Probert had just said made my blood run cold. They couldn't admit to a phone tap, but he wanted me to know they *were* listening, they knew everything I was doing, every word I was saying. Now I said nothing, just punched the code into the security pad on the garage wall. The motor whirred as the doors lifted.

The sweet aroma of methanol fused with silicone and exotic fluids wafted out. Both detectives stepped into the garage, like children eager to enter Santa's grotto. 'What have we here then?' Detective Probert asked.

I looked down at the sensual scarlet curves formed from carbon, aluminium and Kevlar, all that now remained of Trans-Atlantic Ltd. A pair of gleaming, day-glo red projectiles, capable of firing a man from zero to 240 mph in less time than it took the detectives to say '*We know your type!*'

Since the first raid, rumours had spread like shockwaves from an earthquake. One by one the team's backers had withdrawn or were simply not available, or had reconsidered their marketing strategy, or were having cash flow problems, or were reconsidering their positions, or, or... Well, trust is everything in this business; without trust there simply is no business. Trans-Atlantic collapsed – its foundation destroyed. With no money to pay for storage, the cars had been parked up at the house since November 1993, a few weeks after the curtain had finally dropped on the Trans-Atlantic team, four weeks after I had attempted to pull the plug on my own life.

We'd hoped that at least one of the Lolas could be sold to clear the team's debt, but the detectives had other ideas. 'We're confiscating these cars as the proceeds of crime.' The second officer stepped over and tapped the front Goodyear with a sturdy boot before adding with a chuckle, 'At least you'll be able to get your car into the garage tonight. Er, don't suppose there's any chance of borrowing the team's truck to move the cars?' I didn't bother to answer.

The judicial system requires that all defendants accused of heinous crimes attend regular pre-trial hearings, hosted by the Honourable trial Judge. In my case, such events were informal affairs at which the learned judge would amuse the court with legal anecdotes and tales of corruption in which I was the central character. On such occasions, Judge McGaea's speculation inclined towards how I'd funded my former life.

A regular topic of debate and conjecture was the judge's apparent belief that I might in fact be some kind of drug baron and that hauls of booty were likely to be secreted around the world in various numbered accounts. DC Barnet had needed little encouragement. He would happily have nipped to Switzerland to get his Timex fixed if the taxpayer was covering the bill. The hard-working lawman had been despatched, globe trotting in search of my hidden millions. They were never found; none existed.

On these little get togethers, rules of court etiquette decreed that I sit quietly with my mouth firmly shut. Equally, convention expected the learned judge to reach decisions based on fact, not outside influence, suspicion or conjecture. George Lampton McGaea was not a conventional judge, and the reasoning behind his next ruling would only become clear much later in the proceedings during his summing up.

'It has come to my attention that Mr Toby Jackson, the Defendant's solicitor, provided legal advice to the Defendant in matters relating to the Prize Indemnity scheme. I am not happy for Mr Jackson to continue to represent Mr Middleton at trial.'

At the time nobody thought to ask a very obvious question; how could His Honour possibly know that Toby had provided the legal advice on the Prize Indemnity? It had happened some eighteen months earlier and the advice given by Toby had been at a face to face meeting. Nothing appeared in any court bundles, so how could the learned judge be aware that Toby Jackson was the solicitor who provided the legal advice?

Toby's law firm was not a big practice. It comprised just three lawyers but had recently expanded and now had offices in both Southampton and Salisbury. Jackson, Evans and Crowthorp were undoubtedly the biggest of the local practices and had a good reputation in the community.

They had acted for Team Capricorn, my old race team for many years, and during the last months of its life had vainly attempted to recover the outstanding accounts from reluctant debtors who had one by one, during the turmoil and financial burnout of the late eighties, gone bankrupt. With their knowledge of Team Capricorn's collapse, they had been the natural choice to defend me following my arrest for defrauding WPA. For over twelve months Toby had worked, cross-referencing exhibits and becoming familiar with all aspects of the case. Now, with only weeks to go to the start of the trial, McGaea had edited out my only ally.

6

There are some acts of justice which corrupt those who perform them.

(Joseph Joubert)

London, September 1994

The shops were still shuttered when we arrived in London. The journey from Climping had taken less time than expected. It was 9.30 am on the first day of the trial and my defence team had not yet arrived. A mixture of excitement and apprehension flooded through me as we entered the drab court building. I was still expecting the trial to be dropped at any moment and offers of compensation to be put forward.

A plume of smoke hovered around the small group of security officers that stood relaxing by the reception desk. 'Middleton ... Will Middleton,' I stammered nervously.

The officer drew heavily on his cigarette, then examined his clipboard. 'Court One ... but there's no point in going up till ten at earliest.'

The building had originally housed a carpet warehouse until the mid 1980s when the apparent huge increase in crime had resulted in the need for additional courts. The conversion of the former warehouse to a Crown Court was intended only as a temporary measure, but the spectacular collapse of the economy had clearly tightened the public purse, as well as forcing the liquidation of my former racing team. It was now ten years later and completion of the new Crown Court buildings was not expected until the following year. This was a desperate, depressing place.

I welcomed the opportunity to clear my name. Eleven months had passed since my suicide attempt, some eighteen months since

31

the horrific day in February the previous year, when the still of the Sussex morning had been shattered by the dawn raiding party. 'Operation Coverall', Detective Barnet had named it, and he was proud of his creativity. Of course, it's everyday practice for the police to give a code name to such activities, a name that reflects the nature of the operation. 'Operation Coverall' appeared to refer to my having insured family and self against every eventuality, not in itself a criminal activity. We could not help wondering if in truth the operation was a euphemism for something altogether more sinister, an internal operation to sanitise a massive police bungle.

When a storm breaks, we all follow our own nature: some, like a rabbit caught in a headlamp beam, freeze in abject terror; others flee; some may try to hide. Rob Allan my former co-driver was in the first category. Having been raided simultaneously, he was terrified and had been jumping at shadows ever since.

Of course they could have begun an inquiry in a far less dramatic way than with a dawn raiding party, but then it was all part of the tactics ... to establish how serious the matter was. For the raiding party, there were the health and safety issues to consider, the risk assessments, a need for back up officers and support personnel. Equipped with radios, blue lights flashing, the raiding party struck both our homes simultaneously under cover of darkness, like the SAS storming the Iranian Embassy. Nobody could have been in any doubt they must have been dealing with a very serious criminal, certainly not simply a disputed insurance claim. In the sleepy village of Climping it was big news and the news spread quickly.

Unfortunately for the raiding party, both Beth and I had been away for the weekend and weren't due back until midday on the Tuesday, so my mother, who had lived with us since my father's death, had to contend with the interrogation. She was over eighty and scared to death when, at five in the morning, they forced their way in, flashing badges and warrants at her and my sister Sue.

On our return we discovered the office furniture had been moved. Books had been taken from their cases on the wall and now sat in piles, their pages flickering in the breeze of the still open window. Someone had attempted to use the Xerox machine, but it had jammed in protest. It hummed testily on the table, its power still switched on, its display flashing error. Files lay where they had been thrown in heaps; a snowstorm of papers fluttered across the once organised desk.

Since that day, and at the insistence of the Honourable Judge, every detail of my past life had been systematically dissected, scrutinised, filtered and documented. Disappointingly for the Crown there had been no trace of foreign bank accounts, no deposits of gold bullion, no shares in offshore companies, no hoards of drug money, nothing.

The cost of the investigation to the taxpayer of around two million pounds somehow suggested the depths of my deception. The cost to me and my family had been much higher. Our life lay in shreds, the investigation had stripped away all foundation of dignity and credibility. Rumour and speculation abounded.

I flicked a glance at my watch: 9.40. Beth and I strolled hand in hand to the court canteen to await the arrival of my defence team. My new solicitor, Jonathan Barker, had arrived and was sitting studying the latest batch of prosecution papers which had only been delivered the previous day.

My heart sank at the sight of a huge pile of new documents that the Crown had served only hours prior to the start of the trial. It ran to several hundred pages and had been prepared meticulously by a crack team of Crown Prosecution lawyers. There were too many documents, and they'd been filed way too late, but the Honourable Judge McGaea had magnanimously made the concession after apparently hearing strident arguments from the Prosecution. From the outset I had been portrayed as a major criminal causing the Crown considerable additional work, and His Honour had judged it was only right that such arduous labours should be rewarded and admitted into evidence – hours before the trial.

I viewed the fresh mountain of papers with all the apprehension one might reserve for a mugger. At the sound of our footsteps Jonathan looked up; clearly sensing my mood. 'Don't worry, the last-minute disclosure of documents is a favourite trick of the Prosecution,' he explained. 'At the last possible opportunity, especially in the week prior to trial, they simply unload an extra

33

van load of papers on the defending solicitor's desk. It's purely tactical. They're just trying to rattle you. How are you feeling?'

For somebody with an outwardly blustery personality, the truth was that I was rattled, overwhelmed and secretly out of my depth. Mixing with big groups of people, and being expected to give evidence in public to a court full of strangers, was to me a terrifying and daunting prospect. I have never been one to show feelings easily, and away from the spotlight of the race track tended to be quiet, laid back and in truth a bit of an introvert. Fortunately, the Prozac and Propanarol, prescribed by my GP, were fighting a gallant battle for the control of my jangled nervous system. 'No problem,' I replied.

'All parties in the case of Middleton to Court One,' the tannoy announced.

My stomach, trying masterfully to control a rather greasy bacon sandwich, leapt to attention. Beth rose and started towards the door as I fumbled for my briefcase and pulled out a small plastic bottle of pills. After a moment of toying with the child-proof cap, I extracted a pink pill and placed it in my mouth. It tasted bitter and I had no drink to wash it down.

Leaving Jonathan to gather his papers, Beth and I rode the elevator to the third floor, walked down the corridor and shouldered open the double mahogany doors that led to Court One. The room was immense, walled in hessian with a high ceiling. The courtroom was still filling yet eerily hushed. A diet of transatlantic courtroom dramas had led me to imagine that I would be permitted to sit with my solicitor in the relative obscurity of the body of the court, but this was London, not LA.

Beth kissed me gently before taking her place in the public gallery. The knot in my stomach tightened as I was led past a reinstated and grinning Detective Barnet, surrounded by his impressive array of files, each boldly emblazoned 'Operation Coverall'. The contents were merely papers, which might or might not contain information of relevance, but Barnet had spent many weeks preparing his impressive library and was keen that it be given a position of prominence.

The dock was raised some three feet and enclosed with toughened glass. Within, two rows of six seats faced forward towards my accusers. A prison officer ushered me towards a seat in the front row. Peering down from my glass box I surveyed the packed rows of bewigged and gowned legal figures assembling before me like flocks of long-legged birds preparing to feast on carrion. On my left the Prosecution, headed by the cumbersome figure of Mr Antony Paterson-Smythe. To the right stood Giles Adams, my defence barrister, lean and aristocratic, with sharp features and intense eyes that peered through dark wire-rimmed spectacles. He was in his early thirties and dressed impeccably in tailored suit and gown. Behind Giles sat John Peterson, the newly appointed junior.

Giles was originally to be just the junior, but when my senior barrister's prior case was bizarrely delayed, Giles, with only seven days' notice, had been exalted to the position of leader. Since discovering we had drawn Judge McGaea, he'd been acting very jittery. 'Hell ... of all the judges out there, what are the odds of getting this one? The first damned trial I'm going to lead. He was my tutor at my first chambers. He used to delight in setting "little problems" for all the juniors to solve. He gave everybody grief.' When agreeing only last week that Giles could take over as Leading Counsel, I had never considered he might be afraid of the judge. 'We've got our work cut out,' he continued. 'If we piss him off he'll make life hell for weeks.'

For the first time it had occurred to me that for Giles, and for that matter the whole system, this trial was just a few weeks' work. I was no longer a person; I was simply a pawn in a much larger and more complex game. To me each witness would be vital and each day critical. To the players, each day was just another day.

7

The devil hath power to assume a pleasing shape.

(William Shakespeare, *Hamlet*)

I'd first met Giles some weeks earlier at his cramped but functional Surrey chambers on the first floor of a modern office complex. Jonathan had driven me through the rain to the meeting that was destined to last several hours. There was plenty to discuss.

With the obligatory greetings over Jonathan began. 'We will clearly require a number of conferences prior to trial, and time is getting short. I have documented three distinct areas: the injury claim, the redundancy claim and lastly these new charges involving Prize Indemnity.' He paused, 'As the injury and redundancy overlap, I suggest we leave this latest Prize Indemnity charge to a later meeting.'

Giles peered up from his papers, his brow furrowed. He looked concerned. 'You're planning to plead *not* guilty then?'

'Naturally.' I replied, feeling slightly taken aback.

'Yet you don't deny making these PPI claims?'

'Of course not, what's the problem?'

He raised his eyebrows. 'I can see we could have a few problems with this case,' he said, glancing over to Jonathan. 'Mr Middleton was claiming for this horse riding injury, but then began a secondary claim for redundancy payments? Is that correct?'

'It is,' Jonathan replied.

'How is any jury going to acquit a defendant claiming to be unwell, so presumably unable to work, when at the same time he's claiming to be redundant and must therefore have been trying to find work?'

'I wasn't unwell!' I snapped, trying hard but failing to control my irritation. 'I was injured; I'd broken my back in two places.'

'Oh, I see...' Giles turned to Jonathan. 'Do we have testimony to collaborate this?'

'Oh, yes, quite conclusive, doctors' reports, specialists, x-rays, CAT scans. It's all documented in your bundles. Initially the injury was considered temporary; the extent wasn't diagnosed at the time of the accident; in fact it was WPA's own specialist who pointed out that Mr Middleton had broken his back when he fell from the horse. We even have a photograph of Mr Middleton riding the offending animal.'

Giles stirred his coffee slowly while staring at his notes. 'How can you *not* diagnose a broken back.' There was a degree of cynicism in his tone.

'Very easily. You're thinking of a classic spinal break, where the cord itself is severed and the patient is confined to a wheelchair. But in this case the break occurred below the spinal cord at level L5, S1...' Jonathan reached around, indicating the area in his lower back, just below his belt. Giles glanced over while continuing to take notes. 'According to the specialist, the whole area is now unstable and has already moved by more than half an inch; it's what's known as a spondylolithesis. It's not that Mr Middleton can't race, it's that he shouldn't ever race again according to WPA's own specialist. The damage to the spine is simply too severe.'

'Remember, the accident happened on an island off Malaysia,' I added, 'so I was never taken to a hospital. I just saw a local doctor who gave me a pile of painkillers. Then for years I obtained repeat prescriptions for increasing amounts of painkillers every time I got back into a race car. What made the situation worse was that after each bout of pain I visited an osteopath who, without realising my spine was fractured, manipulated the broken area causing further instability and damage.'

'According to WPA's own specialist, the sciatic nerve was also damaged,' explained Jonathan, 'which causes Mr Middleton to lose feeling in his right leg. With rest and painkillers however, the pain and symptoms can go away almost completely, but then Mr Middleton gets back in a race car and the whole cycle starts again.'

'How long has this gone on for?' Giles interrupted, turning to me.

'Almost five years, since December 1988.'

Giles looked aghast. 'But ... you haven't been claiming that long, have you?'

'No. I first claimed around a week or so after the accident in 1988, but only for a couple of months. But then over the five years I had an on/off claim running three, maybe four times – whenever the pain was such that I couldn't race and the doctor insisted that I rest.'

Giles looked relieved. 'But I understand from the Prosecution that you did in fact race again.'

'That was before we knew the extent of my injuries, and it was a local *non-professional* race. I did it because it might have led to a paid contract. If anyone acted criminally, WPA did, by sitting on the report.'

'This whole situation only developed into a criminal investigation because for months WPA hid the report that confirmed Mr Middleton shouldn't ever race again, therefore being eligible for a big lump sum payout,' Jonathan added. 'Mr Middleton was more or less forced into finding some way to race again. With no other formal qualifications, he had to earn a living for his family.'

Giles carefully placed the papers on his desk. 'That's all good stuff but I still don't see how this helps us with the redundancy claim. The fact is you were receiving sickness payments while claiming for redundancy payments.'

'I was claiming from an accident policy, not a sickness policy. It paid out regardless of whether I was employed, unemployed, sick, looking for work or retired; it confirms that in the policy. And in any event I checked it with them at the time...' Giles turned to Jonathan, who nodded in agreement. 'After the collapse of Team Capricorn, it was obvious I was going to be out of racing for some time, possibly years, so I went to the Job Centre and was told in no uncertain terms that if I was capable of doing *any* work, regardless of my back injury and previous occupation, I had to sign on as available for any suitable work. So I did what I was told.'

'Interestingly,' Jonathan chipped in, 'the redundancy policy could have been used to claim for his injury also, as it has an injury section. Had Mr Middleton done that, he could have simply sat back with his feet up for years and done nothing, but he took the route of signing on to get back into some kind of work.'

'What was the total amount claimed from WPA, over the period of the indictments?'

'I was getting around two grand a month, so no more than thirty-six thousand pounds, over some eighteen months.'

Giles took a deep breath and exhaled loudly. 'Is this everything? If so, *why?* Why are they bothering with all this? Surely there has to be something more than this. The injury is beyond dispute and your redundancy was beyond your control, so why are they going to all this trouble? This case will cost the taxpayer millions, and all you've claimed is two thousand pounds a month? You must have seriously pissed somebody off...'

We had pleaded with the learned judge to delay the case for just seven days to enable my original senior barrister to return, but to no avail. His Honour, having already disposed of Toby, my original solicitor, was not willing to countenance a postponement, pointing out that he was due to commence another trial in November, therefore any delay was out of the question.

Jonathan Barker now entered the hushed arena clutching his tower of papers and strolled stern-faced to the glass cube. 'Good morning Pooh, said Piglet.' He spoke in the third person, as if narrating or reading from the A.A. Milne book, his appearance impossibly straight. As he spoke, his stern expression broke into a broad grin. The moment was humorous, wonderfully out of place and served its purpose; my tension broke, just a little. Perhaps the little pink pills had also started to work. Over the past year I'd swallowed more chemicals than I cared to think. The thrill of the battle ahead had replaced my former anxiety.

Quite when the A.A. Milne characters had first entered the drama is difficult to recall, but our nicknames had added a degree of comic relief to the interminable weeks of preparatory work, and seemed strangely to represent our various characters: Giles Adams, my barrister, was 'Rabbit', always busily rushing from place to place, attempting, as diplomatically as possible, to steer clear of long conferences with Pooh. John Peterson, the new junior barrister, was 'Tigger', enthusiastically bounding around in his own little world. Jonathan Barker, who had become more of a friend over the past six months, was 'Piglet', who never quite knew how to avoid getting drawn into yet another long discussion of little immediate importance with Pooh but, not wishing to hurt Pooh's feelings, always managed to find the time.

I was a little unsure of my own character, 'Pooh' the somewhat rounded little bear who was always getting into trouble.

DC Barnet wandered nervously around the court like a pot-bellied commander reassuring his men before the off. This was the biggest case of his career and a result was urgently needed to maintain morale and the credibility of both himself and his men. He had enjoyed the months of globe-trotting for the investigation, but today was D-day and he smiled at his animated team of men and women.

The usher, a tall, cadaverous court servitor whom we had dubbed 'Lurch', positioned the judge's chair to precisely the right angle before descending into the body of the court. Clearing his throat, he took his position to the right of His Honour's bench. 'All persons having business within this Crown Court stand forth and give their attention!' he barked.

The dock officer to my side leaped to his feet. As I rose, His Honour Judge George Lampton McGaea made his entrance, a pallid, slim-faced, almost transparent man with lips set in a thin grim line. Resplendently attired in crimson with mauve sashes, he glided gracefully to his pre-positioned throne.

I had first come before him some months earlier, at a pre-trial meeting when His Honour had decided to start a debate on why I had been granted legal aid for my defence. 'How can a man living in a half-million-pound house possibly qualify for state assistance?' he'd indignantly demanded.

I'd fought to control the rising prickle of resentment at his attitude. An investigation had been ordered and I was requested to complete a further legal aid application immediately which the learned judge would study personally.

It did not appear to cross anyone's mind that our home for the past ten years might not amount to quite the opulence that the Crown had been suggesting. Piglet and I had tried to find out where the absurd valuation had come from, but to no avail. But there had been a tabloid article some months prior to the police raid entitled 'WPA Bank pays racing driver £4000 for bouncing cheque'. The article had fleetingly referred to living in a half-million-pound manor house, the wildly inaccurate figure printed for impact, not fact. The real facts were that I was more than £30,000 overdrawn with no employment.

I had never wanted to rely on state hand-outs and it was for precisely such reasons that I had, some years previously, acquired a package of personal insurance policies including Redundancy, Accident, Sickness, Medical, Life and a Family Legal Costs policy from WPA. I'd been shocked when Piglet had delivered the bombshell. 'Will, WPA have declined cover on your Legal Protection Policy.'

'What? That's ridiculous, I've been paying into that policy for years. It specifically states it covers both civil and criminal proceedings. I've checked.'

'Will, that may be the case but they're saying that this decision has come down from their head of claims. We've already appealed to him but WPA are quoting some bizarre small print. Under the circumstances they say your success can only be determined after trial and are arguing that as the Crown are obliged to prove they have a good prospect of success *before* commencing proceedings, you can't have.'

'That's ridiculous.' I was incensed. 'This sounds more to do with the fact I'm charged with swindling their damn policies than anything else.'

With personal legal costs estimated at up to a quarter of a million pounds, no work, and the bank threatening to foreclose, I would indeed need to rely on state aid. WPA did however magnanimously agree that if the charges were successfully defended, they would consider a refund to the Legal Aid Board.

8

This is a court of law, young man, not a court of justice.

(Oliver Wendell Holmes, Jr.)

It was Rabbit who had recommended Jonathan Barker, also known as Piglet, as Toby's replacement. Jonathan was a partner in a practice that specialised in criminal law. I had known Toby, the family solicitor, for years and was anxious about making changes at this late stage, so I was a little on edge at our first meetings. Jonathan was in his mid thirties, a tall, slim man with a pinkish complexion and an organised desk. 'My pen is poised,' he said, 'we have a lot of work to do, so let's make a start.' He opened a fresh legal pad and wrote the time and date at the top of the page.

I began with a race at Brands Hatch in July 88 which led to Roy's invitation to drive in Australia. Then our holiday in Malaysia and subsequent riding accident; the diagnosis only years later of the original spinal damage. I moved on to the collapse of Team Capricorn in November 91 and my redundancy, and finally my father's death. I tried to speak slowly. It was important he took it all down.

'The judge seems to be very interested in your past for some reason,' Jonathan said. 'Tell me about your home, and the purchase of the Old Granary.'

Our home, object of His Honour's scrutiny, had as its name suggested, started life as a Granary, built around 1890. For a barn it was unusually elaborate, constructed of red brick in a Gothic style and set in the grounds of an old farm. It was in September 1984 that we were to discover the ramshackle building. Beth had noticed the for sale sign first. Since our first meeting in 1976 we had always dreamt of finding an unusual property, perhaps in need of restoration; an old barn or even a windmill, something we could make our own.

The barn was set back from the road, bordered by a low weathered fence behind which ponies roamed nonchalantly. 'Oh Will, it's wonderful,' exclaimed Beth, her words hushed. I pulled the car over onto the grass verge in front of the barn. Beth unfastened her seat belt and stepped from the car. We both stood staring at the building in awe. I slipped an arm around her waist, her brown eyes shone with delight in her small face, framed with a few wayward curls of long brown glossy hair, the balance tied in a pony tail. She wandered off towards the gate and patted one of the curious ponies. She turned and smiled, the picture will remain with me always. An almost magical expression on her face, she was wearing tapered blue jeans, red and blue plaid shirt and white trainers. Behind her bounded Cossie, coat glistening, tail wagging happily, nose twitching as he searched out the local wildlife.

The building was full of character but unfortunately its general condition was not good, and it was only an empty shell. The brickwork seemed sound enough though, but broken tiles littered the ground, the roof seeming to bow inwards in an unhealthy arc. A disused road ran around the front of the building, long grass squeezing its way through the cracks.

Beth tugged at my arm. 'Let's look around the back.' She was off again, rampaging through the deep grass like an eager child. I smiled, there was no need to ask her impression, it was obvious. From the back the barn appeared to be built on a slight rise. I looked back into the natural dip and in my mind's eye envisaged a pool with patio, kids playing in the water and me tending a barbecue, overlooking for a moment the likely cost of such a development, satisfied just to savour the illusion. Beth had already left me to explore the inside. She appeared from a side opening, partially obscured by tendrils of ivy. 'Will,' she called, 'come and see, it's incredible inside.' I joined her and was as affected as she was. Sunlight shone through the huge gothic arches. 'This would be our lounge, and through there the dining room,' she enthused.

We sat on a straw bale and gazed out for a moment, the surrounding countryside like a perfect watercolour. I placed my arm around her shoulders and hugged her to me. 'Beth, if we were to get a place like this it would take every penny for the next...' I paused, 'ten years to convert; we wouldn't be able to afford to go out, no holidays. I'd have to sell my car.' I looked lovingly in the direction of my old, rather battered sports roadster. 'There's no water, no electricity, no drainage. We'd have to live out of a caravan for the first year or so.'

'But just look at this place, Will, it'll be worth it,' she said longingly. 'It's what we need, the place is perfect.'

I tried to sound impartial, I pulled her close. 'Look, it's a warm sunny day today, but what about when the winter comes and it's freezing and we're cut off with snow?'

'Hmmm,' she breathed, cuddling up, 'we could be cut off for weeks, we'd have to snuggle under quilts, just think of what we would have to do to keep ourselves warm.' Her eyes sparkled, she had a way of putting things that made it difficult to resist.

The next day I phoned the agents. 'In the region of £68,000; the sale's in three weeks' time,' the auctioneer told me, 'sealed bids only, to be received by midday on the first of November.'

There'd been no time to lose. I'd only been racing for four years, and my income had been far from regular, my ten-year-old roadster being my only real asset. In reality, with more than 100,000 miles on the clock, it was more of a liability, demanding most of my spare time just to keep on the road, but on days when the sun shone and the temperamental electrics didn't fail, I'd considered the extravagance worthwhile.

On November 1st, along with five other hopefuls, we submitted our sealed bid of £76,000. Two hours later we signed the sale agreement. We now owned a Victorian Gothic barn ... at least we would do, as soon as we found the £70,000 balance.

Coming up with just the £6,000 deposit for the barn had used all our spare cash, as well as stretching our overdraft to the limit. Since signing the papers I'd had more than three weeks of sleepless nights, as each mortgage company in turn rejected our application. The problem wasn't just my lack of regular income, it was the barn itself; none of them considered it to be a house, so it simply didn't qualify for a mortgage. My latest idea was therefore to try for a short-term bank loan and as soon as the barn was considered habitable, switch the loan to a more manageable mortgage. If we couldn't come up with the balance within the next week, we'd lose not only the barn itself but our deposit as well.

'What if we don't get it?' Beth asked nervously.

'We will,' I replied, 'everything's going to be fine, it's all under control.'

She didn't buy it.

To my amazement, the bank agreed to give us fifty grand over ten years. All I had to do then was find a buyer for the roadster, then see if we could borrow the difference from our parents.

One week later, loaned up to the hilt, we became the proud owners of the barn, set in two acres of Sussex countryside. Four weeks after that, with George only eighteen months old, we moved into the unconverted hay loft, with no running water, no heating and not even a front door. It was paradise, but it took more than a year before we could persuade a mortgage company to switch our loans to an affordable mortgage. Over the years that followed we slowly converted the old barn into what would become 'The Old Granary'.

Our former home had been minuscule by comparison. You could have fitted all the furniture into just the lounge of the Granary and the expense of furnishing the place was a factor we'd never really considered. We decided that it would be sensible to get as much as possible from house sales and auction rooms; an area in which neither of us had much experience. Over the next few years I regularly returned home with a whole series of fascinating little acquisitions until Beth finally put her foot down as I struggled through the door with a seven-foot grandfather clock balanced on my back and a stuffed beaver under my arm. 'Darling, it's really nice, but, don't you think,' she tried to keep a straight face as Cossie tentatively investigated the beaver, a low growl rising from his throat, fur lifting on his back, 'we should concentrate on a few basic essentials first.'

This change of tack brought considerable distress to the local auctioneers, who had become used to welcoming me on my regular visits where I'd happily bid for the more obscure lots: a collection of ornate chamber pots, an unusual hat stand, an antique bed warmer with a missing handle.

9

*Quite often the truth was the casualty in the process of convicting criminals.
I think there was a time when a minority of officers were prepared to
bend the rules. I think they were prepared to massage the evidence ...
elaborating on things that were said in a way to make sure that the case
had the strongest chance of going through to a conviction.*

(Metropolitan police commissioner, Paul Condon.
BBC Panorama, 5th April 1993)

'So when was the first sign of real cash flow problems with the
old team?' Jonathan asked.

'Black Monday happened three years earlier but the consequence
of the economic slump didn't hit us until mid 1991. Two of
Rob's sponsors had contracted directly with Team Capricorn and
then both got into financial difficulties. One was a property
development company, the other an exotic car outlet. The property
market had gone into freefall and the yuppie market in sports
cars was careering downhill faster than Thatcher's economy could
slide into recession. The result was a debt to the team of over
£40,000. Added to that, Team Capricorn was owed another £30,000
by various other creditors.'

Jonathan raised an eyebrow. 'So the team was owed around
£70,000 in total?'

'Yes, and as the recession deepened, we couldn't get any of it
in. We'd already taken four companies to court and secured
judgements but then Rob Allan's sponsors just collapsed; the
sports car company went bust and the Inland Revenue wound
up the property development company.'

'So in effect your co-driver Rob Allan brought down your team,
yet the Prosecution are calling him as a Crown witness.'

'Yes, although to be fair it was his sponsors, not Rob directly,
that brought down the team, and who could have foreseen the
collapse of the economy? The monies owed to the team remained
on the books as assets, until they became unrecoverable. It was

when they were written off that Team Capricorn became insolvent. There were more than fifty thousand small businesses a week going bust at that time. I certainly didn't blame Rob.'

'How much did the team owe its creditors?' Jonathan asked.

'No more than forty thousand, tops. Most of it was owed to newspapers for advertising and the Savoy Hotel in London for a big promotion we'd done for the coming season.'

'Could you pinpoint when the team's cash flow became critical?'

'Money was always tight, we never made big profits. If we had, the backers would have trimmed back the budgets. Lots of businesses around that time were having big cash flow problems. Team Capricorn's were no worse than many other small companies. Why is all this relevant?'

He studied me for a few seconds. 'Giles had a conference with the Prosecution last week...' He paused as though considering how best to break another batch of bad news. 'It seems the Crown is going to suggest that the collapse of Team Capricorn was in some way contrived – by you.'

'What? They're suggesting I masterminded the collapse of my own company?' I spluttered. 'Why? I did everything in my power to keep it afloat. Besides, the Official Receiver has all the original documents, we can prove I had no control over any of the collapse.'

'Unfortunately, the Prosecution can suggest whatever it wants, within reason. You had redundancy cover with WPA. If they can make a jury believe you deliberately brought down your own company, they've proved motive. You're a man of previous good character, there are no previous convictions, not even a minor misdemeanour, they have to try to slur your previous good name somehow. Our problem is that the Official Receiver has for some reason destroyed all the company's records.' He laid down his pen. 'Quite bizarre! Normally official documents of that kind would be kept for at least seven years.'

'Brilliant, just brilliant!' I blurted out. 'So how do we prove anything?'

'Well they're not actually charging you directly with another offence, so they don't need the records. They're just throwing mud. We're the ones that need the records to prove that didn't happen. Did you try to raise capital to keep the company afloat?'

'Jonathan,' I replied, 'I did everything that anyone could have done, but the team was owed around £70,000. Remember, companies were going bust everywhere. Two had already succumbed to the deepening recession, owing Team Capricorn £40,000. How do they imagine I conjured that up? The team was insolvent; it's illegal for a limited company to trade once it's insolvent. Hell, if we'd had in what was owed, we wouldn't have been in any debt at all. In fact, we'd have been in credit to over £30,000. I acted as any responsible director would.'

Jonathan sipped his Earl Grey thoughtfully, sighing with pleasure at the delicate scent of Bergamot; he replaced the bone china cup carefully back in its saucer. 'Will...' he rubbed his eyes, 'tell me about these new charges. We need to look at the Prize Indemnity.'

He caught the flicker in my eyes, the fleeting look of concern. The Prize Indemnity charge bothered me more than all other charges put together. It was not that the race team had done anything wrong; Prize Indemnity was common practice in professional sport. It was just extremely complex and something that most people would never have come across. When overlaid with the other charges it also threatened to distract from the simplicity of a physical injury and the reality of redundancy. It muddied the waters, obscuring clarity and could derail the defence.

I sat back, took a breath and began. 'It was to be the start of a new career for both Rob and myself, particularly for me given the collapse of Team Capricorn and my redundancy.'

Jonathan checked his notes. 'Whose idea was it?'

'It was either Rob or his American partner; it's difficult to remember for sure, but definitely not me. The first time I heard of it was when Rob competed in a Prize Indemnity race at Le Mans.' I picked up a paper clip from the desk and set about untangling the curves. 'It was sometime early in 1991 I think, I was at their office in Bristol, we were just chatting generally. It was something to do with them creating a contractual liability, if Rob finished in the top six in the race. They explained that they had insured against the risk, which meant if he *did* finish in the top six the insurance paid out.'

It had been around the time when a new and relatively unknown driver had just started to make headlines. At only 22 years old, Michael Schumacher had been drafted into the 7-Up Jordan Formula One Team as a last-minute replacement for Betrand

Gachot who was in Brixton Prison following a conviction for assaulting a London taxi driver.

Jordan had been in the headlines through 1991, and Rob or his partner Stuart had had some kind of contact with the team. I was told: 'It's the way they're funding the new team. The bulk of the 7-Up sponsorship is covering Prize Indemnity premiums. The team insure with specialist underwriters against the risk of finishing in the points. As long as they do finish in the points, they generate income for the team from the policy. Schumacher's good, very good, but at the moment, he's an unknown in Formula One so it's working like a dream. He'll be World Champion one day. It's just that nobody's worked it out yet. It's all been in the papers – it's basically like gambling.'

'Hold on a minute.' Jonathan was looking perplexed. 'I'm sorry, I still don't follow. You say it's like gambling?'

'Yes in a way, although strictly speaking it's not allowed to be called gambling as that would breach insurance rules but everybody knows it is. In fact some of the big gaming companies offer almost identical schemes to the Division One football clubs. In those cases the gambling is blatant but they are licensed to gamble. In the case of Prize Indemnity, the risk has to be specifically linked to a commitment of some kind.'

Jonathan's pen stopped. Again he lifted his eyes. 'I'm sorry ... I still don't follow.'

'Look at it this way. Anyone can insure against an insurable risk. Prize Indemnity underwriters are specialist insurance companies that will calculate a premium based on the risk of a "commitment" having to be fulfilled. In the case of Trans-Atlantic, Track Star Insurance, which was selling the Prize Indemnity policy, needed a legally binding contract in place whereby Trans-Atlantic would have a "commitment" to Rob and me if either of us achieved a specific result in a race. Trans-Atlantic's "commitment" would be to employ us to drive in a further series of races, but of course in order to carry out that "commitment", Trans-Atlantic needed to be set up with all the equipment and would have to either lease or buy a suitable race car – such as Mamet's Porsche.'

'Mamet?' Jonathan flicked a few pages of text. 'Ah! The American you later fell out with?'

'Yes, Mamet's the owner of Trans World Racing in Florida'

'So the "commitment" was to you and Rob to drive either Mamet's Porsche or some other suitable car?'

'Yes. But remember it was only a potential "commitment". It depended solely on us getting the required result in the race. That's why I say it's like gambling; the premium you pay is effectively the stake money, and the claim or payout for us would be employment as drivers with Trans-Atlantic for a full season.'

Rob had first operated a Prize Indemnity scheme in the 1992 Le Mans 24 hours. That had been just weeks before we flew to America to see Mamet. Rob had been driving a Kremer Porsche. The policy had been arranged through the same Les Heath, specialist insurance broker, who was to later sell a similar policy to us. Rob had paid a premium of around £2000. If he then finished in the top six, the insurers would pay a bonus of £20,000. Unfortunately for him he wasn't in the top six, but it was due to that race that we decided the idea was worth giving another shot.

The whole concept to run an indemnity scheme around Mamet's Porsche Spyder developed out of Rob's Le Mans deal. I had now been redundant for seven months and had not worked since mid August the previous year due to ongoing problems with my back. My GP had arranged physiotherapy at the local hospital and I was personally funding osteopathy sessions and ultrasound treatment. The symptoms had, to a great extent, subsided but I was still in pain and scheduled to see WPA's spinal specialist later in July.

Our Prize Indemnity concept was simple. It was strongly rumoured that David Mamet had a huge tax bill, owing over $250,000 and needed to sell his 962 Spyder to pay the IRS. Flying to America when I was unemployed and desperately short of cash was not something I particularly wanted to do. A return plane ticket to Florida would cost just under £300, hotels, food and a hire car would also be expensive, but the idea of establishing a new team, Trans-Atlantic, with potential employment was compelling. If we could persuade Mamet to invest in the Prize Indemnity idea, Trans-Atlantic could then afford to buy the equipment it would need, Mamet's 962 for example, and employ Rob and myself as team drivers. Everybody would be happy.

American Trans Air flight T2557 touched down at Orlando International Airport on cue at 5.20 pm local time. We cleared customs, collected the convertible Ford Probe from the hire company and set off down Interstate Four.

No sooner had we settled into our journey than a great clap of thunder broke over us as a precursor to a full tropical rain storm. The skies opened, deluging the car and highway in a continuous sheet of water, a liquid wall of noise made worse by our attempt to drive through it. The windscreen wipers slapped feebly back and forth barely making an impression.

The storm grew in intensity, the torrential rain flooding the parched ground, sending clouds of mist boiling from the roads. It was late, we were tired, fed up and badly in need of a beer, and couldn't see a thing. More than enough excuse to seek out some friendly oasis, preferably an alcoholic one. Lightning exploded across the blackened skies in an iridescent crackling of electric blue energy illuminating the road ahead. 'There's a place!' I shouted.

Through the watery torrents assailing the screen, I had seen the vague outline of a neon sign flashing its welcome. Rob swung the car in the general direction of my frantic gesticulations. The building slowly came into view through a veil of rain as Rob turned into the parking area, positioning the car as close to the door as he possibly could. 'Run for it!'

As we yanked the door open, a mixture of smoke, stale beer and cheap perfume immediately assailed our senses, stinging our eyes, offending our noses, while the clamorous beat of a band or juke box did its best to deafen us. Thus we were welcomed to The Foxhole. Rob stated the obvious, 'This place is definitely not a hotel!'

As our eyes slowly grew accustomed to our gloomy surroundings, the evidence for that observation became even clearer. A small cluster of 'leg breakers' leaned menacingly against the bar. Cigarette ends littered the floor. The air was wet with humidity; the air conditioning system hadn't worked in years. The rain fell harder on the roof, staccato beats competing with the music inside.

Heavy rock blasted its melodious beat. A red glow flickered from the buzzing 'Budweiser' sign that hung over the bar. A girl, scarcely older than eighteen, slowly unsnapped the clasp between surgically sculptured symmetrical breasts. Seductively she gyrated, tantilisingly removing the last remnants of clothing as the jeers of the drunken men grew louder.

Rob was an accomplished drinker who smoked like a chimney and had a proclivity for drawing women like flies to a camel's butt. I on the other hand was an infrequent drinker. The last ten months had been brutal and I desperately needed this break. By my eighth Bud I finally relaxed and could happily have talked the hind legs off a giraffe. Like most men in that state I too believed talking to be of the utmost importance.

A young brunette, with pouting vacuum-nozzle lips, strutted past and perched herself on a stool next to the bar. Without a word the bar man placed a tall stemmed glass next to her. A middle-aged man in a business suit strode over nonchalantly and took the adjacent seat.

The brunette was in her late teens with silicon breasts exploding through tight fitting lycra and a skirt that reached up to her crutch. I watched as 'the suit' moved in, drawn on as if by an unseen magnet to the exploding cleavage. The girl slowly licked her lips, like a cat, every movement choreographed to sexual perfection, each action intended to taunt, to thrill.

She touched her breasts, then reaching for her glass, toyed seductively with the stem. She licked a finger and ran it around the edge of the glass. 'The suit' moved closer...

'You on your own?' A voice made me jump. The voice sat down next to me. She was strikingly beautiful, probably early twenties, with bronze skin and hazel or green eyes. It was difficult to tell in the dim light. Her blonde hair hung to her waist. She wore a brief, low-cut T-shirt that appeared almost transparent in the ultraviolet light and scarcely covered what were clearly expensively fashioned breasts. The short skirt left very little to the imagination. She crossed never-ending legs. 'My name's Joy. What's yours?'

It had to be, I thought. 'My name's Will.'

'Where are you from, Will?' she smiled, an innocent child-like smile that formed deep dimples in her cheeks.

'England. We're here for a few days.' I looked around for Rob but he'd vanished. There was something surreal yet fascinating about being surrounded by scantily clad, synthetically enhanced American Barbie dolls. 'We're going south tomorrow.' I tried to keep it short. She re-crossed those legs; the girls did that a lot here. My stomach somersaulted. *Oh God I felt weak!* I tried to think of something innocent to talk about. *Forget it!* I ordered a couple more Buds.

'I've got to dance,' she squeezed my thigh, 'but I'll be back.' A voice in my head said run like hell, you're happily married. Something else told me to relax – it's just a bit of fun.

She was now on stage, the skirt had been discarded and all that remained was about to be removed. She crossed her arms and lifted the bottom of the T-shirt over her head while her hips gyrated to the hypnotic rhythm. Blonde hair fell in cascades over the bronzed shoulders, the spray-tanned breasts seeming even bigger. She flashed a perfect American smile and threw me the discarded T-shirt. It was warm, soft and fragrant. Maybe she would just go away; perhaps the stage would collapse and swallow her up. *Oh shit, doesn't this country have anything but natural blondes!*

'Come on Will,' an insistent voice cut through my daze, 'come on; we'd better go.' Over Rob's shoulder, I noticed a pair of leg breakers striding purposefully in our general direction. Something had clearly grabbed their attention.

'Where did you get to?' I asked.

Rob grinned sheepishly as he hurried me towards the door. 'I think there's a "lookey, lookey but no touchy, touchy" rule. Err ... I think I may have touched ... a bit!' he said with a telling smile. 'I'll fill you in later. Let's get out of here!'

I furtively glanced over his shoulder; the leg breakers had stopped but were watching intently. On stage, Joy flashed another wonderful smile and blew a vacuum-nozzle kiss.

Next morning dawned around 11 am as we struggled awake with hangovers the size of the national debt. We'd somehow made it to an inexpensive motel in the vicinity which was surrounded by strip clubs, fast food joints and flashing billboards. The room had cost $35. We wisely avoided breakfast. A meeting had been scheduled with Mamet for later that day, the plan being to persuade him to let us use his Porsche 962 Spyder in the Prize Indemnity scheme. We donned dark glasses, dropped the hood of the hire car and set off with the traffic on Highway 95.

The sun was bright, the storm had long since blown itself out and the scorching rays burnt my temples as we cruised south.

Springsteen bellowed from the speakers. I felt great; my back pain had subsided and as my fitness had returned, so had my need for action. At last, we were doing something positive.

We'd already explained the basic theory of Prize Indemnity to Mamet over the phone. In essence, we would have to secure a top six position for Trans-Atlantic to win the funds that would enable it to acquire the Porsche permanently. The team would then employ Rob and myself as its drivers. According to the terms of the Prize Indemnity either Rob or myself, or both, could drive in the nominated races.

Four hours later we arrived at the pristine workshops of Mamet Porsche Racing in Florida. Mamet Porsche had a long reputation of dealing with 'gentlemen racers', business men with deep pockets and offshore accounts who were content to leave the management of their weekend pursuits entirely in the hands of Mamet.

Mechanics continued to work on the immaculate rows of cars perched on trestles around the spotless workshop. It was more like an operating theatre than a workshop. 'Well you guys, I'll do it, but I've got to be in control,' Mamet insisted. 'You can provide the main pit crew but I'll be Team Manager, and I want to bring my main mechanic over, and all expenses have to be covered, flights, hotels, meals, and we'll need a hire car.'

I cast a worried look at Rob – money was critical. We'd talked about the running costs and had hoped to save on expenses by using all our own pit crew. We'd also wanted to convince Mamet to cover his own expenses, after all we were putting up the Prize Indemnity premium and if it worked Trans-Atlantic were likely to purchase his car and he'd pick up a cool quarter of a million dollars.

I turned to Rob. 'There'll be a ton of admin to sort out,' I said tightly. 'The car's going to have to be freighted for a start, and there will be temporary export documentation to arrange...'

Mamet's gaze turned to me, his head inclined. 'Temporary export?' he enquired. I could sense a feeling of distrust. 'I thought the idea was that you guys or your new team were going to buy the car, with the proceeds of the prize indemnity?'

'We do have to win it first,' I said. 'If we export the Porsche into the UK as a permanent import immediately, we'll have to pay customs duty on arrival. That would be insane.' I regretted

54

using the word insane as soon as it left my lips. 'No, we import the Porsche initially on a temporary *carnet de passage*, it's the way Team Capricorn used to ship its race cars around the world for World Championship events. To do that we just have to set up a bank guarantee linked to the *carnet de passage*. That satisfies Customs and Excise that they'll get any customs duty just in case the car doesn't return to the States, or if it gets destroyed.' I knew immediately I shouldn't have used the word destroyed.

I could sense Mamet balancing any hope of a sale with the risk of losing his baby forever, like a father watching his young daughter leave for her first date. His gaze rested on me. 'Look, Will, you're used to dealing with all this stuff, so you're going to have to deal with the admin, shipping, *carnet de* whatever. I'll just provide the car, my chief mechanic, and I'll manage the team on race day, okay?' I nodded, but Mamet hadn't finished. 'Will, you haven't raced in over a year so Rob's likely to be quickest, he's just done Le Mans. Anyhow, I'll decide who drives, okay? Whoever's fastest runs the race. That's the deal!'

The deal was struck and I'd keep to it. *We'll find the extra money, I told myself, and I'll be the quickest.*

A simple verbal contract; very straightforward. The new Trans-Atlantic Team would enter Mamet's car in three weeks' time in the first race at Brands Hatch and if unsuccessful, a second attempt would be made at Zolder in Belgium a few weeks later. Statistically we were underdogs, in a new unknown team, but now we had access to a world-class car capable of winning. The Prize Indemnity underwriters would simply see an unknown team and look at our past international results in uncompetitive cars when determining the odds. Only we had the confidence that we could win. In any event a win wasn't important, all that was needed was a top six position. It was as good as the money already being in the bank.

'We'll need authority from you to sign papers on behalf of Mamet Porsche Racing, both here and in the UK,' I added.

With a curt nod, Mamet got up and walked over to a desk. He opened a drawer, removed several sheets of Mamet Porsche Racing letterhead and slid them across the desk. 'Type up what you want, I trust you ... just don't screw me over, okay?'

Rob drove us quickly back to the Holiday Inn and we made our way straight to the bar. I ordered a couple of beers and joined Rob in a quiet corner away from the rest of the drinkers. He looked in deep thought. 'How do we cover Mamet's expenses?' he asked.

I settled into a comfortable chair next to a window and took a deep swallow of cold beer. 'Have you given up on your sponsors?'

'Pretty much. It's just not going to happen in time,' he said in frustration. 'We have less than three weeks before the first race and we have to arrange for the car to be freighted over, a pit team to be put together, a hospitality suite for the few backers we already have and now we've got to sort out accommodation and a hire car for Mamet for around a month. What's that going to cost?'

'And a workshop and a tyre deal and race car transporter and driver to move the car around,' I added. I placed my face in my hands, massaging my temples with my fingers. Rob's eyes were boring into me. 'Okay Rob, let's make a list,' I said thickly.

It took several trips to the bar for refills before the list was finished. At best it looked as though we'd need around ten grand to cover basic expenses, and to pull it off that cheaply we'd have to ask favours and at least get a freighting deal, a hotel chain and hire car company to all take payment in the form of endorsement space on the race car and hospitality at the track.

'So where does the ten grand come from?' Rob asked.

I frowned. 'I could find ten grand.'

'You could?' Rob's voice had an eager catch in it. 'But I thought you were broke.'

'I still have a ten-grand overdraft facility.'

Rob leaned forward slightly. 'You'd do that?' he asked huskily.

'I've worked outside all the normal rules for so long, what's one more gamble? This whole thing is a risk but we're convinced we're going to pull it off, aren't we? I'll cover the ten grand on my overdraft but it has to be repaid into my account as soon as the Prize Indemnity pays out, okay?'

Rob frowned, 'What if we don't pull it off?'

I swallowed the last of my beer. 'If we don't pull it off, we split the loss between us, whatever it is, okay? Oh and it's your round.'

Rob leaned back and smiled. 'Deal ... just one thing, we need to be in the gym getting fit. No more beer.'

Two weeks later, Mamet's Porsche Spyder arrived at Gatwick

on board Virgin Flight VF1. Everything was in place. My overdraft was already exceeding the ten grand.

10

You win some, you lose some, you wreck some.

(Dale Earnhardt)

For hours Jonathan and I talked. I reminisced about the old days, our travels, the old battles on and off the track. Every so often he gently steered the topic back to the relevant points.

'Why were you prepared to risk so much on the Prize Indemnity?' he asked.

'There was simply no alternative work. I'd spent five months looking. I had written to over fifty companies, registered with the Job Centre and stretched my CV to breaking point. I'd had to face facts. I was 38, a severely dyslexic former racing driver ... no, an *unknown*, severely dyslexic, former racing driver; not a particularly employable mix of skills. I'd been driving professionally for over twelve years. I simply wasn't going to find work outside racing.'

The pain in my back had lessened by then and as each day had passed I'd become more determined to return to the track. It was the one place I felt confident I could secure a future for my family and myself.

'Finding work in motor racing,' I went on, 'is not like securing employment at McDonald's; you've got to go out and make it happen. You have to get all the ingredients together first: the sponsors, the cars, the engine deals, the personnel. Trans-Atlantic didn't even have a set of overalls.'

He watched me carefully, his eyes fixed, penetrating. 'And the Prize Indemnity worked?'

'If it hadn't I doubt I would be facing this charge. Rob pulled it off at Zolder.'

'So who received the money?'

'Rob won it under contract to the new team, Trans-Atlantic.'

'So Trans-Atlantic made the claim?'

58

'Yes, and used the proceeds to purchase a pair of race cars and all the equipment to run them.'

'A pair of race cars? What happened to Mamet's Porsche?'

'That's why Mamet thinks I've stitched him up. It was only after we'd pulled off the Prize Indemnity at Zolder that it became apparent there was a serious aerodynamic problem with his car, as well as a problem with the rules running a two-driver team in the Super Cup championships.'

'So what happened?'

'Shortly after Trans-Atlantic's claim was approved we paid off Mamet for the hire of the car and bought a pair of Indy cars. The idea was that Rob and I would then be employed to drive in remaining races of that year's championship, but the payout from the insurers was late, very late, so everything was put on ice until the start of the 1993 season. It was only then that the medical report from WPA's expert finally turned up, confirming the severity of my injuries, and I was told I was effectively permanently prevented from racing. My GP Dr Eve sent a letter to my broker. Two weeks after that the police raid took place, coincidentally just after WPA got the report from the private detective – the idiot that had been watching the wrong people!'

Jonathan looked up, his eyes widening. 'So why charge you? Rob won it, Trans-Atlantic received the money and the contracts had already been approved by the underwriters. You're not a director of Trans-Atlantic?'

'No, but I probably would have become a director later.'

'But that's not the point. You weren't a director and you didn't win the Prize Indemnity; Rob did. So why charge you?' He shook his head. 'We'll come back to the Prize Indemnity later.'

He studied me closely, as if considering how best to phrase the next question. 'Will, I have to ask you this...' He was clearly unsure about something. 'You can be certain the same question will be asked by the Prosecution,' he added, as if as an apology for what was to come. 'Why so much PPI insurance? You had a life policy, redundancy cover, accident and sickness insurance. Even a legal costs policy. Why so much cover?' *The jury may think it all a bit too convenient.* The phrase hung, unspoken.

'You have a mortgage, I assume, Jonathan?'

'Well, yes ... an endowment mortgage in fact.'

'So you have a life policy connected to the mortgage, just in case the unthinkable should ever happen?'

'Yes.'

'So each day you go to work and x times per week you enter a courtroom. Do you expect to be killed or seriously injured when you go to court?'

He stalled, sensing an ambush. 'Well, not killed exactly…' A smile spread across his face. 'Occasionally mauled perhaps, but no … not killed.'

'Yet you still have life insurance. And accident cover?'

'I think I have some form of accident cover provided by my credit card company. I like to ski, so it's useful, just in case. However, it wasn't a policy that I actively sought. It was offered to me as an existing client.'

'Snap!' I exclaimed. 'WPA Bank offered me my policy some five years after I first applied for their card. Guaranteed acceptance it said, regardless of occupation. Covered me for sickness also, and a lump sum if an accident prevented me from performing my professional occupation. The legal costs policy was provided the same way. I only took cover following the birth of my sons and we also had a big mortgage to buy the Old Granary. You presumably have some sort of redundancy and sickness package from your employers?'

'Okay … point taken,' he said with a grin.

Yes, I had plenty of insurance, but then I had a family; a wife that I loved and two fantastic sons. I had to consider all eventualities. The world of motor racing is litigious, legal contracts are fraught with ambiguities. A legal protection policy was, in my opinion, a prerequisite to signing anything. Then there were the cars. Most of the cars I raced were little more than high-octane coffins. Flash past a braking point doing 180 miles per hour, explode onto the brakes and when a 50-pence bolt snaps your legs get turned into a bleeding pile of mush, the ensuing fireball providing instant cremation. Not many people have to consider that each time they go to work.

'Anyway,' I threw in, 'I either cancelled or cut back the policies as soon as Team Capricorn ran into cash flow problems.'

Jonathan's pen stopped more sharply than a Le Mans car braking for the Mulsanne hairpin. His head jerked up abruptly. 'You *reduced* the benefits payable under the policies prior to your redundancy?'

'Yes...' I said, trying to recall any other fragments from my tangled brain. 'Didn't I mention that before?'

'No! Let me get this straight. Team Capricorn is on its last legs; it's owed some £70,000, cash flow is critical, so to save money you cut back on your insurance premiums and cut the cover?'

'Yes, not the wisest of things to have done in the circumstances, but I was cutting back on everything I could; money was tight.'

He sat back, letting his pen fall to the desk. His face twitched into a jubilant grin. 'This defeats the premeditation factor; the Crown's contention that it was all planned, that you somehow created some complicated fraud. Why would anyone planning an elaborate scam to swindle their insurers reduce their policies and the impending booty a matter of weeks before making the claim?'

There were still gaps and holes to fill, but Jonathan had unearthed an important point. How many more were there hiding somewhere in my scrambled head? Jonathan was in a happy mood. I was shattered, mentally and physically.

11

A jury consists of twelve persons chosen to decide who has the better lawyer.

(Robert Lee Frost)

His Honour turned his attention to the pool of prospective jurors. Smiling attentively, he explained the role of the jury, pointing out that ultimately one of the chosen twelve must be appointed foreman. Much to the dismay of the assembled group, he advised that the anticipated length of the trial was to be at least two months and checked, at Rabbit's request, that no prospective juror was currently employed by the corporations I was alleged to have defrauded.

The pool of prospective jurors appeared a varied bunch. Their ages ranged from girls scarcely out of their teens, to men old enough to draw an old age pension. Some had prepared their alibis carefully. Employers' letters attesting to their unavailability. A family holiday to Tenerife that had been paid for months before. An important doctor's appointment that couldn't be missed.

McGaea excused a single mother and several others for illness, age, hospital appointments, and those with pressing compassionate problems. A girl with a back condition explained that she had difficulty sitting for any length of time and was immediately excused. Pity, I thought, she might well have sympathised with my injury. Economic problems and small businesses that would be damaged by the length of the trial were not considered suitable grounds to be excused service. The learned judge delighted in lecturing any who attempted to extricate themselves from his grasp with the flimsier excuses, delivering a stern lecture on their responsibility as British citizens.

When he had concluded, eighteen prospective jurors remained. The eighteen names were written on slips of paper. Lurch drew twelve of the slips and began calling the chosen few. One by one the jury of my peers rose, each a member of the public, and each juror from a different walk of life: an administrator of around fifty, a hairdresser, a nursery nurse, a chef, a slightly balding gardener, a window cleaner, one young mother, one student, one builder and two retired people. All took their seats in the jury box, their remaining colleagues relaxing as the twelfth name was called at last. What, I wondered, was their combined understanding of the world of professional motor sport?

Juror number 4, a plump lady in her late 40s, continued to complain that her outside commitments would be unfairly disrupted by the predicted length of the trial, but His Honour's decision was final. Lurch stood before the box as twelve disappointed faces swore the oath.

McGaea turned to his jury. His head nodded sagely. 'Ladies and Gentlemen, you have been selected to serve as jurors. You have vowed to try all matters presented to you. I will instruct you on matters of law; it is up to you to determine matters of evidence.' His tone dropped and he looked intently at the jurors. 'You must not discuss this case with anyone, not even your husbands or wives.' He cast a look pointedly at the dock, and the guard by my side stiffened. 'Furthermore, if you are approached by anyone, you must report it immediately.' His Honour returned his glance to the jury and smiled reassuringly. He continued to hammer the point home for a few more minutes just for good measure, while I mused over what he was implying. A juror glanced in my direction. I attempted a meek smile.

The jury appeared dumbfounded. I scrutinised the faces of the seven women and five men. Could these people with no knowledge of the law, who were clearly intimidated by the process, possibly be expected to understand and adjudicate the weeks of conflicting legal arguments that lay before them? I felt a sudden outbreak of sweat as the wave of anxiety coursed through my body. I could feel my shirt cling to my back.

I tried to imagine what was going through their minds on those initial days. My life had been so different from theirs, a world of machinery of such power and cost that it remains an enigma even to many who have worked half their lives within it. Would the jury understand or simply accept the picture the Prosecution had been trying to paint to my former friends and colleagues over the past 18 months? My future lay in the jury's hands and yet I could only talk to them via Rabbit who, in common with his counterpart, seemed to have adopted some form of new language that was quite foreign. If only I could explain to them face to face for just a few minutes. But that was not allowed, the arraignment was completed, the jury empanelled. The trial had begun and must run its course, the end of a chain of events that had begun more than four years before.

Climping, Sussex, England. 21st July 1988 (4 years and 6 months prior to the first police raid)

Powering up the Gazelle took a little time and followed a precise process. Its 1970s electronic systems and avionics pre-dated microprocessors and computer-controlled systems in later helicopters. All pre-flight checks completed, I adjusted the intermediate pitch stop for thirty degrees. Booster pump primed, I flicked the toggle from run to start. The turbines spun into life. I studied the hand of the on-board chronometer ... ten ... fifteen ... twenty seconds, the amber ignition light flashed on and the turbine exhaust temperature climbed rapidly towards 700 degrees, accompanied by the smell of kerosene and the distinctive whine of the gas turbine jet engine.

I carefully drove the throttle control forward as the turbines gathered speed, 15,000 ... 20,000 ... 25,000. The blades of the French-built Gazelle blurred overhead as the airframe twitched under the enormous torque. The main rotor and turbine needles combined on the gauge at 30,000 before peaking at 42,100 rpm. Taking care not to over-torque the engine, I fully engaged the clutch well within the designated 40 seconds.

Harry, the managing director of Saunier Duval, sat alongside me somewhat nervously. Over the years he'd become both a friend and a second father. Harry had first taken me under his wing more than three years before, agreeing that Saunier Duval, his heating company, would sponsor my foremost years in motor sport. But until now he had not trusted me to fly him to a race meeting, preferring to take the somewhat more sedate Citroen to Brands Hatch. He adjusted his headphones and spoke with unease into the boom microphone which protruded from his

headset. 'How much time have you had in one of these things?'
'Oh, it's about 7.15 Harry.' I smiled evasively. Saunier Duval had
hired the Gazelle to entertain some important clients during the
lunchtime intermission, but Harry was not happy to be on board
himself.

I released the friction and gently lifted on the collective. Harry's
fingers tightened uneasily on the seat swab as we gently lifted
into the hover. I pressed the cyclic mounted transmit button.
'Goodwood, this is Helicopter Golf Mike Alpha November, lifting
from Climping en route to Brands Hatch, Visual Flight Rules
heading zero six zero, two on board.'

There was a moment's pause, followed by two clicks. 'Helicopter
Alpha November. Good morning Will, you're cleared en route
to Brands Hatch, QNH one zero one four, Squawk four three
two one good luck in the 1000 ks.' There was another short
pause. 'Try to keep clear of Gatwick today, old boy.'

The mottled greens of the Sussex countryside spread before
us as we rose into the bright blue sky. Beth and the boys waved
from the lawn below as the house disappeared into a distant
dot.

I swallowed hard. Why was I going to risk my neck again in a
car that stood absolutely no chance of winning? A car that was
about as reliable as a Korean Rolex. A car with a sloppy chassis
that hadn't been competitive three years ago when it was new.
World Endurance racing was far riskier even than Formula One.
Group C2 teams, as we were often called, could not afford the
luxury of the Formula One carbon fibre survival cells, yet our
top speeds at circuits like Le Mans far exceeded those of the
safer Formula One circuits.

In the past two years, three WEC (World Endurance
Championship) drivers had been killed, one, Stefan Bellof, directly
in front of me at Spa in an horrific crash which shocked everyone.
And he'd been driving a car prepared by a front-running, big-
budget team, not one built with somebody else's worn out bits!
Would I come home today?

My thoughts turned to my son George. He was just five, and
for the first time that morning, had seemed to sense the danger.

'Are you going away again Daddy?'
'Daddy, when will you be back?'
'Can I come too, Daddy?'

'Daddy, are you going to drive your racing car?'

'Why do you drive a racing car, Daddy?'

The answers were becoming increasingly difficult to find. All I knew was I loved this sport with a passion that only other drivers could ever understand. The winter months, spent desperately searching for that elusive sponsor, were always rewarded when the first race of the season arrived in March each year. So I would take a few more chances; push harder on worn tyres that were two seconds off the pace; urge myself and the car beyond the limit, somehow qualifying it at the back of the pack. One day perhaps, if the sponsors kept backing me and the barriers didn't claim me, one day I'd get to drive for one of the big Porsche teams, maybe. And by then, well, shit … then I'd be pushing forty!

The ground continued to speed beneath us at a rate of three miles every minute. It had taken less than 40 minutes to fly the 60 miles to Brands Hatch at a speed of over 180 knots. Harry finally relaxed his grip on the seat. He was now enjoying his uneventful journey. I liked him and could never resist enlivening his visits to the track – after all, that was why he sponsored me.

'There Harry. You can see the circuit just to the left, about two miles ahead and over there to the north,' I pointed, 'there's a parachute school. We have to keep well clear of that. You can just see it south of the railway line.'

The circuit's car park glinted like diamonds, the bright sun reflecting from the cars three thousand feet below. To the south a pair of navigation masts rose 1300 feet into the early morning sky. A silver Goodyear airship hung just above the track like an enormous beached whale, and in the distance a wall of cumulus nimbus rose, with the threat of rain.

Harry leant forward in his seat, peering ahead through the perspex canopy. I gently eased back on the cyclic and lowered the collective; the air speed washed off and Harry froze, his gaze fixed dead ahead. The nose of the Gazelle lifted and for a moment we appeared almost stationary, suspended by the spinning silver disk. Then, with little warning, the Gazelle rolled steeply to the right; the horizon immediately inverting through the perspex. 'Oh shit!' Harry screamed. I quickly centralised the cyclic, easing back to effect recovery into wind, then again drove forward the control. Our bodies became momentarily weightless as Harry flailed frantically for the grab handles.

The Gazelle nosedived like a stone, the mottled greens blurred as we spiralled groundwards, the hands of the altimeter unwinding like those of a demented clock. Instinctively my mind registered time, speed and distance as we seared towards terminal velocity … 1000 … 800 … 500. Harry let out another blood curdling scream … 300 feet. I pulled the collective hard past the indent, stamped on the right yaw pedal and eased back on the cyclic. The air boiled from the rotors' downdraft, gravity sucked the blood into our boots and the old 1970s airframe creaked in horror as our body weights multiplied several times with the enormous G force, then with a surge of power, the Gazelle rocketed skywards before rolling out, almost on its back, 2000 feet above the circuit control tower.

'There Harry! Your first loop … well, it's not really a loop, it's called a wing over; if I'd put it completely on its back, it would have chopped its tail off!'

Harry had lost his spectacles, and his headphones had slipped down below his ears, he looked decidedly unimpressed. He fumbled for the lost spectacles with hands that shook. 'You bastard! I thought we were going to die.' His voice was hoarse, 'I didn't think you could do that in a helicopter.'

'You can't! At least, that's what the book says. But then you know me, I'm dyslexic!'

I banked the Gazelle through the thin morning air, its airframe shuddering with the increased power as I descended into a hover, before gently touching down on the grass pad. Harry peered out at the clouds of dust being thrown up by the beating blades as I ran through the shutdown procedure. Several minutes later we stepped out and I led the way through the circuit's tunnel to the team's garage at the end of the pit lane.

The mechanics had been working all night and Roy the team manager had been up plying his trusty crew with coffee since 5 am. This was not an unusual state of affairs for the vastly underfunded Roy Baker Tiga Team. As this was the first time I had driven for the team, I had arrived some three hours early to be fitted to the cramped car and to check that Harry's Saunier Duval decals were correctly positioned on the Tiga's sleek bodywork.

I donned my new red, white and blue Nomex overalls, freshly

embroidered with my regular sponsors' logos, pulled on Nomex race boots and adopted my driving position in the car's cramped monocoque, seated on a large black bin-liner into which the mechanics poured a two-part epoxy foam mix. As the warm foam expanded and set rapidly around my body, forming a mould of my torso, mechanics rushed about repositioning steering, pedals and gear lever to accommodate my six foot frame. The entire fitting process is far more complex and time consuming than most people would ever imagine; the foam moulding must fit perfectly and be as comfortable as possible, extending from beneath the knees up to the shoulders, in effect supporting the entire body.

12

Power corrupts. But it does more than that. Power attracts the corrupt, then corrupts them further.

(Don Matthews)

Anthony Paterson-Smythe, born Paterson-Smith, a middle-aged man in a tattered black gown, lumbered to his feet like a gargantuan lizard rising from the heat of the morning sun, lined face and heavy jowls displaying a disdainful and imposing demeanour. 'If Your Honour has no objections, I will commence my address from the end of the bench so I may face the members of the jury,' he began.

The learned judge could appreciate the vital importance of Mr Smythe's positioning for both his delivery as well as his girth. McGaea nodded. Smythe acknowledged somewhat obsequiously, 'Your Honour, I am much obliged.'

The members of the press sat with pens poised, a hush fell over the courtroom. Paterson-Smythe stepped purposefully forward, removed his spectacles, and for dramatic effect leaned menacingly against the lectern which creaked under the strain. He stared at his audience, brows arched like threatening storm clouds, his milky eyes dwelling on each face in turn. He returned the spectacles to his nose, momentarily adjusting the lower rims to accommodate the baggy pouches below. Juror number 3, the pretty girl in the front row, swept the long strands of hair from her face and shifted uncomfortably in her seat making a loud creak.

Smythe began. 'Members of the jury, over the coming weeks you will be expected to listen to a considerable amount of information. I must make it quite clear that whatever I or my learned colleague may say to you, does not amount to evidence. The evidence comes from the witnesses in the witness box. It is what they say that is important, and it is what they have said that you must consider when ultimately contemplating your verdict. You will find before you a grey lever arch file. There should be one between each pair of jurors, also a yellow highlighter pen like the one I am holding.' He held aloft a fluorescent yellow marker pen. 'One of these should have been provided for each of you. This will enable you to mark up relevant sections of the exhibits as we progress. Now, for those of you that have not come across one of these before, I would just point out the importance of replacing the cap in between use, as they do have a nasty tendency to dry up.'

The jury, wide awake with anticipation, were clearly grateful for this important piece of advice. Almost without exception they studied their yellow Stabilo Super Plus 24s, occasionally removing, then studiously replacing the black plastic caps with a loud click. Paterson-Smythe continued his address as though speaking through a mouthful of sticky treacle, his eyebrows occasionally flashing above his thick spectacles. He carried on addressing the jury as though speaking to a party of juveniles with hearing disorders. 'You may find the files a little difficult to master at first. If you open your files, you should find a chrome mechanism with a lever. Now,' he continued, 'by lifting upwards carefully on said lever, you will hopefully discover the jaws of the file open, to enable documents to be placed within.'

Smythe's colleague sat alongside, scribbling furiously on a legal pad apparently trying to record his learned friend's every word. The situation was close to being amusing. The Prosecution, having carried out the investigation and with the brief compiled, then transcribed each other's words which were being taken verbatim from the brief they'd compiled in the first place. Smythe was in no hurry, the clock continued to tick. The legal eagles could each charge the taxpayer £1500 per day for this little double act, and so far Smythe had only explained how to use a highlighter.

Time had little significance as the speech droned on. The whole court seemed to drift into a state of coma as Smythe laboriously painted the Prosecution's picture. I became transfixed, my eyes drawn to Paterson-Smythe's lips as if by some hypnotic force, his words at times appearing no more than meaningless sounds. What was the man up to? There was no denying his intelligence, but what he was saying was simply untrue.

'In the years from 1987 the Defendant had taken out a number of policies with WPA, a world renowned insurance corporation and bank, in order to safeguard himself against unemployment and sickness. What the Crown complains of is this: he claimed against his sickness insurance, maintaining he was too *ill* to work, while simultaneously claiming against his redundancy policies. Policies which required him to be available for work.'

I glanced over to the press bench and noticed the feverish scribbling of the assembled scribes. I quickly scrawled a message to Piglet on a yellow Post It note – 'I was claiming for my injury off the accident policy – not sickness.' I underlined the words 'accident' and 'not sickness' several times. I folded it and passed it to the officer to hand to Piglet. He studied it but did not pass it to Rabbit – he already knew the facts.

I had been brought up with a strong sense of justice and naively imagined the judicial system would deal honestly, logically and factually with the evidence. However, Paterson-Smythe, now in full flow, was giving a masterful performance. Like an illusionist he drew the jury's attention away from the facts with a slant here and another there. The indisputable facts were that I *was* injured and had been made redundant. I continued to listen in sheer disbelief, for the first time in my life wondering if I could possibly have done something illegal.

'Furthermore,' Smythe continued, 'in the summer of 1992 he used a form of insurance called Prize Indemnity to obtain $250,000 to finance his racing. The Crown's contention is that this claim was fraudulent and in addition amounts to clear evidence of both employment and remuneration.'

He shifted his enormous weight from one foot to the other while momentarily examining his pad. 'To understand this case in its entirety requires a careful look at Middleton and his businesses over a period between June 1991 and early 1993, for the purposes of (a) opening an overall chronology of that period and (b) a consideration of his claims to WPA, to be too *ill* to work.' He paused for a moment to enhance the dramatic effect.

I hurriedly scribbled another note to Piglet 'I wasn't ill!' Piglet took the note, scanned it quickly and nodded reassuringly at me.

As the oppressive steam roller of justice rolled on relentlessly, mowing down all reason, logic and fact, His Honour Justice McGaea sat high behind his elevated bench. When appropriate, his facial expressions would change: a knowing smile, a grimace, a frown. Sometimes his expressions would be accompanied with a nod or a shake of the head. Occasionally, his mouth would gape open in a form of soundless protest at my apparent crimes.

The jury were engrossed. In the press box, pens continued their fluttered frenzy across pads of lined paper. My failures were exaggerated and my successes attacked. Paterson-Smythe had my proverbial nuts in his vice-like grip and was slowly performing a public castration. The press lapped it up.

The usher we had named Lurch deposited a series of charts on the jury's bench with a thud. 'There should be one for His Honour, one for the Defence and a copy between each pair of jurors,' commented Paterson-Smythe smugly, before adding in a distinctly muffled tone that the document was of course not an agreed document, by which he meant the Defence had already proved it was hopelessly inaccurate.

Indisputably, the flow chart was an impressive-looking document of some 44 pages, prepared meticulously by D.C. Probert with nicely coloured encapsulated sleeves. It purported to accurately detail my movements and activities from the riding accident in November 1988 through to late 1993. A number of helpful colour-coded references had been added by the thoughtful detective to guide the jurors to specific exhibits and dates of apparent meetings.

The chart had been one of the sets of documents concealed by the Crown until just before the start of the trial. While it contained a vast quantity of accurate data, it also contained a great deal of inaccurate and highly misleading information. Rabbit had not considered it to be a threat. 'Don't worry Will, I can deal with it during cross examination,' he had confirmed confidently. Trouble was, Rabbit had never led a trial of this magnitude before and this document was a killer. It portrayed a false image, the Prosecution's representation, and Paterson-Smythe was purposely making a big issue of it. The document was now being treated as the inviolable pronouncement of truth, a factual account of my past life. Of course we, the Defence, would not be allowed to enlighten the jury otherwise for weeks.

The court reporters tirelessly continued their task of recording Paterson-Smythe's every word. He mopped his brow, breathing heavily from the exertion of his morning's work, then turned to the learned judge. 'I wonder if this might be a convenient place to adjourn for luncheon?' His Honour smiled appreciatively, nodding in agreement yet again.

'All stand!' Lurch barked.

I had never before raised my voice to Rabbit, but no amount of Prozac or Propanarol was going to control me now. I had been forced to sit through a three-hour character assassination and the indignant rage I had struggled to contain for the past eighteen months finally blew like an erupting volcano. 'The bastard is lying. He's just not telling the truth, why the hell did you let him get away with it?'

'Calm down Will! He's not lying. He's just doing his job, presenting the Crown's case. This is the Prosecution's opening, I can't object at this stage.'

'But he's not telling the truth! He started off by telling the jury only to consider what the witnesses say and then spent the next three hours spoon-feeding them pure fiction. A load of total crap! And what about that flow chart thing? You've proved to the judge it's inaccurate, yet he's brainwashing them with it! They all think it's a bloody factual document!'

'He's not doing anything that he's not allowed to do.' Rabbit did not sound convincing. 'The first few days will be tough Will. You've just got to sit it out, our time will come. Just calm down. Go with Tom and get some lunch. I'll be down in a minute. I've just got to have a cigarette and gather my thoughts.'

'But the jury! The press! They're all taking it in and they don't know me from Adam. They think I'm some kind of real criminal.'

'That's the idea. That's what the Crown pays Smythe to do. In fact that's all he ever does. He works full time for the CPS. He never defends. And he's bloody good. By the time he's finished there'll be little doubt in their minds that you're as guilty as sin. It's all a big game, truth doesn't enter into it. The charges are like a declaration of war by the Crown, but we'll get our turn soon. Just play the game Will, play the game.'

'Game?' I blurted. 'This is my future. My family's future. Guilty or not guilty. Acquittal or a bloody prison sentence ... it should be about truth. Will we be able to show how guilty they are?'

'Will. You've got to get a grip ... don't let them see you're rattled. Try and relax. We have to win the war, not get bogged down with minor skirmishes.'

DC Barnet strolled confidently from the court, smirking at my obvious distress. With a frown, Rabbit addressed me, 'Will, this is not the right place to be talking like this.' He turned to Beth. 'Take him downstairs and try to get him to relax.'

In the canteen an assistant behind the counter demanded to know what we wanted for lunch. He poured a mug of hot brown liquid which I was assured was coffee. Tigger led the way to a sticky plastic white table and sat down. Beth stirred a mint tea bag into a cup of boiling water as I sipped cautiously from my mug of steaming liquid. She and Piglet watched anxiously like laboratory technicians overseeing a dangerous experiment. Having seen no immediate signs of convulsions or botulism they too sipped carefully from their mugs.

Five minutes elapsed before the assistant reappeared with four plates of steaming faggots. I had no idea what poor creature had laid down its life for the creation of our gastronomic lunch but Piglet was paying so I was grateful, whatever it was. I conveyed a morsel of the glistening faggot to my mouth and nibbled thoughtfully while Tigger gave serious consideration as to what to do with a mouthful of gristle. After brief contemplation the sinuous morsel was swallowed with a degree of obvious discomfort.

Rabbit returned from taking his wig for its morning constitutional and sat at the end of our table.

'Sorry about that Giles! I lost my rag for a few minutes, I'm okay now,' I said, trying hard to hide a large faggot behind some mashed potato.

'Don't worry. It's only to be expected. You've been under enormous strain. But if you feel like blowing again, at least try to hold it in until we're away from the court! Remember, the Crown have an uphill battle; not only are your injuries and the redundancy transparently clear but you are a man of previous good character, you have no previous convictions, you look like a decent guy and you sound convincing. This is only the start! They are going to fling mud and try to make you look as dishonest as they possibly can, any way they can!'

'It's just that pompous Smythe! He just winds me up.' I stabbed violently at a soggy sprout but missed, my fork ricocheting off one of the two remaining faggots which in turn offered a glancing blow to the other one. It left the plate in a graceful arc, bounced majestically along the table, missing Rabbit by inches, before tumbling to the tiled floor with a forlorn thud.

13

The press had been turned away and the court remained closed when we returned from lunch. The jury box was empty, the jurors detained in their room with additional tea and biscuits courtesy of His Honour. With the public gallery cleared and only Counsel in place, Judge McGaea entered and made his way to his seat, glaring in my direction. Both Prosecution and Defence Counsel bowed solemnly.

'It came to my attention during the recess,' His Honour began, 'that Channel 4 intends screening a so-called *investigation* into the activities of certain insurance companies and their alleged mis-selling of unemployment protection policies. Having carried out my own *investigation*, I have discovered that WPA is to feature in this programme which is due to be screened this evening at 8 pm.' He fired a look in my direction. 'Mr Adams, I am not prepared to countenance a defendant trying to manipulate the British justice system. Perhaps you could enquire of your client what he knows of this mysterious twist of fate?'

Piglet and Rabbit made their way uneasily to the dock. 'It's nothing to do with me,' I said, trying to hide my delight, 'but I'm sure it will make riveting viewing for the jury!'

'Will,' Piglet began, running a hand through his hair, 'this isn't a joke! Let me make it very clear, the judge has asked a specific question and I suspect from what he's said, that he's already been in contact with the broadcasters. Can you assure us that you have had no contact or involvement of any kind with this programme?'

'I can guarantee you I have had absolutely nothing to do with *that* programme,' I replied evasively.

'What do you mean, *that* programme?' Rabbit asked sotto voce.
I shrugged, 'Oh, nothing of any importance.'

'Will, can you see how this looks?' Piglet pleaded.

'Yes. It looks as though the judge is making assumptions he
can't support. It also looks like there are hundreds, maybe
thousands more people out there like me, being shafted by WPA.'

Rabbit turned to Piglet and nodded sombrely. 'Okay, Will,'
Rabbit said turning back to face the judge.

The judge held up a hand. 'I think we all heard Mr Middleton's
assertion,' he began tersely, 'but let me make it very clear that
if your client is found to be connected in any way with this
programme he will find himself in a prison cell before the day
is out.'

Paterson-Smythe rose from his bench, eager to add to the
debate. 'Your Honour, might I suggest that the jury be sequestered
overnight in a local hotel with all televisions removed?'

'I dare say,' replied His Honour drily, 'that even if we managed
to locate a hotel with sufficient space at this short notice, there
would still remain the risk of family or friends revealing the
broadcast before the conclusion of the trial. No, the programme
must be stopped. I will call a recess for the rest of the day. In
the meantime, I will prepare an order preventing the programme
being aired until these proceedings have been concluded.'

14

Sunday 24th July 1988

The helicopter remained parked on the lawn, as Harry had insisted on taking his Citroen to Brands Hatch instead. It was 8 am when we pulled into the rear paddock entrance. The roar of racing engines echoed hauntingly around the half-empty amphitheatre. The smell of exotic fluids permeated the crisp morning air. On this day the first tenuous link would be forged in the chain leading to the dock.

Despite the qualifying engine's 540 horsepower we had only achieved a disappointing twenty-second place on the grid amid a host of technical problems including a lack of appropriate tyres. We were running Dunlop rubber, the big budget teams had superior Goodyears which gave a clear 1.5 seconds advantage in the dry, even more in the wet, and Saturday had been very wet. It was rumoured that the new wet-weather Goodyears could disperse a staggering seven gallons of water per second, something we could only dream about as we'd slithered around in search of grip.

Despite the conditions, Sauber Mercedes had qualified on the front row using Michelin tyres that were exclusive to the German factory team, Mauro Baldi taking pole from Jochen Mass who lined up alongside in the sister car. The three Silk Cut Jaguars had been bumped to fourth and sixth with John Watson a poor eighth debuting the new 48-valve car. Watson had been unhappy with the car's handling from the first session, which had ended abruptly with the car embedded firmly in the tyre wall on the exit of the revised Dingle Dell corner.

I had not met Andy, my American co-driver, prior to Brands

Hatch, and was annoyed that the Yank had managed to squeeze almost .8 of a second more out of the Tiga than I had achieved. I told myself I had not driven the Tiga previously whereas Andy had raced the car regularly for Roy in America. Anyway it had been wet during most of my qualifying sessions. Dark clouds were already gathering overhead and rain was again forecast for the afternoon.

Inevitably the crowd was down on last year's race but such was the appeal of the keenly fought Jaguar versus Mercedes battle that more than 30,000 spectators spread round the vast curve from Clearways, past the start-finish line to Paddock Hill Bend, to view the mighty clash of the titans. As fate would have it, it was all to be in vain.

Roy strolled from the pit garage. 'Will, I've been thinking, I'd like Andy to start.'

'But the deal was that I would start.'

'I know, but it's going to be a wet race, Andy knows the car. I'd like him to do the first stint and you to do the morning warm up.' What he meant was that Andy had been the fastest.

Brands Hatch was a difficult home circuit which I knew like the back of my hand. Roy had reasoned that Andy, who had never seen the place before, should have the bulk of the qualifying time. Trouble was, that left me with only a handful of laps, in the wet, to qualify myself in an unfamiliar car. 'Roy that's ridiculous,' I exclaimed. 'Andy's never driven in a World Championship race before! He doesn't know what to expect from the C1 drivers. He's out of his depth to start with.'

'Then it's up to you to talk to him.'

Andy was one of the many wealthy amateurs who frequented sports car racing. Nothing wrong with that, it was the amateurs that made up over half the grid in these races and gave the pros someone to race. The amateurs also made the pros look good, though that's not necessarily how the pros saw it, of course. The top professionals had better equipment, bigger budgets, better tactics. They were fitter, had more time to train and therefore had quicker reflexes. Their whole approach was more intense, more finely tuned; racing was their business as well as their pleasure. For Andy it was merely his pleasure, a weekend away from the office, a chance for a guppy to swim among whales.

The majority of professionals considered their amateur opponents to be unfit nuisances that got in the way, caused accidents and risked lives. The Brands Hatch race had been billed by *Autosport*, the bible of motorsport, as 'The Clash of the Titans', the battle between the British Jaguars, the German Porsches, and the privately entered Swiss Sauber Mercedes.

I felt Roy's decision was wrong, but I was new to the team and there was no point in arguing with him once his mind was made up. Anyway, at least I was going to get a few extra laps in the warm-up section, this time in the dry.

I crawled into the cramped cockpit, snapped into the six-point harness and pulled on my helmet. Roy's voice crackled over the headset. 'Just five laps to scrub the new tyres. Then straight in.'

Roy's instructions continued in short bursts: 'Remember this is a different spec motor to the qualifier, it's got a low-pressure crank, 40 lb oil pressure.' Click.

'With the Zytec fuel management you should have 60 lb of fuel pressure.' Click.

'We've put in a slightly shorter top gear and gone 150 lb up on springs all round with two clicks more rebound.' Click.

'The wing's down one degree and we've dropped the ride height slightly.' Click.

'Don't take it above 9000 rpm, watch the top end with the lower ratio.' Click.

'Just see what she's like. Torque will be well down on the other engine.' Click.

'If it rains we will have to re-think the set up.' Click.

I flicked the booster pumps on; 60 lb registered instantly on the gauge. I gave a circular motion with my right hand to a watching mechanic. The signal was immediately relayed to another technician at the rear of the car who inserted the starter pack into the car's electrical system. The rev counter flickered as the engine roared into life.

Paterson-Smythe had enjoyed the previous day's early recess but was back in full flow with the learned judge nodding his support. Smythe turned to His Honour. 'If it will please the court, there is a letter from which I would like to read some extracts.'

'What is it?' asked the judge.

'A letter dated 7th April 93, by the Defendant to one of his insurers. Written some seven weeks after the intervention of the police.'

'Any objection, Mr Adams?'

'None Your Honour. Although it might assist the jury if the letter was read in its entirety.'

'Do you have any objections to that Mr Smythe?' McGaea queried.

Paterson-Smythe flinched ever so slightly. 'Er ... it's a very long letter Your Honour, some six pages.' Smythe sounded almost apologetic. He removed his glasses, polishing the thick lenses somewhat anxiously with the edge of his gown.

'Yes. I'm aware of the document Mr Smythe.' His Honour snapped.

Rabbit rose to his feet, giving the judge a small but gracious bow, for once looking taller, more purposeful, like a small vulture rising to the distant whiff of a bloody kill. 'If it may assist the court, it would be my intention to read the letter of 7th April in its entirety at some stage, Your Honour. Perhaps now might be as good a time as any?'

'Yes, Mr Adams.' The learned judge sighed deeply through pursed lips before continuing in a melancholy tone of deep regret, 'Mr Smythe, it may save us some time if we got it over with now. Proceed Mr Adams.'

The dejected barrister lumbered back to his bench and flopped heavily into his seat which complained audibly under the strain.

Excellent. Bloody excellent. Well done Rabbit. This will give them something to think about and right in the middle of his opening speech. I was impressed and felt like blowing Smythe a raspberry. Rabbit rose slowly, looking as if he'd breakfasted on a bucket of rotten eggs. But he quickly controlled his nerves, collected his thoughts and walked to the lectern.

'Your Honour, the letter was written by the Defendant to WPA, some weeks after the first raid on the Old Granary. This was in reply to the insurer's request for additional information, to enable them to decide whether or not to continue paying the Defendant's redundancy claim. It reads: "*I am concerned that with the police involving themselves in what is clearly a complicated insurance claim the legitimate facts behind this matter are being entirely overlooked.*

Perhaps this is to the benefit of certain parties but clearly this is very detrimental and extremely unfair to me...".'

Paterson-Smythe appeared to shrink, just a little.

'*"I am therefore pleased to summarise my position and would be grateful if you would, once acquainted with ALL the facts, please advise by return whether you intend to honour my continuing unemployment claim or whether you believe I should be claiming under the sickness/disability heading of the policy."'*

McGaea surveyed the dock with a high degree of antagonism. He was clearly a page or two ahead of Rabbit, who was making unhurried deliberate progress and relishing every word.

'*"One of the major events which they accuse me of working on while unemployed in fact took place at the Savoy hotel in London on 7th August 1991 some 5 months BEFORE I was made redundant. This was a function laid on by Team Capricorn, my former employers in preparation for the new season (the police have for reasons known only to themselves ignored the date. Doubtless I will be accused of being cynical but surely this can only help them persuade the CPS there is a case to answer). These are facts which can easily be substantiated."'*

The learned judge listened with growing impatience, occasionally flicking a glance of distaste at Counsel for the Defence. Rabbit pressed on. '*"The allegations that I have been working are simply a quite absurd distortion of the true facts."'*

Paterson-Smythe fidgeted uncomfortably within the confines of his seat which emitted more loud creaks.

'*"As you are aware, a number of years prior to being made redundant I had injured my back and made a claim on the PPI injury policy, a policy I have held since the mid 80s. However, no benefits whatever were received until mid November 91, just at the time I was being made redundant! The injury, resulting from a riding accident, prevented me from performing my usual occupation."'*

Rabbit continued in smooth, effortless style. *I glanced at the jury. Yes! They looked impressed, good. I turned to the press bench. They'd gone. The bastards had left. They'd got their story, at least Smythe's sensational version.*

'*"DHSS records will show that I disclosed I had the back problem,"'* Rabbit continued in clear, polished style, any past hint of nervousness had now vanished, each syllable clearly articulated.

'*"Perhaps nobody involved in a professional sport has previously been hit with two such situations which overlapped. I had a back injury (now confirmed by x-rays and five independent medical experts) and thus a legitimate claim as this specifically prevented me from performing my job as a professional racing driver. Following my redundancy, I believed (and still do!) I had an additional claim for redundancy."'*

The jury seemed to relax and even risked the occasional glance in the direction of the dock. Juror 3, the pretty girl on the front row, smiled reassuringly in my direction as if to say, don't worry, we know there is another side to all this.

For the first time in 18 months, I relaxed just a little. Perhaps this was the first glimmer of hope.

15

Beth stood by the pit wall, her eyes searching anxiously in the direction of Clearways. Roy studied the display on the Heuer chronograph. 'He's not going to try anything silly Beth is he? This is just the warm up.'

The car was understeering like a pig but I knew the track surface would change halfway through Clearways. The rev counter flashed to 8500, I snatched fourth gear. The clock registered a drop of 1500 revs. The momentum carried me hard through the corner, my neck muscles straining to hold my head upright against the invisible forces that tore at my limbs like a giant unseen magnet. The tyres suddenly bit, launching the Tiga like a projectile onto the pit straight.

The crew held out the pit board: L4, my last lap. I scorched the straight, over the brow, 160 mph, 8900 revs. I exploded onto the brakes and entered Paddock Bend a fraction deeper than usual. Wisps of smoke churned through the venturis. The right front tyre clipped the apex, making the back end twitch violently. My weight multiplied as I rocketed downhill towards Druids, a shower of sparks bursting from the underside of the car as the G forces contracted my spine and pinned the Tiga violently onto its skid blocks. The smell of scorching metal singed my nostrils as the steel blocks made contact with the track's surface.

I stamped on the brakes, second gear, 7000 rpm. The Tiga drifted in a perfectly balanced slide out of the horseshoe of Druids downhill using the downward momentum and shortened gearing to shift straight into fourth gear – damn! The rev drop was too high, 2800. Roy was right, this engine couldn't pull the skin off a rice pudding.

A hard smack on the brakes, into third for Surtees. The car switched from understeer to power oversteer, twitching wildly. Down the back straight into Hawthorns at 170 mph, the water temperature registering 100 degrees; 5 degrees into the danger area. *Just hang in there for three more corners.* Dingle Dell flashed by as Martin Brundle zapped past in the TWR Silk 'cat', 105 degrees. One more corner to go. Third gear into Clearways for the last time, 110 degrees, 8700 rpm. I grabbed fourth at the apex as the impetus carried me wide across the track, past Roy holding the pit board with a bright yellow 'IN' in four-inch letters.

I checked the mirrors and lifted immediately, the tell-tale needle registered 9400 rpm. *Shit, I'm going to get a rocketing!* The radio crackled in my ear, 'Will, that was a 1.25!'

I knew it was going to be quicker than my previous times, but then my wet qualifying session had been a joke. Anyway a 1.25 still wasn't quick compared with current times. But for a two-year-old very tired shit-bucket it wasn't bad either. Had I been allowed to do it in qualifying, we'd have moved six places up the grid, just ahead of my usual co-driver Rob Allan. A broad grin of satisfaction spread under my Nomex balaclava: a full nine seconds quicker than dear old Andy eh? *Stuff that one in your pecan pie, old boy!*

Rabbit concluded with a final fluid burst of eloquence. The jury had been listening intently. He had nicely stretched the allotted time to consume the bulk of the afternoon. I checked my watch. 3.50 pm.

Paterson-Smythe examined his watch, and finding it was time for a meal rose slowly to his feet, his frayed robe hanging from his shoulders. 'Your Honour will have noticed it is now ten minutes to four. I wonder if this might be a convenient point to adjourn?'

'Yes, Mr Smythe. The time had not entirely escaped my notice.'

The jury exited quickly. His Honour turned to Rabbit. He waited until the last juror had cleared the court. 'Mr Adams,' he said in a markedly unfriendly tone, 'during your address I could hardly help noticing that your client was, on occasion, nodding in agreement with the various passages of text. It might be appropriate to have words with your client and point out that this is not the done thing. It can give quite the wrong impression to a jury.' Rabbit, suitably rebuked, nodded.

The learned judge turned to the Prosecution and smiled reassuringly. 'Mr Smythe, roughly how much longer do you expect to be addressing the jury?'

'I must admit Your Honour, I do have a tendency to, er, open long, but close short.'

'Oh, that's quite all right,' reassured the judge. 'I was just wondering whether we might get around to calling any witnesses by tomorrow?'

'I would hope to conclude my address by luncheon tomorrow. Perhaps we could commence with witnesses in the afternoon?'

'Oh, excellent, excellent. Please don't think I'm trying to rush you at all.'

Paterson-Smythe bowed reverently. 'Your Honour, I'm most grateful.'

Rabbit rose simultaneously, offering another slow and gracious bow, as though the pair were participating in a little dance together. 'Your Honour, the Defence would like to submit to the court a set of accounts and a report by Messrs Merton and Collins in respect of Mr Middleton's financial affairs covering the past six years.'

Lurch scuttled forward and collected two bound copies, delivering one to Paterson-Smythe and one to His Honour. The learned judge flicked through a few pages and opened one at random. 'Takes me back to my accountancy days.'

16

Justice denied anywhere diminishes justice everywhere.

(Martin Luther King, 1929-68)

Based on the charges, it had been considered prudent to prepare detailed personal accounts. I was at the offices of Merton Collins in Staines.

'What do you need?' I asked the senior partner, Tom Merton.

'Everything you've got.' He leaned back in his chair and smiled.

'How far back do you want to go?'

'Six years, for a start.'

'Not a problem.'

A second partner, Michael Collins, entered the room. 'Good morning. Mr Middleton?' he inclined his head.

'Yes. Hello.' I stood for a moment as we shook hands.

'We've been instructed by your solicitors to produce detailed personal accounts covering the past six years. We haven't much time. I understand the trial is due to commence in a fortnight. What are your records like?'

'I keep everything on a computer. The records should be good. I can account for just about everything going back at least eight years,' I said proudly. I could tell they didn't believe me, this was going to be fun. I unpacked my briefcase and deposited six years of detailed computer printouts onto the table.

'My personal computer is in the car and, if you need to examine original documentation to support the entries, I've also got three boxes of files, bank statements, cheque stubs, counterfoils and receipts in the car.' For some reason I'd always liked keeping detailed financial records. It was more than just the feeling of order and symmetry it provided; it somehow gave me a sense of security, in a world that was anything but secure.

*　*　*

'All stand,' yelled Lurch.

Rabbit and Piglet struggled from the court laden down with files as we made our way to Rabbit's makeshift office on the second floor. 'What do you think then?' I asked eagerly.

'Well, it was a start. Some basis on which to build. And we seem to have quite a good jury. By that I mean at least they're awake.'

Two hours of dazzling analysis and intellectual debate followed, and it was late by the time Beth and I eventually stepped from the court building into the dark shadows. Suddenly the darkness erupted into a blaze of flashing lights. I squinted against the dazzle as cameras clicked and flashed like an arsenal of automatic weapons. A voice shouted from the darkness, 'Come on mate, stand still for a minute! You don't want to look like a criminal in tomorrow's papers.' I smiled into a retreating lens. If only I could have attracted this level of interest on the track!

Winter had come early and the big house was cold when we arrived home. Despite having liquidated any viable assets, money was now in desperately short supply. The bank letters had started arriving by Recorded Delivery. We had not been able to afford our heating for the past year. Derek and Hilary, two of our few remaining friends, welcomed us home. Amazingly they had left London, jobs, home and all, to temporarily relocate to Climping to take care of our boys for the duration of the trial, however long.

The boys stampeded downstairs. 'Dad! Dad! Is it over? What happened? Do you have to go again tomorrow? Are you okay?'

I knelt down and hugged them. Beth's hand appeared on my shoulder. My voice cracked. 'Yes, I'm fine. A few more weeks, then it will all be over, I promise.'

I gazed, almost mesmerised by the blue shadows that flickered from the muted television at the end of our bed. Flashes of my past life, the good and bad times darted through my mind. I was cold. Beth wrapped another blanket around me. Tiredness made my eyelids droop, I drifted into a deep disturbing sleep.

The night was troubled, a voice within my head whispered my

name. 'Will ... Will.' My thoughts drew me into the chill of consciousness. I looked at my watch: 5 am. My father's voice called again. 'Will ... Will.' I sat up wiping the tears from my eyes and gazed at the shape just discernible by the bedroom door. I was intrigued more than afraid.

'Dad!' I exclaimed.

The room was damp, cold and in near darkness but the moon was bright and shadows of light twisted from the window in a soft lilac veil across the room. The hushed almost sibilant whisper called again. 'Will ... don't worry.'

I sat for a moment hoping the voice would rouse Beth, but she remained perfectly still, her sleep serene and untroubled. I whispered her name but there was no response. My body dripped with sweat, scepticism merged with fascination. 'Dad ... but you're dead!'

Slowly but purposefully the dim shape moved silently through the shadows. I stared in disbelief, wiping cold sweat from my face with the back of my hand. I wanted to speak but my throat was parched with emotion.

A chill breeze flickered across my face, freezing the droplets of sweat. My father leaned forward and kissed my brow. 'Don't worry, son. Everything will be okay!' I woke with a start and sprang out of bed, my heart was pounding.

'Beth! Beth! I've just seen my father!'

Her eyes fluttered open. 'Darling, calm down ... it was just a dream.' She roused herself and reached for the light switch. Sitting back against the headboard, she smiled reassuringly. 'Darling, you're soaked! Go and have a warm shower, I'll make you a hot cup of tea. We have to be up soon anyway.'

It could have been a dream that my disturbed mind might have invented, but something inside told me that it really had happened. That it was a sign of hope, real hope transcending the void of mortality, time and the reasoning of man.

17

English criminal justice is in a crisis without precedent, its solutions uncertain and its effects deeply damaging. At a time when the crime rate has reached an all time high, the system often fails to identify offenders: it locks up the innocent while the guilty go free.

(David Rose, Home Affairs correspondent of the *Observer*,
In the Name of the Law)

It was 9 am when Beth and I arrived at court for day two. Paterson-Smythe was already in the canteen busily chasing the remnants of fried eggs around his plate with a slice of toast. The jury, who used the same facilities as us, sat huddled in two groups around a pair of tables, heads buried deep in the day's tabloid fiction.

Rabbit and Tigger collected their coffee and joined us with the usual assortment of files, mobile phones and laptops. 'Giles, all this stuff they're suggesting about orchestrating my redundancy...' Rabbit nodded towards me in acknowledgement as he sipped his coffee. 'Well, the Official Receiver, who'd had access to all the records, agreed we'd done everything possible to save the company. Even if they've destroyed the documents, they must have a record of his findings.' Rabbit took a mouthful of toast, washed it down with coffee, then shook his head. He paused for a moment as though in thought.

'Don't worry about it. I can't imagine they'll get anywhere with that line of argument.' He paused briefly again. 'It just helps confound the jury. The accountant's report proves you did nothing wrong. It's all the speculation that gets me. I've never come across a case with so much rumour, buzz and speculation. At the pre-trial the judge seemed to think you were involved in drug dealing of some kind. Where the hell did that come from? McGaea has a reputation; he sees himself as a champion dedicated to uncovering the truth. He's a bit old school. But he's known to give either side hell. If he thinks you're guilty, he won't let you get away. But he seems to have had the impression you were guilty from day one and he *specifically asked* to hear this case. Why? Are you sure somebody hasn't got a grudge against you?'

'Are you trying to scare me?' I retorted, with a frown.

His eyes met mine. 'Will, WPA went through four sets of private detectives before they could find one who sent in a bungled report. The police must have known it was a case of mistaken identity as soon as they saw the report; it was so obvious, it even included a set of photos of the wrong family, yet they still went ahead and raided you, not once but twice. They've rifled your bank accounts, involved the FBI and Interpol, tracked halfway around the world and possibly bugged your phones – not that we can prove that.' He paused, taking another mouthful of coffee. 'Why? At the end of the day you've claimed on your redundancy and accident insurance. Lots of people make claims, lots of claims get turned down; not many claimants get what you're going through.'

'But this is the Crown; the CPS; the judicial system,' I said incredulously. 'How could they be involved in anything underhand? They're the good guys. The ones that eliminate crime, not create it.'

'I'm not suggesting it's the CPS,' he paused, as if uncertain whether to continue, '... maybe somebody in the CPS? Somebody with influence over someone in the CPS, or somebody in the Met?' He shook his head, 'I don't know, but someone certainly seems to have it in for you.' He finished his coffee, removed a cigarette from its pack and lit it. 'This investigation will have cost a fortune. By the time the trial is over we'll be talking well over a million, maybe even two.'

Outlandish, impossible, I told myself. There had to be something else. I pressed my fingers to my forehead as though trying to stimulate my memory. Rob Allan and his girlfriend Anna came to mind. I dismissed the thought as quickly as it flared, I didn't want to go there, it was too embarrassing especially with Beth there. I closed my eyes and racked my brains. An image flickered in my mind's eye. After the TV programme debacle, I cringed at the thought of mentioning it! A smartly dressed reporter speaking directly to the screen: '*Tonight – a Consumer Alert special... Have you been mis-sold a mortgage protection policy?*' – Cut to smart female reporter – '*Tonight, Consumer Alert investigates the growing boom in Redundancy and Mortgage Protection Policies.*' Cut back to the male reporter, his face now stern – '*During the latter part of the eighties, tens of thousands of such policies were sold to unsuspecting home owners. But as the recession deepens, and claims stack up we ask, are the policies worth the paper they are written on? We asked the head of claims of WPA, the UK's biggest supplier of these policies to join us in the studio, but he declined our invitation...*'

My mind cast back to my letter to the BBC and the time just prior to the police raids; the shadowy shapes that had drifted in and out of our lives, spooks, figures in the darkness. The strange events that had followed my being charged, the odd echoey phone call from Toby, who was then effectively dismissed from the case days later by McGaea.

I shivered, my voice tightened. 'Did I mention that I reported WPA to the BBC?'

Rabbit lifted an eyebrow. 'No, you did not.'

'Well...' I began, 'WPA were originally dragging their feet over my redundancy claim. I'd written to them several times, we were coming under increasing pressure from our mortgage provider. Months went by and WPA refused to pay anything. So I wrote to the BBC, to their Consumer Alert programme and sent a copy of that letter to WPA. A week later, they reviewed the claim and started paying.'

'So your case featured on Consumer Alert?' Rabbit asked.

'No. As WPA had started to pay us my case wasn't featured, but dozens of cases were and it clearly lit a fuse at the BBC. They dedicated a whole programme to WPA and payment protection policies, then ran follow-ups over the next few weeks.'

Piglet's eyes widened. 'This was before or after you sued WPA Bank, using a WPA Legal Costs Policy?'

'I didn't sue; I threatened and they settled.'

Rabbit looked enquiringly at Piglet, his head inclined. 'What?'

Piglet didn't look up from writing his notes. 'WPA Bank bounced one of Will's cheques by mistake. A cheque for eighteen pounds I believe. Will received a settlement of £4000.'

'Let me get this right. You sued WPA Bank for £4000?' Rabbit queried.

'I didn't sue; I threatened to sue.'

'Whatever!' he waved a hand dismissively. 'You got four grand

92

out of them for an eighteen-pound bounced cheque. Then a few months later you lit a touchpaper under them and the BBC did a massive PPI exposé.'

Piglet was frantically scribbling some figures on his legal pad. He looked up. 'Consumer Alert referred to several hundreds of unpaid WPA claims. Assuming each PPI claim ran for just six months and each claimant's monthly mortgage payment was around five hundred pounds, that's a net liability to WPA of around one and a half million pounds. One and a half million they might never have had to pay.'

'Unemployment was running at over three million at that time,' Rabbit added. 'If claimants were out of work then, it was likely to be long term, probably eighteen months or more. WPA's liability could have topped five million just on the unpaid claims highlighted by Consumer Alert.'

I sat awkwardly, a twinge of embarrassment displayed on my face; a fly caught in my own web. I bit my lip. 'Power of the little guy? Sock it to them?' I offered feebly. 'Hmm ... where does this take us?'

Two sets of eyes bored into me. You fool! The words weren't spoken, but I heard them. The disapproval was unanimous and well deserved. 'Have you ever considered Russian roulette?' Rabbit spoke with a degree of sarcasm. 'It might be safer.' Under the table Beth's hand crept into mine.

Piglet finally broke the uneasy silence. 'What happened to WPA's stock value?'

I shrugged. 'No idea.'

Piglet turned to Rabbit. 'It's just...' Piglet paused, 'you agreed to McGaea presiding over the case. McGaea admitted at the pre-trial review that he is a client of WPA. We took that to mean a policy holder. But what if he's a stockholder? As a customer or policy holder, it's debatable whether he should be allowed within a mile of this case, but if he's a stockholder...'

Rabbit flushed slightly. 'Nobody told me about Consumer Alert!'

The tannoy above our heads mercifully interrupted. 'All parties in the case of Middleton to Court One please.'

* * *

93

'All persons having business within this Crown Court stand forth and give their attention!' Lurch announced.

The court attendants stiffened to attention. McGaea entered the hushed arena, dropped into the high-backed chair and with an imperious wave, seated the court. For a moment he surveyed his domain before settling his gaze on the twelve citizens of the jury, his face instantly spreading into a broad welcoming smile.

'Good morning ladies and gentlemen. I trust you all slept well?' Then he turned to the Prosecution. 'Mr Smythe, please continue.'

18

It is necessary to relax your muscles when you can. Relaxing your brain is fatal.

(Stirling Moss)

July 1988, Brands Hatch

Harry stood by the pit wall watching as the mechanics flapped around making final checks. Andy, swathed in Nomex, sat at the wheel of the Tiga, sucking a chilled isotonic drink through a tube that protruded from his helmet. Roy fastened the safety harness and plugged in the radio link and medical oxygen that would provide twenty seconds of life-conserving air to Andy's brain in the event of a fire.

The grid was lined up ready for the first of the scheduled 240 laps, a distance of 624 miles, equivalent to three Grand Prix. Andy was scheduled to make the first refuelling stop on the fifteenth lap, at which point I would take over. The klaxon sounded. Thirty seconds to go. Twenty four engines roared into life.

Mauro Baldi led the formation for the rolling start, the cars weaving like frantic serpents, twitching from side to side in their attempt to generate heat into their tyres.

The lights changed to green, Baldi botched the start and Mass reached Paddock Bend first: Jelinski second, Baldi third. On the second lap Jelinski in the Joest Porsche 962 out-braked Jochen to take the lead and by lap five held an impressive 3-second advantage. Andy had moved up four places and was closing on his next target, but by lap eight the leaders were poised to lap the back markers.

Mass in the Sauber Mercedes had closed the gap on the Porsche 962 which zapped past the Tiga at Clearways. Andy, taken off guard, moved left to allow Mass through – a serious error.

95

Travelling off line at over 80 mph he hit the loose stuff, the debris scuffed from everybody's tyres, little roller bearings of rubber lying there waiting to snare any that strayed off the racing line. The Tiga veered sideways. Mass saw the gap and went for it, but left insufficient room. The Tiga was already drifting back onto the race line.

Bang! The Tiga struck the Sauber's left rear. The car slewed as it turned, scorching molten black strips across the track. The tyre wall exploded as the Sauber hit, the impact tearing out the engine and causing an instant flash fire before pitching the car high into the air and back across the track.

Mauro Baldi in the sister car was close behind and narrowly missed the carnage by throwing the Sauber into an impressive 360-degree spin before not quite so impressively stalling the car in the middle of the track. The Silk Cut Jaguars driven by Niesen and Lammers threaded their way through the mayhem into second and third place.

I turned to Harry, my sponsor. 'I think Andy has just lost Mercedes the World Championship. It might be time to make ourselves scarce.'

The yellow caution flags came out while the track was cleared. Roy's men collected the Tiga and courageously set about rebuilding the front end, a task destined to lose us more than thirty laps. Mauro's car was fortunately unscathed but lost two laps as a result of his smoky spin, stalled engine and the need to replace all four flat-spotted tyres. A somewhat shaken Andy appeared in the pit garage hotly pursued by Jochen Mass. 'What the hell do you think you were doing out there? Are you blind?' A TV crew sensing blood, arrived to film the commotion. I felt sorry for Andy. He looked lost, shaken, embarrassed. 'Don't you have fucking mirrors? You shouldn't be out there if you can't drive! You could have killed me!'

Things were getting out of hand. For a minute I thought Mass was going to physically lay into Andy. It had been a wrong decision to allow him to take the start but Mass had to take some of the blame; there had been two car-widths to pass, yet he had cut in far too close. It was a typical racing accident, typical of a C1 driver not giving a C2 driver room to breathe.

Roy ran from the pit garage. 'Will, get your helmet on. We'll be ready for you in five minutes!'

It had been a huge accident and the Tiga had handled like a pig before the crash. Now it was frightening; still capable of over 180 mph but with a tendency to 'sledge', as the altered ride height affects the under-body air flow and thus the car's ability to stick to the track.

Fear bit deeply into me that day. I fought my way back up the field, finally finishing thirteenth despite additional dramas on the last lap. At the approach to Clearways, the scene of the previous accident, at around 120 mph the right front wheel decided that enough was enough. It detached itself completely from the still mangled hub, bouncing its way over the pit wall. Luckily I managed to carry on, completing the last five hundred metres as the fastest three-wheeler in Brands Hatch history. It had not been a good day and despite finishing thirteenth on the track, the officials decided not to classify the result as the mechanics had pushed the damaged Tiga back to the pits following Andy's accident.

Roy helped me out of the car. 'Will, you drove well today. I want to talk to you about Sandown, the Australian race. I'd like you to drive for me.'

Australia, eh? Sun, sea, racing cars and a stopover in Malaysia. Wow! Perhaps it hadn't been such a bad day after all.

19

Paterson-Smythe gave the jury a welcoming smile. A smile vaguely reminiscent of a baby with colic.

'Ladies and gentlemen, before I proceed further I will spend just a few moments reviewing the ground we covered yesterday.'

The officer by my side was aware that Mr Smythe's 'few moments' would, most likely, amount to a considerable time. He removed a paperback from his pocket and settled down for a relaxing read.

Smythe was determined to erase any memory of Rabbit's orations of the previous day. Slowly he polished the thick lenses of his spectacles before returning them to his nose. He took a few paces to his lectern to address the jury. 'Ladies and gentlemen, would you please open your files and refer to the flow chart provided to you yesterday?'

Paterson-Smythe droned on slowly, stirring the corrosive cocktail, which was of course not classified as evidence, gradually infusing the lethal brew into the deepest recesses of the jury's minds. Occasionally he would attempt to crack a joke in a bid to relieve the boredom. Other times he would direct Lurch to hand out pre-punched copies of exhibits to the jurors, Smythe carefully pointing out which sections should be highlighted yellow prior to insertion in their respective files.

His Honour listened with obvious satisfaction, head nodding. Occasionally he would glance with revulsion at the felon in the dock, projecting subliminal messages to the audience gathered below him.

I wanted to remind His Honour not to nod his head, as it was not the done thing and could give quite the wrong impression to the jury. Also that the court-appointed stenographers were quite unable to record His Honour's terse and obvious signals – but then this was a fact he knew only too well. Unfortunately the role of the victim in a mugging is passive, and court etiquette required me to sit quietly with my mouth firmly shut.

Paterson-Smythe paused to frame his next words tactfully. Now was an opportunity for the Crown to gain potential points with the jury, to show the Prosecution's courtesy, their respect and compassion. Smythe knew when to be cautious; the jury would be offended by any harsh treatment at this stage. The learned barrister had spent many years looking into the eyes of juries; his father was a High Court judge, his friends the judiciary, his training was impeccable.

He turned to the dock and flashed a disconcerting smile, the sickly smile of a schoolboy creeping to his housemaster. He spoke directly to the jury, his voice sugary, slow and deliberate, a man who earnestly cares.

'Ladies and gentlemen,' he paused and looked in great pain. 'Sadly it was at this stage in the activities that Middleton's father unfortunately died. There is no doubt that the Defendant, a good and devoted son, was clearly overwhelmed by the loss of his father.'

I had loved my father and deeply resented his memory being drawn into the Prosecution's theatrical performance. I had been devastated in October 91 when cancer had reappeared in a further attempt to claim his life. He had courageously fought the disease since the mid 1960s. I had been only eleven when my mother explained that he had been given barely four months to live.

In November 91 Team Capricorn went into liquidation, but all my energy was directed for the next three months into duelling with the medical profession who'd seemed more intent on saving money than life with the expensive drugs necessary for my father's survival.

It was at this precise time, according to Smythe's impressive flow chart, that I, having never before been in trouble with the law, was supposedly orchestrating the elaborate fraud involving the collapse of Team Capricorn, my resulting redundancy and injury claim.

* * *

It was the 3rd of February 1992. I'd been redundant for 2 months and claiming for the injury since September the previous year. The day was dark, rain poured in an unrelenting torrent. Wind shook any remaining leaves from the trees. My father was in a private room, flowers adorning the sparse furnishings, in a quiet back section reserved for the dying at the small, friendly hospital in Sussex. Dad had been unconscious since midday when, for just ten minutes, he had woken and we talked. He knew he was dying.

'Hello boy! How long have you been there?'

'Oh not long. How do you feel?' A stupid question. My voice cracked and my eyes began to water.

'Oh I'm okay, son. Don't cry. It comes to us all in the end.'

Three months earlier, when he was again struck down and it became clear his battle was being lost, a family decision was reached; both my mother and father would move to Climping. A new extension would be built onto the Old Granary where they could live out their days. The architect had only that day completed the plans and I had taken them to his bedside knowing his desire to see my mother securely settled. Dad and I sat and studied the architect's drawings for the apartment he would never see. For ten minutes we talked. I explained where my mother would be, where her lounge and bedroom would be built, and how she would be looked after. He seemed to relax as he drifted into the sleep from which he would never wake. I sat holding Beth's hand, watching the rhythmic rise and fall of his chest.

It was 7 pm and my mother and sisters arrived to take over for the evening vigil. A nurse arrived and placed a stethoscope against my father's chest, his breathing had become far more laboured and irregular.

'This is it,' she said, 'he's going. Speak to him! Hearing is the last sense to go.'

I wiped my eyes and held his hand. I kissed his forehead and, swallowing the biggest ever lump in my throat, I whispered, 'I love you, Dad.'

The nurse continued monitoring his heart. I could see no movement. His breath had left him and taken with it his life. My sisters supported my mother. 'Oh, my darling...' were her only words.

Tears dripped from my chin. The nurse looked up. 'I'm sorry

... he's gone.' Suddenly, in keeping with my old-fashioned upbringing, I'd become the leading member of the family, yet with all the uncertainty of the company collapse and my injury, I couldn't even support my wife and children.

Paterson-Smythe rambled on, mercifully finishing by 12.30. By the time he had concluded, the jury were totally bewildered and praying that someone, anyone, would get around to calling a witness.

McGaea turned smiling to the jury. 'Until 1.15 pm then, ladies and gentlemen.' He rose and departed for the sanctuary of his chambers.

Cigarette smoke wafted from all directions as we wove our way through the hallway, past reporters, lawyers and defendants huddled in small groups, past smalltime hoodlums dressed in their best suits, past the weeping wives and girlfriends whose lives had just been judicially shattered by an enforced separation from their partners.

In the canteen, Beth brought me coffee. 'Darling,' she said, almost in a whisper, 'have you noticed the jury over there? They seem very interested in something in the paper. From their reactions, it's got to be something about the trial.' A man was handing around an open copy and every so often an icy glance would beam in my direction. Beth left in search of a newsagent.

Ten minutes passed and Beth returned with an open newspaper. 'Darling, it's not good.' She handed me the open page. 'They've just printed everything the Prosecution said yesterday, as if it's fact.'

The story was written by a veteran court correspondent who had reported on crime over many years. Juicy stories were guarded zealously and Antony Paterson-Smythe's tale of a corrupt racing driver had all the hallmarks of a bonanza story. The words spoken by Smythe the previous day leapt from the page: *'Racing driver in back injury fraud.'*

Racing driver Will Middleton allegedly cheated WPA, the worldwide insurance company and bank out of more than £40,000 by fraudulently claiming he was too ill to drive. Middleton also falsely claimed he had been made redundant when in reality he was setting up sponsorship for his new racing team, said Mr Smythe, prosecuting.

Earlier in November of that year his previous team, Team Capricorn, was liquidated and he started the new team. He later dishonestly gained money from WPA by taking advantage of these developments and embarked on a web of deception.

Beth was indignant. 'How can they get away with publishing these lies?'

Piglet took the paper, examined the content, and shrugged dismissively. 'If you read it carefully, they're not saying anything that is legally incorrect, it's the way it's phrased. It doesn't confirm that the events actually happened, it makes a statement and then adds *said Mr Smythe* or *it was alleged.* It's basically libel-free doubletalk. The tabloids get away with maligning people every day because it's not, strictly speaking, libel. It's not slander if a barrister says something in court and then the paper reports that a barrister says something. You can't then sue for defamation.'

On the sixth floor in a darkened London office, a hunched figure sat behind a cluttered desk. The past month of restructuring at WPA had been a busy and worrying period for Fin as the number of high-risk PPI policies on their books had become clear. Fin had had to delete more than one hundred thousand policies, clients now considered too high a risk. In fact anyone who had *ever* been offered a WPA policy with *Guaranteed Acceptance, Regardless of Occupation* was now out of the security plan. They were people he'd never set eyes on. Many were in occupations he denigrated; military personnel, actors, builders, steeplejacks, window cleaners, foundry workers, miners and anyone in professional sport. To Fin they were simply numbers, not individuals and families that had believed and trusted in WPA – *future cover denied*, security erased and all in the name of WPA's bottom line.

A secretary knocked. 'Enter!' He spat the word without lifting his eyes from his papers.

'The newspapers you ordered, Sir.' The secretary turned and left quickly. Myopic eyes hurriedly scanned paragraphs, bony fingers impatiently flicked pages.

A pause ... a deep satisfied sigh; eyes focused through heavy horn-rimmed spectacles. The wrinkled face broke into a malevolent grin. 'Very nice. Very nice indeed!'

20

The only power any government has is the power to crack down on criminals. Well, when there aren't enough criminals, one makes them. One declares so many things to be a crime that it becomes impossible for men to live without breaking laws.

(Ayn Rand)

His cream coat was duller now, the broad head and velvet muzzle turning a distinguished silvery honey, his movements slow, considered. Dinner time was no longer the most important time of his day, that had been the first sign. After that he'd swiftly gone downhill, becoming increasingly listless; disinterested. But he still loyally followed me everywhere.

It was only weeks since my father's death and I instinctively knew what the vet was about to say. 'I'm so sorry, it's cancer.' She'd had to handle situations such as this many times before, but each time was clearly as painful as the first. 'He's an old boy,' she said, 'and the cancer has spread to his chest. He's had a good innings at twelve years; there's nothing more we can do.'

Cossie lay on his side on the floor, his breathing laboured, eyes dull but still he watched me, his friend. I stroked his head as the vet gently shaved a small area of soft fur from his right front leg. He watched, still curious. The vet rose, selected a syringe and inserted the needle into a vial of turquoise-coloured liquid, decanting a carefully measured dose. She returned and spoke gently to Cossie. 'You're a very good boy, aren't you, Cossie?'

At the sound of his name, his head cocked and he raised his shaved paw offering it to the vet. 'His only trick,' I said, tears running down my face.

Cossie turned his gaze to me. Not a flinch as the needle went in. I kissed his head and closed his eyes. Beth and I had talked about this moment, and whether or not dogs have souls. I wanted to

104

believe they did and for a few precious moments I held my old friend tightly and spoke silently to him, just in case.

The past months had taken their toll and left me drained and in shock. Somewhere around this time I switched off. In fact more than switched off. My mind left its enforced world of lawyers, creditors, insurance companies and doctors. I was in pain, I'd lost my father, my company and now Cossie ... perhaps also my career. I could not train due to the pain in my back and had started to gain weight.

I desperately wanted to return to the track and weight is a critical factor; one kilo of extra body weight in a 700 brake horsepower race car equates to approximately a third of a second a lap at a typical track. That can be the difference between the front and back of the grid. In terms of a visible disadvantage, around one metre per lap for every extra kilogram. For a couple of months my living corpse drifted in time. As my weight began to increase I resorted to a quack doctor who prescribed some medication to maintain the illusion of fitness; attenuate dospan and thyroxine – a lethal brew.

'That one.' Beth said excitedly. The tiny retriever stood up on wobbly hind legs, resting big stubby front paws on top of the pen. The nose wrinkled and he growled bravely. His tiny body was a golden cream, the short but already powerful tail wagged excitedly, causing the little rump to sway eagerly from side to side.

When Cossie died I'd decided never again to have another dog. I had loved Cossie so much but the house was so quiet without him and Beth had talked me round. It was only eight weeks, I still felt unfaithful and disloyal but knew it was the right decision. 'This one's almost nine weeks, his name's Fudge.' The breeder spoke with the air of a Crufts judge. The puppy's nose twitched inquisitively and the oversized paws paddled frantically in the empty air as I lifted the little bundle from the security of its mother.

A sense of new life came over me; Fudge was beautiful and seemed to instinctively take over Cossie's old duties, following me everywhere.

I had never before experienced so much grief in such a short time as over the past months, and had not known how to handle it. I had to pull myself out from under this veil of pain and depression that had cloaked our lives for the past eight months. We had still not received WPA's report despite repeated requests and I decided there and then I would return to driving. I could handle it, nothing is impossible. As the saying goes 'If you can conceive it, you can achieve it.' Bugger the doctors, I told myself. It'd take my mind off the past months and give me somewhere to direct my energies.

I wandered aimlessly around the cold house, lost, tired, yet unable to sleep. I re-heated coffee and sat mulling over the first days of the trial; my despair at Smythe's opening, 'Noddy' the judge, Rabbit's triumphant entry into the fray, shortly followed by the bloody press. My youngest son Jonathan wandered sleepily into the lounge snuggling a stuffed bear. His face was pale and his sunshine hair stuck out in all directions. For an hour we sat cuddling each other, his gentle snuffles merging with my thoughts for what the day ahead in court would bring.

McGaea seated the court and spent the next fifteen minutes explaining to the jury how the ensuing procedures would take place. Paterson-Smythe finished scribbling something onto his legal pad. He polished his spectacles to kill a few more moments before rising to his feet. His words were thick and slow. He turned to the Honourable Judge. 'Your Honour, the Crown would like to call its first witness, Mr Lee Burton of the WPA Insurance Company.'

Paterson-Smythe smiled reassuringly at the witness. A smile of trust, a smile of wisdom. 'Are you Lee Edward Burton of the WPA Insurance Company?'

'Er, yes.'

'Mr Burton. If you could just speak up a little and direct your answers to the jury.' The witness nodded apologetically. Smythe smiled reassuringly.

'If you would like to refer to your notes, I don't imagine His Honour will object. Mr Burton, am I right in saying you are based in offices in London?'

'Yes.'

'Could you advise the court which policies the Defendant held with your company?'

'WPA held a PPI Plan in the name of Mr Will Middleton. It covered accidental injury, sickness, redundancy and provided benefits of £1000 per month for temporary disablement, plus...' he paused, studying his notes, 'a provision for a lump sum benefit of £75,000 in the event the policy holder was permanently prevented from working in his professional occupation due to serious injury.' McGaea wrote it all down. Occasionally a point of particular interest would be underlined.

'Did you hold any other policies in the name of Mr Middleton?' Paterson-Smythe made a check mark against something on his legal pad.

'Yes, we held another policy in the same name which remained in force until August 1991 when it was cancelled by Mr Middleton. This was a WPA Sports and Leisure PPI Policy covering accidental injury and providing a further benefit of £100,000 in the event of a claimant being permanently prevented from working in their professional occupation due to injury.'

Smythe flinched slightly. There is a golden rule; never ask a question of a witness unless you know with certainty the answer. Smythe had made a small tactical error. He moved on swiftly, not asking the witness why I had cancelled a policy worth £100,000 only weeks before I would, if planning a fraud, have claimed.

McGaea cleared his throat loudly and poured a glass of water. Paterson-Smythe glanced down at his notes. 'Did you receive any claims under the first PPI policy Mr Burton?' His delivery was slow, allowing the members of the press a reasonable chance to transcribe his words fully.

'Yes. There were a series of claims on that policy in respect of an injury.' He held up a copy of the claim form and the attending physician's statement. Lurch darted forward and collected the exhibits. The jury was spellbound. Mr Burton continued. 'We subsequently paid £1000 per month to Mr Middleton for a period of four months.'

Paterson-Smythe continued to cajole the witness. My every action was made to seem questionable. Burton didn't know I was a racing driver. Was this deception? How could I be unemployed, apparently looking for work, yet injured all at the same time? That wasn't possible. Or was it? Smythe established, with an air

107

of satisfaction, that I had claimed previously on the policy in 1988 after the riding accident in Malaysia. *What was wrong with that? I didn't ask to fall off the damned horse!*

Australia, November 1988

It was 11.45 at night. Qantas flight QF1 landed at Sydney International Airport, eight hours late. Rob had joined us for the sun, sea and fun. Originally he'd planned to co-drive with me in the Sandown race, Andy having fled for the sanctuary of the United States following his Brands Hatch disaster, but Rob's backer had pulled out at the last minute, so he'd decided to just come along for the ride and planned holiday in Malaysia following the race.

The flight was delayed and we arrived at our Melbourne hotel 18 hours later. It had not been a good day. I had been due to meet with our sponsors, Hilton International, the previous day and qualifying was scheduled to start later that day. I was tired, jet lagged and the day was hot, the height of the Australian summer.

It had been kind of Roy to invite me to drive in Australia after the fiasco of Brands Hatch, but I was in two minds about the race. There was no way the Tiga could win and, to date, this had been the best year of my career. In 1988 I had concentrated on a national championship; a championship that, for once, my team's budget could accommodate. I had been rewarded not only with my first decent salary but also four wins and five lap records. Now I was in Australia and this was a world championship again; Roy's team didn't have the budget to compete on equal terms. All I really wanted to do was head for the pool.

Qualifying was as uninteresting as it was unsatisfactory. My new co-driver had insisted on the car being set up soft. As a result, we qualified seventeenth on the grid but this time Roy had agreed I would start.

Jean-Louis Schlesser lined up on pole, co-driving with Jochen Mass in the AEG Sauber Mercedes. As the lights changed to green, Schlesser made it to the first corner ahead of Mauro Baldi in the sister car, then Lammers and Cheever in the Silk Cut Jaguar.

Any reservations I held quickly dispersed as I hurtled deep into the first corner at unabated speed, balancing the old shit bucket on the razor's edge of adhesion, on worn tyres, through the quick corners and drifting through the tedious second-gear esses.

By lap ten Schlesser had stretched his lead to three seconds and Lammers had dropped twenty seconds behind in third place.

The rev counter flicked. I accelerated hard out of the esses and down the Club straight. The DFV-powered Tiga roared, effortlessly scorching to 170 miles per hour as I approached the end of the straight for my 56th lap. The 200-metre board flashed past in a microsecond, my right foot twitched across to the brake pedal. I snatched third gear. Mass in the Mercedes shot past in a blaze of bellowing turbo fire.

With the suddenness that makes motor racing the most capricious of sports, the car twitched. There was no warning. One minute I was in control, a microsecond later the car slewed sideways scorching black rubber across the track. The Armco barrier only yards away on my right grew large as I ran wide across the grass. My race was over. The last race of my 1988 season had ended with suspension failure.

21

The modern susceptibility to conformity and obedience to authority indicates that the truth endorsed by authority is likely to be accepted as such by a majority of the people.

(David Edwards)

Malaysia, December 1988

The bleached coral sand radiated a shimmering glow as we moved slowly forward, the water welcoming us like a warm embrace, the silence broken only by our breath. We had last dived the West coast of Malaysia on our return from the 1985 Shah Allahm race at Kuala Lumpur. It was nice to be back in the warm Malaysian waters. I had scuba dived since the age of 15 and always jumped at any opportunity to get beneath the waves.

I glanced to my left where Beth was gently finning by my side, silvery bubbles rising with each exhalation like tiny jellyfish to the surface, wobbling as they expanded into the shimmering light above us. A pair of deep blue surgeon fish fluttered around in Beth's bubble stream, taking an impromptu jacuzzi. Out into the blue, a school of tuna and trevelly watched curiously as we continued our descent. We checked our gauges and consciously slowed our breathing to preserve air. All around the colours bleached away to grey as we descended further, deeper, the colours absorbed by the increased density of the deep water.

Fifty minutes later our gauges indicated time to return, and we slowly ascended into the light above and the stunning beauty of Batu Ferringui beach, a two-mile stretch of coral sand washed by the waters of the Straits of Malacca, and backed by a green hinterland of rain forest, a haven for hundreds of species of wildlife, exotic birds and plants.

We had planned to dive the next day but the weather was not good, tropical storms had been forecast and the previous day's light sea breeze was threatening to turn into a typhoon. It was Sunday 11th December and with no diving, and energy to burn, I turned to my next love – horses.

The riding stables were only minutes from the hotel with direct access to the beach. Beth had concerns and wanted me to relax but I was too preoccupied with the thought of riding the Arab stallion one last time. I had taken the ex-steeplechaser out three times over the previous week, each time more fun, more exciting than the last. Today would be my only chance for a final gallop.

I hoisted myself up into the saddle and gathered up the reins. I leant down and adjusted the leathers, slipping my feet into the stirrups. Sweat glistened on the black coat like pearls and he bucked irritably. I rode out of the stable yard and onto the beach, waving to Beth as she snapped a picture for the holiday album. At my first command the stallion set off at a sideways trot.

The stormforce winds had all but gone, and the sun seared down as we trotted briskly past beach merchants, sun bathers and parasailers. Away from the crowd, I tightened the girth and patted the stallion's neck, then with a touch of my heels I sent the animal off across the sand at full gallop, his neck stretched out horizontally.

Sweat stuck the shirt to my back. The soft afternoon breeze drifted along the beach wafting with it the smell of spices, lemon grass and barbecued meats. My stomach growled; I'd missed lunch. I reined in the stallion, raising the back of my hand to my eyes, squinting to examine my watch. It was 4.30 pm, I'd been gone for more than two hours, and it was time to go back.

I began trotting back along the beach, narrowing my eyes against the fading afternoon sun. Directly ahead a small group had gathered. I reined to a standstill a few metres from the crowd and watched as a group of merchants yelled instructions to a fat European punter who was swinging around perilously beneath a large red parasail. '*Kiri. Kiri. Tulak kiri!*' the beach merchants called, but the tourist didn't appear to understand and squinted down helplessly beneath the canopy. I continued to watch as one of the beach boys attempted to climb one of the ropes but a sudden blast of wind quickly jerked him from the cable and he landed with a harmless splash in the warm azure sea below. The parasail shot skyward yet again.

Then without warning it happened. A sudden violent gust of wind hit, immediately inverting the red canopy, instantly sending it flapping into the sky before dropping its cargo with an enormous splash into the sea. The stallion's response was instantaneous. He leapt sideways in horror and reared up. The ground rushed up, everything went black momentarily.

I came to with pain radiating throughout my body, feeling as though I was about to throw up. All feeling in my right leg had vanished. A hoof whizzed over my head, another missing me by millimetres as the stallion galloped away, kicking, bucking.

A group of tourists and beach merchants arrived as sand swirled around me. They placed hands under me, attempting to lift me to my feet. I recoiled with the pain that shot in spasms down my back. 'No ... don't ... hold on a minute.'

'Any broken bones?' one asked.

'I don't think so,' I gasped through shallow ragged breaths.

The next day Beth crammed the cases with the various treasures, trinkets and bargains we'd picked up, while I lay flat on my back mulling over my misfortune and worrying about the winter testing programme.

She wrapped some ice packs in a hotel towel and placed them against my back. I struggled to sit up but could barely move despite the painkillers I'd been given by a local doctor. I didn't relish the idea of the flight home the following day in a cramped economy class seat.

'Yes. Thank you, Mr Burton. Just wait there will you, in case my learned friend has any questions.' Paterson-Smythe subsided with an air of great satisfaction. Rabbit rose to his feet, smiling.

'Just one or two, Mr Burton,' Rabbit began. 'Could you explain to the court just how the WPA policies are marketed?'

'Yes. We have an arrangement with our Banking Division, WPA Bank and our WPA credit card. Mr Middleton would have received an offer of cover with his WPA credit card statement.'

'Ah, I see.' Rabbit glanced at the jury to ensure the point hadn't been missed. 'So Mr Middleton did not approach WPA to request cover, WPA approached Mr Middleton?'

'Yes.'

'Would this be the sales document that you're referring to?'

Rabbit held up some glossy papers. Mr Burton examined the leaflets.

'It's rather difficult to comment. I didn't join the company until after these were printed.'

'I see! Well Mr Burton, would you take a look at the text for us? Is this a WPA document?'

'It would appear to be,' he responded evasively.

'And am I right in saying that it is an offer of a WPA PPI plan to Mr Middleton?'

'Yes.'

'I believe the marketing term is "direct mail". And the second policy, the one Mr Middleton cancelled.' Rabbit held aloft another exhibit. 'Likewise this was an offer from WPA to Mr Middleton of an additional PPI accident plan?'

'Er ... yes.'

'So Mr Middleton didn't go out of his way to seek that policy either? It was in fact offered to him by WPA via a further mail shot?'

'Yes, apparently.'

'And if we look at the policy, we see that Mr Middleton in fact accepted the standard cover, which provides benefits of £100,000 in the event of a serious injury that prevented him from working, as opposed to the premier plan that would have provided benefits of £150,000.'

'Yes, that's right.'

Rabbit glanced at the jury with a bewildered expression, a look that begged the question – If he's planning to defraud the company, why miss out on another £50,000? Or for that matter, why cancel the second policy, worth £100,000, prior to planning a claim?

Rabbit turned back to the witness. 'Mr Burton, you advised the jury that you were not aware that Mr Middleton was a professional racing driver.'

'Yes.'

'If we look at the sales leaflet does it not say, "guaranteed acceptance for all WPA card holders regardless of occupation".'

'Er, er ... yes.'

Rabbit pressed on. 'Is it correct, if we look at the application form, that it does not in fact ask the occupation of the applicant?'

'Er, no it doesn't.'

'So it's irrelevant?' Rabbit asked rhetorically.

Burton answered anyway, 'I suppose so,' a little quieter than before.

'Is it not also true,' Rabbit relentlessly continued, the bit firmly between his teeth, 'that six months after the raid on Mr Middleton's house, this condition was withdrawn and your policy now states that professional sportsmen are specifically excluded?'

'I can't comment on that. It was after the portfolio transfer in October 1991.'

'Mr Burton, you informed my learned colleague that it was not possible to be prevented from racing due to injury, yet seeking employment.'

'Yes, I did.'

'Mr Burton, as you are aware, my client's normal work involved the driving of racing cars. You are also aware that prior to seeing the surgeon's report, his back injury was considered to be only temporary. Mr Middleton was therefore, on the advice of the DSS, seeking alternative employment outside his normal field.' The witness nodded in agreement. 'By way of an example,' Rabbit continued, 'a concert pianist with a broken finger could not play, but if he were then made redundant, he'd be perfectly capable of doing alternative work. Mr Burton, would you now accept that within the meaning of the policy, it is possible for my client be claiming from it for an accident, while also attempting to find alternative work?'

'Well ... yes. In those circumstances, yes.'

His Honour's face contorted at the witness's admission, which undermined the basis of the Crown's case, and he turned directly to the jury, thin lips parting as he silently articulated, 'What?'

It was an important admission, particularly coming from a Prosecution witness; a tennis player's wrist, a musician's finger, a pilot's eye or a boxer with a detached retina, and equally, a racing driver's back – all would quite reasonably be expected to find alternative work, despite being prevented from working within their professional occupations. It was an admission that penetrated the heart of the Crown's case.

* * *

'Call Mrs Margaret Pickup.' Lurch called out.

Margaret Pickup entered the court and smiled sheepishly at the assembled congregation. Paterson-Smythe flashed a sympathetic smile. 'Are you Susan Margaret Pickup?'

'Yes.'

'And are you employed by WPA in the capacity of Claims Manager?'

'Yes, I am.'

'Mrs Pickup, could you explain the section of Mr Middleton's policy handled by your department?'

'Certainly, my department deals solely with unemployment and redundancy.'

'And did you receive a claim under the redundancy section of this policy?' asked Smythe confidently, this time knowing the answer already.

'Yes. On 12th November 1991 we received a claim relating to his unemployment from a firm called Team Capricorn.'

'Could you advise the court,' Mr Smythe continued, 'was your department aware that Mr Middleton was already claiming under the injury section of this policy, stating that he was in fact ill and unable to work?'

'No.'

Smythe pressed on. 'Had you been aware, would the company have continued to make redundancy payments?'

'Had we known that Mr Middleton was in receipt of medical certificates, then payments under the unemployment section would have ceased and a claim would have to have been submitted under the sickness section of the policy.'

'Thank you.' Smythe sat down.

As with the previous witness, my every action had been given the appearance of deception or trickery. Smythe steadfastly refused to use the word injury, preferring always to substitute the word sickness whenever possible.

My only ally in the farce that enveloped me rose to his feet to suggest another series of values for the equation. 'Mrs Pickup,' Rabbit began, 'could you explain how the WPA unemployment and redundancy policies are marketed?'

'No. I'm sorry. I work in the Claims Department, I have nothing to do with the marketing side.'

'I see. Could you take a look at these documents? Is it not

correct that Mr Middleton was the recipient of a mail shot which actually offered him an unemployment and redundancy policy? In fact I believe there is a PS on the bottom of the letter which says, and I quote: *You never know when the unexpected is going to happen, that's why you need to be covered now and why we'll reward you for acting promptly with one month's free cover if you apply before the end of the month.*'

'Er, well, yes, that's right.'

'So Mr Middleton did not "seek out" insurance cover, it was not premeditated. He, presumably in common with many others, received the circular in the post?'

'It would appear so,' Mrs Pickup replied a little hesitantly.

'Mrs Pickup, would you take a look at this document for us?' Rabbit held out three copies and Lurch again shuffled forth. 'There should be a copy for the witness, one for His Honour and one for my learned colleague. Mrs Pickup, is it correct that in an effort to cut the premiums at a time when his cash flow had become critical, Mr Middleton, on 9th August 1991, just twelve weeks prior to his redundancy, reduced the level of cover on this section of the policy and in so doing, any potential benefits payable – from £1500 per month down to £1030 per month?'

Smythe sprang to his feet. 'Your Honour! Calls for speculation as to the Defendant's motives.'

The jury was stunned by the sudden movement and the officer by my side woke with a loud snort. His Honour turned to Rabbit. 'Perhaps you could rephrase, Mr Adams.'

Rabbit nodded. 'I'm obliged Your Honour.' He turned back to the witness and paused for effect. 'Let me put it simply. Did the Defendant, my client Mr Middleton, reduce the level of cover on the redundancy section some twelve weeks prior to his being made redundant? Please take your time and do feel free to study your WPA file.'

Mrs Pickup looked disconcertedly to Smythe for support, but he had suddenly become engrossed in the state of his fingernails. The witness shuffled slightly then reluctantly returned her gaze to Rabbit. 'Yes,' she said, 'it would appear he did.'

Rabbit turned to the jury with a look of triumph.

'Mrs Pickup,' Rabbit continued, 'you advised my learned colleague that if Mr Middleton was in receipt of medical certificates, his unemployment claim with your company would have ceased and a new claim would have had to be instigated under the injury section of the policy. You stated it was not possible for the defendant to be injured yet actively seeking employment.'

'Yes, I did.'

'Mr Middleton was a professional sportsman, a racing driver.' Rabbit paused. He turned, as though now speaking to the jury. 'Assuming a claimant was seriously injured, prevented from performing his usual sporting occupation, not sick, but injured,' he paused allowing the jury to absorb his words, slowly turning his eyes back to the witness, 'and say the individual were to be advised by the DSS that he should seek alternative work outside professional sport,' he paused again. 'In such circumstances, would you accept that it is possible to be claiming unemployment under your policy, while also claiming for the accident under the accident section?'

'In those circumstances ... yes!'

We made our way back to Rabbit's makeshift office. My mood had lightened but Rabbit still seemed tense. I had known nothing of him until weeks prior to the trial, when having just been forced to take on a completely unknown solicitor, out of the blue my senior barrister had also suddenly and bizarrely become unavailable. Rabbit, then junior barrister, the only member left of the original defence team, had been elevated to leader by default. 'Have you ever led a case like this?' I had asked him meekly. 'I've won more cases than I've lost,' was his only reply. Never had inexperience sounded so good I'd thought, but I'd had little option other than to push ahead. McGaea had been adamant he would not countenance a delay.

Suddenly today, though, Rabbit was my hero. I saw him in a new light. If the Crown thought they were going to have an easy ride, they were very much mistaken. In a matter of days, and during the Crown's opening, he had totally slaughtered the entire basis of the Prosecution's case, and we had yet to call a single witness of our own!

Piglet, Tigger and I sat, but Rabbit remained standing. His adrenalin was still pumping. He lit a cigarette, inhaling deeply.

He began pacing around the small room. 'Today was good,' he said, 'very good. I'm wondering if we should ask for a dismissal.'

There was a short silence. I turned to Piglet. 'A dismissal?'

Piglet looked from me to Rabbit and back. 'It means to ask the judge to dismiss the case. No case to answer.'

'Do you think they'd do that?' I asked excitedly.

Rabbit exhaled a blue cloud. 'Hmm ... might be a bit soon. We haven't yet answered the Prize Indemnity charges.' His mobile phone rang, and he answered it. He stood as though stiffly to attention. 'Yes, but I'm in conference at the moment ... no ... I haven't left the building yet.' A pause, the voice on the other end sounded insistent. Rabbit sounded defensive. 'I'll be straight over.' He clicked the phone closed, suddenly looking a little unnerved.

'I have to go. Go home Will, get some rest and try to relax.' Without further comment he turned and was gone.

22

It was Friday 30th September, the weekend lay ahead. Beth had saved some money and as a surprise ordered a takeaway pizza. I removed my jacket and loosened my tie. Beth refilled our wineglasses and gently rubbed my shoulders. 'You're still uptight.'

'I know. It's been a tough week, but we're getting there. Rabbit was good today, don't you think?'

'Yes, he was great,' she smiled.

Beth chose a CD and Louis Armstrong crooned *All The Time In The World* softly from the speakers. The lights were low and the boys upstairs asleep. I sat slowly sipping the glass of wine, now for the first time in months feeling far more relaxed. Beth curled herself into the recliner. Within minutes we were both asleep.

The weekend seemed much like old times again. We were relaxed, convinced the trial would crumble within days.

We arrived at court enthusiastically on the Monday, still with the hope of the case being dismissed. Rabbit's makeshift office was on the first floor directly opposite the barristers' robing rooms. I made my way up the stairs and along the corridor. Detective Barnet appeared, striding confidently in my direction. 'How's the house of cards doing?' he smirked as he passed.

'Quite nicely,' I replied smiling. 'How's yours?' He smirked again and continued down the corridor.

I arrived at Rabbit's office, and knocked. The door was opened by a very troubled-looking Tigger.

'Where's Rabbit?' I knew instinctively something serious had happened.

119

'Will. There's a problem. We've lost Giles.'

I joked, 'To lose one barrister is careless, to lose two...'

Tigger's expression remained deadly serious and my brain suddenly registered that he had used Rabbit's real name. He was serious.

'You're kidding.' His brow creased tighter and he shook his head. 'Oh, my God.' The words left my lips before registering in my brain.

'Jonathan's due in shortly,' he said. 'I've already spoken to McGaea. He's agreed to an adjournment until after lunch but Crown witnesses are already lined up for this afternoon and he's insistent that we proceed.'

The door opened and a tired-looking Piglet arrived. 'Good day team, or should I say, what's left of it.' He sat down and removed a legal pad from his briefcase. 'There is a tide in the affairs of men...' he began, but stopped.

I met his eyes, nausea rising in my throat. 'What happened? We were doing so well.'

Piglet's voice cut through my bewilderment. 'Giles phoned me on Saturday morning...' he stopped mid-sentence. 'You're not going to believe this, but he's *injured his back.* I didn't feel there was any point in calling you over the weekend, it wouldn't have achieved anything. I'm still hopeful he'll be back before the end of the trial, but we don't know.'

I drew in a long deep breath, trying to come to terms with what was being said. 'This is simply unbelievable. If it were a film script, I'd sack the script writer!' For a moment we looked at each other, not knowing what to say.

'Good point,' Piglet finally answered. 'You have to make a difficult decision. I think you should sack Tigger.'

Tigger flinched noticeably, he looked back and forth in confusion, but said nothing.

I frowned. 'What are you suggesting? Why sack Tigger? Then I'll have lost my entire team, except you.'

'Precisely. If you sack Tigger, McGaea will be forced to call a mistrial. Walk away, Will, get a retrial,' Piglet urged.

'But last week was so good. We were talking about a dismissal on Friday. If we force a retrial, what will happen about Burton and Pickup's evidence?' I shook my head. 'We can't stop now; someone's trying to wipe me out. If we force a retrial, the Crown

120

will change tactics with the Burton and Pickup evidence and it's critical to my defence.'

Nobody spoke. I got up and started pacing around the small room. 'I've got to ask this,' I began nervously, 'it's been going around in my head for weeks now, but it is going to sound ridiculous. It's just that,' I paused, my voice becoming tighter, 'there's been a load more in the news this weekend about it; some committee of MPs, a Home Affairs Committee and an inquiry into Freemasonry.' I looked back and forth between Piglet and Tigger, hoping for a spark of positive acknowledgement. 'There's some QC talking about Freemasonry in the police and judiciary, and trying to find out the number of Masonic judges.'

'That simply won't happen,' Piglet responded, just a little too quickly. 'The Lord Chancellor has already ruled out a register of Masonic judges.'

'But the system is shrouded in Freemasonry, isn't it?' I asked awkwardly. 'Could our judge be a Freemason?'

Silence hit the room. Tigger was the first to speak. He looked horror-struck. 'If you think I'm marching into Court Number One and accusing McGaea of being a Freemason, well, I'm not waiting around to be fired, I'm resigning!' he exclaimed sharply.

Tigger turned to Piglet for support and Piglet looked at Tigger. The previous eerie silence again enveloped the room.

'Well,' Piglet finally spoke, 'I'm certainly not a Freemason, so it's not something I could answer. What are you suggesting?'

'It's all the coincidences. They're multiplying like rabbits. Every one says the charges against me are bizarre and I keep being asked if somebody has a grudge against me, and well, what about WPA? If that Consumer Alert programme cost them anything like we estimated, am I being set up by somebody that can pull strings?' I sat back down, a lump rising in my throat. 'You think I'm delusional, don't you?'

Piglet leaned towards me. 'No, I don't. Freemasons are certainly not individuals I'd choose as opponents, and yes, I do think something strange is going on, but I also think this is a discussion for later.'

'But if we can prove...' I began, but Piglet cut in.

'If we could show the judge was a Freemason and all the police officers behind the investigation and even point a finger at somebody at WPA, what does that prove? Only that they all belonged to the same club. That's not illegal.'

'It would certainly be another coincidence!' I added brusquely.

Piglet sighed. 'Time is against us and McGaea is adamant, he wants us back in court after lunch. You have to make a decision.'

I looked over at Tigger. He looked back, almost pleading to be put out of his misery; more like an office junior ready to deliver a memo than a legal eagle prepared to defend me from some malevolent conspiracy.

A pained look crossed my face as I shook my head. 'We have little choice, we have to keep going. Tigger will have to take over.'

Tigger was a junior and had only entered the saga a few weeks earlier when Rabbit had moved up the ranks to become leader after we lost my first senior barrister. Although Tigger had qualified almost six years earlier, he'd never led, or even assisted in a trial of this size. Now he was expected to take centre stage as the leading barrister, with only Piglet to help, in a trial that Judge McGaea had already acknowledged needed a pair of trial lawyers. He stood nervously before the witnesses, anxious only that he might fail to adequately represent me. Paterson-Smythe made the most of his free reign of power. At times he would leap to his feet in a fit of premature exasperation at Tigger's smallest error.

Tigger pushed ahead with all the purpose of a spring lamb, as the days came and went, and with them numerous Crown witnesses. McGaea agreed that the sequence of Crown witnesses could be changed, the less-important ones called first, the rest left for Rabbit's hoped-for return. But still Rabbit did not come back. The jury were trying to solve a mystery, but to solve any puzzle you must have all the available facts and without Rabbit, important facts were being left out.

How convenient it all seemed; so many of our team had been swept aside with a wave of the judicial hand. Now Tigger stood alone, unaided, expected to take over the defence.

A full week went by and Rabbit remained absent. Tigger did his best, but his knowledge of the case was limited. It was not just what he said, it was what he did not say, and what he did not ask. Paterson-Smythe continued to interrupt wherever possible. At times the courtroom exploded in exasperated clacking as the pair clashed like excited geese. With each eruption, McGaea would modify his gaze from benevolent to a cutting frown, in the direction of my only remaining aide.

Each night our little team retreated to our small room to run over the day's events. Tigger was exhausted and spoke with a pained expression etched across his face. 'If I push, McGaea might agree to a week's adjournment. I can try again. Given another seven days there's a chance Giles will be back, but he's drugged to the eyeballs.'

I sighed. 'If there's an adjournment, how's the jury going to follow what's gone on? Will they remember the points Pickup and Burton admitted? And what state will Rabbit be in if he comes back?'

Three days later I finally bowed to the inevitable. A very timid Tigger stood before His Honour and successfully argued for a week's adjournment.

23

Somebody recently figured out that we have 35 million laws to enforce the Ten Commandments.

(Attributed to both Bert Masterson and Earl Wilson)

23rd July 1992

David Mamet arrived with his chief mechanic from Florida on 23rd July. As agreed, Mamet took over as team manager of Trans-Atlantic. The previous day I had visited Mr Dolland the orthopaedic surgeon employed by WPA, at St Richard's Hospital in Chichester.

Thursday 22nd July had been a bright sunny day. I had arrived at St Richard's early in the hope of avoiding the usual hospital queues. That was not to be. I was destined to spend the full day undergoing various tests and examinations, or sitting in the waiting room ploughing my way through the various outdated magazines.

It was now early afternoon. The nurse was pretty and in her mid 20s. She escorted me into the x-ray department. Mr Dolland had already carried out the detailed examination earlier that morning. She examined her clipboard. 'Mr Middleton?' she enquired, flashing a wonderful smile.

'Yes.'

'If you could just remove your clothing and put on the gown, I'll be back with you in a moment.'

I'd been in exactly the same changing cubicle seven months earlier, on that occasion helping my father. All the memories flooded back. He'd been in such pain; it put my own pain into perspective.

Mr Dolland was Head of Orthopaedic Surgery at St Richard's. He stood by his desk and ushered me into the room. The certificates on his walls proclaimed him to be a Consultant Orthopaedic Surgeon (MA, FRCS). He was of medium build, in

124

his late fifties with greying hair, and he walked with a slight limp. A middle-aged nurse sat on his left taking notes. He deliberated over the x-rays on the light board.

'Mr Middleton, you have two areas of trouble. The first is in your thoracic spine and is not a serious problem. I would suggest bringing you into our day clinic and treating you under a general anaesthetic. Basically the procedure involves a series of injections into the affected areas of your spine, followed by some pretty strong manipulation.'

'Does it have to be done under general anaesthetic?' I asked. I had never liked the idea of them.

'Yes it does. I can assure you that you would not like the procedure performed without one.'

'When can you do it?'

'There's a fairly long waiting list. It could be another six months. The second problem is more of a dilemma and somewhat more serious. You have what is known as a spondylolithesis in your lumbar spine. These can be genetic but in your case it's undoubtedly traumatic and would have been caused by the riding accident.' He got up and walked to the light board. 'There is a general build-up of scar tissue which would have occurred over the past few years. If you look at the vertebrae themselves, a slip forward has occurred of about quarter of an inch. This area...' he reached around, pointing to an area of his back just below his belt.

Looking back towards his light board, he pointed with a pen. 'The little wings here and here on the side of the vertebrae, can you see?' I nodded. 'A small section is broken and there are a series of fractures in the vertebra here.' He tapped the light board with his pen. My mind flipped back four years to the holiday in Malaysia and that fall, that bloody stupid fall from a stationary horse.

'Imagine the vertebrae as a tower of building blocks,' he went on. 'The spine has to flex so each vertebra or block sits on a flexible cushion of fluid.' Again he pointed to a light area between each of the vertebra. 'A bony hooking mechanism behind each of your vertebra keeps the tower stable and prevents it from collapsing. Unfortunately, the fall from your horse broke the bones that form the vital hooking mechanism; it's as if the whole tower is simply resting on a foundation of blancmange. The slightest bump and the base of the tower slips further, sending the muscles of your back into spasm. You can't afford to let it slip any further.'

'What can you do?' I asked with a shudder, the image of a collapsing spine already imprinted in my brain.

He returned to his seat. 'Well, I suggest you don't ride any more horses for a start.' He paused for a moment. 'The normal procedure would be to fuse the vertebrae but in your case the damage is in a very vulnerable area, it's also a major operation. We don't like to operate if we can possibly avoid it. We can help reduce the pain you're experiencing but this is a serious injury. How are you coping with the pain?'

'Okay I suppose, it's improved a lot over the last few months, since I haven't been testing or competing.'

'Competing?'

'Oh, just my work,' I replied evasively. 'I'm involved with racing.' I never liked to deliberately start a discussion on motor racing, as it inevitably led to a depressing pattern of cliché questions.

His expression darkened. 'You're going to have to refrain from any heavy lifting or bending and you shouldn't be doing any testing or competing, if it puts strain on your back. I'll give you an appointment for the appliances department. They'll fit you up with a surgical corset.'

'A surgical corset!' I frowned. I felt it a little foolish to mention that I'd just rejoined a gym and started training again. I also decided against telling him that I'd convinced a quack doctor to prescribe me Attenuate Dospan, a derivative of speed, and thyroxine, a medication designed to speed up the body's metabolism, in my determination to get back to the track. Along with painkillers, the effect had been to switch me into overdrive. The results were dramatic. Within a matter of weeks I'd shed 14 pounds and my body fat dropped to below six per cent; I looked super fit and, with the pain masked, felt great. In fact, better than great. I felt euphoric, energised, as if I was living on pure caffeine. As my strength had returned, so had my determination, a determination so deep it was as though it had been specifically reserved for this task. I could sense that familiar thrill, the tingle, the *I'll show them who's beaten* that had been hidden just beneath the surface.

Dolland leaned forward on his desk. 'Your insurers, WPA, have asked me to produce a report. I'll be writing to them within the next week or so.'

Until that moment, I had not seriously questioned the possibility of having to give up racing permanently. As far as I was concerned everything had, until that moment, just been temporary, a setback. I had generally, throughout my life, maintained an ability to consider carefully any significant actions and for that matter, most minor ones too. I loved racing, it had been my dream since I'd been a child. I didn't want to give up; the excitement was my narcotic. I felt like an addict with the Prize Indemnity fix within my grasp, being told I shouldn't have it.

I returned home devoid of energy, despondency deepening. I poured a large glass of Medoc and sat contemplating what to do. Mamet was already on board the plane, due to arrive tomorrow. What of our commitment to him? And his race car was already here, everything was arranged. I'd agreed to pick up Mamet's expenses, my overdraft was already well over the ten grand and I needed Trans-Atlantic to repay me. Chances were I wouldn't get to race anyway, Rob was bound to be quickest. I hadn't driven for over a year; but what if he wasn't quickest? Was there anything wrong in trying? There are times when you need something so much that price or circumstances cease to be obstacles. I had dreamed of returning to the track, but it wasn't my only intention; to occupy my mind after the traumas of the past twelve months was also of paramount importance.

I'd lost my way for so long. A typical day involved sitting about waiting for the next meal long before it was due; there was just nothing else to do. It was as if my life had ceased and I'd been forced to retire before my time. All I had to do was sit around, pop painkillers and be at the beck and call of doctors and insurance assessors – my life-force seemed to have dried up. Like a parched river bed, I needed to return to the source. When I thought of the chance of returning to racing my skin tingled with goose bumps. I could almost smell the excitement and sound of the track; it sent a rush of adrenalin coursing through my veins. Mamet's Porsche was the best car I'd ever been given the chance to drive, an opportunity which was not going to arise again. It was, in effect, the same type of Porsche as the famous Rothman's cars which dominated Le Mans in the mid eighties, but this one was fitted with open Spyder bodywork.

It was rare that I had no answers to the questions that I posed myself. *One day at a time* I thought, *one step at a time.* The specialist's report had not even been written. It would be weeks before WPA got it. I felt good and if I did get to drive, it was possible I'd be fine ... it was not as though I was being paid to drive.

For a few weeks my life was intensified, sharpened. I felt vital and charged with new energy. I had a function, a purpose, and an objective. To get fit and to be quickest. I did not for one moment consider that the decision I'd taken would later be interpreted as a criminal act. It was also the final link in the chain leading to Court Number One.

The week's adjournment passed in a blur and in no time at all we were back in court. Beth and I wearily climbed the stairs to the second floor, my heart beginning to pound in my chest, not from exertion but from anticipation; was Rabbit back? I dreaded the thought of the trial continuing without him. Tigger had done his best, but at times he'd been virtually buried in the Crown's mud-flinging avalanche.

We paused outside our makeshift camp on the second floor, and I pushed open the door. Two heads turned in my direction. 'Ah, Pooh...' said a joyously familiar voice, 'come in and sit down; we have lots to discuss since my little break.' Rabbit continued, removing his reading glasses, his face twitching into a broad smile, 'Good morning, would you both care to join Tigger and me for some juice?'

'That would be great, thanks,' I replied with a smile of relief.

'Just some water for me,' said Beth.

'The team is back together then,' I added, as Beth sat down.

'It would appear so,' he replied with a dry smile, placing his plastic cup silently on the table. 'Just one thing, the judge has insisted we make no mention of the reason I was away. Is that clear?'

'I suppose so, but why the secrecy? Surely the jury will be curious as to where you've been and why the case was adjourned.'

Rabbit looked back at me from beneath a thatch of black eyebrows. He shook his head. 'All I can say is that McGaea is adamant, the jury are not to be told, at least not until after the verdict.'

Piglet arrived carrying a cup of canteen coffee and took his usual place at the table. 'Good morning Team,' he said. 'Good to see everyone is back.' He set the coffee down and started unpacking his briefcase. 'Now, I have been mulling over this idea for a dismissal.'

I leaned forward intently. 'Can we ask today?'

'What are you thinking?' Rabbit asked.

'*Mens rea*!' Piglet replied with a flourish.

'Men's what?' I asked.

'It's Latin, literal translation, guilty act or mind.' Rabbit leaned back in his chair, adding dryly, 'Proof of guilt requires not only that the act occurred *actus reus* but also that it was performed with the appropriate mind-set – that is, with the aim of performing a crime.'

Tigger turned in my direction. 'It came into English law sometime around 1600 when judges decided that the act itself did not construe a crime unless it was accompanied by a guilty state of mind. For example, a theft involving physically taking something *actus reus* must be combined with the objective *mens rea*, that is, the intention of permanently depriving the owner of whatever it is that is being taken.'

I looked back and forth in confusion. 'That's great but how does this *mens rea* get me a dismissal?' Despite the week's adjournment my brain still seemed to be working very slowly.

Piglet unpacked the last items from his case. 'It comes down to your state of mind, Will. The Crown appears, begrudgingly, to be accepting that the riding accident happened, and much to their annoyance, WPA have agreed under cross-examination that you were eligible to claim under both unemployment and injury headings. That leaves them with one chance; the Prize Indemnity. My point is this; when you got involved with the Prize Indemnity, assuming you were wrong to do so, and I emphasise, *if* you were, what was your state of mind when making that decision, and what was the motive? Did you intend committing a crime? The Crown's argument appears to be that if you knew you were seriously injured and were already claiming or were planning to claim a lump sum, then driving at Brands Hatch was fraudulent.'

'But that's simply not the way it happened!' I blurted out. 'I saw Dolland on the 21st of July, when the Porsche was already over here and Mamet was literally on the plane, arriving within hours. I drove at Brands Hatch five days later on the 26th. Dolland didn't write his report until the 10th of August, and I hadn't even told him what I did for a living. It was only after driving at Brands, when I was in such pain, that I got my broker to contact WPA for a potential lump sum in place of the on/off monthly payout and it was another six months before he finally got hold of the bloody report. I couldn't possibly have known the situation prior to driving at Brands Hatch.'

Rabbit gave me a look, and then leaned towards Piglet, his face lighting up into a beaming grin. 'Brilliant! First-rate. You were right, he knows his dates. I think the jury will like him. If he can do that in the witness box we might just win.'

I glanced back and forth between Piglet and Tigger with a sudden surge of anxiety rising in my chest. 'I don't understand, I thought we were talking about *mens rea* and applying for a dismissal, not me going into the witness box.'

Piglet cleared his throat. 'We were, but we can't make the application for a dismissal until after Dolland gives his evidence, as it proves the sequence of events and obviously you'll have to go first to set the scene as he's one of your witnesses.' Absentmindedly he took a second sip of coffee, grimaced, and set down the cup. 'Oh, and on the subject of *mens rea*, you just proved my point.' He sat back in his chair. 'When you went to Florida to see Mamet, you couldn't have possibly known the extent of your injuries because you hadn't yet seen Dolland and after you did see him on 21st July you could only have had the first inkling that the back problem was serious. It was only by taking part in the race that Dolland's words became significant. Dolland will be giving evidence for us and will confirm not only the date of the all-important examination but also that if you continued racing, you would most likely have ended up in a wheelchair. That in itself would make the entire Prize Indemnity self-defeating wouldn't you say? If anyone knew that by taking part in a Prize Indemnity race they were going to end up in a wheelchair, would they do it? They obviously wouldn't be able to take advantage of it, if they did pull it off.'

130

24

Judge McGaea, with his quick command of unknown facts and a degree in hindsight, knew more of Regina v Middleton than any man alive; at least, he believed he did. He sat relaxing under his dusty wig, his demeanour as dry as his morning bran. The chamber seemed strangely lacking in air. A fly buzzed in a spiralling vortex against the corner of the dock.

Paterson-Smythe was again on his hind legs, preparing to coax his latest prodigy, a Mr Jack Carter of the National Charter Bank. A line of sweat appeared above the eyebrows of the witness for the Crown. Jack was a nervous man. He knew precisely what questions were about to be asked and had anxiously sought reassurance from His Honour before commencing his evidence. McGaea smiled reassuringly at my former bank manager, as if to a long-lost friend. His Honour clearly had every sympathy with the delicate position in which the bank found itself.

'You are Jack Carter of National Charter Bank?' Smythe queried.

Jack rolled his eyes in the direction of the judge. 'Yes I am.'

Paterson-Smythe smiled encouragingly. 'Mr Carter. Is it correct you were the manager of the Brighton branch where Mr Middleton held a number of accounts?'

'Yes.'

'Would you please advise the court which accounts Mr Middleton held? If you would like to refer to your notes I am sure His Honour will not object.' Smythe fixed the jury with a serious look.

The witness relayed the required information. 'Mr Middleton held a current account with a £10,000 overdraft facility, a £20,000 joint home improvement loan and a US dollar account.' McGaea

131

nodded studiously and wrote it all down, wiry eyebrows rising at the mention of the dollar account.

'Mr Carter. Did the Defendant's company, Team Capricorn, bank at the same branch?' Smythe asked.

'Yes, until November 1991 when it went into liquidation.'

'And were there any transfers between the Team Capricorn account and Mr Middleton's personal account?' The nervousness was starting to subside, Jack's enthusiasm was returning.

'Yes, sir. There was a regular transfer of £1,200 per month.'

'I see. Mr Carter, could you look at the audited accounts of Team Capricorn.' Smythe held up a cluster of papers and Lurch scurried forth to retrieve the exhibit. The jury were fully attentive, expecting at any moment to be shown the significance of the information and its connection with my back injury. 'In the accounts, under remuneration, what figure is shown for Mr Middleton?'

Jack studied the bunch of papers. 'Just £3500 for the year.'

'I see!' The learned man did his best to look shocked. The eyebrows flashed above the thick pebble lenses. Suddenly he seemed in deep pain and totally perplexed. His face distorted with bewilderment. 'I'm confused ... please help us, Mr Carter. If we look at Mr Middleton's current account for that year, what is the turnover?'

'Approximately £41,000.'

Paterson-Smythe turned to the jury with an expression of contentment.

What was now being suggested was that I had been paid £41,000 in the year Team Capricorn had collapsed, yet declared just £3,500 and therefore must have fiddled my tax returns. Logically, according to the Crown, if I had done that I was likely to have also claimed fraudulently against WPA.

'Mr Carter,' Smythe continued, 'did the Trans-Atlantic Team also hold an account with your branch?'

'Yes.'

'And were there any transfers between that account and Mr Middleton's personal account?'

'There were two transfers in October and November that year, the first for £6,900 and a second in November for £2,800.'

Smythe turned to the jury, his words intended for the witness but directed at them. 'I'm sorry Mr Carter, I'm a little confused again. Are you telling this court that the Defendant, who maintains he was redundant at that time, in fact received almost £10,000 in remuneration from Trans-Atlantic?'

'Yes Sir, he did.'

'Yes. Thank you, Mr Carter. Just wait there please, in case my learned friend has some questions.' Paterson-Smythe trotted back happily to his seat. Rabbit rose, smiling.

'Mr Carter, is it true that the National Charter Bank ran a major feature in its quarterly magazine in 1989/90 entitled "High Speed Success!", featuring Mr Middleton?'

'I believe we did.'

'Come Mr Carter, don't be modest. I believe you arranged it, didn't you?'

'Yes, I believe I did.'

'And when you arranged for this major glossy feature to go into the bank's prodigious magazine...' Rabbit placed particular emphasis on the adjectives, holding up a copy of the shiny periodical, 'did you consider there was anything improper with Mr Middleton's accounts and business activities?'

'No, not at all.'

'Do you now?'

'Well, er, no, not really, although he is heavily overdrawn, and well over his limit.'

'That may well now be the case but we're talking about then, Mr Carter.' Rabbit paused for a moment, then turned to the jury as he continued, 'Mr Carter, you advised my learned colleague about the turnover in my client's personal bank account prior to his redundancy, saying this amounted to £41,000 for the year in question, and that his salary was shown at just £3500, is that correct?'

'Yes, it is.'

'Could you tell me how long have you been a bank manager, Mr Carter?'

'Approximately twelve years.'

'And during those twelve years of service can we assume you have agreed many facilities; loans, overdrafts, mortgages, for the bank's customers?'

'Yes I have.'

'When agreeing a facility, what do you look at before deciding how much a client can borrow?'

'Aside from the usual credit checks, we would look at their

earnings and their expenditure and their ability to repay the loan.'

'I see. And how do you determine what their earnings are?'

'Normally we would look at their pay slips or something from their employer to determine earnings.'

'So you would not simply look at what had been paid into their bank account?'

'We would certainly take that into account as well, particularly in terms of account activity and to see that the account was well managed, that it was being run within agreed limits, but it's the actual earned income that is important.'

Smythe suddenly decided it was time to look for some papers on his desk and became engrossed in sliding documents around. Locating one of apparent interest, he moved it around the desk with all the subtlety of a puppy discovering a long lost toy. Rabbit ignored the distraction and continued. 'I see Mr Carter. So in terms of earnings,' he paused, eyeing Smythe with a degree of contempt, 'you would look at pay slips or something from their employer? In the same way you looked at my client's accounts just now to determine that he in fact earned only £3,500 that year. Why?'

Carter forced a smile. 'Because what appears in the bank account as a credit could be anything: a refund, a transfer between accounts or something of that kind. It could also be something they sold, a car for instance. I understand for example that Mr Middleton's father sadly died and he received a small inheritance. Clearly none of that would be considered as earnings.'

Rabbit turned directly to the jury. 'I see. So you're saying that turnover isn't the same thing as earnings. Is that correct?'

'Yes.'

Smythe grimaced and shifted in his seat. Rabbit continued. 'Mr Carter, do you have any idea what the monthly transfer of £1,200 from Team Capricorn was?'

'Er, no.'

'What about the sum of £10,000 from Trans-Atlantic?'

'No, other than it was paid into Mr Middleton's account – we would have no way of knowing what it related to.'

'Did either Team Capricorn or Trans-Atlantic have their own company credit card accounts?'

'No, they did not.'

Rabbit held out a bound set of documents and Lurch scuttled forward to collect it. 'Perhaps you could take a look at these detailed accounts prepared by Messrs Merton and Collins. These fully audited documents specifically relate to Mr Middleton's personal financial affairs. If you turn to page four you will see that the sum of £10,000, paid to Mr Middleton by Trans-Atlantic, is broken down and cross-referenced to a list of transactions paid on Mr Middleton's personal credit card. Perhaps you could now enlighten us a little further?'

Carter examined the papers. 'It would appear that the £10,000 relates to a repayment for some items purchased by Mr Middleton on behalf of the Trans-Atlantic Team, using his personal credit card.'

'I see. Can you be a little more specific, Mr Carter?'

'Well, part of it appears to be a refund for two flights to Orlando for Mr Middleton and a Rob Allan. Then there's a receipt for a hotel in Florida and a Ford Probe hired from Budget Rent a Car...' He looked up from the documents. 'They appear to relate to a trip to America. There's also a long list of items that were paid for on behalf of a Mr Mamet.'

'I see. Perhaps you could give us a little insight now as to what these were.'

'Well, it's a very long list.'

'That's not a problem Mr Carter, we have plenty of time.'

'Well, there's two, no three return flights, then there's two hire cars, a number of hotels, a long list of restaurant and bar bills, some laundry expenses, petrol receipts, a few more bar bills.'

'And all these expenses were incurred by Mr Mamet?'

'Well, yes, and there's a lot more. Should I carry on?'

I stifled a snigger. 'Oh, yes, please do, Mr Carter,' Rabbit replied cheerfully.

'Well, there are some bills for some Porsche racing car parts air freighted to Brands Hatch, some telephone calls, more restaurant bills, in fact lots of restaurant and bar bills, an invoice for a Porsche nose frame and a radiator and a wishbone and a turbocharger service kit and a front BBS wheel...'

His Honour decided it was time to step in. 'Mr Adams, I think the jury have got the picture.'

Rabbit nodded. 'I'm obliged Your Honour.' He turned back

to the witness. 'So, aside from the trip made to the workshops of Mamet Porsche in Florida, this £10,000 amounts to a long list of bills incurred by Mr Mamet but paid for by Mr Middleton. Is that correct?'

'Yes, it would appear so.'

'I see. Anything there you would consider to be other than legitimate reimbursement of Mr Mamet's very comprehensive expenses? Please do take your time.'

'Well, no, everything does appear to be fully documented against each item of expenditure.'

As before, my every action had been given the appearance of being wrong, dishonest and fraudulent but the reality was simple; as neither Team Capricorn nor Trans-Atlantic had their own card accounts, legitimate expenses had, as agreed, been paid on my personal cards and simply refunded.

Rabbit went on to demonstrate how Team Capricorn had paid the monthly transfer of £1,200 as a nominal sum, aimed at covering the expenses incurred for travel to the various races around the world when I was employed by the team. I had kept all the receipts for anything paid, and each quarter, the team book-keeper had reconciled the transfers. At the end of the financial year the accountant had set the expenses against the transfers that had already been paid, leaving the balance, if any, as remuneration.

The net remuneration or earnings that year had been just £3,500. It had not been a good year, leading up to the team's ultimate collapse. But the Crown was trying to imply that I must have been paid £41,000 and declared just £3,500.

My mind wandered back to my discussion with Rob at the Holiday Inn in Florida, and my agreement to cover Mamet's expenses – my single-minded, bone-headed determination to keep pushing. It would have been the easiest thing in the world to have just given up, sat back and done nothing. Had I done so, I reflected, I would not be sitting here now.

25

... it's like a guy being given an injection. You know, all the pain and everything disappears, ... you lose all relation to grief, to pain, to emotion outside of what you want to do, what you want to get out of that racing car, and every so often the anaesthetic wears off and there you see the cold, hard, horrible world that you're involved in. You know, you see things that you don't want to see, so you really quickly want to have another shot to get back into the comfort and the warmth of your own escape.

(Jackie Stewart. Monaco, 1971)

The race had attracted an excellent field of entries. Prize money was non-existent, competitors raced predominantly for fun. The winner of the weekend's event would receive nothing more than the enjoyment of beating his competitors plus a trophy, on this occasion a pair of Samurai swords. For Rob and myself it was very different; a top six position would provide a massive prize by triggering the Prize Indemnity and thereby guaranteeing a contract with Trans-Atlantic to race for a full season.

I made my way to the circuit office and handed over my RAC International Race Licence and FIA Medical to the official for inspection. She quickly scanned the licence and medical, then looked up and smiled, 'Hi Will.' She slid over the standard track waiver, and I signed against my name. My licence and medical were retained as usual; they'd be returned after tomorrow's race.

We made our way to the pit lane and found our allocated garage. Our quickly assembled pit crew had been preparing the Porsche for the past two days. The atmosphere was electric with anticipation, the smell of exotic machinery permeated the air and occasionally an engine would crackle into life in one of the adjoining pits.

As we entered our garage, it quickly became apparent that Mamet was not happy. His Florida tan appeared to have faded a little. I strolled over to the car. Mamet was astride the Porche's engine, the engine cover removed, a look of deep concentration on his face. Two more mechanics were bent over the massive flat-six air-cooled engine. Mamet looked up, smiled meekly and offered an oily hand. 'Well guys, we have a little problem.' The word was one we never liked to hear.

'What's up?' I asked hesitantly.

Mamet wiped his hands with a cloth and carefully stepped down from the Porche's engine compartment, a pained look spreading across his face. 'It's the turbo, we have an oil leak and we don't have any replacement seals. We need a service kit for a Garrett turbocharger and nobody else in the pit lane is running this single turbo set-up, I've checked.'

I gazed down on the three-litre engine, with its odd single Garrett turbocharger. It was a completely different set-up from any other 962 Porsche; in fact Mamet's car was unique, full stop. Aside from the open Spyder bodywork, it was fitted with an unusual air-cooled engine, a simpler set-up Mamet had said, and completely different from the normal water-cooled 962 cars that ran twin KKK turbochargers. Without the need for radiators and coolant, it was lighter and supposedly more reliable and powerful.

I frowned. 'Can we run it as it is?'

'We can try it, but we'll have to limit the laps. The leak's not bad, but it's still a fire risk; oil flow is critical, and this thing runs hot! We don't want a fine mist of oil spraying anywhere near it at those temperatures. I've already phoned the workshop in Florida; a service kit is being despatched by Federal Express, in fact it should already be on a plane. We can pick it up from Heathrow tonight.'

I dreaded to ask the obvious; what that was likely to cost. I knew it would be me picking up the bill, so I didn't ask.

Rob and I took turns being fitted into the car. Two hours later the set-up was complete and the mechanics pushed the car out of the pit garage. I was to go first; it was agreed that due to the turbo problem we would only have three laps each to qualify. I flicked the booster pumps on and gave a circular motion with my right hand to Mamet, the rev counter flickered and the engine crackled into life. Mamet leaned into the cockpit, suddenly all smiles. 'Take it easy, just three laps; out, one flying lap then lift and bring it straight in. We'll check the turbo and then send out Rob. She's fuelled for just six laps, so she'll be light.' *Not as light as when Rob gets in,* I thought *and I'll have heated up the bloody tyres for him!* 'Don't hurt my baby.' Mamet slapped the top of my helmet.

Cocooned inside my Nomex balaclava, cushioned within my carbon fibre helmet, I looked into his eyes through the tinted visor. The words he'd spoken in Florida came instantly to mind, *whoever's fastest runs the race.* That's the deal. I smiled, took a deep breath and selected first gear. Increasing the revs to 3000, I carefully released the clutch.

Mamet and Rob stood by the pit wall, eyes searching in the direction of Clearways. In the cockpit I swerved the twitching car from side to side, using throttle and brakes to force as much energy into the Goodyears as I could, making sure to avoid spinning the wheels, damaging the tyres or graining the surfaces. Tyre temperature was critical but heat was needed through each tyre's entire carcass to enable them to work properly, ensuring the car would stick to the tarmac for one vital flying lap.

It was my first time in a 962 Porsche and it instantly felt fantastic; for once everything was in the right place; the seating position, the pedals, the gear lever, and it all felt positive, taut, responsive, everything felt natural. I could even see in the wing mirrors ... a total luxury.

I steered the car through Bottom Bend, along the back straight, picking up speed all the time, around Clearways, the tyres suddenly beginning to respond as the heat increased. I hit the throttle; this was my one qualifying lap. The massive turbo kicked in, projecting me down the pit straight. Mamet held out an empty Trans-Atlantic pit board. Down the straight, my vision blurring, over the brow, 160 miles per hour as I exploded onto the brakes, turned in and floored the throttle. In an instant I was at Druids. I stamped on the brakes, second gear, trying to come to terms for the first time with a Porsche synchromesh gearbox, an unheard-of luxury. Seven thousand five hundred revs per minute, taking a classic line, the powerful Porsche drifted perfectly out of the hairpin and downhill. Using the downward momentum and massive torque, I shifted straight from second to fourth for Bottom Bend, along the back straight, a slight lift before flicking into the kink, balancing the throttle, keeping the revs up so the turbo kept producing power. Then, as quickly as I dared, full throttle out of the corner and into the pit straight and past Mamet.

I checked the mirrors and lifted immediately, the revs dropped. I could feel the sweat running down my back. There was no radio link from the pits to the car and with only one flying lap, nothing to see on the pit board; I had no idea of my lap time. I steered the car slowly back to the pits, switched off the engine and removed my helmet and balaclava. Two mechanics took off the engine cover and examined the turbocharger. Mamet appeared by my side, smiling. 'That was a 1.03; not bad for your first flying lap! Currently that makes you the third fastest overall.'

I grinned, it was a reasonable time but I knew the rest of the teams had hardly started; times would drop by at least four to five seconds. But what was most important to me was what Rob could do ... whoever's fastest runs the race.

The mechanics replaced the engine cover; apparently the turbo was holding up well. Another mechanic fitted Rob's seat insert and he stepped into the cockpit. Mamet fastened the six-point harness. The engine fired and Rob exited the pit lane.

I joined Mamet at the pit wall. 'Will, that was good, bloody good. I have to say I wasn't expecting that at all.'

I smiled, not knowing quite what to say. At that moment Rob shot past in a red, white and blue blur. Mamet snapped the button on his stopwatch. 'Okay guys, let's see who's driving tomorrow.'

I strained to see as Rob entered Paddock Hill bend. 'Did he brake later or earlier?' I asked, a little too anxiously.

'Early, much earlier, but it's the speed out of the corner that counts. Smoothly in, quickly out. Get the power on fast; keep the revs up to prevent turbo lag.'

On the track, I could hear the Porsche approaching the kink. I listened for the sound of the engine; was he going to lift or dab the brakes, or take the kink flat? I thought I made out the sound of gear change; a drop to a lower gear. That was bad, but bloody good for me.

We both searched the exit of Clearways. The Porsche appeared, taking a perfect line, a slight drift, then flashed past and down the pit straight. Mamet clicked the stopwatch. I didn't dare ask, just watched as my dream disappeared over the brow in the direction of Paddock Hill bend. Abruptly it registered. He was supposed to have lifted, but he hadn't!

Suddenly in the distance the tyre wall exploded as the Porsche hit, the impact tearing off the nose and flinging it high into the air. Mamet cursed. There was a thunderous bang as the car again impacted with the tyre wall then pitched high into the air, spinning back across the track in a wild arc. The circuit's lights instantly turned red, the ambulance shot out of the pit lane. At all corners marshals waved yellow and red flags, warning the other drivers of the accident. The session was stopped. It was a huge crash.

I sprinted the full length of the pit lane and out onto the track. Rob was still strapped into the car, but he was moving. Mamet was scarlet with exertion and anger. Rob unclipped the harness and stepped from the car, the humiliation obvious.

A truck arrived and began hauling the Porsche out of the gravel trap. A cursory glance suggested that the damage looked worse than it was; the nose, nose frame and oil radiator were smashed and the front left-hand wheel and tyre ruined, but nothing that couldn't be repaired in time for tomorrow's race.

Mamet turned to me. 'Will, assuming we can fix it in time, you're driving tomorrow.'

26

Once an accident has started happening, you've just got enough time to say 'Shit, I'm having a shunt!'

(James Hunt)

The marshal held up the five-minute board. A promotion girl leaned into the cockpit and fumbled around for the safety harness. I struggled to focus my mind but a little voice in my head kept pointing out that she wasn't wearing a bra. The seconds ticked by, a drop of sweat trickled down my back. The mechanics pushed the car into its designated position on the grid. Racing is a combined physical and psychological discipline. In order to compete successfully, you must switch off completely from outside influences and distractions.

The signal reflexes of a fit sportsman travel through the nervous system at a maximum 180 miles per hour. The 962 Spyder's entry speed into the first corner, Paddock Hill Bend, would be close to 170 miles per hour. By the age of 40 a man's reaction speed drops by typically twenty per cent. I was 38. The one thing age provides is experience, giving the ability to anticipate and hopefully counterbalance the handicap.

Your mind must be focused. Unless it is quicker than the car you are driving, you will never be positioned in the right place at the right time, you will always be braking too late or too early, turning in too soon. Your mind must become one with the machine. You must be confident enough to balance the car on the limits of adhesion at speeds approaching 200 mph, stare into the eyes of death, smell the stench and still be prepared to push harder.

Kremer had entered their new CK7 Porsche Spyder driven by 1989 Le Mans winner Manuel Reuter. The combination was going to prove impossible to beat, but then we only had to come in the top six.

Reuter had qualified on pole and been totally dominant in practice. Unlike Mamet's 962, which had been built to the American IMSA rules, the CK7 was designed to World Sports Car Championship specification. Basically this meant the CK7 was lighter and more powerful.

The klaxon indicated 30 seconds to go. A fragile shell of fibreglass and aluminium encased my body like a second suit. I lay practically horizontal, swathed in fireproof Nomex, arms and legs outstretched. Behind my head 800 horsepower throbbed angrily as the six sets of pistons opposed themselves like fighters in a ring.

As the lights changed to green I floored the throttle and the familiar force, a force resembling an express train, hit me in the back. My life blurred; in an instant I'd returned to my former world.

The Kremer car led from pole, leaving team-mate Almo Copelli a distant second in the wrong gear. In the confusion, Copelli struck Eddie McLurg's March, the damaged machine slewing sideways before re-collecting Copelli. I'd qualified eleventh and in the melee and confusion immediately moved up to seventh just behind Johan Rajamaki's Reynard Can Am.

All I had to do was make up one position and hold it. A sense of freedom enveloped my mind, freedom from the past months of sadness losing my father, the turmoil of Team Capricorn's collapse, liquidators, the loss and the thought that I would not race again.

The turbulent air boiled from the Reynard's wings. Dust, grit and shrapnel collided with my visor as I forced my way into the vacuum of his wake. I was locked into the Reynard's slipstream, the one obstacle that lay between me and our prize; a full season's driving. I had to finish sixth or better.

Despite taking half a bottle of dihydrocodeine, the pain in my back was already unbearable. Within three laps the old injury in my thoracic spine was preventing me from holding my head up. By lap eleven I couldn't feel my right leg. I'd swear the bumps were moving, every jolt seemed like a knife in my spine but my adrenalin continued to pump. If you blink at 180 miles per hour, you've travelled around twenty metres with your eyes shut.

In the hospitality suite the guests enjoyed cocktails, assorted canapés, savoury cheese cups and champagne. Rob had carefully ensured that the faces and names, some old sponsors and a few new potentials, were all easily distinguishable with name badges proudly proclaiming the wearer to be a VIP guest of Trans-Atlantic, all guests hopefully witnessing the birth of the new team.

Back on the track, my only provision was a cocktail of painkillers, thyroxine, Attenuate Dospan and adrenalin. The volatile mixture coursed through my veins sending my mind racing; I had to finish sixth. I had to get through Clearways quicker on the next lap. The G forces tore at my limbs, my legs felt as though they were stuck in treacle, the pain in my spine was unbearable.

I entered Surtees alongside the Reynard at 8000 rpm. Into McLaren the 962 was handling like a soggy pudding, the crispness gone. Through Clark curve. I was on the inside so had to run fractionally slower through the sweeping turn, less than one hundredth of a second separated me from our goal. I glanced to the pit wall for any messages. Mamet leaned over, frantically gesturing me on, totally involved, all caution now dissolved, living the race through his eyes.

I clicked on two more turns of boost, and over 700 horsepower projected me down the pit straight, over the start/finish line up the brow, 170 miles per hour into the blind right-hander Paddock Hill Bend. I out-braked the Reynard into sixth place, the car switching alarmingly from entry understeer to mid-corner oversteer.

Rajamak tried to come back on the outside as I accelerated out of the corner, carefully feeding every last ounce of power to the rear wheels, the car switching back from oversteer to understeer. We rocketed downhill side by side, sparks showering from our cars as the G forces pinned us to the track and tried to wrench the helmets from our heads. I stole the inside line into Druids, exploding more than 180 pounds into the brake pedal at the last second.

A spasm of pain shot up my spine. Was I on the brake? Suddenly I couldn't feel my right leg, all feeling had gone. In the micro-second of confusion, the Porsche veered sideways across the grass sending up a spray tail of dirt, the car spinning through 360 degrees, dust and grit swirling in a storm around the cockpit as the car came to rest on the infield. But I'd declutched and the engine was still running. In an instant I'd selected first gear

144

and was back on the track as Rajamak and six other cars shot past. I was down to thirteenth place.

The race commentator told the spectators what they could already see, the Mamet Porsche was rejoining the track. Rob, in the hospitality suite, closed his eyes and cursed me. In the pit lane Mamet closed his eyes and thought of his tax bill. Beth, standing next to him, simply closed her eyes and prayed.

The underside of the car was clearly damaged and the usual mid-corner understeer had switched to alarming oversteer. I powered the car back downhill into Bottom Bend, into third gear, along the short back straight momentarily shifting to fourth gear. I outbraked a Lola, shifting back to third gear for the kink, the car alternating between oversteer then understeer then into power oversteer, sliding wildly as the track surface changed part way through Clearways. Mamet held out a pit board ... just two laps to go, P12. The Porsche rocketed down the pit straight, gaining rapidly on the white Roy Baker Tiga.

Over the brow, 160 miles per hour, 8500 revs. Using my left foot I exploded onto the brakes, outbraking the Tiga into eleventh place. My right front tyre hit the apex, forcing the back end to step out violently. In an instant I corrected the slide as the Tiga attempted to edge past on the inside, both cars rocketing downhill side by side towards Druids, sparks showering from the car's skid blocks.

The Tiga's 500 horsepower was no match for the 700 horsepower of the Porsche but the run up to Druids wasn't long enough to despatch it. I was on the outside as the lighter and more nimble Tiga tried to ease up the inside, deliberately attempting to block me. Again using my left foot I hit the brakes a fraction later than the Tiga into second gear, 7000 revs per minute. Taking the classic outside line the Porsche drifted in a perfectly balanced slide, as the Tiga on the inside line drifted wide out of the hairpin. I aimed the Porsche at the apex, applied full power, the Porsche's superior performance taking me into tenth place.

The rev counter flashed to 8000, I snatched fourth gear and turned in for Bottom Bend, my neck muscles straining to hold my head up. The tyres bit, launching the Porsche into the back straight. One more corner to go. Third gear into Clearways. Ahead two more dicing cars touched, a storm of expensive carbon bodywork erupting as both cars spun wildly into the waiting gravel trap. I grabbed fourth gear at the apex, the momentum pushing me across the track and past Mamet holding a pit board with a hastily added P9. It was too late. Directly ahead the chequered flag waved; I'd failed. Everything was now down to Rob in the second heat.

In the pit garage I groaned with the effort of trying to sit down. The muscles in my back fought in conflicting waves of spasm, twitching, throbbing and contracting. A promotion girl massaged my aching neck as the Citroen AX drivers entertained the crowd. 'Ow! That's it! A bit lower.' She only had little hands but they were powerful. A marshal appeared in the garage with Mamet.

'Who's driving in the second heat? Middleton or Allan?'

'Allan,' I replied firmly.

'You realise he'll have to start from the back of the grid?'

A bolt of pain shot up my spine as I jerked my head in the direction of the marshal. 'What! Why?'

'In the Super Cup the finishing position in the first heat determines the starting position in the second. Middleton has finished ninth in that heat so he's qualified ninth for the final. If Allan drives, he'll have to start at the back as he doesn't have a qualifying position.'

Terry and Rob arrived in the pits and a discussion ensued. I was in agony. The sweat still dripped from my forehead, the cockpit temperature had been over 40 degrees Celsius. The adrenalin was still pumping. I reached into my overalls and pulled out a plastic pot of pills, extracting and swallowing a quick handful. My spine was stiffening up and I had to move my whole upper body to turn my head. I was still confident I'd made the right decision to try, but now I knew it was impossible. 'Look Rob, I can barely move. I can't drive another heat.'

'You don't have a choice mate!'

'Rob, I can't hold my head up. It's not just the G forces, it's the damage to my back. I can't feel my right leg. Half that heat, I was using my left foot to brake. I don't think I should have driven to start with.'

'Just hold it in ninth place. If three drop out in front, we've won.'

David Mamet rigged up a leather strap to hold my head up and Rob located a neck brace. I was anchored firmly into the car by my head. If I crashed I would never get out. I drove the second heat. I was concerned I was doing myself permanent harm. Nobody got past, but equally nobody dropped out. I started ninth and finished ninth.

With the adrenalin still flowing and a bottle of painkillers, I'd coped with the pain, and even driven in the second heat, with difficulty. But with the battle over, pain took the place of exhilaration. Pain was telling me something was very wrong. It had not been lack of fitness, or the effect of the G forces, just a simple matter of mechanics. Despite the circuit being less than an hour's drive from the Old Granary, I spent an uncomfortable night at the track's Thistle Hotel, my back too painful to contend with even the short drive home.

The surgeon had been right, I shouldn't have driven.

It was the day after Brands Hatch. I picked up the telephone and dialled the number for Ned, my broker. I'd last spoken to him months earlier. At that time it was just a general chat, as the claim had been ongoing for some time. Now I was feeling this could well be permanent, and I needed to push forward with the claim.

'Yes Will, I've got a copy of your file in front of me. It seems quite clear from what is being said that this injury is serious, very serious and most likely permanent. I sent you some forms to fill in months ago, why didn't you go ahead then?'

'I didn't want to accept the situation. I still don't, I'm still not sure. I saw the specialist only last week and he's saying the injury's definitely severe but we haven't seen his report yet, he's sending it directly to WPA.' I hesitated. Should I mention that I'd foolishly attempted the comeback? It was an important fact, but facts were one thing, truth was different. The truth was I had a serious injury, I knew that now. I had been a fool to have attempted the comeback. I decided not to say anything.

'Look,' Ned continued, 'if the specialist is saying you have a serious injury like this you should leave the matter to me. It sounds like you have a strong claim for disablement from your occupation.' He sounded eager, excited, as if he'd hooked a big deal. 'These companies will try anything to avoid settling a claim. Send me any information you have and leave everything to me.

I'll contact WPA's specialist and get a copy of his report. We'll work on a contingency basis and charge ten per cent of the eventual payout. The sooner we start, the sooner you get paid. Big corporations move slowly.'

When I woke the following morning it was still dark. I slipped silently out of bed, found my clothes and put them on. In the kitchen I swallowed a handful of dihydrocodeine, ground some beans and brewed a pot of strong coffee. Sitting alone by the window, I sipped from my mug as I watched the dawn arrive and considered carefully Ned's eager words.

Despite all the problems, the past few days had been fun and the happiest since the collapse of Team Capricorn. Did I truly want to give up now? Perhaps I should give it a few more weeks...

27

Zolder International Race Circuit, Belgium, 8th August 1992

The mist still hung in the surrounding forest and campers were starting to rouse themselves. The occasional crackle of a race engine stirred the dawn. The sounds and smells of daybreak drifted through the Belgian woodland.

The local air was clear and clean. The smell of pine needles merged with the sweet scent of local pastries and fresh coffee, the combination drifting in a mouth-watering potpourri through the Zolder paddock.

It was qualifying day and the weather was bright and sunny as I visited the pit lane memorial to one of my heroes, the late Gilles Villeneuve. He'd been killed almost six years earlier, in an accident not vastly dissimilar to the disaster at Brands Hatch with Andy. Beth, the boys and I had travelled over in the Shogun to support Rob. It was his last chance to shine as Trans-Atlantic's sole driver. It was also the fledgling team's last chance for the Prize Indemnity to work.

Young boys clasped the racetrack barricade, their fingers gripping the steel web of netting, dreaming of the day they too would be strapped into the fire-breathing monsters with wheels. Rob was nervous. 'What happens if it fails again?' he asked.

'I don't know. I haven't considered that. We'd... No. *I'd* be totally in the shit. My overdraft stands at over ten K.'

David Mamet was happy to be back in Europe for another stab at the Prize Indemnity. He'd arrived flourishing a fistful of expense chits. He strolled over to the Shogun with a wry smile. 'Will, do you want to do a couple of laps, just to warm it up?'

It was a silly question to ask. Although Rob had been entered as the team's sole driver, my race suit and helmet were still in the truck from Brands Hatch. Every racing driver always ensures his race gear is on board, even if he knows there is absolutely no chance of driving. I didn't need a second's thought, despite the pain after Brands Hatch. Two weeks of painkillers had anesthetised both my body and brain and now I was feeling good – what harm would a couple of warm-up laps do?

The track resounded to the roar of racing engines. It was the first session, un-timed and unofficial. Mamet gave his standard lecture. 'Just four or five laps, okay?' Good, it had increased from just a couple. 'Take it easy; no dramatics! Just get it warmed up for Rob.'

'Yes. Fine.' It's always the same routine. What every team manager wants is for you to go out and blitz the fastest lap of your career. But he tells you to take it easy just in case you destroy the car, that way he's always got the last word and can rant and rave about how you didn't obey team orders.

For weeks the trial droned on. The jury were treated to highlights of hours of taped police interviews and crackly recordings of bugged telephone calls from the private detective. Paterson-Smythe was particularly pleased with a recording of a detective asking, 'So, Will, you're still involved in motor racing then...' and my apparent incriminating and somewhat distorted voice replying, 'Well, I used to own a racing team.'

With each day that passed, I seemed to slip further from reality. I gazed at the faces in the packed court, but saw no one. I watched the lips of the witnesses as they came and went, their brief moment in the drama spent. It was all proving too much for the old boy in the back row, Juror number 11. His eyes had already shut and his head had fallen to his chest, which now rose and fell gently, his lips producing a pronounced but gentle purr.

DC Barnet was called and recounted the events of the raid and subsequent interviews, with regular refreshing glances at his notebook. When Paterson-Smythe had finished, Rabbit rose to cross examine.

'Detective Barnet, I'd like you to cast your mind back to the morning of the first raid. How many officers did you feel it appropriate to accompany you, to arrest one man on suspicion of making a false insurance claim?' He paused. 'Two, three?' he added helpfully, when Barnet failed to answer.

Barnet faltered a little longer, so Rabbit went on, 'Maybe it was four?'

'I believe it was nine officers,' Barnet replied somewhat sheepishly. 'We are required to undertake a risk assessment when planning a forced entry.'

Rabbit turned to the jury. 'Oh, nine officers. To arrest one man, with no previous convictions at five in the morning. Are you *sure* it was only nine officers?' he asked, flicking a few pages of an official-looking document.

'There might have been a few more, if you include the back-up provided by the local force.'

'How about thirteen?'

'Yes, that's probably about right,' Barnet reluctantly conceded.

'So. At five on the morning of the raid, under cover of darkness with your blue lights flashing, you and twelve of your colleagues forced your way into my client's home and arrested him in relation to an alleged insurance fraud. Is that correct?'

'Yes, er ... well.'

One or two of the jury suppressed a giggle. 'It must have been quite a drama for the sleepy village of Climping,' Rabbit added, before Barnett could continue. The officer shrugged dismissively.

'So, you did arrest Mr Middleton, that morning?' Rabbit continued.

Barnet looked slightly embarrassed. 'Well no, not at that point. He wasn't home, so after removing some documents, I left a calling card and asked him to get in contact.'

A few more of the jury suppressed giggles. Rabbit looked aghast. 'Thirteen of you forced entry into Mr Middleton's home, when he wasn't even there? Didn't you think to check first?'

Barnet gave another shrug. 'That's not the way we do it.'

'Evidently not! So, who *was* there, Detective Barnet?' Rabbit asked, already knowing the answer.

'The Defendant's mother and his sister were present.'

Paterson-Smythe's seat creaked as he shifted uncomfortably, looking as though he was about to rise but His Honour gestured for him to remain seated.

'Ah, Mr Middleton's mother!' exclaimed Rabbit. 'I believe she'd moved in with her son and daughter-in-law following the death of her husband. Can you tell us what happened to this eighty-year-old lady, when the thirteen of you forced your way into her home at five am?'

Barnett hesitated. 'She collapsed ... but she'd already got a weak heart.'

A further series of creaks indicated Paterson-Smythe's growing discomfort.

Rabbit turned to the jury. 'Quite correct, the shock was simply too much.' He paused. 'Did you allow for this scenario, when carrying out your risk assessment?'

'Well, no ... but then we were unaware that she was living at the property.'

Bastards! I said to myself, closing my eyes and recalling the effect on my mother. Already in poor health, she had been confined to a wheelchair from that day on, never able to walk unaided again.

Rabbit placed a mark against a point on his legal pad, then spent a few moments studying the notes he'd made earlier that morning. 'And this raid took place simultaneously with a raid on the home of Mr Rob Allan?'

'Yes.'

'So a similar number of officers would have been employed in that raid also?'

'A similar number,' Barnett agreed.

'So overall we're now up to around thirty officers?'

Barnett shrugged. 'I suppose.'

'But you decided to charge only my client and have employed the services of Mr Allan as a witness for the Crown. Is that so?'

'Yes.'

Rabbit turned away from the witness, and returned to his seat. 'I have no further questions Your Honour.'

His Honour turned to Paterson-Smythe. 'Do you wish to re-examine, Mr Smythe?'

Smythe rose and gave a slight bow. 'No thank you, Your Honour.'

His Honour glanced at his watch, then turning to the jury added, 'This might be a convenient point to break for lunch. Shall we say, until one thirty?'

'All rise,' boomed Lurch's familiar tones.

28

In my sport the quick are too often listed among the dead.

(Jackie Stewart, 1973)

My mother had been devastated following the death of my father. They'd lived in a small bungalow in Southampton for 15 years. She was 80, had a weak heart, walked with a stick and frequently fell. In the past year she'd been found in a variety of locations slumped around the bungalow or garden. It was only a matter of time before she was found upturned in the fish pond. It was obvious she would not be able to remain alone.

The offices of Dalton and Evens were based in Portsmouth. They'd acted as my parents' solicitors for as long as I could remember. The senior partner stood behind his desk and welcomed us into the office. I helped my mother to a chair. 'Mrs Middleton. This is a very sad occasion; your husband was a wonderful man. How are you coping?'

'I'm not. I feel totally lost; we'd been together 50 years. I only wish we could have gone together.' She wiped away a tear.

'I'm sorry. I can't begin to imagine what you're going through. Have you reached a decision about moving in with Will and Beth?'

'Yes. The plans were drawn up just before my husband died. We were planning to move in together.'

I put my arm around her and took up the conversation. 'We've had the plans scaled down considerably. Instead of the original design, the idea is to now convert our existing gym into a downstairs bedroom, then construct a new lounge and kitchen onto the end of a new pool enclosure.'

'And the cost?' Mr Dalton enquired.

'Mum will pay £36,000 and we're going to borrow a further £20,000 to build the pool enclosure, from National Charter Bank. It will be on a general home improvement loan.'

He frowned. 'Mrs Middleton, are you happy with that? It does

154

mean you're contributing around two-thirds of the overall building cost.'

She nodded. 'Yes. It's only fair that I pay the biggest lump, after all I'm going to be taking over the kids' gym room as my new bedroom and they're going to move Will's gym equipment to the pool.'

'Fine. I've already taken the liberty of looking into the most tax-efficient means of making the funds available from your late husband's share portfolio. If the family are all in agreement, the best method would be by a Deed of Family Arrangement that could be registered with the Inland Revenue and should result in a zero tax liability on the transfer of funds for the building works.'

The four or five laps had turned into six. Rasping through the gears I dipped the Porsche into a 1:34.02 for my final warm up lap. Despite a few twinges in my lower back, I felt great. I stepped from the car to be embraced by Mamet. 'That was fantastic, Will. You braked later for Turn One than Reuter!' he exclaimed. Despite the fact that my right leg had again gone numb, I was beginning to wonder if I had just been away too long at Brands and hadn't pushed myself hard enough in training. My confidence continued to rise, I felt really good. Like the feeling you get after convalescing from a protracted illness, everything seemed invigorating, intensified. I'd done it all before but time had dulled my senses, I felt alive again.

Rob looked disheartened, even apprehensive as he settled himself into the confined cockpit for official qualifying. He pushed on the clutch and brake pedals, gripped the wheel and scanned the instruments. 'Can you bring the brake pedal forward a quarter of an inch?' he asked. A mechanic quickly removed a carbon fibre inspection panel and set to work. I joined Beth and the boys on the gantry high above the pit road, keen to watch the qualifying session.

Rob entered the track second behind Reuter in the Kremer Spyder but, as the cars completed their first lap, he'd dropped four places and was slipstreaming Richard Dodkins in the McLaren. As he approached Turn One for the first time, he pulled out of the slipstream, cleanly outbraked the McLaren, turned in and in an instant lost it.

In a contemporary ground-effect race car you mustn't let the car slide through the high speed corners. The aerodynamics of a modern race car generates several tons of downforce. By abruptly lifting part way into the corner as Rob had done, the 962 drifted off line, became unbalanced and pitched forward, cutting the airflow through the venturis. Added to which it was his first lap and the tyres weren't warm. As it begins to slide off line, the car yaws, as the leading edge of the wing points in a different direction from the way the car should be heading. Suddenly the car dramatically loses its downforce, the force giving the grip. One minute you're in control, the next you're not. Bye-bye world!

Fortunately for Rob, a gravel trap designed to safely retard unruly cars had been positioned on the outside of Turn One. The 962 slowed abruptly as the friction of the gravel gouged at the underside of the car. The energy spent, the car finally arrested in a cloud of dirt and dust, a glutinous gold liquid oozing from the ruptured oil coolers.

The red danger lights flashed on around the track and the circuit's ambulance shot out of the pit lane like a scalded cat, siren wailing. With the session officially stopped, two marshals leapt the barrier waving their yellow flags, attempting to give the following cars a critical few seconds warning of the melée ahead. Mamet was not amused; Rob had smashed his little darling for a second time.

The 962 was dragged unceremoniously from the gravel trap and returned to the pits by the circuit's recovery wagon. The mechanics busied themselves releasing the car which hung pendulum-like beneath the jib of a crane. They knew better than to speak at a time like this.

Simon, one of my former mechanics who had worked for Team Capricorn, strolled over from the nextdoor pit, surveyed the damage, winked in my direction and with a resigned shrug walked away. He'd seen me do it a few times before, but today it wasn't his job to pick up the pieces. Mamet surveyed the damage. 'Damn it, Rob, you did this at Brands, what the hell were you doing out there? It was only your first bloody lap, the tyres weren't even warm!' The shock, frustration and embarrassment were written all over Rob's face, I felt for him, but it wasn't my place to make excuses. Mamet continued to lay in. 'I want Will to drive. Your mind is just not on the job, this was our last chance to pull off the Prize Indemnity and you've qualified us on the wrong end of the bloody grid!'

The prospect of driving again was stimulating, my pulse quickened at the thought. I would dearly have loved to drive, but after the turmoil of Brands Hatch three weeks earlier, when I'd been forced to compete in both heats, we had agreed that Zolder would be Rob's, it was only fair. Besides, I was by no means certain that my back would hold up for a full race distance. Mamet was not impressed with our logic but as far as I was concerned, a deal was a deal.

The mechanics quickly tidied up the car, removing the gravel that the air scoops had trawled up. It was evident that heat was already affecting the reliability of the lower-budget teams. By the end of qualifying, almost half of the low-budget teams had already dropped out and would not be taking the start.

Manuel Reuter, in the Kremer Porsche Spyder, had fulfilled his role as favourite, setting the quickest time of the session, a 1:30.32 taking pole position. The Reynard Cosworth of Lawrence Jacobsen secured second place on the front row, with Walter Lechner lining up on the second row. Rob had qualified the 962 two-thirds of the way down the grid.

The lights changed to green and Manuel Reuter took the lead. Otto Altenbach shot from sixth on the grid to claim third position before the first corner just behind Walter Lechner in the Horag Lola. Rob had dropped to ninth. As the last of the pack disappeared into the heat haze of the first corner, we held our breath. Vividly I imagined what was happening out on the track.

In my mind it was me driving. A quarter of a million dollars of high-tech machinery pumping out 800 highly stressed horsepower behind me. Through the first left hander. Right into the bumpy Sterrenwachtboch corner, accelerating flat out through Kanaalbocht, down the back straight through the chicane, bracing myself as I scorched over the blind left-hander, plunging downhill into Sacramentschelling, the car vibrating as I run a wheel along the entry kerbing, attempting to straighten out the tight chicane named after Villeneuve. Slipstreaming down the pit straight, inhaling the fragrance of raw speed, then like a slingshot pulling out into the braking areas to pass two cars, into sixth place.

Ahead, a pair of dicing cars touch sending sections of bodywork spinning idly, almost in slow motion into the air. Then, in a split second, they accelerate overhead as I duck. My heartbeat hits 190 per minute, a trickle of sweat stinging my eyes...

Suddenly the sound of the three leading cars in tight formation drew my mind back into real time. There was a pause, then three more cars, another gap and another six cars. I turned to Beth. 'Shit! He's missing!' I sprinted to the pits.

29

If in Doubt - Flat Out!

(Colin McRar M.B.E)

Terry Thompson was the managing director of Trans-Atlantic and a friend, yet bizarrely he had been called as a witness for the Crown. He strolled confidently to the dock and swore to tell the truth, the whole truth and nothing but the truth. 'Are you Terence Ernest Thompson?'

'Yes,' Terry replied confidently.

I had known Terry since the early 80s. His claim to fame was the creation of the KAO PLC Group which included Diamond Loudspeakers Ltd, the company that had sponsored me as a driver for some eight years. Terry was also a local magistrate – unlike the other witnesses, the court setting didn't intimidate him.

'Were you present at Brands Hatch when the Defendant drove the Porsche Spyder?' Smythe asked.

Terry turned and directed his words to the jury. 'Yes, I was.'

'And did Mr Middleton appear to suffer any difficulty while driving?'

'Yes. He was wearing a neck collar because of the G forces; I think that was because he hadn't driven for a long time. He span off in the first heat and as a result came ninth but I recall he was in some considerable pain with his back.' Paterson-Smythe shuddered as though he'd just swallowed a nasty dose of medicine. It was not the answer he'd hoped for. 'There was later a discussion in the pits,' Terry continued, 'that was primarily related to his back problem.' Rabbit struggled to contain his delight. Tigger found a few scribbles on his legal pad to interest him. 'He didn't want to do the next heat,' Terry pressed on, 'but the problem was he'd qualified the car, and if Allan drove it he'd have to

159

start from the pit lane which would be a big disadvantage to the Prize Indemnity.'

It was another important admission, every bit as significant as Mrs Pickup's earlier acknowledgement that I was correct to have claimed under both the redundancy and injury policies. It penetrated the heart of the Crown's case. McGaea carefully wrote down Terry's words.

A short blast from the warning siren directed our attention to the pit entrance. The 962 was limping up the entry lane like a wounded animal. The front left wheel was partially detached, emitting an audible howl of protest as the steel hub ground mercilessly into the magnesium wheel. The new Trans-Atlantic Team crew erupted in confusion as marshals directed the limping car in. Simon, my former team manager, cast me a knowing glance from the adjoining pit.

One of the Trans-Atlantic mechanics inserted an air line into the car's hydraulic system and the 962 rose instantly onto its air jacks. Mamet, displaying all the lightning reactions of an iced doughnut, waved his arms about, directing mechanics in his attempt to take charge of the simple task of replacing the wheel. A TV crew arrived, trying to film the mechanics as they struggled to remove the half-detached wheel from the mangled hub. Finally, in desperation, Simon ran across from the adjoining pit, pushed aside a fumbling mechanic and attached the new wheel himself.

Rob was gesticulating frantically from the cockpit. 'The bloody thing just came loose, I didn't hit anyone!' he shouted. Three painful minutes elapsed before the car finally rejoined the race. We were last, two laps behind the nearest car. Simon returned to his own pit smiling sardonically.

As the leading pack weaved its way around the 962, the awful truth dawned: Mamet's Porsche was just too slow. Rob was with the other cars and even faster than the majority through the corners, but they simply romped away on the straights. 'Will, you've got to do something!' It was Mamet, frantically trying to get my attention. 'You can't just stand here doing nothing. Go and talk to the other teams.' I ignored him. 'Will!' I turned and looked at him. 'Will, you've got to fix something, talk to the other teams, you know the team managers, this is show time! If you do nothing, we all lose.'

'David, I stand to lose more than everyone. I've carried the team on my credit cards for both these races.' Manuel Reuter in the Kremer Porsche flashed past. There was no sign of Rob.

'I'll drop the price by fifteen, no, twenty thousand,' Mamet went on. 'Use it to get a couple of teams to drop out, or at least hold back. All they'll have to do is call their drivers in for an extra pit stop.'

'David, have you ever heard the quote about never giving up? Never give in, never give in, never, never, never. The race isn't over and I certainly haven't given up yet. This Prize Indemnity thing has been a massive gamble. When I made the decision to carry on despite Rob's crash, it was intuitive and probably madness but, as I saw it, it was our, no *my* only chance. If we've failed, then it's me that's lost everything. At least I'll know I gave it my best shot. I'm not making another mistake, and I'm certainly not getting involved in fixing something! Do you understand me?'

He shook his head in disbelief, turning his back on me as he walked to the back of the pit.

By lap twelve, aided by a number of legitimate retirements, Rob had worked the Porsche up to eighth place. The car slid wide through the Ickx chicane, the rear wheels sending up a shower of dirt as he used every inch of track. Down the pit straight, past the start/finish line, our only hope was for some more of the cars in front to fall off or blow up. Rob, sensing an aerodynamic problem, nipped in behind Gellini in the Tiga and stole a tow by letting the less-powerful Tiga Cosworth punch a hole in the air and suck him along in its vacuum. It's a technique that works fine for the straights but can be disastrous in the corners as the lack of air acting on the wings causes the car to feel as though it's skating on ice.

As Gellini hit the brakes, Rob shot out of the slipstream into the left-hander, the wings grabbed some air and he accelerated hard through Sterrenwachtbocht, the 400-horsepower advantage of the Porsche pulling out two hundred yards on the Tiga, before latching onto the next available tow. Gradually, lap by lap, Rob was pulling his way back up the field.

By lap 18 he was running sixth, still one lap adrift from the main pack, none the less a position which at Brands Hatch would have secured the Prize Indemnity payout. But, here at Zolder, there were only 15 starters so we had to secure a top five position, and with only a handful of laps to go the situation still looked hopeless.

Altenbac was running second in the number-two Kremer Porsche but losing precious time jostling with the division-two car of Walter Lechner, the effect being to close the gap between the leading pack and Rob as he clawed his way up through the field. Lechner, third overall, courageously out-braked Altenbac into Turn One. Lawrence Jacobsen in the Can Am Reynard attempted to follow Lechner through on the inside, braking even later.

It happened directly in front of us, in the blink of an eye, a mental snapshot I will always remember. There was a sharp intake of breath from the crowd as Altenbac on the outside turned in, and Lawrence, still running off line at over 100 mph, simultaneously drifted into the much heavier Porsche. The first impact sent Lawrence's bright-red Reynard hurtling harmlessly through the air like a swatted bug. Time seemed almost to cease. The car pirouetted in mid air, discarding sections of bodywork. Then with a loud crack it returned to the track, spinning helplessly into the gravel trap, disgorging wheels and suspension as it tore itself apart. The hopes and dreams of driver, sponsors and team obliterated in fractions of a second of mayhem. Altenbac, delayed only momentarily, continued to the flag.

We all stood transfixed, nobody daring to say a word. The tension was unbearable, my mouth felt as dry as blotting paper and my heart pounded in my chest. I was well over £10,000 out of pocket on this gamble and on the verge of bankruptcy. I felt the sweat run cold in my armpits. I turned to Mamet. The Florida tan seemed to have drained from his face. 'Without Lawrence Jacobsen, where did Rob finish?' I asked. He looked unsure, the pit lane hushed.

The commentator concluded his commentary, his voice rising excitedly, trying to compete with the roar of racing engines. 'Raijmaki in the Judd fourth, Rob Allan in the 962 Spyder fifth.'

Mamet let out a bellowing yell of victory. 'It worked, we've won!' He grasped me and danced me about the pit lane. I struggled to release myself from his grip.

A broad smile spread across my face. 'Well of course it worked, did you ever doubt it?' I looked at him, trying to hide my relief. 'I think Trans-Atlantic's just won a Porsche.'

Rob swept into the pits in a vortex of dust, unclipped his safety harness, removed his helmet and tore off his balaclava. He ran from the car to join us, a look of uncertainty on his face. 'Where did I finish?'

Mamet grinned, 'You did it; fifth place.'

Rob punched the air exuberantly and let out a loud 'Yeah!'

'So what happens now?' Mamet asked eagerly, turning to me.

'We put in the claim with Track Star, I suppose. We'll need a copy of the official results and some sort of sale document from you to Trans-Atlantic, and then once it's agreed, we'll have to import the car permanently and pay the duty.'

'Well, you've got some of our letterheads – if you need anything else let me know, just don't screw me over on this, okay?'

David Mamet left the Zolder circuit a happy man and well ahead of the rest of the team; he had a hire car to return and a pre-booked flight to Florida to catch. He sat somewhere high over the Atlantic, sorting his last cluster of expense chits and dreaming of the imminent sale of his Porsche for a quarter of a million dollars.

It was dark; gone 10.30 pm when our ferry finally edged its way out of Calais. We signed for our cabin keys and Beth settled the boys quickly into their bunks; it had been a very long day. Just along the corridor, we joined Rob in the Promenade Restaurant and sat watching the lights of the harbour as they disappeared. Waiters moved around taking orders and dispensing drinks. We ordered a bottle of Moet to toast our success.

A voice made me turn. 'So, you guys pulled it off then?' It was Simon, my former chief mechanic. He smiled and strolled over to join us. 'So you'll be running the Porsche in next season's championship then.'

'Hi Simon, thanks for your little intervention during the pit stop,' I said. 'Yes, we pulled it off by just 1.3 seconds. I doubt we'd have done it without your help. Would you like a glass of champagne?' I beckoned to a waiter for another glass.

Simon sat down. 'Always pleased to be of service. Are you

going to use the same crew to run it next season?' There was a degree of sarcasm in his voice.

'I doubt it, but we haven't begun to work that one out yet,' I replied.

'Well, when you do, give me a call; maybe we could do a deal.' He faltered slightly. 'You know that car needs a fair amount of development if it's going to win races.'

'Why do you say that?' I asked.

'Well, you do know it's not really a Porsche, don't you.'

'What?' We replied in unison.

He hesitated, as though unsure whether to continue. He coughed and cleared his throat. 'You know it's not a factory-built Porsche 962, don't you?'

'No I didn't!' I exclaimed, an empty feeling opening in the pit of my stomach.

Simon took a sip of his champagne. 'In total, Porsche manufactured around a hundred 962s, but bizarrely, they aren't sure. Sixteen were their official factory team cars and some eighty or so were sold to private teams. That at least is clear, but then it gets more complicated. A few 956s were rebuilt as 962s, and a few more 962s were rebuilt from written-off cars. A few more cars were even given new chassis numbers by Porsche after reconstruction. In some cases, however, parts from one written-off car went into several privately built 962s. It's all a bit confusing, but I think your car is in the latter category. That is, it was built from bits of other crashed cars. I'm pretty sure the chassis was never built by Porsche; it was built by a company called Fabcar in the United States. It certainly doesn't look like an original Porsche chassis.

'What's more, the engine looks like it's from a late 1970s Porsche 936; a 2.65-litre single turbo unit. I'll grant you it's powerful, too powerful for the States. Over there they've run it with restrictors...' He took another sip of champagne, 'You could take the restrictors off and it would give you over 1000 horsepower. That might help overcome some of the aerodynamic problems, but it would also make it more likely to blow up, and finding parts for a 936 engine would be difficult and expensive. The only bit that looks like it's original Porsche is the badge.'

'Shit!' I turned to Rob. 'Did you know any of that?' He

164

shrugged. 'Did you feel there was an aerodynamic problem in the race?' I persisted.

'I did feel there was something wrong; even the lower-powered cars seemed to romp away on the straights. It's as though it reached a speed and just couldn't go beyond it.'

Simon shrugged. 'I think there's a fundamental problem with the Spyder bodywork. Just look at its track record in the States, at best it's a midfield car. At Daytona, in the 24 hours, it struggled to qualify, even with a former Le Mans winner doing the pedalling. If you're looking at running it in sprint races, it needs to be lighter, more nimble, and doesn't want to be held back with any aerodynamic problems.' He downed the last of his champagne. 'Anyway, if you want to talk about running it, give me a call.' He got up and headed for the door.

I excused myself and made my way out onto the top deck. I'd thought everything had worked out as planned, minus a few hiccups, but I hadn't reckoned on this. I felt like a fool; how could I not have realised? The truth was I wanted this to work so much that I hadn't considered Mamet might have been trying to screw us. I needed to clear my head, think through all the options.

A warm night breeze blew in my hair and the diesel engines churned a wake through the dark waters of the Channel. I stared into the darkness, exhaustion taking the place of euphoria, the previous excitement quickly fading into an uneasy fatigue. With a sudden jolt of foreboding, WPA and the surgeon's report drifted into my thoughts. With all the excitement of Rob pulling off the Prize Indemnity, I'd completely forgotten about all that. Once we got his report it was possible, even probable, that I wouldn't be driving next year anyway. My head ached at the thought of it.

A voice made me turn. It was Rob. 'If the Porsche isn't going to work,' he began, 'what about an old F1 car modified to comply with the Super Cup rules? All we'd have to do is fit it with Can Am style bodywork like Lawrence Jacobson's car. It would be light, nimble and incredibly quick.'

'It would also be prohibitively expensive to run,' I added dismissively. For me, the thrill of Zolder was already starting to fade; reality beginning to dawn. 'Rob, we haven't even begun to look at costs yet, and particularly Mamet's expenses. Whatever the bottom line is, it's all been stuck on my overdraft and credit cards. That lot has got to be cleared before we do anything and then we've got to pay for the cost of the damage after the shunts. I've got no income and the bank is going to start pushing me. I don't know if we'll even have enough to pay Mamet what he's asking anyway.'

Rob shook his head. 'I know. That's why an F1 car might be a better bet. Just think about it; it would be cheaper to buy and it would be unbeatable in the Super Cup. We could get a Lotus or an Arrows and run another Prize Indemnity linked to next season's championship points.'

'What are you thinking?'

'Simple; we get Track Star to underwrite a policy of say £1,500 for each championship point in each race in the Super Cup, and then, say £100,000 for winning the overall championship. All we'd need to find would be a sponsor to cover the cost of the premiums and the basic running costs. Simon used to work for Lotus; he's bound to have the contacts. His workshops are based in Norwich, just down the road from Team Lotus. I bet he could get a team of guys together and run it from up there.'

The image of a black and gold Lotus Renault 89T popped into my mind; one of the most powerful Formula 1 cars ever produced, with a 1.5-litre turbocharged engine developing more than 1200 horsepower in qualifying, wrapped up in a carbon fibre chassis, the overall package weighing in at just 600 kilos; half the weight of the Porsche. They were adrenalin-fuelled rockets. My heart accelerated at the thought and I grinned like a schoolkid.

The turbo era of Formula 1 had just ended and Rob was right, there was a glut of the exotic machines lying obsolete around the world. Bizarrely, an old F1 car might work out much cheaper than Mamet's Porsche, leaving enough money to cover all the expenses. But the thought of chopping one of those legendary cars about was sacrilege. 'You're forgetting Mamet,' I added depressingly. 'What about the 962 and the deal with him?'

Rob shrugged expressively. 'Pay him off.'

'It's not as simple as that; we have a deal,' I replied hopelessly. 'Anyway, a Formula 1 car would be too temperamental and we'd have no back-up or help from manufacturers and no support from engine suppliers...' I paused for a moment, the seed of an idea beginning to germinate, 'but what about an old Indy car! They're less complex, even cheaper to buy and run, and manufacturers like Lola might be quite supportive. We could also get parts off the shelf rather than having to get everything made.' It was impossible to disguise my excitement.

Rob looked back, a grin spreading across his face. 'You know, we could probably run a *pair* of Indy cars for the price of running just the Porsche or one F1 Car.'

'If we ran a two-car team, tactics would come into it and it would overcome the two-driver problem in the Super Cup,' I said. 'We could make a killing if Track Star agreed to another Prize Indemnity.' I was now ignoring any question of me driving.

Rob's expression hardened. 'You know, there was an option in the agreement with Mamet to pay a rental for the Porsche, rather than buying it.'

I frowned. 'He'd go ballistic.'

'So? It looks to me as though we're the ones that have been taken for the ride. Talk to him, you're good at that.'

'He's American, Rob; he'll sue. Anyway, he already seems unnerved; he keeps talking about me screwing him over, it's as if he distrusts me.'

Rob gave a helpless shrug.

'There's something else Rob...' I went on. 'After Brands Hatch, I don't even know if I'm going to be able to drive any more with my back problems. It might be time for me to give up, there may only be a need for the one car.' I shook my head, pushing the thought away. 'I reckon we should leave things as they are for a few days. I'll get the paperwork together and up to Track Star. In the interim, I know a lawyer who could take a look at the contract and give us some advice. There's a lot of money involved here. I don't want to speak to Mamet or Track Star or anyone else until we know exactly where we stand.'

'Will, if you couldn't drive, I think I know somebody that would want to take your place.'

I had dreamed of making it as a professional driver for so many years; of joining the ranks of the elite. For many, just by competing I'd achieved that dream, but to me without a competitive world-class team and a car capable of winning, the dream was no more than a shadow on a distant horizon. I wanted to be up there with the big boys, part of the gang!

It hadn't been for the lack of trying and had not been without some rewards: there had been fantastic times in the National Championships with good cars when I'd won races and earned enough to pay the mortgage, but more often there had been the difficult times when we'd struggled to pay even the food bills and I'd driven unreliable cars in underdog teams without any chance of winning. Yet I had tasted the glory of winning and still dreamed of making my name at the front of the grid as a top British driver in a World Championship team, flying the Union Jack. Suddenly, Trans-Atlantic was a reality and maybe, just maybe, there was a light at the end of my tunnel. The team had a budget to at least start the championship, but what about my injuries, WPA's report, and Mamet's Porsche?

Until these issues had been resolved, planning for the future was next to impossible. WPA might reject the report on some technicality. Moreover I was being put under increasing daily pressure by them to return to work, but Track Star could also throw out the Prize Indemnity for some reason. Let things settle, I told myself, let the experts take over. Toby Jackson, my solicitor, could look at the contract and we'd wait for WPA's report however long it took, a week, a month, whatever; then I'd make a decision.

Racing was more than a job; it was my passion and had been my childhood dream but all the uncertainty brought with it insecurity. I enjoyed my association with Trans-Atlantic, it gave me enthusiasm, my spark had still not yet been doused; I wanted desperately to keep going. In the meantime I resolved to continue to help set up and prepare this new team for its opening season in 1993 ... as long as Track Star accepted the Prize Indemnity. Only then, if there'd been no response from WPA, would I go ahead and drive; in Mamet's Porsche or any other car or cars the team purchased. But if WPA agreed that I should no longer compete, I'd give up my dream as a driver ... and then, well, who knows, maybe I could take on the role of team manager.

That decision, so trivial in nature, so terrible in effect, would forge the final link in the chain of events leading to Court Number One.

30

Justice is incidental to law and order.

(J. Edgar Hoover)

Smythe turned to Terry. 'In August 1992,' he continued, 'is it correct that both you and the Defendant attended a meeting with a solicitor by the name of Toby Jackson at the offices of George Evans and Crowthorp in Southampton?'

'Yes, that's right.'

'And did this follow the fifth place at Zolder?'

'Yes. After Rob's crashes at Brands Hatch and Zolder, and Mr Mamet's expenses, there were insufficient funds to buy the 962 Spyder. There was also a big question over the competitiveness and the pedigree of the Porsche itself.'

'Yes quite but...' Smythe tried to interject, but Terry had more to say and wouldn't be stopped.

'We wanted to check the contract and the provision to simply pay a rental for the Porsche, and to look at the possibility of buying alternative cars.'

Terry went on to explain that Track Star had been faxed about the possibility of purchasing alternative Indy cars, after Toby Jackson had confirmed it was legal to do so, and this had led to the expected dispute with David Mamet.

He confirmed that Trans-Atlantic had received the Prize Indemnity payout, and that a rental figure of $40,000 from the fund was paid to Mamet for the use of his 962 Spyder. Terry made it clear that I had received no payment to drive, but that Mamet's expenses, paid on my credit cards on behalf of Trans-Atlantic, had been refunded. 'All such transactions appear within the audited accounts of Trans-Atlantic for 1992 and are cross-referenced to the actual receipts for the items paid by Will Middleton,' he added.

By the time Smythe had concluded his examination he looked

169

a little unnerved, his posture slightly deflated, but still he finished his patter by introducing Rabbit in the usual way, and once again they performed their little dance routine, ending with Rabbit rising courteously to commence his cross-examination.

Our defence team had been aware for some time that Detectives Probert and Barnet had approached a number of witnesses including Terry, prior to the trial, using questionable tactics. But Terry, being my friend, a magistrate and the director of Trans-Atlantic, had immediately alerted us to precisely what was being said. However, the problem was how to bring this to the attention of the court.

'Mr Thompson,' Rabbit began, 'were you approached just prior to giving your evidence by the officers investigating this case?' Rabbit had clearly decided the only way to deal with the sensitive issue was to be blunt. A little too blunt for His Honour who appeared somehow to know what was coming next and rapidly intervened.

The jury were despatched while His Honour, clearly disconcerted by any suggestions of the police doing anything underhand, addressed the problem. 'Mr Adams, I will not have a word said against these good officers in my court. Is that clear?'

It was, and the matter ended before it was allowed to begin.

Rob and his girlfriend Anna had arrived at Heathrow unusually early. I'd grown accustomed to seeing him arrive at the check-in desk, always at the last minute, in a plume of grey cigarette smoke. But today he was relaxed, standing by the counter waiting for me. In his hand he held a large artist's presentation case containing illustrations he'd produced of the new Trans-Atlantic cars which were to be shown at the Super Cup presentation. Anna looked up and smiled. 'Hi Will.'

Anna was in her late twenties, five foot six and very slim with a body so curvaceous it might have come straight from a teenage boy's fantasy. She wore tight-fitting blue jeans and a white T-shirt. A tousled mane of dark-brown hair hung simply to her shoulders, her features were delicate, her eyes dark, and her cheekbones high. She was stunningly beautiful.

For over two years she'd lived with Rob, often turning up at the European races, but their relationship had become distant, and they'd begun to argue publicly, so I'd been surprised to see her at the check-in desk, particularly as she hated flying.

Beth and I checked our luggage through the crowded number three terminal and the four of us made our way through the jostling crowds past security to the departure lounge and ordered hot drinks from a harassed waiter at Garfunkels. An hour passed as we sat waiting for our flight to be called, but when no announcement came we ordered more refills. No sooner had these arrived than the tannoy system, announcing our flight, finally interrupted.

We downed our refills, found our way to Gate 35 and awaited instructions to board. Half an hour later we boarded the aircraft, found our seats and the aircraft taxied to its designated runway. Anna clung desperately to Rob, her nervousness obvious. She pushed a hand through her hair and smiled in my direction, her smooth olive complexion flushed slightly, then she lowered her eyes demurely. Rob caught the glance, his eyes darting jealously between us. If only I could read her thoughts – we had barely spoken since the weekend of the incident. Did she still think about that night, I wondered? An icy finger of guilt ran down my spine, the chill of disloyalty that I would always live with.

As we climbed to 10,000 feet, the 'Fasten Seatbelts' sign extinguished. Beneath the port wing the Sussex countryside spread out in all its late autumnal glory. I peered out of the nearside window: the weather was bright and the horizon sky-blue. Below, I could clearly make out the mottled greens and browns of the Downs, Devils Dyke where I'd played as a child and the contours of Brighton with its cream-edged beaches and two piers, one now only a relic, its metallic skeleton collapsing into an unfriendly sea. My mind wandered back to my childhood days, the day I'd met Graham Hill, and the day I'd first decided to become a racing driver. Decisions had been so easy then.

At 5.30 pm we touched down at Salzburg International Airport. As the 'Fasten Seatbelts' light extinguished, Rob and Anna joined the usual mad rush for the exits. Beth and I remained seated. I flicked through my copy of *Autosport*, waiting for the mass of passengers to disembark. We were now running more than an hour late.

We headed for Passport Control, where we queued for five

minutes before being waved through. Luggage had just begun to circulate around the carousel by the time we arrived. We joined Rob, Anna and fellow passengers, all scrutinising the bags as they lurched past. With Customs cleared, we collected our red BMW M3 hire car. Beth and Anna climbed into the back. Rob, in the passenger seat, unfolded the free courtesy map from the glove box. We set off briskly in the direction of Salzburg.

The thick snow still glistened under the dying rays of the sun, the wheels crunching as we wound our way past the baroque churches and towers of Salzburg over the river Salzach and out into the beautiful countryside, moving as swiftly as we dared up the slopes and down into the valleys, through dense forests of pine.

It was dark by the time we arrived at the Kaufhaus Juhasz, a small Austrian hotel nestling in a valley. We checked in to our respective rooms, and after a quick freshen up and change of clothes, made our way down into the basement section which housed the elegant function rooms. A sign welcomed the 1993 Super Cup Teams, the rest of whom had already arrived more than an hour earlier.

We pushed our way through the swing doors and I glanced around the room. I knew most of the faces by sight but few of the names. I nodded to a waiter in a black evening jacket and was directed to a reserved table. Paul Goppart, the German president of the Super Cup Championship, noticing our arrival, came over and introduced himself. Paul spoke three languages fluently, and all with a deep German accent. We shook hands and the conversation quickly moved on to what he wanted to hear; Trans-Atlantic would be running not one, not two, but three cars in the 1993 Championship.

A waiter arrived and placed a bottle of Mouton Cadet on the table. When he left, Paul leaned over and in his excited German accent enquired, 'So what cars will the team actually be running?'

The conversation quickly moved on from the Indy cars to topics of team sponsorship, engine type and tyre deals, and finally to who would be the third Trans-Atlantic driver. The waiter returned and slapped down our starters, '*Klachelsuppe,*' he announced with a flourish. 'Pig soup!' Paul translated with a grin.

The Klachelsuppe was surprisingly good and the veal that

followed excellent. Finally Paul rose to start his presentation. Coffee was served and his address concluded with an announcement that a new, three-car British team was being launched; Trans-Atlantic, which would be competing in the forthcoming Super Cup.

The stuffiness of the dimly lit room suddenly hit me and I beckoned to the waiter for the drinks bill. Rob rose, stubbed out a cigarette and led the way out into the moonlight. I pulled the collar of my new Trans-Atlantic race jacket around my neck as we strolled out into the formal gardens now shrouded in the shadows of the night. I pulled Beth close. The snow crunched under our feet, still more drifted downwards out of the colourless sky, settling in a light dusting on our shoulders, the bright moon reflecting from the flakes as they fell like tiny diamonds.

I breathed the cold night air deeply into my lungs, a mood of excitement reminiscent of Christmases long past flooded through me. We were happy and content the gamble had paid off. I'd taken on a horrendous financial risk. We could have lost everything and might even have been forced to sell up and lose our beloved granary, but in a last throw of the dice everything had slotted into place and we'd been rewarded with a gift only money could provide; a fresh start in a brand new team. The excitement of it made me realise how much I'd missed it all; the sounds, the smells, the thrill, the speed, and my friends. Beth leaned closer, snuggling up, and smiled, a few flecks of snow rested on her cheeks. I looked deeply into her eyes, 'I love you lots, you know.'

Despite pulling off the Prize Indemnity and the creation of the new Trans-Atlantic Team, Christmas that year was strange. In place of the usual hundred or so corporate Christmas cards, now there were just those from family and friends, the most significant absence being my Dad's. There was also no news from WPA, specifically no report from the surgeon and now little likelihood of receiving anything until after the New Year break. Anyway, following the launch in Austria, I somehow dreaded its arrival and what it would say. Christmas and the New Year was a time for making fresh resolutions; for the first time I realised that I didn't particularly want to see the report, not today, not tomorrow;

perhaps never. The mood around the house was warm and peaceful; each day merging into the next. The January 1993 New Year celebrations came and went.

Beth handed me the stack of post; it had been piling up over the past week but we hadn't wanted the festive mood to end. It was now mid January, the boys were back at school and we needed to get back into a more normal routine. I flicked through a mass of junk mail, magazines, catalogues, credit card statements and complementary calendars from the local takeaways. WPA's report was in the last envelope. It had been face down at the bottom of the pile. I flicked it open, pulled out the six-page document and started reading.

'Well?' Beth asked after some minutes, drawing out the word.

'It's dated the 10th of August. That's two days after Rob pulled off the Prize Indemnity at Zolder. How could it have taken until now to get a copy?' I continued slowly down the pages. 'Here,' I stabbed at a paragraph of text, 'it's confirmed. I broke my back in two places when I fell from that bloody horse; and according to this, the lumbar area of my spine was knocked forward by a quarter of an inch.'

Beth winced. She started to say something but stopped. The room darkened with a heavy silence. I dropped the report into my lap, making a helpless gesture with my hands. 'That's it, they can't fix it; my career is over.'

Beth placed her arms tenderly around me. 'My darling,' she said, 'I'm so sorry.'

31

Rabbit fired up a cigarette and inhaled deeply.

'Well, that went well then,' I said with obvious sarcasm, as we headed back for the usual debriefing. 'How can this trial be fair and unbiased, if the judge is stopping us presenting our evidence?'

'He's a Crown Court judge; he can do what he likes,' said Rabbit, drawing heavily on his cigarette. 'We have to move on; tomorrow's a very big day. The Crown has got both Rob Allan and the Prize Indemnity broker giving evidence. If we have a good day tomorrow, it could blow the Crown case clean out of the water.'

We entered our makeshift office on the first floor and sat down. I drew in a deep breath, and sighed. It must have been a fairly prominent sigh, because when I looked up, Piglet was eyeing me curiously. 'What's up, Will?' he enquired.

'I do have a few concerns about Rob,' I said.

Rabbit stabbed out his cigarette tetchily. 'How so? Is there something we need to know?'

'There is a potential problem...' I hesitated, glancing at Beth. 'Well, there *could* be a problem.'

Tigger blinked at the first mention of a problem. Rabbit took a deep breath and rubbed his eyes. 'If there's something relevant to what Rob Allan might say in evidence tomorrow, then we need to be pre-warned.'

'Well, it's not as easy as that; I don't know for sure. Rob and I haven't spoken for almost a year. Not since shortly after the second police raid and things had been a little fraught even before that.'

'I thought you were good friends,' Tigger interjected.

'We were, but after the second raid he broke off all contact.

175

He just didn't want to talk, or meet up. He said he'd been advised not to talk to me. But there was a lot more to it than that. There'd been a lot of rumour and speculation doing the rounds.'

'Would you care to elaborate?' Rabbit asked.

I paused, unsure how to explain. 'Well, there was a sort of *incident* between Rob's girlfriend, Anna and me.'

All three faces looked back at me blankly. The room went uneasily quiet for a moment, no one daring to make eye contact with Beth. Her hand crept onto my knee reassuringly. 'Go on, Will,' she said, 'it's okay, we've dealt with all this. Tell them what happened.'

'So, what *sort* of incident?' Piglet finally squeaked in a remarkably neutral tone.

'I suppose you might call it a sort of *fling.*'

Piglet winced noticeably. Tigger drew in a sharp breath and frowned. Rabbit's jaw dropped, and he went suddenly very quiet.

Rabbit placed his head in his hands while drawing in another long deep breath. He looked back at me through splayed fingers for what seemed like a very long time. 'A *fling…*' he repeated, with obvious distaste, as if it were an infectious disease. 'Are you telling us that you had an affair with Rob Allan's girlfriend?'

'No, it wasn't exactly an *affair!*' I said.

'Did you sleep with her?' Piglet asked.

'No! Well, not exactly.'

'So what are you saying *exactly*? Do you think he's going to stab you in the back?' asked Rabbit bluntly.

'I don't know what he's going to say, but yes, I am a little concerned.'

'His evidence could make or break the Crown's case,' said Piglet, eyeing Rabbit intently. 'Remember, this is the person who dreamed up the idea of doing the Prize Indemnity. Correction … actually ran a Prize Indemnity, and only months before Trans-Atlantic did. That evidence is critical. The Crown is trying to say it was *all* Will's idea,' he turned back to me, 'and part of the overall scam involving the collapse of Team Capricorn. But if Rob agrees that it was *his* idea and that *he* ran Prize Indemnity months earlier, what is the Crown left with?'

'But this is a double-edged sword. If I use this latest revelation to discredit Rob, assuming we need to, it's tantamount to judicial suicide for Will. We need the jury to *like* Will, not think he's gone behind his friend's back and had an affair with his girlfriend. Half the jury is female.'

'It wasn't an *affair*!' I blurted out.

'Okay,' Rabbit interrupted resignedly. 'Well, if it wasn't an affair, what was it? Tell us what happened, *exactly*.' Six eyes bored into me.

'Well ... it sort of happened at Le Mans ... in 1992,' I stammered ruefully. 'It was the weekend that Rob first ran his original Prize Indemnity...'

Rob was entered to drive in the 1992 Le Mans 24 Hours. I was not taking part; it was the year after Team Capricorn collapsed and I was out of work, but had driven over at the last minute after he'd phoned asking if I could bring Anna to watch the race. That weekend everything changed; how could it not, after what happened.

Qualifying had finished on the Thursday before, and by the time we arrived late on the Saturday, Rob was being strapped into the car for the start of the classic 24-hour race.

Anna and I made our way to the gantry above the pits to watch the start. I couldn't help but notice the admiring glances of envious men, impossible to ignore her beauty, her smiles.

Following the collapse of my team, it was so strange to be back at a race track with nothing else to do except chat to Anna. Beth and the boys had been the centre of my life but the racing had been what held everything together, the house, the lifestyle, my dream. Racing had been more of a way of life than a job. Nothing else gave the same excitement or drama. With the collapse of the team and the loss of my father, I found myself in some kind of void. Not that my life wasn't fulfilled at home. I loved Beth, the boys and our home. It was just that the adrenalin of the race track somehow brought me to life.

For hours Anna and I wandered around the paddock area, chatting and watching the pit stops. We'd always been just platonic friends, but the longer we spent together, the more attracted to her I was becoming. The way she nibbled her bottom lip when she was unsure. The dimples that formed in her cheeks when she smiled, her vulnerability.

Clouds drifted lazily overhead, the waning sun sank lower on the horizon until darkness descended suddenly, like a blanket. A light drizzle began, a precursor to the swathes of mist that would later arise, drifting menacingly in unpredictable patches along the infamous Mulsanne Straight where Rob raced at up to 250 miles per hour, in the darkness.

It was late and we'd not eaten since early that morning on the ferry. We left the hustle and bustle of the track behind us and drove the short distance to the famous 24 Hours restaurant.

It was after 10.30 pm when we made our way into the crowded restaurant, situated just yards from the Mulsanne Straight. She paused outside, as if unsure what to say next. 'I don't know how much longer Rob and I will be together,' she said, her eyes misting over. I put my arm around her and pulled her close, her cheek brushing against mine. I turned to meet her brown eyes and before I knew what was happening, we kissed. A rush of excitement, like electricity, coursed through me, a strange nostalgia from batchelor days. Gently I ran my hands down her back, tracing the outline of her bra. Abruptly, she broke off, 'I'm sorry, I didn't mean that to happen, I'm sorry.'

Almost reluctantly, on the edge of making the biggest mistake of my life, I looked into her deep brown eyes. 'It's okay,' I said, 'I'm not.' She looked back at me, the pain of the recent months with Rob obvious. A pain that I knew only too well existed and doubted would ever heal. She kissed me again, at first gently but then more passionately, her lips parting, her breasts pressing against me, her arms wrapping around my shoulders.

She broke off again. 'I always thought Rob was the one. I thought we were going to settle down, grow old together, have kids, but...' she hesitated, then she suddenly lost control. She snuffled, wiping the tears from her eyes. I held her close. I knew what she wanted to say, but couldn't let on that I knew.

For too long I'd been in the unenviable position of having both Rob and Anna confiding in me. For months Rob had made it clear to me that his relationship with Anna was over, yet he couldn't quite get round to leaving her. But as Rob's friend, I couldn't let on to Anna what was known by most of our racing inner circle – that Rob was having a string of affairs, with a different girl receiving his attention in whichever country we happened to be racing in. But I was the only person who knew he was now serious about one girl in particular; an American with white ankle socks and her own private plane. Dawn. More difficult still was that Rob had confided to me that only weeks earlier Anna had had an abortion. 'There's no way I'm the father,' he'd insisted. 'We haven't been that way for more than a year.'

'Would you like me to take you back to the house?' I asked her, not knowing quite how to handle the situation.

'No, we're here now,' she said. 'Let's get something to eat.' She pulled out a tissue and dried her tears.

We pushed open the door. The place was packed, a solid, steaming mass of humanity, some 200 or more partygoers, all vying for the attention of the handful of waiters that darted between the rows of trestle tables. Only yards away, the sound of the cars was deafening as they blasted past, their headlamps sending flashes of light flickering across the room.

As quickly as we could, we ordered the set 10-franc menu and a carafe of red house wine. Anna toyed with her food but ate little, concentrating more on the wine. By the second carafe, she'd relaxed. 'Mmm...' she purred, holding her glass with both hands. She smiled, raising her eyebrows, waiting for me to say something.

'You know, I've got nowhere to stay tonight,' I said. Rob's business partner, Stuart, had hit on the idea of renting a house for the team personnel and sponsors for the Le Mans week, but by the time Anna and I had arrived every square metre of the place had been taken. The only room available was Rob's, but Rob was otherwise engaged, on the track.

She grinned, still toying with her glass. 'I've got a room you know.' She paused. 'Just as long as you're going to be good.'

'I'll try,' I lied, pushing away any thought of what might happen if we were to share a room, or even a bed together.

I paid the waiter and we made our way to the car. We drove the short journey through the tiny country lanes to the house. I parked the Mitsubishi and we entered the house. The place was full and heads turned as we entered but we barely noticed the familiar faces we both knew so well; sponsors, friends, Rob's business partner Stuart, as I followed her quickly to a downstairs room.

She pushed open the door and beckoned me in. The room was large with a pair of double doors leading off to a private patio area. 'It's got its own pool,' she said, closing the drapes. 'We could take a swim in the morning.' A large unmade double bed dominated one wall, along another was a mirrored wardrobe and off to one side a makeshift uncomfortable-looking single camp bed had been strewn with an assortment of Rob's clothing. An en-suite bathroom led off from the far side of the room. 'I'm just going to take a quick shower,' she said.

A few minutes later she returned, draped in a thick white bath robe, a towel wrapped around her damp hair, water droplets glinting on her cheeks.

'I think I'd better take a cold shower.' I pushed open the door to the bathroom and turned on the shower, letting the cool water flow over me. What was I doing, I asked myself, what was I getting myself into? I mustn't do this, just go back in there, get into that single camp bed and go to sleep! I stepped out of the shower, pulled a towel from the rail, wrapped it around my waist and returned to the room.

She was in the bed, lights turned down low, the white quilt pulled up high; bare shoulders just showing. Her damp dark hair fanned over the pink pillow. I pushed away my thoughts of just minutes earlier, gently tugging back on the quilt. 'No, Will, we mustn't!' she grinned, a dimple forming in her cheek. A brief tug-of-war that she had no wish to win ensued. She released the quilt, quickly placing an arm over her breasts.

She was naked except for a pair of sheer black panties. She was exquisite, fragile, vulnerable, her body warm, sensuous, inviting. Her vulnerability touched something hidden within me. I sat down on the side of the bed and kissed her. Again she responded. Slowly I moved my lips down to her breasts.

'Will, we shouldn't,' she murmured. I flicked my tongue over her hard nipple, a slight sigh lifted from her throat, her breath becoming more ragged. My fingers moved down, gently caressing the inside of her thighs; she let out a groan. I touched her lightly, almost teasingly, through her sheer panties, she closed her eyes, releasing a gasp of breath, her back arching, hips lifting, body beginning to tremble.

I kissed her again, my hand slipping back over her taut stomach, gently hooking a finger into her panties. She blocked me, this time more decidedly. 'No. Will, we mustn't do this...' she said, gathering her wits. 'We shouldn't be doing this at all; you're married and I'm still with Rob, this is a huge mistake!'

Rob's name, and the reminder that I was married, happily married, jolted me back to reality. The sudden realisation that I was in his bed had a more sobering effect than the shower. What the hell was I doing! And what's more, Rob could walk in on us at any moment, what would I say? *Hi Rob ... just taking care of Anna for you!*

We kissed again, but this time without the passion. A kiss to say we could just be friends.

I spent an uncomfortable night on the camp bed, waking again to the emotional turmoil at 7 am, having slept for less than six hours. I hadn't the faintest idea what to do next. We had not been unfaithful – well, not really, I told myself. But I could not live a lie, we'd crossed a boundary and I'd broken a trust, to both Rob and to Beth. I would have to tell her the truth, but what the hell could I ever say to Rob? If I was to say anything, it would guarantee the split that was likely anyway.

In the time that followed, Rob would regularly ask about what happened that weekend, but that was as far as it ever went. All that was left was an awkward blush of embarrassment, but Rob knew what had happened; at least he thought he did. One day, when it mattered, I couldn't help but feel I would be made to pay for my breach of faith.

32

Rob Allan stood in the dock wearing his finest suit. Gripping a Bible in his right hand, he swore to tell the truth. He looked terrified. He'd been running scared since February 93 when his flat had been raided; his attitude had only seemed to intensify police interest. The detectives had sensed an ally in Rob and pursued him relentlessly. The last time we'd spoken had been almost a year earlier. He had been terrified then.

'Will, they're telling me all the phones have been tapped.'

'You're kidding!'

'You don't believe it?'

'I don't know. It just seems so fantastic, maybe it's one of those private detectives. I just can't believe the police would bug a person's phone.'

'Will, this was a Metropolitan Police Officer, and if he says all our phones have been bugged, I believe him. They also said that they have evidence from your bank that you've been fiddling your income. They keep saying you're going down for a long time. I just don't need this. I don't want any more to do with Trans-Atlantic, Mamet's Porsche, the Indy cars, anything. Okay?' The line clicked and went dead. We hadn't spoken since that day.

Paterson-Smythe began in his usual fashion. He introduced the witness, and asked him to address his answers directly to the jury. He asked about Rob's background, where and how we'd originally met, and enquired, with apparent interest, about the cars Rob drove. Rob stumbled over his words nervously, but each time he hesitated, the learned barrister smiled back reassuringly. Smythe studied his notes then glanced back at Rob, and smiled once more. 'Whose idea was the Prize Indemnity?' he asked.

Rob's eyes narrowed a little and he cast a glance at the dock. 'That was Will's idea.'

'That's a lie!' I blurted.

Smythe turned to His Honour with a slight smirk. His Honour scrutinised me for a moment. 'Mr Adams. Please instruct your client to remain quiet.'

Smythe smiled with obvious satisfaction and the carefully coordinated avalanche continued. 'Thank you. Mr Allan, I think you were telling us that the Prize Indemnity was the Defendant's idea, is that so?'

'Yes ... that's right.'

'And whose idea was the Trans-Atlantic Team?'

'That was Will's as well. He came up with the idea after his previous team, Team Capricorn, collapsed.'

Slowly and purposely the Crown continued their examination, a hint of something suspicious here, an actual fact there. Smythe moved on to the new team. 'And did you have any involvement with the setting up of the Trans-Atlantic Team?'

'Nothing in particular. I attended a couple of meetings, and I went to Florida to see David Mamet. The idea was that I might be one of the team's drivers, but that was about it. Will dealt with all the day to day activity and all the set up.'

'Yes. Thank you, Mr Allan. I expect my learned colleague might have a few questions.' Paterson-Smythe returned happily to his seat as Rabbit rose on the other end of the legal see-saw.

'Just one or two questions, Mr Allan,' Rabbit began. 'You told my learned colleague that the Prize Indemnity was my client's idea. That was simply not the case, was it Mr Allan?'

Rob looked shocked. He turned and glared at me in the dock. 'I don't know what you're suggesting. I didn't know anything about Prize Indemnity until Will came up with the idea.'

Rabbit wasn't prepared to give in quite that easily. 'Mr Allan, is it not true that you drove in the Le Mans 24 Hours in 1992?'

'Yes.'

'And in that race, is it also true that you had taken out a Prize Indemnity policy worth twenty thousand pounds, with Track Star, the same firm that you later used for the Brands Hatch and Zolder races with Trans-Atlantic?'

Rob stiffened noticeably, as though attempting to hide something behind his back. His eyes flickered momentarily back and forth between Rabbit and me. He hesitated just a moment longer, then replied, 'Absolutely not!'

The more Rabbit pushed, the more unclear Rob became on details. It was all very strange. Facts, events, timescale, everything that had happened, it all seemed to have dulled with time and Rob simply insisted it was all down to me.

It was all valuable testimony for the Crown. The truth was that we had all helped to create the new Trans-Atlantic team, there had been no crime in doing so. Rabbit was not suggesting that Rob had done anything *wrong*. But what had been suggested by the Crown was that I was the mastermind behind the team and working full-time, while claiming to be injured and redundant. Rob hadn't been charged with anything because he wasn't claiming redundancy, but his distancing techniques meant only one thing. If he'd done very little, I must have done a hell of a lot. Of course the Prize Indemnity was another matter. If there was anything wrong with that, he knew he'd been every bit as involved as myself and Terry, but by distancing himself it again made it look as if I must have been totally in charge.

Rabbit's interrogation continued, but his progress was mostly negative and the deeper into the maze they went, the more Rob distanced himself and the deeper the anger swelled inside me.

Rabbit decided to change tack. He held up a large file. 'Perhaps you could take a look at this file, Mr Allan.' Rob nervously flicked a few pages. 'Could you tell us what this is please, Mr Allan?'

'It's, er, it's my working file. My Trans-Atlantic file.' Rob suddenly looked anxious.

'I see! And what is your "working file", Mr Allan?' Rabbit asked, smiling in the direction of the jury.

'Well, it's my designs for the Trans-Atlantic logos, team clothing and stuff like that.'

Rabbit eyed the witness blankly for a few moments, before exclaiming, 'Oh, I see! So you produced the designs for the new team?'

'Yes.'

'Why? Why would you do that, if you were not directly involved with the team?'

Rob shrugged, 'Somebody had to do it. It was needed for the Super Cup presentation in Salzburg.'

'I see. Did you attend the presentation in Salzburg?'

'Well, yes I did.'

'I see. And if we look at the graphics you produced,' Rabbit waved some additional copies and Lurch collected the exhibits for the jury, 'there appear to be not one, but three cars. Is that correct?'

'Yes,' replied Rob nervously.

'So, which of these cars is Mamet's Porsche, Mr Allan?'

Rob scanned the page. 'Mamet's car isn't there. These are the two Indy Cars, and the one in the middle is the Scorpion. We ... well Will had decided not to purchase Mamet's Porsche by this point.'

'Oh, I see. And you say the third car, the one in the middle of the picture, is the Scorpion. Where did the Scorpion come from?'

'It was a sports prototype, endurance racer. Will had been involved with its development some years earlier. The idea was to run the Scorpion for a paying third driver, to help fund the overall running of the new team.'

'Who owned the Scorpion?'

'It was owned by one of my sponsors; Sub Zero.'

'That was very kind of *your* sponsors to provide this *third car*, for an additional *third paying driver.* Particularly as you say you weren't directly involved with the running of the team.'

Smythe leaped to his feet. 'Your Honour, might I have a few words?'

His Honour studied his watch for a moment, an expression of exasperation speeding across his face. 'Yes, I am aware of where we are heading, Mr Smythe.' He turned his attention to the defence, pinning Rabbit with a hard stare. 'I think you are moving into a difficult area Mr Adams.' He paused for a moment, his gaze rising to the ceiling, as though the pending dilemma might be resolved somewhere high up within the bland plasterwork that occupied so much of his attention. 'You will be aware that there are no charges on the indictment that relate to the 1993 season.' He hesitated. 'It would therefore be inappropriate to introduce evidence from that period. Is that clear?'

The jury looked bemused. Smythe, unable to repress his delight and clearly grateful for His Honour's ethical vigilance, subsided with a satisfied smirk.

Rabbit remained on his feet frowning in contemplation for a just a few moments. Finally he spoke. 'But, Your Honour...'

'Mr Adams!' His Honour shot back, eyes narrowed, brow furrowed. 'We will discuss this matter later, in my chambers, is that clear?'

'Certainly, Your Honour.'

Rabbit pushed on, refocusing his attention on the witness. 'If you turn to the back section of your file, there appears to be a series of letters to sponsors. Could you tell us who wrote those letters?'

'Those are letters that I sent to some potential sponsors.' Rob's voice suddenly sounded a little hesitant.

Rabbit tried to look surprised. 'Oh, so you were actively involved with finding sponsorship for the team as well?'

Rob shifted uncomfortably, faltering just a little. 'Er ... yes.'

Rabbit rushed on. 'Was that before or after you attended the meeting in Florida with David Mamet?'

'Before ... er ... no after ... yes, I think it was after.'

Rabbit frowned, and shook his head in disbelief, for the benefit of the jury. 'And was that before you designed the company logos and letterheads?'

'That was after, yes, that's right, after.'

'And then you drove, and crashed Mamet's Porsche at Brands Hatch?' A silence hung between them for just a moment, before Rob finally found his tongue.

'Yes,' he replied in a subdued tone.

Rabbit frowned, and hesitated for a just moment, before asking, 'Was it then that you raced the car at Zolder and finished fifth, winning the Prize Indemnity?'

'Yes.' Rob looked uncomfortable.

'But you still maintain you were not involved with the setting up and operation of the team?'

'Yes. I mean no, no I wasn't!'

'Mr Allan, I would like you to cast your mind back to the meeting you attended in Florida with the Defendant at the workshops of Mamet Porsche Racing.' Rabbit paused. 'Is it not true that during that meeting a discussion took place concerning a bank guarantee and a *carnet de passage* that would allow the Porsche to be temporarily imported into the UK?'

'It may have done, but I can't recall.'

'I put it to you that it did, and that you both also requested authority from Mamet Porsche to sign and produce any necessary paperwork for both the importation of the car itself and any potential claim documentation for the Prize Indemnity.'

Rob's brow furrowed. 'Again, it's possible, but I can't remember.'

'Is it not true that in this respect, Mr Mamet then provided you with a quantity of Mamet Porsche Racing letterheads?'

'No, definitely not!'

Rabbit returned to his seat. I looked across the courtroom at my former friend Rob. As soon as he noticed my stare, he looked away.

His Honour turned to the Prosecution. 'Would you care to re examine, Mr Smythe?'

Smythe rose to his feet, smiling. 'Just a couple of questions, Your Honour, if we have time.' His Honour shot a look at his watch, then nodded his approval.

Smythe turned to the witness, his voice deep, clear and soothing. 'Just to be clear Mr Allan, you said the Prize Indemnity was the Defendant's idea. Is that correct?'

'Yes it is.'

'And you had never heard of the term "Prize Indemnity" before and had never operated such a scheme yourself in any previous race, such as the Le Mans 24 Hours. Is that correct?'

'Yes.'

'Thank you. And you said you had no recollection of Mr Mamet handing over any company headed paper or letterheads while you and the Defendant were in Florida at the headquarters of Mamet Porsche Racing, is that correct?'

Rob exhaled deeply. 'Yes, absolutely.'

'Thank you, Your Honour.'

His Honour nodded in acknowledgement. 'Thank you, Mr Smythe. I believe we have Mr Heath, of the Track Star Insurance Company, giving evidence tomorrow. Is that correct?'

'Indeed it is, Your Honour.'

At the mention of Les's name, Rob flashed a momentary glance in my direction. I caught the worried look in his eye and managed a wry smile back. He opened his mouth, as though about to say something, but then caught himself. His Honour continued, 'I would like a few words with both Prosecution and Defence, in

187

my chambers before you leave court today,' he paused for a moment, 'we won't require the services of the stenographer.'

33

A good lawyer must be a great liar.

(Proverb)

9th August 1992

The ferry was about to dock at Dover by the time Rob had finished explaining his idea.

'It simply won't work,' I said.

Rob drew hard on his cigarette. 'Why not?' He exhaled a small blue cloud of smoke in frustration.

I shook my head, 'Well for one thing, the guy won't have an International Race Licence and he's only ever raced in a junior formula.'

'If he enters a UK international-class race before the start of next season, he'd be eligible to apply for one. There's bound to be something scheduled before the end of the year.'

'But a Group C racer is a massive jump up, and the Scorpion was hopelessly uncompetitive when I raced it back in 1989. It only ever won one race at Thruxton, and that was because there was no other car in the same class. I just don't think he'd even qualify it in a Super Cup event.'

Rob dropped his cigarette, squashing out the burning ember with the heel of his shoe. 'Qualifying is down to him, but if we got a pair of Indy cars and ran the Scorpion as Trans-Atlantic's third entry, I think I could get Sub Zero to put up the bulk of the team's running costs, providing they appear as prime sponsor on the Scorpion, and we get to keep any driver revenue.'

There was no doubt that the deal was lucrative, and in the dire financial climate of 1993 it could prove essential to the successful operation of the team. In essence, Simon, my former team manager, would prepare and run the Scorpion alongside the Porsche or two Indy cars, modified to Super Cup rules.

189

General team sponsorship, covering preparation and transportation for all three cars, would be provided by Rob's sponsors, the Scorpion's owners: Sub Zero Refrigeration. The additional revenue, brought in by the Scorpion's driver, would cover the cost of the Prize Indemnity premium for Rob and myself. Providing we got the results, we would pick up around £2000 per month each plus a healthy bonus at the end of the year, as long as one of us secured the overall championship.

Tuscany, Northern Italy, June 1993 (10 months later)

Mugello International Raceway

A blue and white flash blurred past. Car number 21, Trans-Atlantic's third entry for the 1993 season, the aptly named Scorpion. The howl ebbed away into a distant scream. 'The Scorpion's on its last lap,' said Simon, the new team manager, into my headset. 'Just do five laps and in. Just feel your way into it Will. Okay?'

Simon stepped to the front of the car and indicated to two mechanics at the back. One shoved a starter mechanism into the rear of the gearbox, the other placed a heat deflector into the turbo outlet to deflect the exhaust and prevent discharge from incinerating the mechanic operating the starter. The engine coughed, fired, and then roared into life.

The blue and white Scorpion slowed and rolled past me into its pit, its test session concluded. Sunlight glinted off the glass screen. Behind the polished glass the young novice driver lay practically horizontal, bathed in sweat. He removed his helmet and tugged free his Nomex balaclava. It had been his first run in a world championship class race car. His first experience of over 500 horsepower. Prior to that, his only experience of motor racing had been limited to the lower formulae.

Simon helped release the belts and Les, the team's third driver, eased himself from the confines of the chassis, his blond hair, dank and darkened with sweat, clung to his forehead. He strolled over and squatted down next to me. A few specks of oil stained his immaculately tailored race suit. He beamed a politician's smile, the ring of confidence smile. His fingers combed through the lank hair. 'Brilliant, Will, bloody brilliant. It handles better than I ever expected.' Excitement sparked in his eyes, a look of anticipation spreading.

In truth the Scorpion was about as exciting as a dose of haemorrhoids, but to Les it was a big step up the ladder from racing a junior formulae. I raised my voice above the sound of my warming Buick Indy engine. 'Later Les ... we'll talk later. Okay?'

A pair of mechanics pushed Rob's day-glo red Lola from the pit garage. Les straightened up, collected the pit board and strolled over to the pit wall to help time our first practice sessions.

34

To protect and excuse ourselves while visiting serious vengeance on others, corrupts justice and demeans office...

(Ann Widdecombe, MP)

'There's been a useful development,' Piglet announced happily. 'Your old mate Rob Allan phoned the court this morning and apparently he's had an amazing return of memory. He now recalls taking part in the previous Prize Indemnity at Le Mans, and admits it was arranged with Les Heath of Track Star.'

'Fantastic!' I said. 'But you know why he's suddenly admitted this, don't you.'

Rabbit looked up from his notes, 'Well, I suspect he's not trying to do you any favours.' He spoke with a slight air of distaste. 'Most likely today's witness, Mr Heath, has read Allan's transcript of evidence and phoned him.'

'What transcript?'

'It's produced by the Watching Brief,' Tigger intervened merrily.

'The watching what?'

'The Watching Brief. She's the rather attractive young lady sitting behind Paterson-Smythe. It's her job to take a daily brief for WPA and Track Star.'

I was about to explode, but Rabbit stopped me. 'Hold on a minute, before you say anything, they're simply recording witness statements to confer internally. It's perfectly normal in trials of this kind, especially when the insurance industry is involved.'

I was incensed. 'You're saying that the insurance witnesses are all receiving transcripts of what their colleagues have previously said, *before* they step into the witness box to give evidence? That's not conferring, it's blatant collusion!'

'Well, when you put it like that it sounds a little underhand, but it's not meant to be. They're just protecting their position. They might wish to pursue a civil claim, so they need a record

192

of what everybody has said. Anybody can sit in court and take notes, it's a public trial. It's not against the rules to show those notes to a potential witness.'

I placed my head in my hands and closed my eyes. 'Are we going to recall Rob Allan?' I finally asked.

'I don't think that would be very wise,' Rabbit said. 'He's already attempted to stab you in the back once, and Smythe is insistent he has Les Heath in the witness box this morning.'

'Will,' it was Piglet. He glanced at his watch and was surprised to see that it was already ten minutes past ten. 'I know this all sounds strange, but we need to move on, we have to be in court in twenty minutes. The judge will inform the jury that Rob Allan phoned and that he made a mistake about his previous Le Mans Prize Indemnity race.'

I looked up and turned to Rabbit, 'Why did the judge ask to see you and Smythe in his chambers last night?'

Rabbit let the question hang for a moment. Somewhere, in the distance, a mobile phone rang. He shook his head, as if trying to clear his thoughts. 'It was to do with Mr Heath giving evidence today. He doesn't want any reference being made to him being Trans-Atlantic's third driver. He says he doesn't see the relevance.'

'The relevance is bloody obvious!' I blurted. 'Les Heath was present at each of the damn races. He was our third bloody driver, so he obviously knew we were running Indy Cars and not Mamet's Porsche. Shit... It was his policy that set the team up in the first place.'

'They may be trying to protect their position. But we have a copy of the fax that you sent to Track Star about wanting to change cars from the Porsche to the Indy cars. I think I can prove they did receive it, so we should be able to show there was no infringement of the policy. If Les volunteers it in court, that he was the third driver, then we can pursue that point, but otherwise we can't.'

At precisely 10.30 the Prosecution called to the stand Mr Les Heath, the insurance agent who had brokered the Prize Indemnity Policy purchased by Trans-Atlantic.

Les was a director of Track Star, at least he had been a director up until the latter part of 1993, when the Crown had decided to focus their attention on the Prize Indemnity. At that point he'd made a career change more rapid than any politician making a U-turn.

Les swore on oath to tell the truth. He told the court that I had arranged the Prize Indemnity and that I was personally its beneficiary. Paterson-Smythe moved on to the Indy Cars that had been acquired in place of Mamet's Porsche.

'That was an infringement of the policy,' Les said. 'We had no knowledge that an alternative prize had been obtained. The contract called for the purchase of the Trans World Racing Porsche.'

Les's evidence was important, clean and straightforward. Smythe didn't want to complicate matters. His Honour liked the cut of this young man's jib and used his mobile expressive features to convey his pleasure to the jurors.

Rabbit rose to cross-examine. Les, a man unrestrained by truth, smiled back from the witness box. His priorities were simple, don't get rattled, and don't get tripped up. He took his time as each question was laid before him, considering the permutations, the equations and consequences. If he answered yes to a question, then it might imply doubt to an answer he'd given a few moves further back. Yet if he were to disagree with a question, it might lead on to a series of subsidiary questions, which might lead him back to Rabbit's previous area of challenge. Then there was another factor. Rob Allan's evidence.

Rabbit pushed on. 'Could you tell the court when you first became aware that the Prize Indemnity had been won?'

'Well, the first I heard of the claim was when I received a phone call from the Defendant advising us that Rob Allan had secured a fifth place at Zolder.'

'I see. And could you explain how the claims procedure worked?' Rabbit asked.

'Well, we naturally carry out our own checks, but I advised the Defendant that we would need an official result sheet, signed by the stewards and a copy of the invoice from Trans World Racing for the purchase of the Porsche.'

'And did you receive that information?'

'Yes, it was faxed to us a day or two after the Zolder race. I believe we then received a hard copy in the post.'

'I see. And then what happened?'

'I waited for the official race results to be published in *Autosport* later that week before submitting my file to our underwriters. They subsequently sent out a cheque for a quarter of a million dollars.'

'And who received the cheque?'

'It was sent to Will Middleton.'

'But, who was this cheque made out to?'

'The Trans-Atlantic Team.'

'Oh, I see.' Rabbit turned to face the jury, but continued speaking to Les. 'So when you told my learned colleague that the *Defendant* had been the recipient of these funds, you meant to say that the cheque was sent to him, but that it was *payable* to the Trans-Atlantic Team. Is that correct?'

Les spoke a little more softly. 'Yes, that's right.' His Honour frowned.

'Perhaps you could speak up a little Mr Heath, for the benefit of the jury,' Rabbit continued. 'Were you aware that the Trans-Atlantic Team was a company owned by a Mr Terry Thomson, not the Defendant, Will Middleton?'

'Yes.'

Rabbit shook his head while gazing thoughtfully at the table before him, before continuing. Slowly and methodically he began studying some papers. 'You told my learned colleague that this...' he held up a buff file of papers in his right hand, 'is the complete Track Star file Mr Heath?' Heath's back stiffened and he cast a nervous look towards the solitary paper in Rabbit's other hand. Rabbit studied the document thoughtfully.

'Er, yes, I think so, yes,' Les replied, unsure of what might be coming next.

'You advised my colleague that you were unaware that Trans-Atlantic had acquired the Indy Cars instead of Mr Mamet's Porsche and that that was an infringement of the Prize Indemnity policy. Was that right?'

'Yes it was. In fact we'd received a copy of the Trans World Racing invoice, so we naturally assumed the Porsche had been purchased.' Heath's voice rose and now seemed to incorporate a spot of vibrato.

Rabbit waved away the reply, as if it were a bug. 'Quite, Mr Heath, but we'll come back to that. It's the file I'm interested in. Could you tell us, does the file contain copies of all the faxes received?'

195

Les Heath cast an awkward glance at the dock. I tried to resist the smile that was creeping across my face.

'It should do,' he replied.

Rabbit looked surprised and stared at the witness for a few seconds. Seconds that seemed to last minutes.

'Mr Heath, I have in my hand a copy of a letter sent to you by fax, by the Defendant, a few days after the race at Zolder, specifically informing Track Star that Trans-Atlantic had decided to purchase a pair of Indy Cars in the place of the Trans World Porsche. I also have a copy of the fax confirmation from Track Star and a copy of the Defendant's British Telecom itemised phone bill, which confirms this letter was not only faxed but also received at your office. Could you explain how this letter appears to be missing from your file?'

'I have no idea.' Les smiled confidently at the jury, like a politician smiling into the lens of a camera. 'Perhaps it was misfiled.'

'I see.' Rabbit paused for a few moments as he pretended to re-read the fax. 'And you still maintain that you were completely unaware that two of the three cars being run by the Trans-Atlantic Team were in fact Indy Cars?'

Rabbit emphasised the word three, but Les remained unflustered. He stole a furtive glance at the dock, then smiled again. 'Absolutely no idea whatsoever.'

'Mr Heath, let's assume for a moment that what you say is true, and you had no knowledge of the team purchasing Indy Cars in place of the Porsche, would it have any bearing on anything? Would it have mattered to Track Star that Trans-Atlantic spent the proceeds of the Prize Indemnity on the Indy Cars?'

'Well, contractually Trans-Atlantic took out a Prize Indemnity to specifically cover the cost of purchasing the Trans World Racing Porsche, if either of its drivers secured a given position in the races at Brands Hatch or Zolder. I suppose the result was the all-important point. Providing the liability or prize cost was the same, it might well have been acceptable.'

Morning drifted into afternoon. Rabbit landed a couple more small punches, but on the whole Les ducked and dived with the artistic grace of an insurance salesman, which of course he was. There was barely a blow-dried hair out of place.

Had the jury been acquainted with the full facts of Les's

association with Trans-Atlantic, perhaps it might have concluded that I'd been telling the truth all along. But then, as I'd been told on the day the police seized the Indy cars, proof wasn't important, *doubt* was important. By concealing from the jury that Les was one of the Trans-Atlantic drivers, suddenly there was doubt. The police officer's words drifted back hauntingly, '*Proof is not what's important, Will. Doubt's what's important. You'd be surprised at how it works. You will be treated very sceptically; we on the other hand, will be treated very politely.*'

At 12.51 precisely, on Thursday 27th October, Anthony Paterson-Smythe rose onto his hind legs, the great expanse of his frame seeming to inflate with importance. He smiled graciously. 'That concludes the case for the Crown.'

I breathed a sigh of relief. Now it was our turn.

35

During the 30 years I've been studying miscarriages of justice, I've found the most common cause to be over-zealousness on the part of the police.

(Sir Ludovic Kennedy)

With the jury excused, Rabbit rose to his feet to request that the court run just a little late, so as to allow the Defence to open and our key witness to testify. He glanced at his watch, it was 3.55 pm. 'Your Honour will appreciate that if Mr Dolland is *not* permitted to testify now, we will be unable to call him at any other time.'

His Honour was clearly unimpressed. The arduous duties of the court were expected to conclude in time for afternoon tea. 'Mr Adams,' he said with an indifferent tone, his gaze rising to the ceiling, 'how long do you expect Mr Dolland's evidence to take?'

'Well Your Honour, I would hope to get by within ... say, ten to fifteen minutes?'

'Yes, Mr Adams. There will of course also be the matter of your opening speech. How long do you anticipate that taking?'

Rabbit had told us he intended opening as quickly as possible. Smythe had droned on for two days; Rabbit would open in twenty minutes, half an hour tops. The jury would appreciate that. 'No more than thirty minutes, Your Honour,' he replied more confidently.

His Honour turned in the direction of the Prosecution and smiled reassuringly. 'Mr Smythe. How long would you anticipate for your cross-examination of this witness?'

Paterson-Smythe rose ever so slowly as though he'd just concluded the final course of an immense banquet. He inclined his head while lifting a reflective brow, his mind in deep contemplation. 'Probably another ten, maybe fifteen minutes, Your Honour.'

His Honour examined his watch. Turning to Rabbit, he said, 'Mr Adams I am trying to assist you. However, there will need to be the re-examination by yourself.' He paused for a few more valuable moments. Having concluded his deliberations he continued, 'Mr Adams. You may proceed with your opening address and your first witness, providing,' he paused for a moment as though studying a rare species of weevil that just happened to be strolling across his legal pad, 'you can conclude your examination in chief within ten minutes.'

Rabbit bowed in grateful acknowledgement.

The jury took a few more costly minutes to return and settle into their box. Rabbit rose to his feet, and turning to face the jury, smiled. 'Ladies and gentlemen of the jury, we will call evidence to show that the Defendant, Will Middleton, did not deliberately wind up Team Capricorn to enable redundancy payments to be claimed, as has been suggested by the Crown. You will hear from the Defendant's own lawyers of the litigation which led to the collapse of that company. Will Middleton did not plan that liquidation, the exact opposite was in fact the case, a fact that you will hear supported by a firm of independent auditors. My client did everything possible to keep Team Capricorn alive.'

'My client was not *sick* but he was *injured*. Then, with the collapse of Team Capricorn, he became *unemployed*. I would ask you to recall the evidence of two of the Crown's witnesses, Mr Burton and Mrs Pickup. Both witnesses confirmed that you *can* be available for work when injured. For example, a professional pianist with a broken finger could *not* play, could *not* perform his normal occupation as a pianist, but he *could* be available to take part in *alternative* work.

'What, however, if that finger had been severely damaged? Damaged to the point that the bones could never be fully repaired? He would then be permanently unable to perform his professional occupation as a pianist. Clearly the pianist would be capable of some *other* type of work, but he would be unable or disabled by virtue of the damage to his finger to work as a pianist and if he were insured, would be eligible to claim. This, ladies and gentlemen of the jury, was the unfortunate circumstance in which my client found himself.'

Rabbit turned a page on his legal pad, then hesitating for a moment, he picked up a jug and poured himself some water.

He raised the glass slowly, taking a sip, savouring the moment. His Honour stifled a yawn; twenty minutes had already passed.

'Will Middleton,' Rabbit continued, '*was* initially temporarily disabled from his racing career due to a spinal injury. This is an indisputable fact. An injury caused by a horse riding accident some years earlier. The full and serious nature of his injuries were not, however, diagnosed until five years later. Only at that point did it became clear to the surgeons that he should never again step into a racing car. Will Middleton did *not* therefore, at the time of the Prize Indemnity, believe that the pain he was experiencing was from anything permanently debilitating in nature. It was not until after he saw Dr Dolland and later drove in the amateur event at Brands Hatch, linked to the Prize Indemnity, that he realised there was something seriously amiss. And very significantly, members of the jury, Will Middleton did *not* see the WPA medical report, compiled by Dr Dolland that confirmed the permanent nature of his injuries, until two weeks before the police raided his home in February 1993. This was a full seven months *after* the attempted comeback in the unpaid Prize Indemnity race at Brands Hatch. A race that, in all likelihood, he deemed it improbable he would be selected to drive.'

Again Rabbit paused.

'Members of the jury, this case is about two things, honesty and dishonesty. Did Will Middleton act dishonestly?' Rabbit took another slow sip of water, allowing time for his question to sink home. 'By your standards, members of the jury,' he continued, replacing his glass on the bench, 'was he dishonest? This case is about a man who now has his chance to explain things from his point of view. He does not *have* to go into the witness box to prove these things, but he has chosen to do so. Once you have heard him, you will understand him.' Rabbit turned to His Honour. 'Your Honour, the Defence first calls Dr Dolland.'

Dr John Dolland, a heavily built man with greying hair, crossed quickly to the witness box. The time was 4.24. His Honour greeted the expert for the Defence with the look one might bestow on a dog that had just relieved itself on the lounge carpet.

Rabbit ran quickly through the witness's résumé to formally qualify him as an expert. Dr Dolland gave the jury a summary of the examination that he'd carried out at St Richard's hospital. He spoke slowly and clearly, aiming his answers directly at the jury. He used layman's terms wherever he could. Where jargon was necessary, he quickly explained it. 'Did you take any x-rays Dr Dolland?' Rabbit pressed on.

'I did. I x-rayed his thoracic spine, that's the upper part of his back, and this was normal. I also x-rayed the lower part of the spine, the lumbar, from the ribs to the pelvis, and this exposed the damaged area where a number of stress fractures were evident. It was also apparent that two of the vertebrae, or more accurately the hooking mechanism that holds the vertebrae in place, had in fact been broken.'

'Did you form a view as to how this damage had occurred?'

'I would say the injury was traumatic in origin and would be consistent with an impact from a person falling backwards, into a sitting position from a considerable height. I would say that the injuries were consistent with the riding accident experienced by Mr Middleton in Malaysia. We in fact use the term spondylolithesis to describe this kind of condition.'

'We are all familiar with that term,' interrupted His Honour, 'and what it means and need not, as I see it, go into it further at this stage.'

Rabbit rushed on. 'What risk might Mr Middleton be taking if he continued racing, so far as pain was concerned?'

'I considered it likely his pain would get worse.'

His Honour fidgeted in frustration. It was now 4.48.

'And how intense could it become?' Rabbit asked.

'It would become exceedingly painful and certainly painful enough to significantly interfere with his life.'

'So could you summarise for us please, the advice that you gave him about what he should or should not do?'

'There were two problems when I saw him. One was the upper part of his spine and the other was the lower section. The trouble in the upper part, the thoracic, was relatively minor; this condition had probably instigated the referral to me in the first instance, as he was clearly unaware of the serious nature of the lumbar or lower spinal injury. I advised that for the thoracic problem he be admitted to hospital to have injections into his upper spine, and for this area to be manipulated under general anaesthetic. I put his name on a waiting list for this to be done. With regard to his lower back, the spondylolithesis, I advised him to wear a lumbosacral corset and to avoid any activities which he had found in the past to aggravate this area. I also advised that I would be writing to his insurance company, WPA, to further detail my findings.'

'In your view,' Rabbit continued, 'could Will Middleton still get in a racing car and drive it?'

'Yes. There was no reason why he *couldn't* do it, but in his condition, he *shouldn't*. I can't prevent people from doing things, I can only give advice.'

'Thank you Dr Dolland.' Rabbit returned to his seat. It was 4.57.

Paterson-Smythe rose slowly to cross-examine. 'Did Mr Middleton tell you that only four days before your examination, he'd forwarded application forms to compete in two races, one at Zolder and one at Brands Hatch?'

'I have no recollection of him saying so.'

Smythe turned to the jury with the smug satisfaction of a marksman who had just brought down a sitting duck. 'Thank you Dr Dolland.'

His Honour turned to Rabbit. 'Mr Adams, do you wish to re-examine?'

'No, Your Honour,' a somewhat deflated Rabbit replied.

His Honour turned to the jury. 'In that case ladies and gentlemen, we will adjourn until 10.00 am on Monday when we shall reconvene, not in this court but in Court number three, as the Defence will be showing us some video and Court three has the necessary equipment.'

The dock officer opened the gate and ushered me out into the body of the court. I joined Rabbit and Piglet, who were already in deep discussion with Dr Dolland. 'I thought I was supposed to be giving evidence on what a spondylolithesis was,' protested Dolland, 'and why his condition was classified as a permanent disability.'

'We were very limited in respect of time, but we did cover all the relevant issues,' Rabbit insisted.

The witness looked surprised. He reached into his pocket, removing a section of human vertebrae. 'I brought this along,' he said, handing it over to me, 'I thought we were going to show it to the jury, with illustrations, so they could understand why a breakage in the hooking mechanism is such a critical injury.'

202

'We covered everything we could, in the time available,' Rabbit persisted. 'The jury responded well to your evidence.'

Beth arrived from the public gallery. She could see from my face I wasn't happy. 'Was that the extent of the medical evidence then?'

'It was quite adequate,' Rabbit insisted again, somewhat defensively. 'We need to get the picture across the best way we can.'

'But what about the Prosecution's remark about the race application being sent off days *prior* to the examination?' Beth continued. 'He somehow managed to make it sound suspicious. If they'd been sent *after* the examination, perhaps he could have tried to make something of it, but *prior* to it?'

Before anyone could respond, Rabbit's phone vibrated in his pocket. He flipped it open. 'Hello, Giles Adams.' He glanced in the direction of the judge's bench. 'I'm just in the middle of a short conference. Could it wait? Right, yes, I will. Just give me two or three minutes.

'That was the judge; he wants to see me in his chambers before I leave. Apparently the Prosecution are unhappy with what we have planned for Monday.'

36

The following Monday, the hearing for the Defence re-commenced without the jury at 10.00 am in the smaller surroundings of Court Three. Paterson-Smythe was not a happy man. The previous Friday he'd demanded a private assessment of the proof we intended putting before the jury. He knew better than most that video and pictures rarely lied, and after seeing the evidence had already made his feelings clear to His Honour. Strident arguments had been put forward by the Crown, within the privacy of His Honour's chambers, but no official outcome had been agreed. Any legal decision needed to be made in court, and recorded by the stenographer.

Smythe remained on his feet, as the rest of the court officials bowed and sat. 'Your Honour, as you are aware, the Crown is *most* unhappy about showing these videos. The first is some form of video diary and shows the Defendant as a family man. It shows the conversion of the Old Granary. It is clearly intended as a home movie and the Defendant can be seen playing with his children in the swimming pool. The second video is something of a mystery to us all. It shows the Defendant's wife, in the grounds of the Old Granary during a storm. Clearly totally irrelevant to these proceedings. The last video shows the Defendant in some sort of promotional film, at the wheel of a motor racing car, and ends with music. The Crown fails to see the relevance of any of the proposed videos and objects to their showing in the strongest possible terms.'

Rabbit was already halfway up from his seat to respond to the Crown's objection, when His Honour intervened. 'Mr Adams, before you respond, I suggest that I first view the proposed evidence.'

Rabbit returned to his seat as Lurch inserted the first of the three tapes into a machine. All around the court the video screens flickered into life. Beth appeared on the monitors, sitting at our dining room table, flicking idly through a pile of photos of the old barn. The scene was clearly posed, never intended for public viewing. She smiled coyly at the camera. In the background music played. The camera angle changed to one of the photos in Beth's hand. One by one, the pictures then began to sequence through like a slide show, showing the unconverted barn and the gradual transformation of our home. As the pictures flicked by, Beth and I could be seen knocking down walls, shifting rubble and digging drains. The still pictures continued to cycle through before reaching 1992, when we added the granny flat and pool cover and purchased a video camera. The conversion had developed very slowly, over more than seven years. The boys, aged two and six, appeared, splashing around happily in the swimming pool years before it was enclosed. The Crown's argument had been that the pool had been built using funds fraudulently claimed from WPA. But if the boys were two and six, clearly the pool had existed at least three years before the claim.

Lurch inserted the second video into the machine. Beth, this time in the garden of the Old Granary, was being buffeted by a colossal gale, laughing and swirling around playfully. Abruptly the video cut to the roof of the Old Granary, where a large area of tiles had started to lift. The fencing flattened, panels cartwheeled away as trees bent almost horizontal. More and more tiles started to lift and smash to the ground. Suddenly, Beth's voice, 'Oh, no, oh my God, no.' An entire outbuilding collapsed, its corrugated roof flipping end over end, then crashing down to demolish an area of balustrade that the previous video had shown being built.

Lurch stepped forward and silently ejected the second tape. As he did so, His Honour placed the palm of his right hand directly on top of his wig and hunched his head in the direction of Smythe, who appeared to acknowledge the strange gesture.

The last tape was inserted into the machine. This time, there was no music and initially no picture, only the sound of a racing car gradually building up speed. Then gradually an image blossomed on the monitors, in-car footage of a high-speed lap of the Brands Hatch circuit. The camera switched to the outside of the track as the 800 horsepower Group C prototype exited the pit lane in a shower of sparks. Back to the in-car camera as the lap continued, the car impacting hard onto its skid blocks as it exited Paddock Hill bend, sending a shower of sparks bursting from its underside. The pounding G forces, the assault on mind, body and senses, the reaction times and pressures exerted on the driver were clear for all to see and hear, in just a few minutes of video. The picture faded and in its place appeared a still-smiling image of me, dressed in my sponsor's fireproof Nomex overalls. Text began to scroll down the screen, promoting the concept of corporate sponsorship to an upbeat musical score.

The learned judge pursed his lips as though contemplating how best to handle this unexpected evidence. 'Mr Adams,' he began, his words slow and heavy, 'I can see why you might wish to show the jury the video diary and even the last racing tape, but the second video? Why do you wish to show the jury a video of what appears to be a storm?'

'Your Honour,' Rabbit began, rising from his seat. 'You will be aware that there has been much speculation by the Crown as to my client's personal finances. In fact,' Rabbit glanced in the direction of the Prosecution, 'I understand an in-depth investigation was ordered, and the results showed no trace of anything untoward. No foreign bank accounts, no deposits of shares in offshore companies. However the Crown then spent some time producing a report, based on various credits or inputs into my client's bank account.'

'I am aware of the report,' interrupted McGaea, 'but what has that to do with a video of a storm.'

'Well, Your Honour, the importance of the second tape relates to one of the larger credits, highlighted by the Crown. The video was filmed in January 1991, when the south coast of England was battered by the severe storm you saw on the videotape. According to the Met Office the south coast and Channel Islands were in fact hit by a tornado at that time, with wind speeds of some 85 mph and gusts exceeding 100 mph. Scores of properties were devastated with extensive damage amounting to many millions of pounds. The significance of this tape is that the Defendant was by chance filming at precisely the moment when considerable damage was inflicted on his home, the Old Granary, and its surrounding buildings. In fact some £10,000 worth of damage ultimately resulted to the roof of the property. Needless to say, Your Honour, the house was insured and there was therefore a resultant credit entry, for the repayment of the repairs by the building insurance company.' Rabbit again glanced over at the Prosecution. Smythe had perked up considerably at the mention of a new insurance claim and was furiously scribbling notes. Rabbit continued, 'That credit has however been incorrectly identified as "undeclared earnings" by the Prosecution in the report.'

'I see. So you're saying that those funds relate to the proceeds of a storm damage claim?'

'Indeed Your Honour. And if you examine the debit column of the account, in the preceding weeks, you will see that three cheques, totalling more than £10,000, were in fact written to a contractor by the name of S Butler and Sons who carried out the repairs.'

'I see,' remarked His Honour, in somewhat subdued tones.

'I'm sure it will not have escaped Your Honour's notice,' Rabbit continued, 'that this storm occurred in 1991, the same year my client's company, Team Capricorn, unfortunately collapsed during the recession. It was a time when advertising revenues dropped dramatically. We shall be providing evidence to prove that the collapse was due to a series of sponsors and other creditors failing to honour contracts, and in some cases going into receivership. Understandably however, any sums seen to be received by my client around that time came under scrutiny in the Crown's report and might, in the current circumstances, therefore be considered suspicious by the jury. It is for that reason we wish to show the jury this particular video.'

For a few moments His Honour was silent, then he spoke. 'If you wish to proceed with the showing of this evidence, you may do so,' he paused for a few moments, still contemplating the situation, 'but I can see no purpose in doing so with sound. The tapes will be shown to the jury silent.'

Rabbit protested, 'But without sound the jury will not appreciate the intensity of the storm, and without sound the race car footage won't fully portray the demands exerted on the driver, the impact, the ...'

'Mr Adams,' His Honour interjected, 'I have ruled on this

evidence. This court is hardly a *Multiplex*; there is no possible point in inflicting sound on the jury.'

'I must object Your Honour.'

'Your objection is noted and overruled,' replied His Honour. 'If you are not happy with my ruling then it will be a matter for the Court of Appeal, should you deem it appropriate.'

'But that would only apply if the jury returned guilty verdicts, Your Honour.'

'*Indeed* it would, Mr Adams.' His Honour turned in the direction of the usher. 'Bring in the jury.'

The jury took to their seats, oblivious to the past hour of legal debate. Rabbit rose to welcome them, giving a brief explanation of what they were about to see. Lurch inserted the first of the three tapes. The jury watched in a bemused hush as Beth silently flicked through the pictures of the Old Granary. Lurch inserted the second tape. Again the image of Beth appeared and the jury watched as she appeared to laugh silently into the camera. The camera panned to the untidy muddle of broken fencing panels. One or two of the jury exchanged confused glances, missing completely the vital moment when the outbuilding collapsed. They heard nothing of Beth's painful cry. Lurch inserted the last cassette. A Porsche 962 racing car completed a soundless lap of the Brands Hatch circuit.

His Honour turned to face the jury. 'Well that concludes your viewing pleasure for this morning, ladies and gentlemen. I think this might therefore be an appropriate moment to break for lunch.'

'How can he do that?' Beth snapped angrily, as I left the dock. 'This is supposed to be *your* Defence. The judge seems to think you're guilty and he's doing anything he can to stop you getting away with it, whatever it *is!*'

'I just don't know,' I began, my mouth dry, my voice unsteady. 'We were doing so well when the Crown were presenting their evidence. Rabbit was talking about the dismissal.' I drew in the warm stale courtroom air, and tried to slow my breathing. I felt nauseous. Taking Beth's hand, I headed for the door. I just needed to get away from the oppressive atmosphere. 'It's almost as though we'd done *too* well,' I said, my mind still searching for reason. 'It's as if the judge is trying to even things up.' I glanced over my shoulder and through the open doors of the adjoining Court One. Detective Barnet's impressive wall of evidence that informed all visitors that they were entering the Crown's 'Operation Coverall' trial, still occupied the entire entrance. 'I thought this was supposed to be about getting to the truth,' I said, still thinking, 'maybe it's not just me.'

'What do you mean?' Beth asked.

'I don't know; it's just the way they all seem to back each other up. Perhaps I'm not the *only* person this has happened to? What makes us think I'm the only one they've done something like this to? There's so much money invested in trials like this. And all the media interest; 24-hour breaking news. The newspapers seem to think I'm some sort of charlatan, with a phoney "bad back" claim. Maybe the system just feels it *has* to get a conviction, any way it can.'

Before my nightmare began I would have considered such thoughts crazy, that a justice system might scheme to secure a conviction, but now? In my mind I relived the past weeks, shaking my head in disbelief at our broken world and what we'd witnessed. 'If it's only partially true...'

Rabbit and Piglet strolled out of the court, still deep in debate, and seeing us, made a beeline in our direction. Rabbit smiled, hands tugging at the lapels of his black gown. He was trying to look strong, he said nothing, but then he didn't need to.

'Are you okay, Will?' Piglet asked.

'No, not really,' I replied.

37

The system works this way. It isn't to say did a person do it, or didn't a person do it, in respect of the crime. The Criminal Justice System, in our country works [like this] – have the Prosecution proved their case?

(John Cooper, leading criminal barrister, The Bar Council, Channel 4 Interview, 9th February 2006)

His Honour watched carefully as Toby Jackson, my former solicitor, stepped into the witness box, like a man nervously entering a lion's den. Rabbit methodically went through all the usual formalities, before asking, 'Could you tell the court how you know the Defendant?'

'I am a solicitor and partner in the firm of George Evans and Crowthorp, in London Road, Southampton. In that respect, I acted for Mr Middleton's racing team, Team Capricorn, for a number of years.'

'And have you acted for Mr Middleton in any other respect?'

Toby turned to face the judge. 'I acted for Mr Middleton in respect of a number of matters, both business and personal.'

'Is it correct that you were in fact originally scheduled to represent Mr Middleton in these proceedings?'

'That is correct, at least until some weeks ago. We were then advised that His Honour considered a potential conflict of interests might arise and that I might in fact be required to act as a witness. I therefore withdrew and Mr Jonathan Barker, also from a practice in Southampton, took my place.'

'And at the time, did *you* consider that any conflict existed?'

'No, I did not.'

McGaea raised his eyebrows while staring down fixedly at the solicitor before him. The judge selected a pen and scratched furiously across a legal pad. Rabbit removed a tabloid newspaper cutting with the headline *WPA Bank pays racing driver £4000 for bouncing cheque!* from a file in front of him. 'In or around

210

September 1992, did you in fact act for Mr Middleton in relation to a personal legal action against the W... ' Rabbit's words were intercepted by Smythe, who rose with uncharacteristic speed.

'Your Honour, I wonder if the jury might be excused for a few moments?'

His Honour turned to the jury and smiled with the sincerity of a used car salesman. 'A small matter of law has arisen that does not concern you, so this might be a convenient point for a short coffee break.'

Toby Jackson remained in the witness box as the jury exited. His Honour turned to the stenographer. 'I cannot imagine any record will be required of these representations, will they?' Not waiting for a reply, he continued, 'I think you could take a short break also.'

Smythe remained on his feet as the official record taker left the court. 'Your Honour,' he began earnestly, 'I suspect that I know where my learned colleague is heading, but the Crown fails to see the relevance of this line of questioning and strongly objects to the introduction of evidence relating to any previous civil action between the Defendant and the WPA Bank.'

'I am inclined to agree,' commented His Honour swiftly, turning to Rabbit. 'Can you offer any reason for wishing to introduce evidence of the settlement between the WPA Bank and your client?'

'Well,' Rabbit replied, 'the tabloid article is included in the Crown's bundles, Your Honour. And it's not a document disclosed by the Defence, so it must have been released and considered relevant at some stage by WPA and the Crown.'

Smythe rose again, his words a little more pressing than usual. 'This might help, Your Honour. My Junior has just located the original tabloid cutting.' He held up the cutting between thumb and forefinger, as though it might be infected in some way. 'It appears in fact to have been filed amid the Crown's bundles of *unused* material. Clearly, Your Honour, we have no intention of relying upon such a document in these proceedings.'

Rabbit was still on his feet. 'Your Honour, we requested sight of the Crown's unused material many times prior to commencement of this trial, but were only granted access very shortly before commencement. The significance of this document has only recently become apparent and we most certainly *do* wish to show this article to the jury, along with two other clearly connected exhibits; documents 2061 and 2062, that were not filed as unused material. You will find the documents in Bundle J.' His Honour selected a large file and flicked a few pages as Rabbit continued, 'Until the tabloid article was recently discovered, the importance of the two documents, two memos, had never been apparent.'

Having located both memos in his file, McGaea slumped back into his seat. His eyes stared down at the recipient's name and the subsequent reply, his usual pallor turning almost translucent as the blood drained from his face. He redirected his gaze coldly in the direction of the Prosecution. Smythe looked back with raised eyebrows.

Trying to compose himself, McGaea redirected his attention to Rabbit, who was still talking. 'As you can see, the first memo is from Mr Burton's supervisor and states that he is in possession of a newspaper cutting. It goes on to say, "*I am not sure if anything can be done with this, but no doubt you will advise.*" The reply from a Mr Alexander P Finnigan, who appears to be the chairman of the WPA Group, can be found as the next document, in the same Bundle; document 2062, Your Honour, and reads, "*Meeting, my office at 9.45 today. Tell Burton to bring the article and the claimant's file. I need hard evidence that Middleton was working during the currency of the claim; send in surveillance, we will need to attract the interest of the police*".'

His Honour took a sip of water, still in deep thought. His eyes flicked between the two memos, his colour returning slowly. Lifting his head to look directly at Smythe, he spoke with a clear finality. 'Mr Smythe, I can see no reason for troubling the jury with these irrelevant documents.' Turning back to Rabbit he added, 'Mr Adams, we will have no reference made to this tabloid article or the accompanying memos or the civil proceedings in this court, as I feel they will muddy the waters for the jury. Is that quite clear?'

Rabbit was about to protest, but His Honour raised a hand, as if to fend off any plea. Whatever Rabbit had been about to say, he thought better of it, just bowing meekly in acceptance. Paterson-Smythe nodded gravely with satisfaction, whilst carefully folding the offending cutting and disposing of it in his gown pocket.

Toby was still in the witness box, stunned at what he'd witnessed.

The jury and stenographer returned, unaware of what had occurred. To the jury, nothing appeared to have changed. Rabbit moved on, as though little had happened. 'Did you act for Mr Middleton's racing team, Team Capricorn, concerning the collection of outstanding accounts and court judgements, prior to its collapse?' he asked.

'Yes, I did,' Toby replied.

'Could you elaborate?'

'Team Capricorn was owed somewhere in the region of £71,000 by three different companies and each company was refusing to pay.'

'Refusing to pay? Was there some kind of dispute over the sums due?'

'No, the amounts and the contracts were not in dispute. It was just a very difficult time; the economy was crashing and the country was going deeper into recession. The team had attempted to reach compromises but the problem was that it had ongoing contractual obligations and financial commitments itself. It also had binding agreements with other sponsors that *had* paid, so it had to compete in specific races and was at risk, due to the defaulters, of failing in its own commitments to comply with its obligations.'

'I see. And did you advise Mr Middleton of the prospect of success in collecting the £71,000 owing?'

'Well, yes, we did. Team Capricorn had binding contracts and ultimately *had* secured judgements in court, so we advised that he had a very good prospect of being paid.'

'And did you in fact obtain any of the outstanding funds?'

'We obtained an undertaking from one of the company's solicitors, but he also ended up in default.'

'Let me get this clear. One of the company's solicitors that gave an undertaking to pay, failed to do so?'

'That's correct. The solicitor in question turned out to be the company secretary for the business concerned and ended up being struck off. I'm sorry to say we failed to obtain a single penny from the other companies. One by one they simply collapsed as the recession deepened.'

Rabbit paused for a few moments before continuing. 'I would like to take you back now, to 13th June 1991. A time when the events in question were coming to a head. Do you recall making

213

a phone call to the Defendant concerning one of the defaulting companies, Huxley Sports Cars?'

Toby cast a look at me. 'I do,' he replied sadly. 'Prior to breaking the news, Mr Middleton was very happy as I recall; he'd just collected his new car and was on his way to take part in a big race.'

I remembered the period in question so very well; it had been a busy time. We'd just reached an agreement with Sky Television and a big finance company. The overall deal had been worth around £90,000 to Team Capricorn, and with all the old problems seemingly behind us, new business had been even more important. The new agreement had revolved around Sky sponsoring the race team with TVUs, in effect handing over an agreed number of minutes of advertising air time, in return for endorsement space on the car. I would also act as the camera car for Sky, in itself very prestigious. Team Capricorn would then sell the air time on to advertisers, to secure the actual hard-cash funding.

I'd already managed to place most of the TVUs with the finance company, and was simply looking forward to the bit I liked most, the racing. I relished the new challenge.

Sitting in the dock now, I kicked myself for being so naive, but I had actually sat down and worked it all out before buying the new Colt Shogun; cashflow projections, budgets, the lot. After two years of scraping by to get to the point of securing court judgements, life was going to be good again, or so I'd thought. I hadn't allowed for the fact that, despite the recession and people still wanting to borrow, the banks that provided the funds for the finance company's clients would simply dry up, leaving the lucrative TV advertising deal useless.

With hindsight, I'd purchased the new car with little more than increased confidence and a lot of promises. The garage had offered me a protection policy with WPA. As I already had redundancy cover with them, it had seemed a logical choice and I'd accepted the option as part of an overall HP protection package. I'd literally just picked up the keys and was proudly heading north up the A24 in the direction of Snetterton when the mobile phone rang. I clicked a button on the hands-free and the familiar voice came over the speaker. 'Hi Will, it's Toby Jackson.'

'Hi Toby, how are you?'

'Not too good, I'm afraid, Will. We've got some problems over these judgements. One of the partners has just been arrested and the other has apparently disappeared to Spain. I'm afraid it looks as if you've lost any chance of getting what's owed.'

'Shit! Toby, I just don't need to hear this now. I'm on my way up to Snetterton for a big race this weekend; I'm driving the camera car for Sky. And I've just picked up my new road car – I signed a three-year HP agreement for it only thirty minutes ago.'

'I'm really sorry Will, but I couldn't leave this. We'll need to talk next week.'

In the space of the short journey to Snetterton, Team Capricorn had lost over £71,000 and with my new commitment I was suddenly becoming financially unstable. However, at that time my mind was set on other things, the new Sky deal.

Then the next problem arose, this time on the track.

38

My first priority is to finish above rather than beneath the ground.

(James Hunt, 1975)

Esso 24 Hour Race, Snetterton Circuit, Norfolk, 13–16th June 1991

I arrived at the Norfolk circuit, parked the gleaming new Shogun and located the team. I was again co-driving with Rob Allan and, on this occasion, a third driver Angus Mackay. We were competing in the second of the two R&D Motorsport prepared Sierra Cosworths. Alastair Lyall, Dave Carvell and Ken Grundy, the team owner, had secured pole position with a 1:22.60 in the team's number one car.

I was driving the number two car, and as qualifying ended, Rob managed to pip my time by a mere two tenths, to place our Cosworth on the second row with the third fastest time of the day, a 1:23.01.

Rain clouds gathered overhead, issuing a light warning shower, as the Sky TV technicians completed the installation of their on-board cameras. Mechanics busied themselves with their final preparations. The pressure is always high at this point; they know the race will depend on their work.

It was 3.50, ten minutes to go. The mechanics pushed the glistening blue and white Sierra Cosworth with its Sky TV decals into its position on the second row of the grid. The car looked beautiful. The clouds again opened, this time the rain a little heavier and the mechanics donned their bright orange wet-weather coveralls. It was going to be a wet weekend, ideal for the 4x4 teams.

As the lights changed to green, Lyall led into the mist of the first corner. Paul Lee was a close second and Rob third. Lee was determined to take his moment of glory and out-braked Lyall

216

into the second corner. By the end of the first lap Rob had dropped to a disappointing seventh. Within ten laps the rain had abated and the drivers were already settling into their pre-agreed pace. The team called Rob in, refuelled and switched drivers to Angus. I was scheduled to take the third driving stint, but often nothing goes according to plan in motor racing.

Angus exited the pit lane, made it through the first two corners and onto the Rivet straight. Suddenly disaster struck as the automatic electronic extinguishing system triggered itself half way down the straight. Angus fought to maintain control as the cockpit and his lungs filled with nauseating, inert halon gas. The car coasted to a halt two-thirds of the way down the back straight, and Angus was rushed to the circuit medical centre, insisting there were elephants rampaging around the cockpit. It would be another forty-five minutes before the car was returned to the pits. We were now in last place, thirty laps behind the next placed car.

I sat astride a chair in the crew caravan, sipping black coffee from a styrofoam cup. Roger Nevitt the team manager appeared. There was a disheartened look on his face. 'Will, the car's going to be back in five minutes. Angus will be okay, but the officials are keeping him in the hospital, he's still stoned out of his mind. It's going to be down to you and Rob. There's no pressure, we're totally out of contention, just try and keep it together and on the black stuff, okay?'

I've always found something particularly challenging about being in a situation that everybody else thinks is impossible. Why was it impossible, I thought naively. The car was in good shape, the other teams seemed to have settled into their nighttime pace. It was wet again, very wet, positively 4x4 weather, and I was very used to being an underdog, from my low-budget days in the World Sports Car Championship. But unlike those days, this was a good car and a top, well-funded team. It certainly was possible to get back up the field. I always relish it when somebody throws down the gauntlet. Besides, my number-one fan was watching, our son George. He didn't often come to watch me race but Beth had driven him up for the weekend as a special treat and had set up their own little camp, huddled together under ponchos and a large team umbrella close to the team motorhome.

The night was warm; the scent of gasoline drifted in the air, the moon disappeared behind dark clouds. The only light came from the dazzling glint of head lamps as the cars sped past on the pit straight, sending up cascades of grey spray.

Sweat beaded on my forehead as I eased myself into the confines of the car's cockpit. I breathed deeply and glanced across the illuminated instrument panel. The roar of the track muffled into a distant pulse as I tugged the helmet over my ears and secured the strap under my chin. I relaxed as a sedated sense of familiarity flooded through me. Roger leaned into the cramped cockpit to fasten the clasp of the Williams harness. I stretched out, gripped the wheel and watched the mechanics; a swarm of scurrying ants through the misty sparkles assailing the shimmering screen.

Roger gave the start signal. The headlights of the car sliced into the gloom, flickering in time with the coughing engine, then blazed as 350 horsepower of turbocharged Cosworth throbbed angrily into life. A flash of blue light crackled from the side exhaust. The door of my steel cocoon slammed shut and I hit the throttle, exiting the pit lane in a shower of spray. A sense of self-determination overtook me as the turbo kicked in with a huge shove in the back. There was that feeling of independence, of self-assurance, the need to put behind me Team Capricorn's money problems, with a renewed resolution to win.

At the quarter-distance mark, Dave Carvell in the team's number one car radioed in with a high water temperature. Two laps later the engine blew. Kurt Luby in the Team Pirelli BMW M3 was now leading the race. My Sierra cut through the night like a blade, as lap by lap I fought my way back through the field. Hour by hour our thirty-lap deficit reduced.

I remained out on the track for three consecutive two-hour sessions, pitting only to take on board fuel and fresh tyres. I knew I was driving the race of my life but strangely there was no elation, only smooth functioning of machine within machine. Elation would follow later, perhaps.

As dawn crept across the lightening sky we were running fifth overall, the team were ecstatic and any financial problems confronting Team Capricorn were a distant memory. I pitted for Rob to take over. I'd set the second fastest time of the entire race, and done it in the damp conditions and at night!

The track was now dry enough for slick tyres, in fact the clouds had blown away and blue sky had appeared overhead. As Rob completed lap 900 Roger flashed a signal from the pits, second place overall, first in class 'A', seven laps to go.

We were closing at the rate of five seconds per lap on the overall leader, a BMW M3 driven by Will Hoy, but he was still eight laps ahead. After 1700 miles of racing we were running out of time. Like grains of sand in an hourglass, the last minutes melted away, the deficit had dropped to a mere seven laps. Another 10 minutes of race time could have provided an overall win. We had come from thirty laps down in last place, to win the class and finish second overall.

'Did you also provide my client with legal advice in relation to a Prize Indemnity policy?' Rabbit asked Toby.

'I believe we did,' Toby replied, a little less confidently.

'Do you recall the advice you gave?'

'There were a number of areas that I believe we assisted in.'

'I see,' Rabbit paused for a few moments before skirting around the issue for a few more minutes. Then he said, 'Well in that case, Your Honour, I have no further q...'

'I think if you look behind you, Mr Adams,' His Honour interjected, 'your client is trying to gain your attention. Perhaps we should adjourn for a few moments.'

McGaea turned to Paterson-Smythe, 'I think this might be a convenient moment. Shall we say fifteen minutes, members of the jury?'

The jury and stenographer were again excused. McGaea rose but stayed within earshot, in the short corridor between the court and his chambers. Toby remained in the witness box. He knew exactly why I was annoyed. The dock officer released me into the body of the court and I joined my Defence team. Beth watched from the upper gallery. 'Why the hell don't you just ask him the question directly?' I blurted to my legal team.

'I did,' insisted Rabbit.

'You didn't.' I persisted. 'Just ask the question. *Did you provide advice as to whether we had to purchase the Trans World Porsche?*'

Toby stood awkwardly in the witness box, listening as I argued with my barrister. 'Why not ask the damn question?' I said to Rabbit, turning to face Toby, who stared back at me with a look

219

of concern. 'He knows what advice he gave us. Hell, he charged us enough for the damm meeting!' Rabbit and Piglet exchanged glances. 'I know you're all lawyers,' I added, 'but if he's made a mistake, then he's got to admit it. We acted on *his* advice.'

'Okay,' said Rabbit, 'if you're instructing me to put the question to him that way, then I will.'

A few minutes later the judge and jury returned. Rabbit remained seated, unhurriedly drawing up a list of questions on his legal pad. Tigger handed him over a thick file from the stack before him and they conferred as Rabbit flicked a few pages, every so often adding another line of text to his notes. Toby just watched and waited from the witness box, wanting to get it over and done with, and to get out of the oppressive court and back to his cosy Southampton office.

Finally Rabbit stood up and turned to face my former solicitor, who was now looking more anxious than ever. Without seeing Rabbit's list, he knew precisely what was coming. 'Did you attend a meeting in your offices at Southampton...' began Rabbit, 'and provide legal advice to Will Middleton and Mr Thompson, following the race at Zolder, when the team had won the Prize Indemnity?'

'Yes I did.'

Rabbit made a tick mark against something on his list, before asking, 'And do you recall the purpose of that meeting?'

'I do,' Toby replied without hesitation. 'I was asked whether, in my opinion, the Trans-Atlantic Team was legally committed to purchase the Trans World Racing Porsche.'

Another tick mark was added to Rabbit's pad. 'Were you given any explanation as to why they had second thoughts over the Porsche?' he asked.

'Yes. I was told that a number of technical anomalies had arisen over the rules relating to running two drivers in the Interseri Championship. I was also told that the Porsche's engine specification was not as had been originally described and that the car itself was not as competitive as they had hoped. I also believe there was some sort of aerodynamic problem.'

Three more ticks. Toby watched as Rabbit studied his list for several moments. 'Did they advise you as to what they wished to obtain, in the place of the Trans World Porsche?'

'Yes, I was informed that they had seen a pair of Lola Indy racing cars.'

Tigger opened a file in front of him, flicked a few pages and handed it to Rabbit, who quickly scanned the sales invoice for the Indy cars. Then he asked, 'Did you understand the difference between the Porsche and the Indy cars?'

'Not specifically, only that there were a *pair* of Indy cars and only the one Porsche.'

'And what advice did you give to Mr Thompson and Will Middleton?'

Toby shifted his position slightly, then turning to the jury, replied, 'My advice was that, in my opinion, Rob Allan had clearly achieved the result on the track at Zolder and had won the Prize Indemnity. I said that I could see no reason why the insurers, Track Star, would have any concerns as to how Trans-Atlantic spent the proceeds of the Prize Indemnity.'

Judge McGaea's mouth gaped open in a voiceless protest over what he'd just heard, and turning to the jury, he mouthed his objection silently – *What!* – Neither the stenographer nor my defence team noticed, but others clearly did, most significantly the jury.

Rabbit allowed a small grin to cross his face. 'I see,' he replied quietly, turning to face the jury. 'You are doubtless aware that the Defendant has been charged with obtaining by deception, as a result of the team purchasing alternative cars to the one stated in the Prize Indemnity contract, but you are telling this court that he was acting on *your* advice in this respect, is that correct?'

'Yes it is.'

Rabbit placed a tick mark against the last item on his list and turned to the judge. 'No further questions, Your Honour.'

Paterson-Smythe stood and turned to face the witness. 'Mr Jackson, I put it to you that you did not advise the Defendant that he was entitled to purchase an alternative car and that your purpose in giving evidence today is simply to try to assist the Defendant.'

'Absolutely not.' replied Toby, indignantly.

'So you're not here to help the Defendant in any way?' asked Smythe, sarcastically.

'I came here to give evidence and to tell the truth.'

'Most commendable,' was all that Smythe added, mockingly,

before turning to the judge to say, 'I have no further questions for this witness, Your Honour.'

'Do you wish to re-examine the witness?' McGaea asked Rabbit sharply.

'No thank you, Your Honour.'

Toby left the witness box, but before reaching the door, he glanced meekly up at the dock. I nodded a thank you and he half-smiled back. His advice had clearly been wrong, but he had admitted his mistake in the full and hostile gaze of the court.

I looked back to see His Honour scowling intently in my direction, fingers drumming irritably on his bench. He turned to Paterson-Smythe. 'Mr Smythe,' he snapped. 'I would like a few words in my chambers, if you have a moment.' Smythe bowed as His Honour rose and strode furiously from his bench.

39

If you can't convince them, confuse them!

(Harry S Truman)

'The Defence calls Dr Henry Bell,' announced Rabbit, turning towards the door. Dr Bell, a tall man in his late fifties, strode purposefully to the witness box and swore the oath. Rabbit went through his resumé and quickly confirmed him as an expert in the field of learning difficulties. 'Can you explain how dyslexia affects the Defendant?' Rabbit asked.

'Dyslexia is an organising or learning difficulty which restricts the individual's competencies in information processing and working memory.'

'Is the Defendant dyslexic?'

Bell turned directly to the jury, 'Yes, Will Middleton is severely dyslexic, but he also has a very high IQ, within the top ten per cent of the population of his age.'

'I see, and how would this mix affect the Defendant?' Rabbit asked the pre-planned question that Dr Bell was waiting for. The doctor replied with the same answer he'd previously given to the question from Piglet.

'Well, due to his dyslexia, it is reasonable to expect that he'd make frequent spelling errors and would tend to have problems completing forms and the like. He's also unlikely to see subtle variations in similar format from one paper to another.'

'Dr Bell, I wonder if you would examine these two sets of WPA claim forms both signed by the Defendant in respect of his redundancy claim?'

Rabbit held aloft a set of papers which Lurch relayed to the witness.

'Looking at the two forms, we can see that they are both A4-size printed documents,' Rabbit coninued, 'both headed *Continuing Unemployment Claim Form*. Both forms have three sections, the first section giving the name and address of the claimant, the second section being a declaration for completion by the Department of Employment and finally, the third section on each form is a declaration of continuing unemployment which has to be signed by the claimant.

'To all intents and purposes the formatting on both forms looks identical. However, if we examine the text of the declaration on the second document, WPA has changed the wording. A change that coincidently happened at precisely the point WPA instructed a private detective to monitor the Defendant.'

He glanced at the jury, to ensure they were following. 'Changed from that of the original, almost identical forms. Formerly it stated: *I hereby declare that I have remained continuously unemployed and not worked.* If we now examine the later form, it reads: *I hereby declare that I have not undertaken any kind of work, either paid or unpaid.*' These WPA claim forms, which were signed monthly by the Defendant, directly give rise to the counts of obtaining by deception, due to the fact that my client *was* assisting with *unpaid* work highlighted by the private detective, namely the setting up of the new company, Trans-Atlantic. Dr Bell, would you expect the Defendant to notice a change such as this in these two forms?'

'Absolutely not, but then it's a mistake that any of us could so easily make. Only a handful of words have been changed.'

'Thank you Dr Bell. If you could just remain there please.'

Judge McGaea turned to Smythe and smiled. 'Do you wish to examine this witness?'

Smythe was busy shuffling important legal papers. He looked up, as though completely unaware that anyone had even entered the witness box. He quickly readjusted his glasses, while rising slightly, his body language suggesting that, as far as the Crown were concerned, the witness was of no significance. 'Oh, thank you, Your Honour, but no thank you.' He hastily lowered himself to the bench and redirected his attention to the far more important legal papers before him.

Our next witness, Harold Morgan from the accountants Ballard Graves and Partners made his way slowly and confidently to the witness box. Rabbit ran through his formal qualifications and established him as an expert in the field of accountancy. 'I understand you carried out a full audit of Will Middleton's financial affairs. I would be grateful if you could explain to the jury precisely what is involved in such an audit.'

'We examined all of Mr Middleton's bank accounts, both personal and business, including the bank accounts of the collapsed Team Capricorn and the new Trans-Atlantic Team.' His words were clear, precise and unhurried. Morgan was a man who dealt in fact, not uncertainty. 'In all, we reconciled transactions dating back to just over six years.'

'Reconciled?' queried Rabbit, as though he had no understanding.

'I'm sorry, reconciling is an accountancy term,' Morgan explained, turning back to the jury. 'It means that we carried out very thorough, in-depth checks against transactions listed on all bank accounts, in this case, going back for more than six years.'

'And was this a relatively straightforward process?'

'Well, we were confronted with one major obstacle. For reasons we were never able to ascertain, somebody within the office of the Official Receiver destroyed every single record and every paper ever filed or belonging to Mr Middleton's company Team Capricorn.'

'Destroyed?' Rabbit, turned to face the jury with an exaggerated look of shock.

'Yes, destroyed,' confirmed Morgan. 'Quite extraordinary really. Apparently the records were destroyed only days prior to our request to obtain copies. Official records of this nature are normally maintained for six years.'

'So let me get this clear. You're saying that *somebody* within the office of the Official Receiver destroyed all records and all paperwork relating to Team Capricorn, just *days* prior to your request to carry out a full audit?'

'Yes, and there was absolutely no explanation from the Official Receiver.'

Rabbit paused to allow the witness's words to register fully with the jury. Paterson-Smythe found a few more important papers that required shuffling.

'Doubtless this hampered your investigation?'

'Indeed it did, but fortunately Mr Middleton had retained copies of some of the records and we managed to obtain copy bank statements, so we effectively reconstructed the events of the company's last years. Will Middleton was in fact the major creditor, following the collapse of Team Capricorn, so stood to lose the most. He was also required to personally repay the National Charter Bank, as he'd signed as guarantor.'

'I see,' said Rabbit, gratefully. 'And could you explain just *how* you carry out such an in-depth audit?'

'Well, we started with the bank statements. For example, each debit transaction was tracked back to the actual goods or services purchased, thereby tying each transaction down to an actual receipt or invoice. On the credits, or monies received into each account, we tracked back to the source of the credit to identify what it was and where it came from. For example, if it was a salary payment from Team Capricorn, we checked to see it was recorded within the company records and that the appropriate tax and national insurance had been paid. If however the transaction was an expenses refund, we analysed the transaction, tracking down and identifying the tangible expense and if appropriate, the split...'

'The split?' interrupted Rabbit.

'I'm sorry, the split is another accountancy term. It relates to when a single transaction is made up of several smaller sub transactions. If say, a sum of forty-two pounds was recorded as a refund to Mr Middleton, it might have been made up of, for example, twelve pounds for postage and thirty pounds for stationery items. We would check that the date of the expense and the sum refunded was identical to the expense incurred.'

'I see.'

'There were also a number of transfers between accounts,' Morgan went on somewhat passionately, 'so each transfer was also analysed and all proved to be correct.'

To the jury, it was all pretty dull. One or two were visibly distracted, and the pretty girl on the front row stifled a yawn.

'I see,' Rabbit repeated, 'and did anything stand out to you as "out of the ordinary" in relation to Mr Middleton's financial affairs?'

'Yes, it did. I would say Mr Middleton had some of the best-maintained records I have seen in all my years as an accountant. All the transactions we checked reconciled correctly and in most cases he even had the original receipts, purchase orders and invoices to back up transactions going back more than six years.'

For more than an hour Harold Morgan provided the jury with his stimulating insight into the world of accountancy. As Rabbit moved into the second hour, most spectators in the public gallery had vacated the court and almost all the jury member's eyes had glazed over. One or two were visibly leaning towards their neighbours as the warm and stuffy air of the courtroom threatened to catch them napping.

'My client has maintained,' Rabbit pushed on, 'that while he was involved with the setting up of the new Trans-Atlantic Team, he did in fact make a number of loans to the new team, on his overdraft. He states that no remuneration was received for any of the work he put in. Having studied the various accounts, can you shed some light on the various sums paid into Will Middleton's personal bank account?'

'The inputs, expenses and reimbursements are all fully detailed in our report,' Harold Morgan replied, flicking a few pages. 'The inputs are divided into four categories. The biggest single input being a sum of sixty-one thousand pounds, paid to Mr Middleton following the death of his father. Those funds were utilised in full for the building of a granny flat. He also borrowed a further sum of just over twenty thousand pounds from the National Charter Bank, to complete the works.' He looked up from his notes. 'There is a full breakdown of the expenditure if required.'

'Just the inputs to the personal account will suffice.'

'Well, there were three other categories: Refunds of expenses paid by Mr Middleton, on behalf of the Trans-Atlantic Team, of thirty-eight thousand pounds.' He hesitated for a moment. 'Again, I do have a full breakdown of what Mr Middleton had paid out, if required.'

Rabbit shook his head, so Harold continued. 'Well, we then have the monies received from WPA: just over ten thousand two hundred pounds for the injuries and then unemployment and redundancy payments amounting to twenty-five thousand, seven hundred pounds.'

'So if we exclude the refunds and the monies paid from Mr Middleton's father's estate, he received a total of some thirty-six thousand pounds in total, during the duration of the claims?'

'That would be correct and that would of course have been over a period of some eighteen months.'

'I see,' replied Rabbit. 'And did you discover any other payments of any kind?'

'No, there were no other payments or income.'

Rabbit paused for a few moments, before asking, 'There has been some speculation by the Crown that my client benefited, or may have even influenced the collapse of Team Capricorn, to enable the redundancy payments to be claimed from WPA. Have you found any evidence whatsoever to support these allegations?'

'We found absolutely no evidence to support such an allegation. Team Capricorn was in fact owed some £71,000, and despite obtaining court judgements, they were unable to collect anything. The team in turn owed its suppliers less than £40,000. If it had been able to collect what it was owed, it would have ended up declaring a profit of more than £30,000 for the year.' Morgan was almost indignant. 'And as I mentioned previously, Mr Middleton was required to personally repay the National Charter Bank, when the team collapsed. All of which would have exceeded any benefit he later received in redundancy payments.'

'Thank you Mr Morgan. If you could just wait there, I expect my colleague might have a few questions.' Rabbit finally subsided, with a look of contentment.

The jury came to life as Paterson-Smythe rose slowly from his bench. 'Mr Morgan,' Smythe began, contemptuously flicking a few pages of the report, his eyes never leaving the witness's face, 'did you check *every* transaction in this report?'

'No, we were only engaged some three weeks ago, so in the time available, it was not possible to check every transaction and as explained, the Official Receiver destroyed...'

'Yes, quite,' interrupted Smythe hurriedly. 'So you didn't check *all* transactions?'

'No, but we did check all the major entries and a random selection of the smaller items.'

Smythe gazed at the witness like a bloodhound that had just been handed a juicy bone. He took a few moments to pour himself a glass of water, time meant very little to the Crown. Finally he took a short sip, then spoke. 'Mr Morgan, I'd be grateful if you'd please refer to exhibit 3002 in bundle E,' Smythe asked.

Morgan flicked his way through a large volume. 'Do you

recognise this document?' Smythe enquired as Morgan scanned the exhibit.

'It appears to be a sales invoice from Trans World Racing in Florida for a Porsche racing car,' Morgan replied.

'I know what it *appears* to be, but my question was, have you seen this document previously. Is this one of your so called *reconciled* transactions?'

'I don't believe it is.'

'I see,' replied Smythe disdainfully. "So would this transaction appear anywhere within the Trans-Atlantic accounts?'

'I'm not aware of the entry, but then I understand the purchase did not go ah...'

'Yes quite,' Smythe cut in sharply. 'But, to reiterate,' he continued, 'all the transactions you *did* check, reconciled satisfactorily?'

The witness nodded, 'They did.'

'*Indeed?*' replied Smythe. He took another sip from his glass and replaced it on the bench, then continued to flick through the report condescendingly. 'So if we were to select one of the *larger* transactions, at random...' He paused, turning pages more purposefully, and running a finger down a column. 'Like this one. £20,000 credited to the Defendant's personal account on 12th June 1987.' He turned to face the jury. 'What was that?'

Morgan turned a few pages. 'Ah, yes, this goes back to the time following the purchase of the Old Granary. It was a transaction on Mr Middleton's personal account and related to the sale proceeds of his sports car. In fact, you can see the vehicle's registration number has been recorded against the transaction.'

'Oh yes, so I see,' replied Smythe innocently, while still facing the jury. He took a few moments to allow the jury to digest Morgan's words. 'And what sports car was that?'

'It was a 1983 Ferrari GT4.'

Smythe, still facing the jury, looked aghast. 'A Ferrari.' he repeated, jowls quivering. He jerked back to face the witness.

'But...' began the witness, but Smythe interjected swiftly, his eyes narrowing theatrically. 'So, is this the type of entry you referred to as being *correctly* reconciled?'

'Yes.'

Smythe shook his head as though in utter bewilderment. 'In

that case, Your Honour, I have no further questions for this witness.'

Why had he selected that entry, I thought. There were literally thousands of other entries they could have queried. My old Ferrari had been my pride and joy. I'd purchased it more than a year before we'd found the Old Granary; at the time, it had cost less than most new family runabouts at just over £5,000, but after the purchase of the barn, amid the upward spiralling prices of the 80s, it dramatically increased in value, and we quickly sold it to cover the costs of the barn conversion. I hurriedly scribbled a note to Piglet – *What the hell's the relevance of all this? They're the ones trying to muddy the waters ... car brought on HP years ago ... did it up and sold for a profit as restoring Granary ... what's this got to do with anything?* – I underlined the word 'anything' several times. Piglet took the note, read it and handed it to Rabbit who nodded back reassuringly. I shrugged angrily.

His Honour turned to face Rabbit. 'Mr Adams, would you like to re-examine, or would you prefer to confer with your client, he appears somewhat agitated?' Several of the jury shot glances in my direction, eager to see the outcome of this interesting exchange.

Rabbit rose, turned in my direction and waved a hand to indicate that I should relax. I nodded back as though I understood, although I didn't. Rabbit turned back to the judge. 'Thank you Your Honour, that is most kind, but I won't proceed with a re-examination at this point.'

Over the days that followed, Rabbit continued to call and questioned various witnesses for the Defence. He shuffled papers, ticked off his lists and followed his script; always careful to only ask questions to which he already knew the answers. Like stepping stones, he laid a path that he hoped the jury could follow.

My GP, Dr Eve, was called, and confirmed that an appointment had occurred in December 1988, following my return from Malaysia, and that the riding accident was fully documented in my medical records. He told the jury about the ongoing treatment and painkillers he'd prescribed and told how the fractures to my spine had not been identified originally. He even recalled the bruising to my lower back following the accident. His evidence was compelling. Smythe attempted to bring the doctor's evidence into disrepute, but failed and quickly gave up, returning to his seat temporarily dejected. On the whole, Rabbit did a good job, but his experience was limited and every now and then Smythe, the Crown's marksman, would simply rise, armed with just a pen, and calmly obliterate a witness with a handful of well-chosen, usually totally irrelevant words.

It was November 1994. Beth sat in her usual seat, alone and away from the other spectators, in the upper-level spectator gallery. Like everyone else, she waited in anticipation for the next witness, but unlike the others she knew who was about to be called. Looking down into the body of the court at the gowned and bewigged figures, surrounded by their piles of books, files and legal papers, she closed her eyes in a silent prayer. Smythe poured himself some water as Rabbit rose silently.

'Your Honour, the Defence would like to call our last witness, Mr Will Middleton.'

40

Time is of the essence ... and I'm very short of essence.

(Graham Hill)

Rabbit had previously carefully considered that the merits of placing me in the witness box outweighed any possible disadvantages. Having spent the time available speaking with me prior to the trial, he believed that if the jury could hear me, they would surely understand me.

But would a jury of my peers ever understand what inspires a racing driver to do what we do? What fuels our mentality? I had planned my dream since the age of seven and had lived that dream, my life, on the edge for more than fourteen years. A life that circled around the quest for ever-improving lap times, a search for bigger and bigger financial backers, the best team managers and engineers I could afford. It was a world where technology and budgets were always stretched to the absolute limit. A world of aerodynamics, mathematics, downforce and G forces, a place where the four-stroke V8 engines screamed in twelve thousand rev symphonic protest, every minute of their brief existence. A world where turbochargers boosted engine outputs to more than a thousand brake horsepower. And in the middle of it all, a very ordinary guy with an extraordinary dream based on little more than raw instinct. It was poles apart from the everyday world.

For almost two years now, my honesty and integrity had been called into question by the investigation; witnesses, former backers and friends, all told that I was a fraud. Gossip and speculation abounded. Rumour will destroy a reputation far faster than any amount of years taken to build it. Never before had I been accused of anything more criminal than breaking a speed limit. My life's ambition had been shattered and the security of my family destroyed. The Prosecution wanted me to appear in the

232

witness box angry, spitting nails. For weeks they'd performed a spectacular character assassination. And I *was* seething, simmering like Mount Vesuvius. Now all I wanted was revenge and was ready to lash out or erupt in an instant.

Pace yourself, I told myself as I walked towards the witness box trying to look as casual as possible. Beneath my facade, my stomach churned and my heart was pounding furiously. Making my way up the single step, I glanced momentarily at the jury, reminding myself not to smile, then up at the judge, who eyed me back intently, like a lion surveying its prey from a high tree. Up in the gallery, Beth watched the now packed court below her.

An expectant hush fell as I swore the oath. Rabbit slowly poured himself a glass of water before turning, smiling in my direction. He began with the basic personal facts; age, birthday, all aimed at trying to get me to relax. We'd been through the questions a thousand times before and I knew every question that I was likely to be asked before it left his lips. Slowly I did begin to relax.

The jury learnt that I was the only male child of the current Middleton generation. There were two sisters, Susan and Jane. I was the youngest and as the only son in a family of old-fashioned values, great things were expected. Unfortunately, by the age of ten it was evident that I was not academically gifted, in fact I was considered by my headmaster, Mr Wickham, to be positively retarded.

Rabbit moved on to the start of the recession, and the collapse of Team Capricorn. He checked his notes again, before lifting his eyes to mine once more. 'When the company's cash flow became critical, can you recall your first actions?'

'Yes, I immediately began cutting back on costs, in an attempt to save the business.'

'And where did you manage to make those cuts?'

'The first thing I did was to reduce my drawings and I cancelled the current marketing campaign. I also cancelled or cut back on my personal PPI insurance cover.'

'I see,' said Rabbit, turning to face the jury, his eyes widening theatrically, wiry brows lifting. 'Let me get this clear, Team Capricorn is near collapse, cash flow is critical, so to save money you cut back on or cancel your insurance policies?'

'Yes.'

'Are these the very same policies that you are charged with defrauding?'

'They are.'

Rabbit shook his head, his face broadening into an enigmatic smile. 'Not what might be expected of a person who was planning to defraud his insurers.'

Smythe leaped to his feet with uncharacteristic speed and exuberance, his arms spreading in a gesture of exasperation. 'Your Honour,' he pleaded, but McGaea was already turning to caution Rabbit and raised a hand to indicate Smythe should return to his seat. Smythe bowed gracefully, as His Honour faced Rabbit. 'Comments of that kind call for speculation as to the Defendant's motive, Mr Adams.' He turned to face the jury and smiled. 'You will disregard the last comment.'

Rabbit bowed. He scrutinised his legal pad for a few moments, just long enough for the jury to take on board his previous comment, then turning to face me, he asked, 'Why, when Team Capricorn went bust, did you sign on as unemployed, when you were already signed off work by your GP with your back problem?'

'I considered that I was unemployed,' I replied. 'My racing team had just collapsed and as a result I was redundant and out of work.' Rabbit nodded but said nothing so I continued, 'But the situation wasn't black and white, it was *grey*. The trouble was I had such an unusual job. We didn't know quite what to do.'

Rabbit flipped a few pages of another file. He thoughtfully sipped some water from his glass before prompting, 'So did you seek guidance from anyone?'

'Yes. Immediately after the collapse I phoned WPA and explained about my redundancy and asked for advice about claiming. I had the car finance and our mortgage to pay, and as far as I was aware, I was insured. It was WPA who told me that if I intended claiming for unemployment I *had* to sign on at the local Job Centre, for any type of available work, as I would be required to get the WPA PPI claim form stamped every two weeks.'

'And did you take that advice?'

'Not immediately. First I went to the Citizens Advice Bureau for guidance. As I said, it wasn't black and white, it was *grey*. Neither was I used to claiming unemployment benefit, but the

Bureau directed me to the local Job Centre. When I got to the Job Centre, I explained about my ongoing injury, and what I normally did for a living, but they told me that I could only be signed off work if I was considered sick.' I turned to Smythe somewhat indignantly, 'Which I most certainly was *not.*'

Smythe turned and offered a curious smile to the jury.

'Would you describe yourself as a competitive person?' Rabbit asked.

'Yes I would.'

'And a business man?'

'Yes. In any type of professional sport, you have to be able to sell yourself. So, yes I would describe myself as business man, as well as a racing driver.'

'I would like you to tell the jury in your own words about your decision to drive at the Brands Hatch Prize Indemnity race, shortly after seeing the surgeon, Mr Dolland.'

'I had been out of work since the collapse of Team Capricorn and had been claiming under the redundancy section of my payment protection policy. There had also been the on/off claim running under the accident section of the policy for my back injury. At that time nobody, including my GP, had diagnosed the true extent of my spinal injury. We had been waiting for months to see the specialist that WPA had appointed but following the collapse of Team Capricorn, I had also been trying to get the new Trans-Atlantic deal together with Rob Allan and Trans World Racing to run their Porsche in the Prize Indemnity scheme...' I paused for a moment, trying hard to find the next words. I fought hard to stop the tears that were beginning to fill my eyes. 'My father had just died, and I'd already lost Team Capricorn.' My jaw tightened, 'then I lost my dog.'

McGaea raised his eyebrows as he turned towards Rabbit then, looking back at me, with incredulity on his face, he intoned, 'You lost your dog?'

Rabbit straightened involuntarily, 'I believe Mr Middleton was referring to the loss of his pet Golden Retriever, Your Honour,' he explained. 'His much loved dog died around the same time.'

McGaea eyed Rabbit sceptically for a few moments, eyebrows still raised, Rabbit held his stare. His Honour glanced at his watch, before looking across to Paterson-Smythe, who was sitting

235

with his fingers pressed against his lips. Looking back at me, His Honour shook his head before adding crisply, 'Continue.'

'It helped having something positive to focus on.' I said. 'I saw Mr Dolland on the 21st of July, five days before the Brands Hatch race. The Porsche was already in the UK by then and David Mamet was on a flight to Gatwick. Mr Dolland didn't even write his report until the 10th of August. He was working for WPA at the time and did not explain precisely what any of it meant.' Rabbit nodded. 'Just that I *shouldn't* compete or put any strain on my back. He told me he was going to send a full report to WPA.'

Paterson-Smythe scoffed visibly at my explanation. He shook his head while making a detailed note.

'And when did you finally get to see a copy of the specialist's report?' Rabbit asked.

'Around seven months after the race,' I said. 'It was literally a week or so before the police raided me and accused me of fraud.'

'How were your symptoms at the time you saw the specialist?'

'I still had a lot of pain, particularly each time I'd seen my osteopath. However, overall it was improving, but then I'd been out of work following the collapse of Team Capricorn, so I hadn't sat in a race car for around a year.'

Rabbit paused for a moment. 'I'd like to get the timing very clear on this for the jury. At the time of the Brands Hatch Prize Indemnity race, were you claiming for the injury?'

'No I was not. The accident claim had to be renewed every month and the current period ended the week before the race weekend, around the same time I saw the specialist.'

'But you *were* still claiming under the unemployment heading?'

'Yes I was.'

'Were you being paid anything to drive at Brands Hatch?'

'Absolutely not! The reality of the way motor racing works is a million miles away from the public's perspective of drivers being paid fortunes to drive. When I was employed by Team Capricorn, I was paid to drive, but even then I would often have to give up my seat to another pay driver.'

'A *pay driver*?' enquired Rabbit.

'That's a driver who brings money into a team, usually from sponsors, to take part in a race. For Brands and Zolder I had

236

loaned the new Trans-Atlantic Team thousands of pounds on my overdraft, just to get it off the ground. If all went well, the deal was that I'd get it back along with a contract to drive for the full season.'

Smythe regarded me disdainfully while listening intently to my every word. Most of the jury were looking totally confused but Rabbit pushed on. 'How did you end up racing at Brands Hatch?'

'We'd spent months trying to put together the deal with Rob, Mamet and Trans World Racing. The deal was simple – whoever was quickest would drive the race. Rob had just come back from doing the Le Mans 24 Hours, and I hadn't raced for more than a year, so when I went to Brands Hatch, I considered it very unlikely I would out-qualify Rob,' I paused for a moment, before adding, 'but I was determined to try.'

'So you knew that at least you'd get to drive in qualifying at Brands Hatch?'

'Yes I did.'

'And in qualifying, who was quickest?'

'I was!' I said, grinning from ear to ear as my mind drifted back to the qualifying session. 'And it was my first time in a Porsche 962.' Rabbit smiled, making a subtle gesture with his right hand that I should remain sober and composed.

'So it was at that point that Mr Mamet of Trans World Racing offered you the drive?'

'Well, sort of,' I began. 'Initially, as I said, I considered it was unlikely that I was going to get to race at all, but in Interserie, the rules allow for two drivers to compete in each of the two heats making up the race, so after qualifying, a compromise was reached whereby I would drive the first heat, as I was fastest, and Rob would do the second heat.'

'I see,' said Rabbit. 'But is it not true that you ended up driving in both heats?'

'That was because nobody at the time realised that in Interserie racing, when a team runs two drivers the second driver has to start at the back of the grid in the second heat. That only became apparent after the first heat and it would have penalised any chance of winning the Prize Indemnity, so Mamet then wanted me to drive in the second heat as well.'

'But doubtless you were pleased to be handed the opportunity to race again?'

'No,' I replied glumly. 'I only raced in the second heat because there was no other practical option. As I said, if Rob had driven, he'd have had to start at the back of the grid. I'd spun off in the first heat because my back had gone into severe spasm within a few laps and my right leg was numb. I couldn't feel a thing and missed the brake pedal for the hairpin at Druids. I was in agony again.'

'But you *did* drive the second heat?'

'Yes, I did. But I was in *real* pain again in my lower back and my neck after the first heat.'

'Your neck?' asked Rabbit.

'The neck problem wasn't the real trouble,' I explained. 'That was simply down to not having driven for so long.'

Rabbit glanced smiling at the jury. 'Perhaps you could elaborate, for the benefit of the jury. I suspect they may be unfamiliar with the effects of racing G forces.'

'The Brands Hatch Indy Circuit is short and predominantly made up of right-hand corners with no real straight. When you enter a corner at high speed, your whole body experiences G forces, the most severe effects being under braking and during cornering. In the corners, your body weight can multiply several times.'

'How much greater would the effect of G force on a racing driver be, than say a member of the jury driving a very fast road car?'

'The fastest, highest-performance roadgoing sports car might pull around one G, but to experience that, you would have to put it onto a race track. At the other end of the scale, a modern Formula One car would regularly be pulling around five G. The Trans World Porsche 962 pulled around three G.'

Rabbit nodded knowledgably, 'And how is a driver affected by this G force?'

'Well, one of the most affected areas, especially when you haven't raced for some time, is your neck muscles. In the corners, the weight of your head and helmet momentarily multiply three or more times in direct relation to the G force being pulled. For most racing drivers, competing regularly, the neck muscles get built up, but I hadn't driven for around a year, so I was having trouble holding my head up in the right-hand corners. But it's not just in the corners. When you hit the brakes at say

160 mph, around a hundred metres before an apex, where you need to be doing around 80 mph, your whole body experiences even higher levels of G force.'

'But none of this had anything to do with your spinal injury?'

'Absolutely not. My neck problem was simply down to not having driven for so long.'

'So how did you cope with that problem?'

'David Mamet got a leather belt from one of the promotion girls and lashed up a strap from the right side of my helmet to the Porche's roll cage, so my head could only move so far. It took the load off my neck.'

Rabbit looked shocked. 'So your body was presumably strapped into the car by the safety harness ... but your head was strapped to the roll cage?'

'Yes.'

'In the event of a serious crash, what would have happened?'

I shrugged. 'That's something you don't consider. If you thought about what *could* happen, you'd never get into a race car.'

'You must have been pretty determined to get back into a racing car.'

'I was.'

Rabbit glanced at the jury with deliberation. 'Did you consider the consequences of what might have happened in the event of an accident?'

'This is unlike any other type of job,' I said. 'If you're preoccupied with thoughts of what might happen or you're worried about getting hurt, you wouldn't do it. That's not to say you don't think about it, from time to time, but you put those thoughts to the back of your mind.'

'Did you ever see anyone seriously injured?'

'I did.'

'Killed?'

I paused for a moment, glancing round the impersonal court. 'Yes.'

'But that never stopped you from wanting to get back into a racing car?'

'No.'

Rabbit turned to the jury as he put his next question in an almost casual manner. 'So, when the WPA specialist, only days before the race, simply said you *shouldn't* drive, what did you think?'

'I thought I could,' I said without hesitation. 'He said he'd send a full report to WPA, but I had no real idea what was going to be in it. Racing was in my blood, it was my childhood dream and the Trans-Atlantic Prize Indemnity project was the biggest opportunity of my career. I thought I'd be okay, but it didn't work out that way. It was only afterwards, having seen the specialist days before and then being in agony, that it began to dawn that my career was most likely over, regardless of what happened at Zolder.'

Rabbit paused for a few moments to allow the jury to take on board what I'd said. 'Mr Middleton,' he finally went on, 'Is that the reason why the injury claim was renewed following Brands Hatch?'

'It was. After the Brands Hatch race, I was in such pain that I couldn't even drive home. I ended up staying in the circuit hotel overnight and saw my GP the following day. The claim was then renewed and I decided to leave Zolder to Rob and wait and see what was in the specialist's report.' Rabbit nodded, waiting for me to continue but I remained silent.

After a few moments Rabbit said, 'I'd like to go forward a few weeks, to Zolder and the second attempt Trans-Atlantic had to win the Prize Indemnity.' I nodded, knowing only too well what was coming next. 'Did you drive at all at Zolder?'

Around me the cold unfriendly walls appeared to recede. Reaching into my pocket with my right hand, I managed to grip hold of the small pot of pills while twisting and releasing the lid with my thumb and forefinger. Tipping the pills out into my trouser pocket, I placed a couple in the palm of my hand. I glanced over at the jury and around the court, then up at Beth in the gallery. More than forty sets of eyes were watching my every move. I coughed, bringing my hand up to cover my mouth, and swallowed the tablets.

'Mr Middleton?' Rabbit encouraged.

'Yes?' I answered but my brain was otherwise engaged. 'Sorry,' I said. 'I think I was having some sort of flashback.'

'Are you okay to continue?' asked Rabbit, concerned.

I glanced up at Beth again in the gallery, she smiled back encouragingly. It was becoming difficult to concentrate, impossible to think clearly.

'Are you okay?' repeated Rabbit, his voice seeming to echo around the court, the sounds crashing in on me. A look of concern was now showing on Rabbit's face. His Honour glared down at me, his face suspicious. Smythe flashed me an irritating mouthful of yellowing teeth. Rabbit continued, 'I'd like to take you forward to the Zolder race.'

'Did you drive at Zolder, Mr Middleton?' Rabbit asked slowly and deliberately.

'Yes,' I replied lamely, 'but only for a few laps.' McGaea cast me a stern look of reproach. 'I know,' I went on, 'with hindsight, it was a stupid thing to do, but David Mamet asked me just to warm the car up for Rob before qualifying started, so I did.'

'How many laps did you drive?' Rabbit went on.

'Just three, maybe four...' I replied glumly. 'But we had no idea what was in the specialist's report at that stage.' I shrugged, shaking my head, pausing for a moment. 'And it didn't change the fact that the riding accident had happened and I was seriously injured.'

'Were you paid to drive, Mr Middleton?'

'No.' My voice tightened. 'I was *never* paid anything,' I said sharply. 'And I had lent Trans-Atlantic the money it needed on my overdraft, so it could keep going.'

Rabbit made a gesture for me to relax. 'I know Mr Middleton, I know,' he said softly. He paused for a few moments, before adding a question that he knew would make me smile. 'Who was quickest?'

'I was,' I replied smiling again. 'Rob then drove, trying to beat my time.'

'But it was Rob Allan who drove the Trans World Porsche for official qualifying?'

'Yes, it was.'

'And in the race also?'

'Yes.'

'And it was Rob Allan who won the Prize Indemnity?'

'Yes it was.'

'So you didn't drive again after that time?'

I shook my head. 'No. After Rob won the Prize Indemnity, I waited to see the outcome of the report that the specialist had sent to WPA, but it was then that the police raided me.'

'But you did return to racing some months after the police raid?'

241

'It was several months after the raid,' I corrected. 'I now had no income at all and there was the real risk of losing our home, so I took the only option open to me. I persuaded my GP to prescribe some very strong painkillers, and took up the contract to drive the Indy Cars for Trans-Atlantic. Whenever I drove, I used a combination of over-the-counter painkillers and the very strong pills prescribed by my doctor.'

As each day blurred into another, Rabbit continued to delicately prise the details from me. I recalled everything as best as I could, explaining how as time went by, the injury, that had originally been diagnosed as simply bruising never seemed to get better. I explained how the pain, at times almost unbearable, returned whenever I raced and always after receiving treatment from Mr Banister, the osteopath who had been due to give key evidence in my defence before reading the reports on my trial in the press.

On the sixth day Rabbit finally sat down and Paterson-Smythe rose to his feet, armed with his trusty pen, his eyes never leaving my face.

Smythe's junior lifted a plain brown paper bag onto his bench and carefully removed a small stack of garish magazines. Each copy had been carefully tabulated with coloured markers. Smythe removed the top copy and held it up between thumb and forefinger, allowing it to fall open at a tabbed page.

'I have a copy of this...' he paused, his milky eyes scanning the two full-frontal nudes in the most explicit poses, 'magazine for Your Honour and a further six copies for the jury.'

Lurch stepped forward, collected the exhibits and began distributing the evidence to judge and jury. Juror number three, the girl in the front row, blushed. The other female members of the jury looked suitably unimpressed, one or two downright disapproving.

Smythe opened his personal copy and returning his gaze to my direction, head shaking in confusion, he asked, 'Mr Middleton, are you familiar with this ... publication?'

41

The court was silent, apart from the occasional flick of a glossy page, and the tick of the clock. The jury seemed curious, if slightly confused, about Paterson-Smythe's latest exhibits. His Honour flicked a few pages of naked flesh, before returning his gaze to the learned prosecutor. I looked over at Rabbit. He glanced back, frowning.

I had explained to Rabbit and Piglet about the magazine and described how 'page sponsorship' operated, but as with Prize Indemnity, 'page sponsorship' was an alien concept to most people outside the world of motorsport. Piglet had searched the agreement with the publishers for any irregularities, but none had been found. The deal was straightforward, even if the concept was unusual and publication somewhat risqué.

Smythe checked his notes and then lifted his eyes to mine. 'You are familiar with this publication Mr Middleton, are you not?' He watched me closely, waiting for my reply.

'The magazine was one of the sponsors of the new Trans-Atlantic team,' I answered.

Smythe's eyes roved over the naked flesh for a few moments, before he turned smiling to the jury. 'And who was responsible for arranging that sponsorship?' he asked with a look of disdain.

'I can't recall exactly,' I answered. 'It was a number of years ago.'

'Oh, you can't recall,' repeated Smythe mockingly, his milky eyes boring into me, 'how convenient.'

'Well, when I say I can't recall exactly, I mean I can't recall who tied up the deal. I do know about the deal,' I said, my mind trawling back through a tangle of memories.

'Ah, so you are familiar with the *deal*,' repeated Smythe, with an insincere smile. 'Is that because it was *you* who negotiated that deal?'

'I certainly met with the publishers,' I said, 'but then I also met with at least two or three other potential backers – over a number of months. The deal with the magazine was simply that it would sponsor the team with advertising pages that could be on-sold or given as part of a marketing package to the team's financial backers. If you turn a few pages, you'll see there's a full page advertisement for an oil company and another for Aztec Finance...'

'Quite, quite,' Smythe interrupted, with a wave of dismissal, but I continued.

'It was a perfectly straightforward deal,' I said, the cogs in my brain turning far too slowly. 'I know I spoke to the oil company and to Aztec, but I just can't recall exactly who tied up the deal with the magazine. I think if you look in the Trans-Atlantic correspondence file you'll find it was Rob Allan.'

Ignoring my answer, Paterson-Smythe rapidly moved on. 'I'd like you to turn to exhibit 3876, your WPA Unemployment Claim form. As we can see, the form is in three sections; the first providing contact information, name and address and so on, the second section is the declaration that you had stamped and signed by the Department of Employment, and finally, a third section with an unemployment declaration, which you signed. Is that correct, Mr Middleton?'

'Yes,' I answered cautiously, already recognising the blind alley I was being drawn into.

'If we study the declaration that you signed, it says *I hereby declare that I have not undertaken any kind of work, either paid or unpaid.* How do you reconcile this with negotiating with magazine publishers, oil companies and finance companies?'

'Firstly, the wording on that form was changed when WPA instructed a firm of private detectives to watch me. I didn't notice the change in wording. Originally the declaration confirmed that I was just unemployed and had not worked. Secondly, the unpaid work that I did amounted to just a few hours over several months.'

'But that was also untrue, was it not, because you *were* working for Trans-Atlantic.'

'As I said, I was helping to get Trans-Atlantic set up and

244

running, but that amounted to only a few hours over several months. I wasn't being paid to do anything and the Job Centre allowed me to do unpaid work of up to sixteen hours per week.'

'Is that so?' asked Smythe knowingly. 'You're familiar with your UB40, are you not?'

I hesitated, my mind going blank. For a few seconds my only recollection of UB40 was of the band. 'UB40?' I enquired.

'Yes,' repeated the learned prosecutor. 'UB40.'

'The only UB40 I know is a band,' I replied innocently. Then meeting Smythe's gaze firmly, I added, '*Dance with the Devil* was their most recent release I think, wasn't it?'

Rabbit placed his head in his hands, willing me to stop. The only juror that appeared to be on my wavelength was the pretty girl on the front row. She grinned, leaving me no option but to add, 'I believe they formed the band when they were unemployed, *did they not?*'

Smythe exhaled slowly, then fixing me with a predatory stare and to everyone's surprise, he added dryly, 'I believe, *Don't do the Crime* preceded it, Mr Middleton.'

Sensing his advantage Smythe pushed on quickly. 'Is it not true that every two weeks you presented this UB40 to your Job Centre to get your WPA claim form stamped?' His junior handed him a small booklet entitled UB40. Smythe held it up for the benefit of the jury.

'Ah, I see ... yes, yes, I did,' I replied. 'Except for the time when I went to Florida with Rob Allan to see Trans World Racing. I specifically signed off then, although WPA agreed I could continue claiming as the trip related to getting back into work. I also filled in a special form at the Job Centre explaining why I was going to Florida.'

Smythe leaned forward on his lectern, his hands clasped before him as if in prayer. The lectern creaked under the strain. He looked at me for a long moment, saying nothing. Then finally he spoke. 'If we look at page sixteen of your UB40,' he flicked through a few pages, 'it states, *On each day since the last date I claimed, I was unemployed and did no work, paid or unpaid.* Mr Middleton, I previously asked you a very simple question, which I shall now repeat. How do you reconcile your actions of signing the declarations we have seen while at the same time negotiating with magazine publishers, oil companies and finance companies, not to mention driving at Brands Hatch, while claiming to be unemployed and *sick?*'

'I'm sorry,' I said, conceding the point. 'I didn't read the UB40. I don't think I even took it out of its plastic wallet and as I said before,' my voice rose with irritation, 'I was *not* sick, I was injured and unemployed and I wasn't paid anything to drive.'

Smythe tried to look shocked, and for the benefit of the jury, his eyebrows shot theatrically into his receding hairline. 'But Mr Middleton, each fortnight you *also* signed a form UB25.'

I hesitated for just a moment, my mouth going dry. 'I'm sorry, what's a form UB25?'

There was another short pause while Lurch handed out copies of the mysterious UB25 exhibit. With each member of the jury now equipped with a copy of the text, Smythe continued. 'The UB25 is your fortnightly signing-on declaration, is it not? It states *I have read and understood booklets UB40 and UBL 18 "Responsibilities of Claimants" and understand what I must do and what I must report when claiming.*'

'I'm sorry, I didn't read that either.'

'How odd, especially as we heard from Dr Bell that your IQ was in the top ten per cent of the population – was that not correct?'

'Well, yes apparently, but I am also chronically dyslexic. I simply didn't read the small print.'

Ignoring my response, Smythe moved on. 'Shall we now look at your *sickness claim?*'

The anger immediately exploded through me. 'I was not *sick*, and I *was* unemployed.' I shot back. 'I was injured because I fell off a bloody horse. The injury was never properly diagnosed. I then paid thousands of pounds for more than six years to an osteopath, before the full extent of the injuries were discovered. Then within weeks I was raided by the police.'

Smythe smiled politely. 'I assume this osteopath will be appearing as a witness for the Defence to corroborate that statement Mr Middleton?'

What could I say; *Banister had refused to testify?* 'Er,' I hesitated, unfortunately just long enough to catch the attention of the jury. Originally Mr Banister had been due to attend court and back up important facts but that was before he'd seen the newspaper coverage of the trial. I knew now that whatever I said, it would be twisted. 'No,' I finally answered. 'We decided it was unnecessary to call Mr Banister in light of all the medical evidence we already have from the specialist and my doctor.'

'Really Mr Middleton?' His tone suggested polite disbelief. 'How peculiar. Well, perhaps you could now explain to the jury what exhibit 3002 in bundle E is?'

There was a pause as I fumbled my way through a particularly large volume. 'Ah yes, this is a copy of the invoice we faxed to Track Star. The original was later thrown away as we didn't buy the Porsche in the end. There's a credit and debit entry in the computer records.'

'Well, I put it to you Mr Middleton that this document, which purports to be an invoice from Trans World Racing, is a forgery!' he said with a flourish.

'That's utter rubbish.' I exploded again. 'You know from your own forensic test that's not correct.'

I got no further. Smythe's anger also visibly erupted and he turned to His Honour. 'Your Honour,' he pleaded, 'I'm having some difficulty with this witness.' My response had not been anticipated and the jury were quickly removed.

'Your Honour,' Smythe said again, this time in subdued tones, 'we *had* avoided the introduction of the forensic report specifically, as we considered the tests to be inconclusive.'

'When you say *inconclusive*,' enquired His Honour, 'what precisely do you mean Mr Smythe?'

'Well, we discounted the report when we discovered that Trans World Racing in fact utilise photocopied letterheads when producing invoices.'

The judge looked a little confused. 'So is the Crown now accepting that Mr Mamet *did* provide the Defendant with letterheads for use in the Prize Indemnity claim? Because as I recall, Mr Mamet's evidence was that he had *not* provided the letterheads.'

'Quite so, Your Honour. Our position remains that the letterheads were forged by the Defendant and used to produce the invoice. It's just that we consider the forensic report to be inconclusive.'

'I see.' His Honour swivelled in my direction with an angry stare. 'Mr Middleton,' he spoke directly at me in a cold, clipped tone, 'you will refrain from referring to documents that are not in evidence.' He turned back to address Rabbit, but I swiftly interrupted.

'Your Honour, I have no legal training or knowledge of what I am or am not allowed to refer to. I swore to tell the truth and that is what I am attempting to do.'

'Mr Adams,' McGaea continued angrily, ignoring my outburst, 'I suggest you have words with your client concerning what is and what is *not* admissible in my court. I think now is definitely an appropriate time to break for luncheon.' He rose and withdrew to his chambers.

My defence team hurriedly escorted me to the canteen, reminiscent of being dragged to the headmaster's study at my old school. Beth and I sat together at one of the Formica tables; Rabbit took the seat at the end and lit a cigarette. His mood seemed strangely dark, all the usual friendly banter gone. 'Are you okay?' I asked.

He shook his head. 'Will, you mustn't speak to the judge like that. He's not easy to get on with and I'll be appearing before him a lot more than you. Remember, he's the one who could be be deciding your sentence if it all goes wrong. Also you can't make jokes at the Prosecutor's expense or refer to documents that are not in evidence.'

'Why not?' I snapped. 'Smythe was the one that brought up the UB40 and the letterheads and the Trans World invoice and it was him that told the jury the invoice was a forgery. The Crown commissioned that forensics report with the sole intention of using it against me. Just because it helps us, and doesn't say what they wanted it to say, they're now trying to cover it up. Why can't we refer to it?'

Rabbit didn't answer immediately. I watched as Piglet arrived carrying a tray of coffee and a plate of curling sandwiches. 'Sorry but they were the last four they had!' he said, placing a couple of mugs in front of Beth and me, handing two more to Rabbit and Tigger. My stomach growled, reminding me that I hadn't eaten anything since last night.

Piglet added a spoon of sugar to his coffee and began stirring. 'Smythe put it to you that the *invoice* was a forgery,' he said, his words more soothing, 'he didn't mention anything about the forensics report. It's the forensics report itself which is not in evidence, so you can't talk about it.'

Rabbit and Piglet exchanged glances. 'We shouldn't even be *having* this conversation,' added Rabbit. 'We're not supposed to talk about anything with you until after you've concluded your evidence.'

'But it was the judge that told you to talk to me.' I said, exasperated.

The sound of shuffling feet behind us, preceded the familiar, uninvited voice of Paterson-Smythe. 'Sorry to interrupt your conference,' he said smoothly. He leaned forward over the table, a chess master, preparing to make his next move.

'Everything okay, Mr Smythe?' asked Rabbit uneasily.

'Oh yes, fine,' replied Smythe. 'I took the liberty of having a few words with His Honour in his chambers and he has agreed that I should make a statement to the jury when we return about the disputed invoice and forensics report. Judge McGaea would also like a few words with you in his chambers,' he smiled politely at Rabbit, before adding, 'alone.'

My fingers tightened on the handle of my coffee mug, threatening to break it. I clenched my jaw as a burst of resentment coursed through me. How had it been '*agreed*' that he was to make a statement? Beth, sensing my irritation, placed a hand on my leg, trying to calm me. Again, I wanted to tell Smythe that the invoice wasn't *forged*, which the forensics report would help to prove, but there was no point.

Rabbit took a final drag on his cigarette, then getting up, stubbed it out next to his uneaten lunch and made his way back upstairs to the judge's chambers. I took a few deep breaths, trying to calm down. But it was difficult. We sat there for the next thirty minutes, deep in thought, part of me thinking this nightmare would surely soon be over, but another part of me wondering if this was just the beginning. What if the jury actually believed it all?

It was a quarter past two in the afternoon when Paterson-Smythe rose to welcome the recalled jury. 'Ladies and gentlemen,' he began, with an enigmatic smile. 'You will have heard the Defendant make reference to forensic evidence that was commissioned by the Crown.' He paused as though deep in thought. 'It is correct that a forensic report exists. Nonetheless, as its findings were inconclusive, we considered it fairest to discount its contents. However, in light of Mr Middleton's reference to it,' he flashed a glance at the witness stand, 'I will explain the Prosecution's previous conjecture.'

Smythe went on. 'The Crown's contention was that the Defendant had utilised another exhibit, exhibit 3121, to create exhibit 3002. You will note,' he pointed with a pen, 'that some marks exist at the bottom of the page of both 3121 and 3002. Our belief had been that the headers and footers of 3121 had been cut and pasted to a blank sheet of paper, thereby producing a blank master letterhead, and that the Defendant typed the disputed invoice on that forged letterhead.' The jury were engrossed. Smythe continued, 'Of course, as soon as we discovered that Mr Mamet was in the habit of photocopying letterheads and that the marks may therefore have originated on *his* Xerox, we decided not to rely on any evidence that related to the letterhead. That was, until the Defendant mentioned it.'

The cross-examination lasted for a further seven days. Yes, I carried lots of insurance. Yes, I was covered for redundancy and injuries. Yes, that was very convenient. Yes, I had claimed on the injury policy once before, for some three to four months after the riding accident in 1988. No, there had not been any other claims. No, I had not claimed on the redundancy policies previously. No, there had not been any prior indication of Team Capricorn's collapse. No, no, no, yes, yes, yes...

On the last day, Rabbit rose again and smiled. There were going to be a few last questions, but this time easy, welcome ones. Questions intended to smooth over any gaps in my evidence. Questions that should help cast off any incorrect images left by the Prosecution.

Some time later I stepped shakily from the witness box, all life sucked from me. I'd aged another five years. The guard ushered me back into the dock. Smythe and Rabbit took turns to sum up. Was this the beginning of the end of my nightmare?

42

The tongue of the wise commends knowledge, but the mouth of the fool gushes folly.

(Proverbs 15:2)

It was Thursday 15th November. Judge McGaea leaned back in his high-backed leather chair and eyed the twenty or so people before him. Paterson-Smythe and his junior were engrossed in some important documents. Rabbit, Tigger and Piglet sat watching expectantly. At the judge's left the jury sat in their booth.

McGaea looked down at his prepared notes and adjusted the microphone in front of him, to ensure all his words would be picked up. He gazed thoughtfully at his jurors and exhaled with great intensity. 'You have paid great attention to this case and I now have to sum up,' he began. 'I have to give directions of law and review the evidence. I am the judge of law, which you must take from me and apply to the facts. You alone are the judges of fact.' He paused for a moment. 'Counsel in this case have made submissions upon the facts and I am very likely to do so also, but it is you and only your view of the facts that count.'

'As with Counsel, I will not plough through every word in evidence, it would take an inordinate length of time. I will be selective. If there is a piece of evidence I pick on and you think it is unimportant, then you may conclude it to be so. For that matter if I, or Counsel, have *not* mentioned a piece of evidence that *you* think is important, then you may conclude that it is important.'

His words were thoughtful, clipped, measured and uncompro-mising. With the exception of His Honour and the gentle tap of the stenographer's fingers on the keypad, the room was silent.

I could hear the laboured breathing of the security guard beside me and the slow measured tick of the clock on the wall.

The jury had taken vows; they needed a legal foundation to support a verdict, assuming a verdict could be agreed. His Honour continued. 'The evidence comes from the witnesses and exhibits. It is not what Counsel say or what I say. It is not speculative, that would be a guess. Do not therefore speculate.'

He spoke with the practised performance of a politician, the words flowing like warm honey. He paused, smiling at his jury before continuing. 'So far as deception is concerned, there are a number of these alleged in different counts. As a matter of law, the Prosecution do not have to prove all the representations in any one count are false, it is sufficient to convict the Defendant if any one part is considered to be false.'

'Mention has been made of the fact that the Defendant does not have previous convictions. This goes principally to a person's credibility; it may also be taken into account in deciding whether therefore, he is less likely to commit an offence.'

His Honour flipped open a legal pad on the bench before him. 'I shall deal with Dr Henry Bell's evidence first. Dr Bell told you that dyslexia is a learning difficulty with reading and writing. He conducted various tests on the Defendant; firstly to see where he stands intellectually and then where he stands with particular skills. His IQ test and achievement led Dr Bell to refer to him as bright, in the top ten per cent of the population. Despite this high IQ, you will recall that the Defence case is that the Defendant's dyslexia resulted in him not being aware of the wording on the unemployment claims form issued by his insurers, WPA, which specifically asked whether or not he'd taken part in any paid or *unpaid* work.

'On the subject of work, what work did he do?' He cleared his throat. 'Consider the work he did for Team Capricorn. Did it differ significantly from the work he performed for Trans-Atlantic, after Team Capricorn collapsed? Recall that the Defence case is that at no time did the Defendant do *any* work, paid or unpaid and that he was not dishonest.'

'He's making mistakes,' I hissed. 'We didn't say that!'

'You must keep quiet,' the guard beside me whispered. 'If you interrupt his summing up, he'll send you to the cells.'

I angrily scribbled a note and handed it to Piglet – *We said that I'd done no paid work! And the work I did do with Trans-Atlantic was allowed as it was less than the 16 hours permitted by the DSS* – I underlined the words no paid work. Piglet read the note and handed it to Rabbit, but he was busy tapping away on his laptop, attempting to record every word spoken by McGaea. By law, it was illegal for the Defence to take a tape recording of the summing up.

'As far as Jack Carter, the Manager of National Charter Bank was aware,' His Honour continued, 'knowing Will Middleton as he did, he said he'd be looking to restart a business as soon as he walked out of the door; to get on with things rather than sit around doing nothing.'

'He's doing it again,' I fumed, just loud enough, I hoped, for the jury to hear.

McGaea leaned forward intently and spoke directly into his microphone. 'In respect of Mr Toby Jackson, the Defendant's former solicitor, you may think the Prosecution believe that he was either a fool or a *knave*.' He paused for a few moments, allowing the word *knave* to hang in the court's temperate air. 'If it is the former, then it is not to reflect on the Defendant. If however it is the latter, then you must ask yourself, why did he give this evidence?'

The summing up continued for hours, sometimes bearing little relation to what a witness had actually said. '... recall the evidence of Mr Burton of WPA. Mr Burton advised us that according to the WPA policy, a claimant cannot claim under the unemployment heading of the policy if injured and unable to continue with their normal occupation.'

Rabbit plucked up sufficient courage to interrupt, and rose cautiously. 'Your Honour, I apologise for interrupting, but I wonder if I could just have a few moments?' The jury were despatched for lunch and Rabbit remained on his feet.

'Mr Adams,' McGaea said, returning his gaze to my defence barrister. 'You're saying I've misquoted Mr Burton?'

'Indeed, Your Honour, that is right.'

His Honour frowned, before switching his gaze to the Prosecution for confirmation. Paterson-Smythe nodded back in agreement. 'Ah ... I see ...' He raised an eyebrow, then motioning in a gesture of breezy rebuff, continued, 'no matter, my memory must have been playing me false. Let me make a note to myself.' He scribbled a few quick lines before looking over to my barrister. 'Mr Adams, I will clarify the position with the jury when we return from lunch.'

Rabbit bowed in acknowledgement and Smythe waddled off quickly in search of refreshments.

Some time after the greasy faggot episode, we had taken to eating lunch just across the road at a little Chinese restaurant that offered a lunch time special at a reasonable price. Rabbit finally broke the gloomy silence as he skewered a piece of pork with a single chopstick. 'He's muddled up the Burton and Brambly evidence.'

'I know,' I replied with exasperation, 'and even if he's going to correct it, the jury has already heard three different versions of the same evidence. Now they're going to be treated to a fourth account!'

'Are you managing to take everything down?' Beth asked Rabbit.

'Most of it,' Rabbit replied, 'and Tigger is making written notes as a back up, so between us we should have most of it.'

'He's made more mistakes than just the Burton and Brambly evidence, a lot more,' I added glumly. 'He's told the jury my Defence was that I hadn't done any work at all, at any time, which is ridiculous! We all know that I was helping to get Trans-Atlantic set up, but that was all unpaid, and for just a few hours. And he's tried to somehow tie that in with an off the cuff comment by my bank manager, and even got that wrong.'

'What was that?' asked Rabbit, pulling out his laptop to make a note.

'Didn't you hear? He told the jury my bank manager had said that I was going restart a business as soon as I walked out of the door. Jack didn't say that, and neither did I. What he actually said was that Team Capricorn had collapsed and that I had the *hope* of setting up a new venture.' I glumly surveyed my uneaten food. 'The hope was Trans-Atlantic.'

Rabbit nodded. 'Yes, I recall that now. He said that under my cross-examination.'

'McGaea's also brought up all that rubbish the Prosecution kept going on about, claiming to be sick. How many times did I say I wasn't sick, but injured?' I continued.

'Will, we are making notes of all this,' Piglet offered soothingly.

'I'm sure the jury will manage to see a way through all the evidence.'

43

A Judge: a law student who marks his own papers.

(H.L. Mencken)

The court reconvened. 'My memory played me false this morning,' His Honour began. 'Learned Counsel has reminded me that Mr Burton *did* in fact accept the Defence proposition that a claimant could be unable to continue with their normal occupation whilst, at the same time being available to do alternative work.' He moved on quickly whilst the jury contemplated precisely where this edit fitted into the overall odyssey. 'I shall now deal with the evidence of Mr Thompson, the managing director of the new Trans-Atlantic team. You will recall that he advised the court that the Defendant didn't appear to suffer any difficulty with his back whilst driving at Brands Hatch.'

Rabbit rose warily again. 'Perhaps, Your Honour, if we could just have a moment?' He remained on his feet until the last juror had left. 'Your Honour, Mr Thompson in fact advised the court that my client had a neck collar at Brands Hatch because of the G forces, as he hadn't driven for a long time, but also that he was in some *considerable* pain with his lower back and didn't wish to drive in the second heat.'

His Honour, clearly unimpressed, studied the ceiling for a long moment. 'And your point is, Mr Adams?'

'Well, clearly Mr Thompson's evidence supports my submissions which I referred to in my closing speech.'

'I see,' replied His Honour with a tone of reproach. 'Well, can I read you *my* note of Mr Thompson's evidence?' He flipped open a legal pad and began to read, '*At Brands Hatch there was discussion as to whether he should drive the second heat and there were two problems. One was the neck collar and some problem with his back?* Hmm ... my note seems a little fuzzy in that area.' He turned to the Prosecution for support. 'Can you assist me Mr Smythe?'

My mind cast back to Smythe's opening words on that first day of the trial almost seven weeks earlier: *The evidence comes from the witnesses, in the witness box. It is what they say that is important and it is what they have said that you must consider when ultimately contemplating your verdict.* Would Smythe stand by his earlier assertion, I wondered?

The Learned Prosecutor rose slowly to add to the debate. 'I have found my note if it helps Your Honour.' He held up a legal pad and started to read, '*He was wearing a neck collar because of the G forces as he had not driven for a long time, and I believe he was in some pain in his back,* is what my note says, Your Honour.' His Honour, for the first time in more than six weeks, looked somewhat embarrassed.

'Ahh … *I believe he was in some pain?*' His Honour repeated.

'Well yes, Your Honour.' Smythe, to my amazement, appeared to be backing up the Defence. 'Well, to read it word for word, rather than adding my gloss, *and I believe in some pain in his back. He didn't want to do the next heat.*'

'*Didn't want to do the next heat*' repeated His Honour softly, as he contemplated the matter for a few moments before deciding how best to address the discrepancy. 'I consider this really to be more of a matter of shading. To give the jury a reminder of what Mr Thompson *actually* said may very well now serve only to confuse at this stage, as between us we have three different versions. I think it best to leave it as I have already summarised.' He gestured to both barristers to indicate that they should be seated.

Smythe gave a curt nod, and subsided with a look of indifference. Rabbit remained on his feet. 'Your Honour, could I ask if it is your intention to run through the accountant's evidence, Mr Harold Morgan?'

McGaea took a sip of water, without taking his eyes off Rabbit. 'Yes, I do intend carrying out a selective review of some areas of the accountant's evidence, Mr Adams. Is there anything specific that you have concerns over?'

'Well, Mr Morgan's evidence was very comprehensive, Your Honour,' Rabbit hesitated. 'It's just that with all the Crown's speculation over my client's income from the insurance policies, and the Prize Indemnity that was paid to Trans-Atlantic, I was wondering if you intended covering the expenses and reimbursements that Mr Morgan dealt with in evidence?'

'If it is your wish, Mr Adams, that I cover that area, then I will endeavour to assist.'

'I'm most obliged, Your Honour.'

The jury were summoned and His Honour continued to sift through the evidence, witness by witness. Sitting in the dock, I allowed my thoughts to drift back over the events being summarised. I knew he was making some glaring mistakes, yet what he was saying sounded so convincing. I glanced at the jury; a number of them were making notes as His Honour continued to speak. Would they simply take what was being summarised at face value, or recall what the witnesses had actually said weeks ago? Listening to McGaea, I even had to remind myself of the real facts – that I had broken my back, and lost my business in the recession.

His Honour moved on to the evidence of Les Heath. 'Members of the jury, the loss adjusters had asked to see the Trans World Racing invoice, and Les Heath forwarded the document that had been provided by the Defendant. Mr Heath stated that there was no reason to believe that the invoice was not genuine. If he had suspected anything, then he would not have forwarded it. The Defendant's case is that the original copy of the invoice was thrown away after a credit had been entered into the computer accounts. However, you will recall the evidence of Mr Harold Morgan, of the accountants Ballard Graves and Partners, was that he could find no such entry.'

Rabbit jumped to his feet as though another brilliant idea had suddenly flashed into his brain. 'Your Honour. I wonder if we might have just a few more moments regarding some documentation?'

McGaea raised an open palm, to Rabbit, as though commanding traffic to stop. Then, turning to his jury, he smiled. 'My apologies ladies and gentlemen, a slight problem appears to have arisen, some documentation to be checked for a point of detail I suspect. We will adjourn for perhaps ten minutes.'

Rabbit remained standing until the last juror filed out. McGaea turned with distaste to my counsel, holding Rabbit firmly in a steely gaze. 'What is it this time, Mr Adams?'

'Your Honour commented to the jury that the original of the Trans World Racing invoice was thrown away after a credit had been entered into the computer accounts.'

'That is correct, Mr Adams, and that was in fact *your* client's evidence!'

'Indeed it was Your Honour, but my point relates to your comment that Harold Morgan could not find such an entry. I understand that the original records are in the possession of the Crown and are in fact available downstairs. Mr Middleton assures me that given five minutes with the printout, he could locate the ledger entries.'

McGaea leaned back in his chair. 'How can that be possible, if the accountant says they don't exist?'

'With your permission, Your Honour, may I have just a quick word with my client?'

'As you wish, Mr Adams.'

Rabbit and Piglet made their way over to the dock. 'Are you certain you can find these entries, Will?' Rabbit whispered.

'Absolutely!' I replied. 'Everything was always recorded, I entered the information myself. There will be a debit entry on 1st September and a credit entry around a month later, sometime in early October, after the meeting with Toby, when the decision was made not to go ahead with the Porsche.'

'So why didn't the accountant know about it?'

'Harold wasn't shown the printout, he was only asked if he knew of the invoice. He simply didn't recall the transaction, without being shown the ledgers.'

His Honour watched us from his bench; every so often he would make a point of studying his wrist watch. Rabbit cast him a quick nervous glance.

He turned back to face the judge. 'Your Honour, apparently when Mr Morgan was asked the question, he was not shown the printouts. Mr Middleton however insists the entries are there, because he entered the information himself.'

'Very well, we will adjourn for fifteen minutes then.'

Fifteen minutes elapsed and we returned to court with a copy of the computer printout, the supposedly missing entries now neatly highlighted in yellow. The jury were still in exile, oblivious to what was going on. Rabbit's eyes sparkled with pleasure. He'd already made Paterson-Smythe aware that the entries had both been located.

'Your Honour, the Crown is now in some difficulty,' began Paterson-Smythe. 'It would appear the Crown were wrong in their submission in relation to the entries of the Trans World invoice. However, whilst we concede that the ledger entries *do* exist, and the date and amount *do* tally, you will see that the description does not specifically state that it is the Trans World Porsche. There is just an abbreviation and a reference: *962*, which I understand from my colleague to be the Porsche model number. I wonder therefore, if we might take a little longer to prepare an agreed admission?'

His Honour decided that an adjournment was in order. Rabbit and Paterson-Smythe went off to a quiet corner to produce a form of words that would satisfy the Crown and then be read to the jury. Beth, Piglet and I waited in the court canteen. An hour later the tannoy made its all too familiar announcement, 'All parties in the case of Middleton to Court One.'

We all returned to the court. Beth kissed me gently. Straightening my tie, she smiled and said, 'This is going to be good.'

I watched as she made her way back out of the court and up into the spectator gallery. Sitting back in the dock, I waited. The jury filed back into their stall. Lurch called us all to order and we all rose and bowed as His Honour made his entrance and sat down. He turned and smiled at the jury. 'There has been an agreed admission,' he said.

There was a small shuffling of papers, before Paterson-Smythe rose, smiling, with all the conviction and plausibility of the righteous victor. He turned to face the jury. In his hand he held the text of the agreed statement. 'It is admitted,' he began, 'that a computerised record of the invoice of the 1st September 1992 was followed by a credit entry on the 5th October 1992.' He paused for just a moment before adding, 'there is however no invoice or credit reference other than 962 and neither the invoice nor credit note supports the entries.' He spoke without punctuation, intonation or stress. His words were bland, a confusing riddle and he knew it.

His Honour was also smiling. 'The additional evidence has now been heard. Now, finally, I have been invited to summarise the income, expenses and reimbursements incurred by the Defendant during the period of the indictments. You will recall the evidence of Mr Harold Morgan of the accountants Ballard Graves and Partners. Mr Morgan confirmed that in total it amounted to some one hundred and thirty six thousand or so pounds.'

'He's doing it again!' I whispered. 'I never earned a penny.'

McGaea flicked a few pages of a legal pad and then continued. 'Mr Morgan told us that the income was in four categories with around sixty one thousand being monies for the building works on the granny flat. There were then three other categories: Refunds of expenses of thirty eight thousand or so, and then ten thousand two hundred and eighty three pounds in relation to his receipts from WPA, and then a further sum for the unemployment and redundancy claim amounting to around twenty five thousand, seven hundred pounds. So if you take out the refunds and the building work figures, *it* is therefore about thirty six thousand pounds in total.'

I was dumbfounded by what I was hearing – what was the '*it*' that was being referred to? *It* sounded as though the jury were being told that my *income* during the period I'd said I was out of work had been thirty six thousand pounds. I wanted to protest and with anger rising through me, I opened my mouth to speak, but the guard by my side stiffened, and McGaea was just finishing. I buried my face in my hands as His Honour went on, 'That is all I propose to say, the witnesses have had their say, as have Counsel and I. Now it is your task to appoint a foreman to act as your spokesman, and consider and return verdicts.'

'All rise!' called Lurch at 12 pm precisely. His Honour rose, everyone bowed and McGaea left the court. A few moments elapsed before the jury filed out to begin their deliberations. Paterson-Smythe closed his legal pad and began gathering up his papers. Piglet wandered over to the dock. I was about to reel out a list of protests, but as I looked up His Honour was returning.

'I would ask Counsel,' he began, 'to please remain within the vicinity of the court and, Mr Adams, the Defendant is not to leave this building. His bail is now restricted.'

Rabbit nodded.

Paterson-Smythe turned to face His Honour. 'Your Honour, does that mean that the legal representatives *are* permitted to leave the building over luncheon, or would you like us to remain here also?'

'No, I think the demands upon the court's catering facilities will be a little greater with the jury in retirement than they might be otherwise, so no doubt you might take the opportunity of stretching your legs at least outside the building.'

Paterson-Smythe smiled. 'I would not seek to put further strain upon them, Your Honour. One final point. I felt it prudent and have in fact taken it upon myself to rewrite the Crown's admission concerning the ledger entries for the Trans World Porsche. Just for the record, you understand.' Smythe's junior handed over the revised admission.

'Very wise, Mr Smythe, I trust it is legible?' McGaea took the revised document and studied it carefully.

'A little more so,' replied Smythe. 'You may wish to replace your original copy with the revision. I have in fact destroyed the earlier versions.'

McGaea nodded and, without another word, walked out of the court.

44

'I've never heard a summing up like it, Will.' Rabbit sat at the
canteen table, smoking a cigarette. He exhaled a blue fog which
drifted gently towards the ceiling, his hands seeming to relax,
just a little. 'I was expecting the usual concise summary of
evidence. Why did he tell the jury Thompson didn't think you
were in pain at the Brands Hatch race? That was the exact
opposite of what the witness said. I just hope the jury pick up
on all the inconsistencies.'

'Giles, I told you at the beginning, this judge has such a twisted
view of me, it's downright scary. Why didn't you object more?'

Rabbit sat slumped in his chair, legs outstretched. 'Will, I
objected when he misquoted Lee Burton and Terry Thompson.
You can't keep interrupting a judge during his summing up.
Especially that judge. We've kept a detailed record of everything
he's said, it's been transcribed directly onto my laptop. If there's
a problem, we can appeal.'

'If by a "problem", you mean a conviction,' I said, 'I'll be in
a bloody prison cell at that point. And what about the Crown's
admission – how can they possibly be allowed to rewrite it, for
the *official* record and *after* the original had been read out in
court. Anyway, I couldn't understand a word of it.'

Nobody replied. Rabbit seemed lost in his thoughts.

'And that summary of the accountant's evidence,' I went on.
'The judge made it sound as if I was being paid a damn salary
of thirty six grand, whilst I was claiming off the policies!'

'That's just the way our system works, Will,' said Rabbit,
unconvincingly. 'We have an adversarial system of justice in this

country. The Crown says one thing, we say another.' His voice was dull and flat.

'Just because that's what we have, it doesn't make it right!' I shot back.

There was a long silence. 'It may not even get to a verdict,' Rabbit finally said. 'If you have three jurors that can't decide, you end up with a hung jury, and in a trial like this I doubt the CPS would consider a retrial to be in the public interest.'

The first day of waiting drew to a close with no sign of any verdict, and McGaea sequestered his jury to a local hotel for the night. The following day, Friday 18th November, we returned to the court canteen at 9.30 sharp to start the waiting process again, jumping at each crackle of the tannoy, playing cards and speculating further on the jury. A door banging in the background would hardly have been noticed days ago. Now it was a jarring jolt that jangled the nerves. Piglet shuffled, cut and dealt the pack. Beth continued reading the paper. Rabbit sat slumped in his chair.

The doors of the canteen swung open and Lurch appeared. 'The jury are returning to court but I think it's just questions.'

We made our way to the court where McGaea smiled at the jury before returning his attention to the bewigged men before him. 'I understand the jury have a question relating to the medication the Defendant was taking.' He held up a note that had been passed by the Foreman, and began reading it aloud, 'Were the drugs being taken by the Defendant legally prescribed or illegal? I think I can answer on behalf of Counsel, that all the medications were legally prescribed to the Defendant.'

'How had they got it into their heads that I might have been taking illegal drugs?' I asked as we returned to the canteen.

Piglet shrugged, 'I'm afraid what goes on in the jury room is something we will never be party to.'

For the second time that day, Lurch strode in. 'The jury are returning once more.'

Again, we made our way back to the court. Again a guard ushered me into the dock.

We all held our breath as the jury filed in and the Foreman rose. 'Your Honour,' he began, voice trembling, 'we have had many hours of deliberation, and were wondering if we could possibly have some sandwiches. It is rather late,' he added, 'and we haven't had any lunch.'

His Honour shot a look of distaste in the direction of Lurch, before replying, 'Certainly. I must apologise for this oversight. The Usher will make arrangements immediately.' He nodded apologetically in the direction of the Foreman, before asking, 'As we are approaching the end of the second day of deliberations, I was wondering if you felt that a verdict might be reached today? Not wishing to rush you, it's just that, being a Friday, we will need to make hotel arrangements for you for the weekend if you feel a verdict might not be reached today.'

The Foreman glanced momentarily at his colleagues, before replying, 'I believe we are getting close, Your Honour.'

'No pressure being applied there, then!' I said sarcastically as the guard released me from the dock.

Two more anxious hours passed before the tannoy system blasted and we all froze. 'All parties in the case of Middleton to Court One.'

'This has to be it!' Rabbit predicted, as we made our way up the three flights of stairs for the third time that day.

I kissed Beth, then pushed open the doors of the court and headed towards the dock. The usher opened the gate, directing me to my usual seat. With my heart in my mouth, I glanced back. Beth was still holding her ground, no particular expression on her face, but for all that she looked oddly vulnerable, lonely and desolate. She smiled and blew me a kiss.

His Honour was already in place. The jury filed into their stall looking nervous, two of the women appeared to have been crying. Rabbit turned to me. 'This is it, the jury have verdicts.' I put my right hand in my breast pocket and retrieved my father's engagement ring. My throat thickened. I closed my eyes.

'Have you reached verdicts?' His Honour asked.

'We have, Your Honour,' replied the Foreman.

McGaea nodded at Lurch, who bowed before turning to face the jury. 'Just answer yes or no,' Lurch began. 'Have you reached a verdict on all counts?'

'Yes.'

'On Count One, Obtaining by deception; do you find the Defendant guilty or not guilty?'

'Not guilty.'

265

McGaea made a slight grimace.

'On Count Two, Obtaining by deception; do you find the Defendant guilty or not guilty?'

'Guilty.'

'On Count Three, Attempting to obtain by deception, do you find the Defendant guilty or not guilty?'

'Guilty.'

'On Count Four, Furnishing false information; do you find the Defendant guilty or not guilty?'

'Guilty.'

His Honour nodded slowly, as if he had known all along. My breathing was becoming shallow; the knot in my stomach seemed to draw its way into my throat, blocking my ability to breathe.

'On Count Five, Obtaining by deception. Do you find the Defendant guilty or not guilty?'

'Guilty.'

'On Count Six, Obtaining by deception. Do you find the Defendant guilty or not guilty?'

Guilty! Guilty! Guilty!

'And are these the verdicts of you all?'

'Yes.'

There were a few seconds of hollow silence before McGaea turned to the jury. 'Ladies and gentlemen of the jury. I would like to thank you for your diligence throughout the past weeks. This has been a long and difficult trial and in view of the duration, I shall be arranging for you all to be excused future jury service for the next ten years. You may previously have heard conflicting arguments for and against the merits of jury trials on fraud cases. Doubtless you now have views of your own. Now, before you depart, some information that was withheld from you. You will recall Mr Adams, the Defendant's barrister, was absent for a period of a week earlier in the trial and that the trial had to be adjourned for a week. This was caused by an unfortunate accident to the defending barrister's back when lifting some files.'

A couple of the jury exchanged glances. In other words, he had been temporarily incapacitated from conducting the case. During his period of sickness, or was it injury, he'd continued to 'work' from his sick bed to discuss important details with

Tigger and Piglet. Even His Honour had phoned to discuss aspects of the trial. There were similarities to my situation, albeit on a lesser scale. If he'd claimed on his accident insurance, might he have been next in the dock, I wondered?

Suddenly the court started to spin. I couldn't breathe. I turned to the officer by my side. 'I don't feel too good.' Time came to a halt. I heard voices calling me. I was floating, drifting, cocooned, somehow suspended from reality. A comforting thumping sound seemed to encircle me; other more distant noises seemed to crash furiously in the background.

Beth's voice. 'I'm here darling. It's okay. Everything's going to be okay.' She was sobbing. I wanted to stay where I was, wherever I was. I ignored the calls. Was I dead? If this was death, it was not unpleasant.

Suddenly sounds, voices, bright lights, pandemonium. I was aware of several people around me. 'He's coming round thank God. Somebody get a doctor, damn it, get a bloody doctor!'

Strong hands lifted me onto a chair. I drew the heavy air into my lungs. I was wet with sweat, and my breath was wildly erratic. Suddenly I broke down completely; I could not stop the tears. I sobbed uncontrollably. My body shook in deep unruly sobs of shock and despair.

Beth whispered, 'Darling it's okay, we'll sort this out.'

45

'It's fish or omelette, dear.'

'What?' I looked from the food trolley to the middle-aged woman who was smiling down at me. 'Where am I?' I stammered, pushing myself up from the armchair.

She didn't answer, just smiled and repeated, 'Fish or omelette, sweetie, you just need to decide. Okay?'

Seeing I was becoming agitated, she turned to one of the nurses. 'Sandra,' she called, 'can you have a word dear, I think this one's a little confused.'

This one, I repeated in my mind as a young nurse came over, smiling. 'Hi Will,' she said, 'have you just woken up?'

I looked anxiously around the room. 'Where am I?' I repeated nervously.

'You're in hospital, Will. You've had a bit of a breakdown, but there's nothing to worry about; you're going to be fine. Okay?'

'What hospital? What happened? I want to see my wife.'

'Just try to relax, Will. I'm going to arrange for the doctor to come and see you and give you some more Diazepam. Your wife is due back any time, she was sitting here...' she broke off, 'oh, here she is, she's back.'

I turned to see Beth coming over to me. 'Will, it's okay, I just nipped out for something to eat, you were asleep.' Reaching me, she wrapped her arms about me.

'What happened, where am I?'

'You collapsed in the court, darling. They got a doctor, who said you just fainted due to shock. We got you home, but,' tears came to her eyes, 'you were acting very strangely. I phoned our

268

doctor and he felt we needed to get you in here. We just want you to get better and to keep you safe.'

Suddenly everything came crashing back, like a wave. 'It's okay,' I said, 'I remember; I was found guilty. Shit, I was actually found guilty!'

'Look, we're going to fight this. Jonathan and Giles are going through the judge's summing up and we're going to appeal, okay? Jonathan is coming down to see you tomorrow. He's only visiting, Will; he's not planning to go through anything yet, not until you're feeling better.'

'What sort of hospital am I in?'

'You're in Sommersdale Ward at Graylingwell, the psychiatric hospital.'

'Graylingwell?' I blurted. 'That's for nutters; I'm not crazy!'

'We don't refer to our patients that way, Will,' a voice behind me announced. I turned to see a grey-haired man in a white coat. 'My name's Michael Matthews, Will, I'm your doctor. You're looking a little better, how are you feeling tonight?'

'Tonight?' I paused, and returning my gaze to Beth, asked, 'How long have I been in here?'

'Darling, you've been in here for a few weeks. It's 1994 now; we've just had New Years' Eve.'

The doctor turned to the nurse, 'I think it would be best to get Will back into bed.' Then turning to Beth, he added, 'Maybe it would be best to leave, Mrs Middleton, perhaps you could come back tomorrow?'

I stood at the window and watched as Beth drove away into the darkness. I felt numb. Tears of anguish flowed uncontrolled from my eyes. The kind voice of the nurse made me turn. 'Come on Will, she'll be back tomorrow, let's get you into a nice warm bed.'

It was a new year, and all around the world people had been celebrating a new beginning. I lay in bed, alone and awake, staring at the wall. Light from the hall outside shone under the door. The Diazepam was starting to work; I felt tired but couldn't sleep. I looked around the dim room. My mind drifted, I thought of my family, the boys, the police, our home, my father, the trial. Then there was nothing but darkness.

* * *

I woke, and found myself in a lounge. It was late morning and I was wearing only a dressing gown; my dressing gown, a present from Beth. How did it get there? I don't remember. I don't remember if I ate any breakfast either; probably not. They seemed to be getting so many of those little white pills down me that my brain felt frozen.

I looked around the room; other patients were all about. I pulled the gown around my legs, I didn't want to talk, I just wanted Beth and the boys. *I'll look out the window, I don't want them to talk to me, I want to hide away; hide inside myself, away from everyone.*

'Hi, my name's Robin.' I turned to see a middle-aged bald man in a green bath robe standing over me. A crucifix was hanging around his neck. He hadn't shaved in a week and his breath smelt rancid. He glanced about to check nobody was listening. 'Have you seen them?'

'Oh, I see you've met our Robin,' a nurse announced in a brisk tone. She looked up at the wall clock. 'It's time for our daily group meeting, Robin. I expect Will is going to join us today?' She glanced in my direction enquiringly.

'No, I'm fine here. Thanks anyway.' I pulled the gown around my legs and closed my eyes.

'Oh, nonsense, Will, you'll enjoy it.'

Do I have any choice? the voice in my head enquired. I closed my eyes and pretended I was trying to sleep. 'Come on, Will.' *Shit, didn't work!* She smiled, looking normal enough.

'I'm fine here.' *Just leave me alone, please, please just go away.* She still smiled, waiting; could she read my mind? I got up and joined the others in a circle of chairs.

'Now,' she began, to the rest of the patients, 'shall we get started with the meeting? Who's going to be chairman today?'

'Will,' a voice called from the door, 'you have a visitor.'

I got up, pulling the gown around myself and headed into the hall. My vision blurred momentarily then cleared suddenly. Piglet was standing there, a genuine look of concern on his face. 'Hey Will, it's good to see you.'

We shook hands. 'Jonathan, this place is full of nutters!' I said. 'I've got to get out of here.'

He smiled. 'Well,' he began, but I butted in. 'No, I'm serious, they're all crazy. I might have had some kind of breakdown, but I'm not mad. I've got to get out of here.'

270

'Will, you've got to get better first. Whatever happened, when you collapsed, it was serious. The doctors here have had you medicated for weeks...'

'I don't care,' I interrupted, 'I've just got to get out and start sorting the appeal.'

'Will, before the trial started...' he paused, trying to find the right words, 'you tried to kill yourself.'

'The frigging police were threatening to implicate Beth and get the boys taken away, if I didn't admit to everything! Being dead seemed the only way I could keep my family safe.' My hands shook uncontrollably as the anger flooded back. 'And that bloody judge wouldn't let us bring it all out in court! Why?'

'I suspect he thought it would prejudice the police in the eyes of the jury.'

I put my shaking hands in my pockets, so Piglet couldn't see. 'Too bloody right it would have, the jury would have realised what was going on. Shit! You know, they don't pull off something like this without someone *very* high up pulling strings.'

This time Piglet remained quiet slightly longer. 'Look Will, do me a favour and try to relax. Do what the doctors want. We've already started going through the summing up, and we will need to talk to you, but not now, not until the doctors say you're ready. Okay?'

Suddenly a crashing of upturned furniture erupted from the meeting behind us. I stood up, and peered through the half glass door. I turned back to Piglet. 'You see what I mean, they're all crazy in here! I don't know what happened to me in that court. I don't remember much after I started giving evidence, except for the verdict, but I'm not crazy, not like that.'

'I know,' Piglet said softly, 'but neither are you in the peak of mental fitness. I was there when you collapsed, remember, and the doctors are insistent you avoid stress. You need time to recover from this breakdown.'

I nodded. He'd made his point.

For almost an hour, Piglet worked hard to keep the conversation away from the trial, but inevitably he couldn't stop me asking the obvious question. 'How come they let me out of the court, after they found me guilty? Surely the judge just wants to throw me in prison?'

'McGaea was forced to adjourn sentencing after you collapsed.

271

He had little choice other than to release you on bail, until you're considered fit to be sentenced. The chief psychiatrist here is insisting you are still not fit to be released, which isn't going down very well with His Honour. But don't worry about any of that. When the time comes, we will be arguing very strongly for a non-custodial sentence and we're already looking into your appeal.'

For a few moments we stopped talking and were enveloped by the quiet, the only sound the buzzing of a broken fluorescent fitting overhead. Finally, changing the subject, I asked, 'Do you remember that chat we had a few weeks back, about Freemasonry?'

'Yes, when poor old Tigger took over, when Rabbit injured his back,' he chuckled. 'You almost gave Tigger heart failure, he thought you wanted him to accuse McGaea of being a Mason!'

'Yes ... well, on that subject, and forgetting where we are for just a moment, how much do you know about Freemasonry?'

Piglet gave me a look. 'Well, as I told you before, I'm *not* a Mason, but I do know a little of their background. They're supposed to date back around three hundred years, but others believe its more like three thousand years, to the masons that built King Solomon's Temple in Jerusalem, around nine hundred years before Christ. I know there's some legend of them building the Tower of Babel.'

'I had no idea they went that far back.'

'If you believe what some people say, the Masons go back to the very dawn of civilisation, way back to Adam and Eve. They say the fig leaves are somehow symbolic of the aprons they wear today in their ceremonies.'

'How do you know all this stuff?'

'A lot of the legal profession are Masons. When I was younger, I was curious, and I did a bit of research.' He paused, giving me time to take it all in. 'Nowadays they're known to attract some very powerful, high-ranking members. Most of the American presidents were Masons. Depending on who you talk to, the Masons are believed to be entangled with everything from the World Bank to the Illuminati, whoever they are.'

The fog in my brain returned and for a few moments I remained silent, waiting for it to clear, then leaning forward, I said, 'I'm very curious about Masons, specifically in the police and justice system.'

46

It was 6.30 am, on 3rd February 1995, the third anniversary of my father's death, and the day chosen by his Honour Justice McGaea to determine sentencing and compensation. A nurse and a taxi had been provided by the hospital to get me to the court. Beth had arrived in good time to allow for a small unofficial detour. 'Darling, do you want to pop into the house on the way through and see the boys?' She sounded unusually strong and in control.

'Yes. If there's time,' I said with more enthusiasm than I'd been able to muster for weeks.

As I stepped from the cab, I was immediately engulfed by both boys. We hugged desperately. Jonathan was too young to understand the situation, to him it was just another goodbye, but George knew and cried a little. I buried my head amongst my family as the nurse watched uncomfortably from a discreet distance. I whispered, my voice breaking, 'See you soon, I love you boys.' I turned to Hilary and Derek, the friends who had taken care of the boys during the trial, and thanked them for their help and support.

Beth gently drew me away. 'Come on darling, we've only got a few minutes.'

Fudge followed me across the room expectantly, the noble head inclined and the warm, gentle eyes watching curiously. I closed the door against his puzzled face and stepped into the waiting car. As we headed down the drive, both boys appeared at the front door and began running behind the car. The driver speeded up, trying not to prolong the agony any longer. I gave one last wave.

JOHN BARTLETT

The journey to London seemed to take forever. We sat in silence and watched the traffic speeding by. I studied the faces of the drivers as they raced to work. I envied them, wherever they were going, whatever their job or walk of life, whatever their stresses. Could they be hauling burdens as formidable as mine? At least they'll be going home tonight I thought; will I?

Beth kissed me before making her way to the public gallery. Lurch opened the gate of the dock and directed me to my old familiar seat. The nurse from the hospital sat behind me. I felt distant, detached, yet somehow I was expected to grasp what was happening around me, to instruct Piglet and Rabbit and comprehend complex matters of law. I sat in dreamlike unreality, my mind like fusing electronic circuitry.

The courtroom seemed to spin momentarily, then stopped. Suddenly, Rabbit was there, leaning into the dock. 'Will, Will! The judge wants to know if you accept that the monies from your father's will were a gift.'

'I don't understand.'

'Okay. He's trying to get his hands on the money from your father's will. He's asking if you accept that under Section 74 of the Criminal Justice Act 1988, it was a gift.'

I tried to understand what was going on. I tried to grasp what Rabbit was talking about. *The Criminal Justice Act*, I thought to myself. 'The whole bloody things an act!' I blurted. 'Everything's just getting switched around to suit their game.' I didn't have the strength to fight any more. 'I don't know any more,' I said. 'I suppose it is, if everyone's saying it is.' My vision blurred and then cleared. Rabbit was off, talking to the judge.

McGaea glared at me as though I were a serial killer. 'Having listened to Mr Middleton give evidence, I am of the opinion that he is not a person to deliberately divest himself of assets. Some seven years ago he placed the Old Granary into the sole name of Mrs Middleton. I believe this was nothing more than a ruse to defeat future creditors. I find therefore that Mr Middleton does own a fifty per cent beneficial interest in the family home.'

He stared at the dock, his face a study in moral indignation. 'In case I am wrong, however, in relation to the Defendant's beneficial interest in the family home,' he paused, as though

274

still pondering a dilemma, 'I reach an order for compensation by an alternative, second route.' Again he flashed a look at the dock. 'The monies transferred to the Defendant in respect of his late father's will, the funds utilised in part to pay for the "granny flat" for his mother, I deem to be a gift under section 74 of the Criminal Justice Act 1988. This is a point the Defendant has himself just acceded to, via his Counsel, and as such, those funds shall be forfeit.' He smiled contentedly in the direction of the dock. 'These proceedings will be adjourned until after lunch when I will address the matter of sentencing and the level of the compensation to be awarded to the insurers. The Defendant will be placed in custody.'

I heard the words, but my belief that justice would somehow still prevail deprived me of the meaning. Our home had been placed into Beth's sole name more than seven years ago, after advice from lawyers. Trans-Atlantic had not even been conceived at that stage. What future creditors could I have been planning to avoid?

One of the dock officers escorted me deep down into the bowels of the building. I was led along a twisting grey passageway and into a holding cell, the door slamming shut behind me. A dense blue haze of cigarette smoke hung low. The cell smelt like a London telephone kiosk, and the walls were covered in graffiti. Two men with ashen faces sat in one corner, deep in conversation. I took my seat at the farthest end of the cell.

They cast me a look. 'What you up for mate?'

'I claimed on my accident and redundancy policies.'

'Oh, nice little scam?' one asked.

'It wasn't a scam!'

'Hard luck mate. What judge you got?'

'McGaea.'

'Shhhhit!' The word was drawn out slowly like escaping steam. He turned to his colleague. 'You hear that? Poor sod's got McGaea!' They both simultaneously made a sign, as if trying to ward off an evil spirit.

'That bastard put a mate of mine away for a four stretch.' He turned back to me. 'Did he do his usual face-pulling at the jury?'

'Yes, and the rest, and he had the nerve to have a go at me for nodding my head once,' I said indignantly.

'I tell you mate, that man is to British Justice what Norman

Bates is to the hotel industry. Piss him off and he'll put you away for life, given half the chance. I kid you not.'

A guard came in. 'Middleton, I've been asked to give this to you, from your wife I think.' He handed over a small, hastily scribbled scrap of paper, doused in perfume.

My Darling Will, They're saying I can't see you at the moment, but we will be together again soon, nothing they do can stop that. Whatever happens, remember we all love you and will fight this injustice. Keep strong. Love Beth and the boys.

The door opened again and a different guard entered carrying a clipboard. 'Middleton, they're ready for you.' I checked my watch, 3.20 pm. The guard escorted me back up the three flights of stairs and through a door which led directly into the back of the dock. I was greeted with an icy glare of hostility from His Honour, dressed in full regalia, already in place and eager to get on.

My strength had long since left me and my mind, frozen with medication, could barely absorb what was happening. I thought of Beth up in the public gallery; oh how I needed her. I felt as though the blood was draining from my body. The nurse entered the dock and gave me another of the little white pills. His Honour indicated with a finger, as though to a dog, that I was to sit. It was important not to inconvenience the court with another collapse.

Rabbit was on his feet. 'Your Honour, you are I believe aware that my client suffered a serious breakdown immediately following the trial itself, and has subsequently been admitted as an inpatient at the psychiatric hospital in Chichester. I have placed before you a letter from the Chief Consultant Psychiatrist for the hospital, Dr Michael Matthews. You will see in his letter, Dr Matthews states that he considers Mr Middleton to be unfit at this time to serve a custodial sentence. If I may, Your Honour, I would like to just read the last paragraph of Dr Matthews' letter.'

'I am familiar with the doctor's letter,' His Honour retorted. 'But I'd remind you that this was written some three weeks ago on 11th January. Unless you have any additional correspondence from Dr Matthews, I think we can safely assume the Defendant has now fully recovered from his "breakdown".'

Rabbit bowed. The room became silent in expectation.

His Honour's thin lips parted and he began to speak. 'Will Middleton,' the words were drawn out like a dagger. 'You have been found guilty of a serious and planned series of frauds against your insurers WPA and Track Star. It is now my responsibility to pass sentence upon you.' For once, His Honour's expressive features were held under rigid control. 'You deliberately set out to create an elaborate web of deceit and deception with the sole purpose of defrauding these Companies. You were driven by your ambition to commit these offences, and in so doing, have brought ruin on yourself and your family. You shall go to prison for a period of four years.

'In addition,' he continued, 'you will pay compensation in the sum of £90,640.00 to be split between the insurers you defrauded, and you shall be disqualified from holding company directorships for a term of seven years. Should you fail to pay the due sum, you will serve an additional two years in prison, this additional term to run consecutively to the first, four year sentence.'

The door at the back of the dock creaked open and a middle-aged warder beckoned me in. A cardboard sign had been quickly erected by the guards, as a welcome for me, the words scrawled in red pen, '*Abandon hope all ye who enter here!*' The door crashed shut behind me.

47

I never saw a man who looked with such a wistful eye upon that little tent of blue which prisoners call the sky.

(Oscar Wilde, *The Ballad of Reading Jail*)

A mist of grey rain rose in clouds from the glistening asphalt. We sat in silence, entombed in the white prison van as it ploughed its way through the streets of South West London.

I knew Beth must have left the court around the same time and I scanned the streets through the smoked glass window, vainly trying to catch a glimpse of her. I watched pedestrians as they scurried along the pavements. I gazed at the shops and buildings as they rose and died away on each side, as we made our way through the streets, in the direction of the prison. The traffic slowed again to a crawl and we pulled up alongside a kebab house. A couple inside paid for a takeaway, it seemed so ordinary. I'd been captive for only hours, but I already longed to be free, to be with Beth and the boys.

It was dark when we arrived at Wandsworth, a prison with a dreadful reputation. The huge security gate wound back and we reversed into the floodlit reception area. Another prisoner arrived in the reception cuffed to a burly guard. The captive tugged at the restraint impatiently like a dog waiting to be released from its leash.

'Middleton!' a warder bellowed. I only noticed the lack of my first name. 'Stand on the mark and look directly at the camera.' He pointed to a white mark painted on the floor. I looked into the lens of a digital camera as a red diode blinked. 'Full name and age?'

'Will Middleton, 40,' I said, almost stammering.

'Middleton, your number is F J 3 8 6 6, remember it!' He scanned a clipboard for a few moments, before placing a mark against a cell number. 'B Wing, Cell eighteen. Pass through and collect your kit. Next!'

I was led to a hatch where I was issued with an ill-fitting blue striped shirt and oversized blue jeans plus a pillow case containing a green towel, a plastic plate, a spoon, a knife and fork, soap and a toothbrush. The inmate issuing this kit plonked a pair of green sheets and green blanket on top of the pile I was already holding. 'Strip and hand over your personal clothing to the orderly,' an officer barked. 'You can keep your watch and wedding ring but everything else, personal clothing, any other rings, jewellery etc. goes into the bags provided. You won't be seeing any of it again for a few years.'

An orderly collected the bags and attached a label that already bore my name and number. 'Sign 'ere mate.' He handed me a clipboard with my personal items all neatly itemised and I scrawled a signature.

Another officer appeared and escorted me to a small office, barely six foot by eight with a barred window. An Indian doctor sat behind a large desk which occupied most of the room. 'Stand there,' ordered a warder, pointing to the centre of the room.

The doctor took a bundle of papers from a file. 'Middleton?' he enquired.

'Yes.'

'You're number FJ3866?'

'I'm sorry, I can't remember.'

He cast me a frustrated glance. 'Give me your full name then.'

'Will Middleton.'

He scanned some papers, then asked, 'And your sentence?'

'Er, four years I think, or it might be six, I'm not sure.'

The doctor removed his spectacles, revealing deep indents in the bridge of his nose. He paused for a moment. 'You don't know how long you've been sentenced? What are you in for?'

'I claimed on my insurance, I fell off a horse.'

'Oh,' the doctor interrupted, 'fraud.' He looked at me in disgust, then replaced his spectacles. 'Any thoughts of self-harm?'

'Right now I could do with a bottle of sleeping tablets, if you've got some.'

He scribbled something on a note pad.

'Are you on any medication?'

'Yes. I was in a hospital, but I've no idea what they were giving me, there should be a report.'

'Yes. Well I've got that here,' he picked up a brown file and flicked a few pages. 'I haven't time to read all that now, it's late and we need to get you lot banged up. What were you on before you went to hospital?'

'Prozac, two a day and some painkillers, oh yes and I was on some sort of sedation, some little white pills.'

'Right, Prozac, forty ml once a day. I'll get back to you over the painkillers. What about sleeping, do you need pills?'

'Eh, yes I will,' I spluttered.

He continued to go through his set patter. All the right words were written down but there was no sincerity, no compassion, and no hint of care. The 'human element' was not his concern. It was late and it had been a long day. I was just another number, an item to be logged in and stored away for four years or maybe six, it made no difference to him. I weighed in at eighteen and a half stone. It was a shock. I'd been thirteen stone before the start of the investigation.

The doctor rang a bell and a screw arrived. He led me away into one of the main wings. The place was like a medieval stronghold filled with passages and half-hidden openings, a labyrinth of totally confusing doors and tunnel-like turnings. Looking up, I peered through tiers of steel netting – a protective web against suicide attempts which was strung across each of the four landings. The landings were narrow with doors on one side and iron railings on the other.

A gate was opened, another portal unlocked. At the far end of the corridor another iron gate led to the centre of the complex. Five wings, each with four landings led off from this central hub, like tentacles of a giant octopus. Another gate opened and we entered B wing. 'No!' the warder bellowed, 'you walk clockwise only around the centre, Middleton, *sun wise.*' What did he say, I thought, *sun wise,* or did he say clockwise? Why could I only walk clockwise? I did not dare ask.

We walked from the centre up a flight of steps and through an iron gate which crashed shut behind me. I continued to follow the screw. We passed an open cell and for a moment I glimpsed inside a pair of dusky outlines hunched together on a bunk.

We were now on the second floor landing. I peered up and down the enormous hallway; it was like being in the belly of an immense ship. To the sides clung the confined walkways with iron railings. All I could see around and above me were other cells, metal, wire and concrete. And the stench! The smell of human filth was everywhere. The place reeked of urine, excrement and sweat, fused with a pungent, sweet, sickly smell, somehow reminiscent of joss sticks.

Most of the cells were fitted with solid steel doors with either a red or white card attached to the outside. A few of the doors had been replaced with heavy iron gates behind which an isolated prisoner stood like a caged zoo animal, devoid of any privacy. 'Observation cells,' commented the screw.

A web of steelwork led high into the roof, twisting from landing to landing. Men scurried back and forth along the walkways carrying slop buckets, some carrying mugs. A door slammed somewhere on the upper landing and I jumped nervously.

A white card was already in place on the door as we approached what was to be my cell. The card denoted name, sentence and cell allocation: B wing – Second Floor – Cell 18, the white card signifying Church of England. The red cards on the neighbouring cells denoted Roman Catholic. The officer unlocked the cell door and I entered. 'New cellmate for you Smith,' he said as I entered. The door slammed behind me with a crash so violent I could feel it.

A man, probably in his mid twenties, his head shaven, body emaciated, was lying face down on the lower bunk, reading. He turned and smiled. 'Welcome to Beirut mate.' He got up, offered a hand. 'Terry Smith.' Releasing my hand, he stepped over to the bucket, pulled down his boxer shorts and squatted, releasing a volley of farts as he purged his bowels. Shocked, I turned away. 'Soon get used to it mate, they give us a lot of beans in this place. No flusher I'm afraid.' He pulled up his boxers and returned to his bunk without rinsing his hands. 'You'll be taking the top bunk mate.' He pointed at the vacant bunk. I looked across at my cellmate. The word 'skins' was tattooed subtly across his bleached forehead, in fact most exposed flesh appeared to have succumbed at some time or other to the tattooist's artistry. His left ear was pitted where once an impressive array of metalwork must have resided, and a week's growth of stubble adorned his chin.

The bunk beds consisted of a pair of four-inch thick foam mattresses resting on a metal frame, bolted directly to the floor so as to prevent it being upturned. I spread the two heavily stained sheets and blanket over the thin mattress on the top bunk.

The cell stank. The stench seemed to be embedded in the walls, floor, the very structure and fabric; even the supposedly clean bedding reeked of festering mankind. The cell was barely ten foot by eight. A single yellow bulb, controlled from outside, hung from the centre of the ceiling. The window was tiny with four layers of bars and a sill that sloped in and down. It was so high up you could only see out by standing on the hard metal-framed chair. A steady drip that occasionally formed into a trickle ran from the top of the barred window down the sill and into a puddle of water.

I pulled myself up and peered through the bars. Clouds of steam spewed from the pipe outlets which protruded from the motley collection of outlying buildings, the mist boiling into an oppressive haze as it defused into the yellow, sulphurous glow of the powerful overhead searchlights. In the distance the muffled sound of a train echoed by.

For a moment I withdrew into myself. I saw memories of my childhood, my parents, and holidays in the sun. The sound of some music drew me back, somewhere in a distant cell, John Lennon's 'Woman' was playing on a radio. The lyrics of that far-off song echoed in my brain and my mind drifted away again to Beth and our first date at that Chinese restaurant all those years ago. '*I know you understand the little child inside your man... However distant don't keep us apart... I never meant to cause you sorrow or pain...*

The peek hole in the door slid open. 'Middleton?' a voice barked, 'You okay?' I jumped like a naughty child caught doing something wicked, then nodded sheepishly in acknowledgement.

I pulled back the blanket, pulled myself up and got into the cold, hard, uncomfortable bed and thought of everyday life. Below me, my cellmate was already asleep, a low persistent droning snore echoed around the cell.

I look around at the cream-painted walls, covered with graffiti. Even the arched ceiling which flaked like festering scabs, was covered with the scrawling of former inmates. *Do your bird, The Governor's a bastard, Fuck the screws*. I added my name *Will Middleton, Not guilty! Sentenced 3/2/95*. I closed my eyes and thought about

Beth and the boys. I thought of the thousands of things free people take for granted. The tablets were working, I drifted into the oblivion of sleep.

A procession of grey, veiled shapes, shadows, ghostly images, swept through my disturbed mind, vainly striving to anchor themselves, to grasp with outstretched arms. Desperately trying to end their journey and return once again into a living world, a world of which they had once been part. 'Middleton!' My eyes snapped open to see the face of a screw, so close I could smell the nicotine on his breath. 'You okay?'

'Yes I'm okay.' I answered. The screw didn't reply, but simply turned and left the cell, slamming the door behind him.

When sleep finally returned it came in brief naps, interrupted with long bouts of gazing at the yellow bulb that was never turned off and listening to the sounds of the night screws as they wandered about the walkways. A thunderous crashing and slamming of doors finally roused me from another disturbing nightmare to a more loathsome reality. The first rays of daybreak crept through the barred window.

A jangling of keys heralded the opening of the door. It burst open and swung back with a reverberating crash letting in more dim rays of light. A moving mass of cockroaches on the floor scurried for cover. Sounds resonated in orchestrated pandemonium. The prison was coming to life. My first full day as prisoner FJ3866 was about to begin.

Terry's shaven head appeared from the bottom bunk. 'We should put in for a cell clean mate.'

'A what?' I asked, propping myself up on my elbows.

'A cell clean.' Terry was seized with a momentary bout of coughing, and then with startling accuracy, spat a ball of yellow phlegm directly into the bucket, without moving from his bunk. 'You new to prison? A cell clean means we'll get to keep the door open for a bit while we mop out.' Pulling back his blankets, he got up, snorting back mucus from a congealed nostril. 'You okay mate?'

'Eh, yes, I think so,' I said. 'Where are we?' I swung my legs around and slid down the bunks onto the cold hard floor.

'You're in B wing, affectionately known as Beirut.'

'Why Beirut?'

''Cos it's the only wing they haven't renovated mate. We ain't

283

even got a karzie. Come on, we've got to get down to the hot plate and get breakfast.'

'No, I don't want to eat,' I replied.

He ignored me, then asked, 'You got any burn?'

'What?'

'Burn! Snout. Tobacco, fags.' He studied me for a long moment. 'Are you for real? You're a right innocent, ain't you!'

'I'm sorry, I don't have any cigarettes. I don't smoke.'

'You soon will in 'ere.' Again the silver mucus reappeared and merged with the stubble of his upper lip. He inclined his head, blocked the adjacent nostril with a stubby forefinger, and with a blast of thrust evacuated a column of silver jelly onto the cell floor. 'I'll get you a cup of diesel, okay?' He pulled on a pair of jeans and donned a prison issue shirt and left, wiping the remaining residue from his lip with a swipe of his sleeve.

The days slowly turned into weeks. For the first seven days I refused to eat and lived on just water and prison tea. The cell had no water, no toilet, no hint of comfort. Terry my cellmate was addicted to dope and I quickly discovered what that strange 'joss stick' smell was; marijuana. He smoked the stuff incessantly, seeming to live in its ever-present fog.

His supplies arrived regularly during prison visits. His girlfriend would simply pass the packages, sealed in a condom, by mouth. Terry would swallow it, defeating any body search, and a day later the consignment would conclude its journey in our slop bucket.

I had never even smoked a cigarette. My repeated requests to move to a non-smoking cell were met with little more than mild amusement. 'This isn't an 'otel Middleton!'

In the weeks that followed, I learnt more about lawbreaking than I had thought possible. How to modify a mortice key to open any mortice lock. How to perform 'undetectable' credit card fraud, and counterfeiting. I hesitated to point out to Terry that the fraud must be detectable by virtue of the fact that he was serving 18 months for precisely that offence.

Each night I lay in bed thinking about my family. Each night I would listen to the steel-capped footsteps of the night screws as they paced up and down the landings, stopping every few strides as they peered into each cell in turn. And each morning I woke to the sounds of fluttering, the soft beating of wings, as my daily visitor, a one-legged pigeon I named Clarence, arrived for breakfast. Every day he came, always around the same time, and for just a few minutes he clung to the grille covering the bars, waiting for a few scraps of bread.

I lived in continual fear. Every night I could hear the thin, agonising screams of people being attacked and raped. A neverending echo of steel-capped boots pounding the metal walkways. The constant noise. Whistles blowing, fights and the desperate, demented hammering on the locked cell doors. The sounds seared down into my nerve endings, the essence distilling into raw fear, fear that I had never before experienced.

The daily regime never changed. Over 23 hours a day, seven days a week locked in a cell ten by eight with a bucket of shit and just Terry for company. All post was opened and read by the inquisitive screws, the only exception being letters from solicitors. These were boldly stamped on both sides 'Rule 37A Solicitor's Letter' and were not supposed to be opened. In fact they usually were. 'Sorry mate, opened it by mistake.'

The jangling of keys and crashing of cell doors heralded the 11.10 call for exercise. We made our way through hallways, the metal doors and gates to the outside yard. I closed my eyes against the powerful glow of the sun, and then slowly opened them as they adjusted to the brilliant light.

Men with skin as bleached as chalk; old men, middle-aged men, young men, downtrodden and lost men traversed in a freakish, revolving kaleidoscope. Mindlessly gyrating round and around they went, again and again in unbroken circles of despair. Six screws spaced themselves around the yard.

I joined the ring of denim-clad figures. 'Nice watch mate!' Six feet of hardened muscle had appeared by my side, covetously examining my wrist.

'Thanks!' I replied naively, as I continued walking.

I scanned the high security fence with its razor wire and daydreamed of escaping.

48

Law is not justice and a trial is not a scientific inquiry into truth. A trial is the resolution of a dispute.

(Edison Haines)

A key turned and the cell door crashed open. 'Middleton, you've got a visit.'

I was led off the wing and down a series of corridors into a waiting area. The walls were plastered with posters warning of the dangers of drug abuse, others warned of penalties of trying to pass anything during visits. I sat and waited. Thirty minutes later a screw called out, 'FJ3866 Middleton.' I jumped up and was immediately directed to a cubicle. 'Stand on the box, legs apart, Middleton,' the screw demanded, before commencing a body search more rigorous than any airport security. With the search concluded, the officer placed a fluorescent yellow sash over my shoulder and secured it around my waist to identify me as a prisoner. 'Report to the desk in Visits,' the screw said, pointing to a doorway.

I entered a huge hall with rows of tables and chairs. I reported to a screw sitting at a desk on a raised platform. 'Will Middleton,' I said, 'I've got a visit.'

'Number!' he demanded.

'FJ3866.'

He studied a clipboard. 'Your visitors are on table B7.'

I set off down one of the long rows looking for Beth. Suddenly I saw her and the boys sitting on the hard chairs, gathered around one of the tables, all beaming directly at me and waving frantically. As I reached the table, all three jumped up and we hugged. An officer appeared, 'Please sit at the table.' It was strange to hear the word 'please'.

'Don't worry Will, you're going to be out of here soon. Jonathan is working on your appeal and a petition has been started to get you released.'

286

'Have many people have signed it?'

'There are a few hundred so far, and one of your old sponsors has produced a "Will Middleton is Innocent" sticker.' They're going up everywhere.'

I listened to all Beth's news for the next 45 minutes, our hands intertwined, her strength flowing steadily into me, recharging me. I hugged the boys and between us we downed two bars of chocolate and two cups of tea. All too soon the speaker system announced 'Visiting time is now over, all visitors must now leave please.' It had taken Beth and the boys more than three hours to travel from Climping to Wandsworth and it would take at least another three hours before they would all be safely home again.

I stood and watched as they disappeared out of the visits room and into a connecting corridor. A few moments passed but I didn't move. Suddenly both boys reappeared at the door. They paused for just a moment, then rushing back they flung their arms around me. We hugged and I tried hard not to cry, but failed.

I looked around for something to do. I was bored; I needed to occupy my mind, it had been more than a week since Beth's visit and I wouldn't be allowed another one for three weeks. Yes, I thought, there were her letters. She'd written twice, sometimes three times a day, every day. Even Fudge, with a little help from Beth, had apparently put pen to paper in an attempt to console and comfort me. I'd read them a dozen times before but I'd read them again. I was still bored; I reached out to the shelf above the bed and selected the nearest book. It was an old hardbacked Bible, probably the first time I'd picked one up since my youth, donated by the Gideons Society.

I flicked a few pages mindlessly as my thoughts drifted again to my school days and the sounds of the morning assemblies echoed through my brain. Whatever faith I had, had taken a severe hammering. That faith had itself been a belief based more on compulsory indoctrination than a coherent philosophy of life and death. The book fell open. Instantly a section appeared to stand out from the rest, as though illuminated in the gloom of the cell. I started to read:

So do not fear, for I am your God. I will strengthen you and help you; I will uphold you with my righteous right hand. All who rage against you will surely be ashamed and disgraced; those who oppose you will be as nothing and perish. Though you search for your enemies, you will not find them. Those who wage war against you will be as nothing at all. For I am the Lord, your God, who takes hold of your right hand and says to you, do not fear; I will help you.

It was a Tuesday. The usual crashing and jangling of keys heralded the arrival of a screw. Tuesday and Friday were shower days. We were allowed to take two quick showers a week. The bath house was situated in one of the outlying buildings and was filthy. Typically fifty inmates were expected to use the facility at once. Within a week my feet were covered with sores and verrucas.

I returned to the cell, the filth of Wandsworth being too deeply ingrained for any soap and water to purge. Sunlight filtered past the layers of bars casting shadows across the floor. I lay on the bed reading, *Empire of the Sun*. I had now been confined for seven weeks in one of Her Majesty's highest security prisons amongst some of the most dangerous criminals. The keys jangled and the door crashed open again. 'Middleton! Dr Good the prison psychologist wants to see you immediately.'

I was ushered to an office on the fourth floor landing. Something was happening. I knocked courteously and entered. The room became instantly silent. Dr Good was sitting closest to the door. She wore a white coat, her iron-grey hair gathered back in a fierce bun. Four other officials sat huddled around a table. I recognised one as the prison doctor. 'Middleton, FJ3866?' Dr Good asked.

'Yes.'

'Have a seat.' She waved a hand in the direction of a chair on the opposite side of the table.

I nodded and eased myself into the chair. The door slammed shut behind me. I studied the dark suits and frowning faces. Two of the group started removing documents from buff-coloured files. The door reopened and a guard entered and stood behind me. 'Finding this place a bit tough?' the psychologist enquired, unclipping a biro from her breast pocket. I started to pay a little more attention.

'Well, yes.'

She took out a pad from the desk drawer and started to make notes. 'We need to know how you're feeling.'

'Well, you know, some days are better than others.' *What did she expect me to say? I was having a ball?*

'Any further thoughts of self-harm?'

I knew that if I told the truth about how I felt I would not be transferred anywhere. 'I don't know. Sometimes I get very down, but I'm better than I was.'

'So you're no longer depressed?'

'Oh, no, I'm fine.' *Silly bitch, of course I'm bloody depressed!*

'I see you live in Climping, Sussex. That's near Ford isn't it?' My stomach flipped. I was going to be transferred to Ford.

'Yes.' I answered eagerly.

'Right, you've been risk assessed as a "D cat", that means you can go to an open prison. We just have to be sure you are not feeling suicidal any longer. Would you like to go to Ford?'

I breathed a vast sigh of relief. 'Yes!' I said. 'It's very close to my family.'

She started to make notes on the pad.

Ford was only ten minutes from my home and almost entirely reserved for so called 'white-collar' criminals. Surely the place had to be more civilised and the regime less rigorous.

'Right, you are down for transfer next week,' the doctor continued. 'You'll be issued with a travel warrant to make your own way by rail to Ford. You're lucky; most inmates have to wait six months or more for transfer to an open prison.'

For the first time in months a broad grin swept across my face. Even the screw smiled. I was leaving this hell hole. At last I could start my fight for an appeal.

It was 9.45 am on Tuesday 14th March 1995. I neared the prison gate with excitement and apprehension, was I truly going to get out? Had it been a mistake? Would somebody suddenly decide I couldn't go?

A screw somewhere in a control room punched a button and the huge security gate obediently whirred back. I walked into the street, a feeling of exhilaration overtaking me. Trees swayed in the breeze, birds sang, leaves fluttered to the ground. To be out in the fresh air after nearly seven weeks was indescribable. It had felt a lifetime. How could a man handle being locked up for years, or even life?

I watched as the buses trundled by on the main road. Women with children in tow strolled past. I listened to the sounds of the London traffic and gulped down the polluted air as though the supply would be cut off at any moment.

I'd never felt more alive. I had always demanded so much from life. I'd spurned the mentality of those who appeared to live less than a minute in their entire lifetime. I had lived that minute, every minute of my life! Yet now all that seemed so unimportant. Could it be natural for a person to feel this good just because they were outside, feeling the sun on their skin? Another inmate had been released at the same time for the trip to Ford. He strolled over to me. 'Hi mate, I'm Carl. You going to Ford?'

I studied the typed instructions on my transfer licence. 'Yes, I've got to catch the bus at the end of Trinity Road, wherever that is and go straight to Clapham Junction.'

'Oh, fuck that. That's what they tell you to do. I fancy a trip to the West End. You coming? We don't have to be at Ford until 3.30. I can arrange a car.'

'No, I live in Climping, it's only ten minutes from Ford. I want to see my wife and kids.'

49

Though you search for your enemies, you will not find them. Those who wage war against you will be as nothing at all.

(Isaiah 41:10 NIV)

Towns and villages divided the countryside and swept rapidly past the windows. Ninety minutes later the train slowed as we approached the little country station of Ford. I quickly grabbed the prison-issue holdall from the seat opposite and stepped onto the familiar platform. I stood for a moment, glorifying in the warmth of the mid-morning sun. I was free, almost home. The liberation made me want to scream with relief. Two other passengers disembarked from the train. A uniformed guard appeared from the last carriage and gestured towards the driver. The train slowly lumbered away.

I checked the time, 11.30. I didn't have to report to the prison for four hours. I set off down the road, fields spreading out on either side, the heat of the midday sun warming my back. I drew in the country air, cleansing my lungs of the foul stench of Wandsworth, my limbs aching with the unaccustomed exertion. On the road ahead a crow pecked feverishly at the deflated remains of a carcass, strands of something sinuous glistened in the bird's beak as it surveyed me nervously. Suddenly it was airborne, flapping off, the strands of gristle dangling from the black beak. The car that had disturbed the bird slowed to a halt, the door swung open and a pair of familiar scuffed shoes came into view, followed by shrieks of 'Daddy!' as the boys caught sight of me and charged past Beth in their excitement.

I bent down and hugged them both, trying hard not to let them see the emotion clouding my eyes. As I stood up, George possessively nestled himself under one arm, Jonathan clinging to the opposite leg. I looked down at Beth. We looked into each other's eyes, I put my arms around her, closed my eyes and held her close. 'I've totally screwed up, haven't I? I'm so sorry,' I whispered.

'It's okay.' she replied softly, 'there's nothing to be sorry about.' She looked up at me, as she ushered the boys into the back seat of the car, her voice also dropping to a whisper. 'Are you all right? What happened in that place?'

I shut the rear door of the car carefully before answering. 'I'm okay, nothing happened. It's just... I know I should've done things differently.'

She looked into my eyes tenderly. 'You didn't have the benefit of hindsight then, Will. You did what you thought was best, at the time.'

'But I shouldn't have done *anything*, should I? I should have just sat back and waited. Not fought to get the new team going. I should've turned down the drive. I just don't know how much more I can take. I'm just not as strong as I thought.'

She kissed me, then buried her head in my shoulder. 'You're not alone, we'll fight this together.'

'I'll always love you,' I said.

Beth drove the short journey to the house. The familiar driveway and facade of the Old Granary loomed. I stepped nervously from the car, as both boys tumbled out. 'Are you allowed to come home?' Beth asked, somewhat uneasily.

I shrugged. 'I doubt it, but they know I live just up the road. 'Nobody said I couldn't, just that I have to be at Ford by 3.30.'

Beth unlocked and pushed open the front door and we all stepped into the hallway. Fudge bounded up to greet me as normal, tail wagging happily, oblivious of the dramas of the past months. As far as he was concerned, I'd just returned from a spot of shopping. I bent down, gave him a big hug, and then opened the door and released him into the garden. I wandered into the lounge. The contrast from the austere, depressing greyness of Wandsworth and warmth of home struck me. In the corner of the room lay a mountain of legal documents, boxes, books, files and loose photos, remnants of the trial. Somewhere in the pile could be the information needed to overturn the conviction. Beth followed my gaze. 'What do you want to do with all this stuff?'

'I'm going to need to get it down to Ford, so I can work on the appeal, but I can't take it down with me or they'll know I've been home,' I said. 'I'm going to need access to my computer as well. It's got all my notes from the trial on it.' I knelt down by the mountain of papers, removing the lid from one of the boxes. No files, just dozens and dozens of old pictures. Racing pictures, images of Beth and myself years earlier, a photo of George as a toddler sitting in one of the race cars, another of Jonathan the day he was born. Pictures of a former life, when life was normal, a life before our world had been shattered.

I got up and stepped over to the patio door. The sun appeared over the orchard wall, its rays shimmering off the lilypad. The chickens strutted about eagerly seaching for worms. It all seemed so normal, so peaceful.

50

Laws are like cobwebs, which may catch small flies, but let wasps and hornets break through.

(Jonathan Swift, *A Critical Essay upon the Faculties of the Mind,*
1707)

The windows of the reception area were opaque and positioned high in magnolia-painted walls. I paused at the entrance; the room seemed to exude a forbidding atmosphere. 'This way.' A guard led me towards a small, open-fronted changing cubicle. 'Took your time getting here, didn't you?' Another short stocky warden rose to his feet, inflating himself like an indignant bullfrog. 'Anything on you that you shouldn't have?' he snapped.

'No. I don't think so,' I replied hesitantly, unsure as to just what might be forbidden.

'Remove your shoes and socks.' The shoes and socks were carefully examined whilst the bullfrog checked the soles of my feet. 'Now your coat, jacket and shirt.' Each item was taken and examined in minute detail, the pockets, the seams and linings. 'Now your jeans and pants.' I'd realised by now that this was all part of the system of degradation and humiliation, all part of the punishment. 'Now lift your arms and turn around.' I tried to switch off from it, but the humiliation seared deep into my soul.

'Okay, get dressed.' The bullfrog threw my clothes at my feet. 'Then go through to Induction.' I stepped out of the reception building and back into the sunshine. A vast expanse of green spread out before me with shrubs and a large aviary where parakeets fluttered and chirped happily, seemingly oblivious to their sentence. Park benches bordered the green, and men sat relaxing in the waning spring sun. A group of visiting children wearing football gear were kicking a ball and chatting happily to a crowd of inmates. Two prisoners rode past on bicycles, another was mowing the grass.

The picture resembled a college campus. Ford certainly wasn't a conventional prison. It was more like a self-contained village with its own shop and a cricket green at its centre. The prison was divided in two by a public road: the east side housed the accommodation which was split into two blocks, 'A wing' holding around 200 men in a mixture of single and double rooms, and 'B wing' which consisted of a collection of twenty wooden huts with between eight to sixteen men in each. The perimeter of the camp was divided from the free world by an eight-foot wire fence topped with barbed wire, the outer boundary shielding the inmates from public gaze with a covering of wood panelling. Inside the periphery a walkway provided a track, allowing inmates to exercise by walking, jogging or running inner circuits of the camp. The west side over the road contained the administration blocks, officers' mess and inmates' employment areas, such as the laundry, maintenance works and greenhouses.

'That's "A" wing,' remarked the screw waving a hand in the direction of a sixties-style two-storey block, 'used to contain the officers' accommodation when it was an airforce base. Now it holds the long-term prisoners, men over 40 and lifers.'

'Lifers?' I enquired.

'Yes, lifers; nowadays we're getting more and more long-termers and violent offenders. We currently hold around forty or so lifers, all coming to the end of their sentences. They've been in the system for upwards of twenty-five years. Probably here for just a couple of years before they're released.'

The screw studied his clipboard for a few seconds before finding and ticking off my name. 'Make your way over to B Wing, induction unit, hut H one,' he said pointing a stubby finger in the direction of a ramshackle collection of huts on the south side of the cricket green. Clearly visible, peeking over the roofs of the dilapidated buildings, just beyond the perimeter fence, rose the steeple of St Mary's Church, Climping.

My thoughts turned to Beth, the sounds of wedding bells filling my head, *With this ring, I thee wed...* Our wedding had taken place there, almost 10 years earlier, on 23rd March 1985. In my mind I turned to see my stunning bride making her way slowly down the aisle to the strains of Jeremiah Clarke's Trumpet Voluntary. She was wearing a beautiful, white, off the shoulder gown set off by a graceful white and gold filigree bead choker.

Her shoulder-length hair had been piled up elegantly on her head, with just a few curls left to dangle down around her ears. I thought of her now, and my eyes filled with tears.

Wednesday 15th March 1995

The sound of heavy rain pounding on the timber roof of the induction hut woke me. I lay on the narrow uncomfortable bed and listened to the rain. Suddenly an unutterably loud intermittent alarm assaulted our eardrums. It was reveille, the signal for morning roll call. 'By your beds you 'orrible lot!' The screw belched out the barely discernible instructions in the manner of an army drill sergeant. He must have been in his mid fifties. The shoulders were bulky, the jowls square and his frame supported a robust beer gut. 'Right! Once you've got the sleep out of your eyes, I want you lot over to the Health Centre on A Wing by 08.30. Orderly will explain where to go. Any of you lot bringing in any legal files?'

I hesitated for a moment, then raised my hand. 'Yes, I've got to prepare my appeal papers.'

He eyed me warily, before strutting over in my direction. 'Thinking of disputing your conviction,' he scanned his clipboard for a name, '3866, Middleton?'

'Yes, I am.'

'Not "innocent", are you Middleton?'

'Yeah, I was... I mean, I am.'

He regarded me with a sceptical stare. 'Well Middleton, you're going to have to comply with our little six-inch rule then, like all the other innocents.' He slapped a ruler into his left hand. 'Total combined legal documentation must not exceed six inches, okay?'

'But I've got a mountain of files and paperwork that I need for the appeal,' I insisted.

'Then you may be unsuitable for open conditions. We might have to consider returning you to Wandsworth.'

'But...'

'No buts, it's for your own good and for the health and safety of your fellow inmates.'

I felt a flush of irritation rising up. 'Health and safety?' I repeated incredulously.

'Yes, *health and safety*,' he repeated. 'Look around you son. Huts are wooden. Can't have piles of inflammable paperwork lying about the place, can we? Fire hazard.'

We made our way out of our hut and across the central green to A Wing, stepping into the hallway, shutting the door behind us. The health care department was just down the hall on the right. We sat down on the collection of hard seats and waited.

'3866 Middleton!' An orderly called my now familiar number. I got up and entered the small office of Dr Patel, the prison doctor. He was in his late forties. He extracted several sheets of typed paper from a file and scanned them for a few moments. 'You're on Prozac, 40 mg per day and dihydrocodeine, is that right?'

'Yes, but I'd like to try reducing it. I need to try and get my head clear.' For too long my character had been controlled by medication. I was determined that must stop. A person's character should come from life, not a blend of chemicals. I'd begun to realise just how easy it was to become hooked. The snappy green and white capsules made reality retreat into the distance. The difficulties were still there but they seemed remote, removed from true life. Perhaps that had been one of the problems at the trial. At the time it had all seemed so unreal.

'Okay, we'll see how you do. Now, I have a report here showing an injury to your lumbar spine. A spondylolithesis. This means you're not wanting to be undertaking heavy manual work, no bending or lifting. Is that clear?'

'Yes, I'm aware of the problem,' I replied with some degree of irony.

'We will certify you as "labour two". This means you will only be given light, non-manual work whilst in prison. I'll try to put you down for work in the Education Department. You have to be careful of conditions like this.'

'Yes, I know!'

I was again weighed, my blood pressure taken, more dihydrocodeine prescribed for the pain. In due course the anti-depressants would be halved and the kindly prison doctor would set about trying to reduce my dependence on the powerful painkilling drugs. The local hospital enrolled me on a course of hydrotherapy and the prison drafted me into the delights of the occupational health class.

For the first week the daily routine consisted of meetings with the chaplain and various officers who dealt with the seemingly endless task of paperwork. They also carried out the all-important risk assessment; a process intended to ensure that only inmates who were not considered a risk to the local community were housed in the low-security camp. I was summoned to a room where an officer dispensed with the problem on a single sheet of A4, all appropriate boxes neatly ticked. The local community were now deemed safe.

I had arrived as part of a mixed intake of five other felons, all selected from various penal establishments throughout the country. Piglet had prewarned me to never ask another prisoner what they were in for, but this group seemed surprisingly happy to discuss their crimes and sentences. There was Matthew, a former barrister from Brighton, sentenced to two years for 'borrowing' from his firm's client account. Carl, the inmate released from Wandsworth with me, was in for two years for so called 'longfirm' fraud. Tim barely nineteen, had been sentenced to six months for faking his income on a mortgage application. Jack, an emaciated lifer with papery white skin and intense deep set eyes, was serving his sentence for rape and murder. Lastly Stewart, a man with a regrettable tendency to crack bad jokes at every conceivable opportunity and whose only obvious talent appeared to be refining flatulence to a fine art. Stewart had been sentenced to eighteen months for identity fraud. 'It's a nice little scam,' he explained, with obvious pride. 'First you pick a suitable address, a large property that's likely to have a lot of equity.' Tim, the youngest of the group, listened intently, leaning forward in his chair, eager to develop his knowledge. Stewart continued, 'Next you pop down to the local post office and redirect their post to an untraceable box number. Two months is usually enough time,' he grinned, revealing a mouthful of yellowing teeth. 'You just filter everything, copying anything useful, and redeliver the resealed post the following morning. They never suspect. Within a month you've generally got everything you need. Then you apply for a duplicate driving licence, and with copies of their bank statements, and a utility bill, you open a new bank account. Next you get their current mortgage information from a credit agency and finally, this is the nice bit, you apply for a nice new second mortgage for 'em!' He grinned,

'Wam bam, thank you mam! I was picking up fifty grand a shot, no problem.' He sat back in his chair, fired up a cigarette and exhaled a small cloud. Still filtering the post each day, he'd wait for the big mortgage cheque to arrive, bank it in his new account, then withdraw the funds in cash, explaining that it was for building works, then vanish!

I sat silently, taking it all in. The thought of the unfortunate homeowner finally alerted to the crime months later, after getting a threatening letter from an unknown mortgage company demanding payment for a loan they knew nothing about was frightening. I shook my head, uncertain what to say. Stewart swivelled his chair in my direction. 'You're very quiet, what you in for mate?'

'Oh, I got six years for falling off a horse.' A few faces regarded me with suspicion. 'Forget it. It's a very long story,' I said, 'I'll tell you about it sometime.' Looking to divert attention, I turned to Jack, 'What happened to you,' I asked innocently.

'I sliced up a kid. Little bitch had been asking for it for weeks, so I gave it to her, good.' We all became very still. I recalled Piglet's warning about not discussing anything with other inmates, but Jack seemed to have no such qualms. 'Bitch got me life,' he went on, looking around the room, intense eyes daring more questions. He waited, but nobody asked, so he continued, 'There was this little place in the woods, I used to go there to watch 'em swim.' He smiled unashamedly at the thought. 'Little bitch was always there, used to go skinny dipping with her boyfriend. I could see it all, and she knew I was watching, dirty little bitch!' For a moment he seemed mesmerised, caught up in his memories. 'Smooth, silky little thing,' he added. Then he went silent again, his chest rising and falling, as though exerting himself. 'I should be out of here within a couple of years.'

Nobody dared speak. Tim the youngest, in for faking his income, looked as if he were about to throw up. Finally Carl broke the silence, 'Well, I've got eighteen months left to do of a two-year stretch for longfirm fraud. I should be out within nine months.'

Hoping to stop Jack from speaking again, I quickly enquired, 'What's longfirm fraud?'

'You set up what on the face of it is a legitimate limited company, and trade normally for a few years, hence the term "long",' Matthew, the ex-barrister explained. 'During that time you establish more and more credit with suppliers and then one day, when conditions are right...'

'Wham bam, thank you mam,' interrupted Stewart, with a knowing chuckle. 'You cream off the assets and the stock, and cash it all in, nice and legit!'

'I don't understand,' I said, 'How can you "cash in", if your company goes bust?'

Matthew shifted in his seat, then explained. 'You skim off anything of value and sell it secretly for cash, before it goes down. Then you stop paying your suppliers and blame it all on cashflow problems. Of course, you go through all the motions first, beg creditors for more time, maybe you even go to the bank for a bigger overdraft, but you know you won't get it. Eventually one of the creditors gets fed up waiting and sues. Official Receiver steps in and winds up the company for you. But because he can see that you've tried to do everything to save your business, you get away scot free.'

Somewhere in the back of my mind, a dim light flickered – wasn't that precisely what the Crown was trying to make out I did with Team Capricorn? The group were silent again.

For the first few days, with the exception of Jack, there remained a strange tendency to stick together, only occasionally venturing out in small groups to explore the terrain outside our hut, whilst keeping a wary eye out for any potentially hostile natives.

After Wandsworth, life in the induction unit was not unpleasant. That is, if you could cope with the uncertain plumbing and competing stereos, all vying to outdo each other for the highest bass level. The furnishings were spartan: an iron bed frame with a thin mattress, a bedside chair and a desk. The walls were plastered with sufficient material to satisfy a college of gynaecologists, the girls being photographed in positions that would have rendered pin ups of Playboy Bunnies more akin to extracts from Beatrix Potter. Within a week or so, five of us, Stewart, Matthew, Carl, Tim and I, were moved to our permanent accommodation, hut B6. Jack was moved into the lifer's long-term A wing.

Work on my appeal had been delayed due to my breakdown and hospitalisation, and the restrictions of Wandsworth, but on 1st March 95, Rabbit had finally filed for leave to appeal against the severity of sentence and the compensation order. The appeal against the overall conviction was to follow, once we'd had a chance to access transcripts of key sections of the trial. The 'drift net' phrasing on the indictments had complicated the task: we simply did not know quite what I'd been found guilty of. Did the jury think I'd created an elaborate deception with the collapse of Team Capricorn, or did they think I wasn't injured?

As winter turned to spring I gradually became accustomed to my new surroundings. The tornado that had entered my life destroying everything in its path, slowly, very slowly, ebbed away. I remained shocked, isolated and distraught. Other inmates asked if I needed help but I just shrugged, still incapable of expressing my thoughts.

51

An illusion of summer descended on the prison. Over the following months, the excess weight I had gained slowly started to fall off, my frazzled brain gradually began to work and bit by bit the concentration became sharper. My rage at what had happened turned to structured thought. Thought as to how I could unravel the nightmare that had overtaken my life and threatened to destroy my family.

Ford was a working prison, that is to say all inmates had to be employed during normal working hours, somewhere within the camp. The word 'work' is probably a misnomer. Aside from the kitchen or laundry, the only jobs were potting plants and pulling weeds on the estates or mowing the grass, for which inmates received the princely sum of £4.50 per week plus a £1 attendance bonus which was paid if you started work on time every day. A fortunate few had their income supplemented by family, friends and the odd Swiss bank account.

We were permitted to spend our meagre wages in the prison canteen which stocked a reasonable range of goods. There was a prison slang for just about everything; cigarettes in packs were known as civvies, loose leaf tobacco for rolling was called burn or snout, matches were known as strike. Other more dubious supplies, marijuana, heroin and assorted amphetamines tended to arrive in the daily 'pigeon post' the gutted carcass of a dead pigeon stuffed with 'goods' and thrown innocuously over the prison fence for collection at pre-arranged times. Occasionally, in the absence of an appropriate bird, a tennis ball or carefully hollowed orange would suffice.

302

I had been assigned 'light duties' due to my back injury and sent to work in the Education Department. The new education block had been built only three years earlier and was staffed with personnel from the local college; there was not a screw in sight. The building was light, airy and modern, completely unlike a prison.

The entire concern was run more in the manner of a modern office complex than a prison department, by a Mrs Addington, a lady in her early sixties, with greyish hair and a warm heart who'd joined the education department some ten years earlier. She was helped by a small friendly staff.

Initially, I was put to work on the reception desk, but my dyslexia was quickly discovered and within days, I vaulted the queue of waiting inmates and found myself in Sue's English class. She was very slim and delicately made, her face was gentle. She was pretty, in her mid thirties with an innocent smile but with a fiery inner strength. She reminded me of Beth.

'Mrs Addington says you're interested in writing a book.'

'Yes, I would like to write about the past couple of years, as, er … as an English project? It would help with my dyslexia and it would be nice to try and achieve something from this nightmare.' I could tell she was sceptical.

'Well, it's been approved for you to type up your book project, but there can be no legal work, no letters to solicitors and absolutely no work on your appeal. That's been specifically prohibited by the Governor. Okay?'

'Prohibited?'

'Yes, any appeal work has to be undertaken in your own time and not using the prison computers.'

I slowly lowered myself into the chair and flicked on the computer, the machine whirred into life and the screen lit up with the message: 'Linked to HMP Ford Prison network, timed central backup.' Big brother was clearly watching me.

The occasional voice filtered in from the hall outside, the machine hummed testily, but otherwise the room was quiet. Over the weeks, hands accustomed to controlling 700 kilos of high-performance racing machinery now sought to turn inadequate words into some sort of phrasing that was both accurate and readable. I had no experience of writing, of punctuation or grammar. In fact, aside from technical manuals which I had consumed avidly, I had only read a handful of books and that had been in my school days, twenty-five years earlier.

Slowly at first, somewhat clumsily, my hands moved over the typewriter keys. For the first time in years I was becoming caught up in something new and stimulating. I became a regular visitor to the prison library, studying the mechanics of writing, its structure and packaging. The famous authors on the musty shelves became my mentors. I discovered how to write metaphorically, how to recreate the imagery, how to portray my emotions. Phrases blossomed in my mind and as my hands became accustomed to typing, the words on the screen before me took on a new purpose. The internalised memories surfaced in all their rancid putrification. I relived every moment of the trial, recreating them like scenes in a film. I researched Piglet's transcripts for the actual words spoken in court. I recalled the voice of His Honour and again smelt the rank decay of Wandsworth, the reek of urine and excrement and that ever present aroma of marijuana.

As the weeks blended into months, the rough notes and scribblings taken during the trial slowly became paragraphs, and the paragraphs pages. Within months those pages turned into chapters. The book wrote itself, the words marching out like ranks of soldiers, soldiers of truth preparing to leap into battle.

52

Justice may be blind, but she has very sophisticated listening devices.

(Edgar Argo)

Tuesday 16th May 1995

The door of the computer room swung open and Mrs Addington handed me a movement slip, a piece of paper which allowed you to move from one place to another within the prison. 'Will, you're wanted in the legal aid office immediately, something to do with your appeal.'

I suddenly had an enormous knot in my stomach. From time to time, the system can hand down a ruling with astonishing velocity. Justice can be fabulously efficient. My stomach was churning like a cement mixer as I sprinted to the legal aid office.

The building was opposite the induction hut. An officer in his late thirties sat behind a small desk studying a batch of papers. 'Ah, Middleton, come in and sit down.' He looked at me in a way that suggested I was most likely infected with a contagious disease. 'I assume you've heard about your appeal?'

'No.'

'Oh well, this is not going to be good news then.' He selected a manila file from his desk, removed some pages and leaned back in his chair. 'The "first judge" has refused leave to appeal. Says it should have been lodged within twenty-eight days of conviction, and you're out of time. He's also blocked you on your appeal against the compensation order. Apparently the trial judge said that if he was wrong in respect of you owning an interest in your home, then there was a second route that was sound. Something to do with your father's will?' The officer shrugged dismissively before continuing, 'The decision was made on 2nd May, it looks as if the paperwork has been sitting up at Wandsworth for a few weeks, bit of a cock up in the system.'

305

I was hit with a wave of emotion. I tried to speak, but the words were lost. I felt dizzy, I was starting to hyperventilate. 'What? How can that be? I'm innocent!' I said, breathlessly. 'Do you mean they won't even listen to an appeal?'

'No, what it means is that the first judge considers that you're out of time. You haven't complied with the twenty-eight day rule, and you haven't shown good cause for any delay. He also considers that the sentence is not excessive.'

'But I was in a bloody mental hospital! I suffered a total breakdown. What more cause does he want?' My words trailed away.

'You could still carry on to the full Court of Appeal, but you'd do so at your own risk, and they'd not allow any legal aid. You'd have to fund any further work privately.'

I hurried away to a quiet corner opposite the cricket pitch where other inmates could not see my eyes. They can't tell so much about you when your eyes are hidden.

Ever since the breakdown I had had to contend with the ever-present danger of a sudden, uncontrollable flood of tears. I had always been somewhat sentimental, but prior to the breakdown had managed to hide my errant emotions beneath a thin veneer, that inbred stiff upper lip that the British are so famous for. Those days were gone. I only managed to regain control when I heard Matthew, the ex-barrister, step up behind me. 'Hi Will. Had some bad news?' he asked.

'Oh, hi Matthew. I'm okay,' I lied. 'Got some grit in my eye.'

He gave me a look. 'Oh, right.'

I cleared my throat. 'Well, I've also just been told that the "first judge", whoever that is, has rejected my appeal against sentence, some twenty-eight day rule or something.'

Matthew frowned. 'Will, practically every application is being rejected at the moment. The so called "first judge", as the name suggests, is just the first official to examine your request to appeal. It's supposed to be his job to decide whether your application has merit to be placed before the full court, but nowadays ... well, they tend to make their own rules, and it's getting very political. All part of the "get tough on crime" ticket that the government are playing, so they're turning everything down. You've just got to push on, make them realise you're serious, that is, if you *are* serious.'

'Oh, yes,' I said, 'I'm serious, very serious!'

Matthew put his hands in his pockets. 'Look, I don't mean to pry Will. But if you want to discuss your case at any time, well, nowadays my fees are a little lower than they used to be. My initial brief fee is a mug of coffee... Okay?'

53

Matthew was looking out of the window of our hut. 'How accurate do you think our justice system is?' he asked.

'How do I know? Based on my experience, not at all!'

'Okay then, prior to your experience, how accurate did you think our justice system was? How often do they get it wrong?'

'Where is this taking us?'

'Just answer the question.'

'I don't know. Before my case, if I was asked, I suppose I'd have said we got it right most of the time, probably 99% of the time.'

'And you got that opinion from where?' It was a rhetorical question, and he continued, 'The TV, the tabloid media, politicians, the endless docudramas? And like everyone else out there, you felt crime was spiralling out of control, but the good guys were sorting it all out.'

I thought about it for a moment. 'Yeah, I suppose.'

'Well, welcome to the real world. The reality is the good guys and bad guys are so intermixed these days, nobody really knows who's good and who's bad. The politicians use the media, the media simply want to sell papers, and the two things that sell newspapers are sex and crime. So we're inundated with stories of crime and corruption and how the government are implementing new measures to keep us all safe.'

'Is this supposed to be helping me?'

Matthew held up a hand. 'Hold on just a moment, there's a reason I'm asking these questions.' He stood up, stretched and wandered over to the window. 'Let me ask you one more question. If the system is, as you say, getting it right 99% of the time, then 1% of the convictions are wrong, yes?'

'Yes, I suppose.'

'Well we currently have a prison population of almost eighty thousand in this country. So, if just 1% of those are wrongly convicted that means there are currently around eight hundred totally innocent people locked up in cells in England, for crimes they did not commit.'

'I thought you were trying to make me feel better.'

'My point is this; if you want to prove your innocence, you've got to fight harder and make your voice stand out louder than the other people that have been wrongly convicted. And incidentally, the generally accepted figure is 4%, that's around 3,200 people locked up that shouldn't be, and that excludes all those held on remand. That figure is growing each year.'

For the first time it dawned on me that this mess was not going to resolve itself, and any resolution that might come along, might not be the one I was expecting. Since the first police raid, I'd naively imagined that everything would somehow get sorted. That I would receive official apologies, be showered with financial compensation and somehow return to my old life. Not as a driver, I knew those days were gone, but maybe on the management side.

But finally the penny dropped; I was convicted, the assets of the team were being held by the Crown, I'd suffered a total breakdown, the bank were poised to foreclose and take our home and I was stuck, indefinitely, in prison with around 400 convicted fraudsters, rapists and murderers, most of whom were also insisting they were totally innocent.

54

An appeal ... is when you ask one court to show its contempt for another court.

(Finley Peter Dunne)

If it had been Matthew's intention to stop me feeling sorry for myself and refocus, then it had worked. The six-inch rule was preventing me from bringing in anything other than a handful of files, but lots of my notes and documentation were also stored on my home computer. Every evening, thoughout the trial, I'd returned home and made detailed notes in Word. In order to carry out any constructive work I was going to need the machine brought into the prison and that would necessitate a visit to Mr Hammond, my wing PO.

A visit to Mr Hammond was not going to be fun, but I knew I had to get his approval before I would be allowed to have the machine. Over the years Hammond had curried favour with those in power and had himself risen high within the prison hierarchy. At Ford he wielded considerable power, ever watchful, always listening, and a manila P16 file on every inmate. Officialdom at Ford quickly formed opinions and compiled files often based on little or no knowledge of the facts.

He sat behind a desk organised with military precision, his lips pursed spitefully. He studied me with sceptical grey blue eyes through wire-rimmed spectacles. His air of disdainful impatience threatened to overwhelm me as I entered the cramped room. Hammond was known to be the most difficult screw in Ford, a man who loved to operate by the book, when it suited him. 'What do you want?'

'You asked to see me Mr Hammond.'

'No. You asked to see me.'

'Oh, it was about bringing in my computer.'

The fierce grey blue eyes glared as he scanned my application, the face barely able to contain its anger. He rose from his chair and removed his glasses. I watched his face carefully; the only emotion was one of hostility and bitterness. He glared again. 'You want what?'

'My computer Mr Hammond, if it's possible? I need it so I can deal with my appeal.'

'Your computer?'

'Yes, if that's allowed.'

'This isn't a bloody holiday camp Middleton. Why do you need a computer?'

I pondered what to say next. Matthew had guided me to a relevant Standing Order in the prison library. 'There's a restriction on legal files brought into Ford; the six-inch rule? A lot of it is on my computer and I need to access my notes from the trial and some letters. I need access to it for my appeal. I understand Standing Order 16, subsection 7 allows an inmate necessary equipment and facilities to be brought into the Prison if he is conducting his own defence.'

Hammond looked up from his desk, clearly surprised by my knowledge of prison standing orders. He had been taken momentarily off guard but he quickly recovered his composure. 'Regulations also state that you can't have any mains-operated electrical equipment unless you are in single room accommodation.'

'Could I bring in a battery-operated laptop?'

Hammond's eyes narrowed and focused on a file of Home Office regulations sitting on his desk. He slowly flicked through a few pages of text. The face turned into a wistful scowl. 'Yes. Yes you can. Providing you don't have a charger.'

'But how do I recharge the batteries?'

The eyebrows flashed above the wire rims and he inclined his head as though pondering an immense problem. 'Regulations state that you can't have any mains-operated electrical equipment unless you are in single room accommodation, so you don't.'

'But that's ridiculous!'

'That's the rules, now shut up and get out.' The meeting had lasted no more than five minutes. I left the office as thousands of others had done before, with anger and fury engulfing me. Hammond made you try to squeeze your case into no more than a dozen words which amounted to the upper limit of his thought process. When you couldn't do it, he ridiculed you and refused your request.

It took three months of bureaucracy, applications, meetings with senior officers and two governors before the request for my computer was finally approved. I could at last get on with trying to sort out the muddled mess that was once my life.

I switched on the computer and waited as the machine whirred and clicked its way through its boot up routine. A few minutes later, accompanied by the Windows fanfare, a familiar picture appeared on the screen, a picture I'd saved as the background: Beth and the boys, a holiday picture taken in Thailand. I smiled at the memory and blew a kiss to the screen. I placed my fingers on the keyboard. *Okay, let's go*, I told myself.

Clicking my way through the various icons and files, I made my way to a Word document I'd named 'File 1092', the number representing the date the whole nightmare began; October 1992. I clicked on the file icon. Inside, I'd recorded my daily notes of the events as they'd unfolded, a complete sequence of events, everything from the time the tabloid article appeared '*WPA Bank pays racing driver...*', to the trial itself, including the more bizarre comments from the judge and the times he'd conveyed such clear facial expressions to the jury, the meetings without the stenographer, and of course all the mistakes I could remember during his summing up.

Within weeks of receiving my computer, the first draft of the appeal was complete. I was pleased with it, the first constructive work I had produced in months. The typing was neat, the phrasing concise, but as always, misspelled. After fifteen years in the highly litigious world of professional motor racing I was fluent in 'contractual speak'. But it was only the first step, there was much more work that still needed to be done. For that, I needed Piglet.

I entered the B Wing block and made my way to see the screw behind the glass sliding hatch in the office. 'I need to make a phone call to my solicitor.' The telephone by the officer's side erupted and he plucked it from the cradle at the first ring. I waited whilst he completed the call.

'Middleton, you still here? What is it?' I repeated my request and went on to explain how it was impossible to make the necessary legal calls on the open inmates' card phone. 'A single prison phone card costs two pounds and lasts for a few minutes. I'm only earning five pounds a week!'

Beth and the boys were surviving on eleven pounds a week income support and donations from the Salvation Army, yet despite our financial status I was being refused all requests for legal aid. The officer shook his head as though appreciating the immensity of the problem. 'You've got no legal aid because you were out of time with your appeal. You'll need to complete an application.'

'An application?'

'Yes. A Miscellaneous Applications Form. Fill it in explaining exactly why you want to speak to your solicitor.'

'Well, it's quite complicated,' I began. 'I need to speak to him about my appeal.' The officer did not look impressed and again his telephone erupted. This time he closed the sliding glass window, isolating him from curious ears. I waited until he had finished the call. He slid open the glass. 'Right, have you completed the form?'

'You didn't give me one.'

'Oh, aren't there any in the rack?' He pointed to a crude wooden rack attached to the wall.

'No, it's empty.'

'Oh well, you'll have to come back in the morning. We're short-staffed at the moment. I haven't got time to copy any more until later.'

The following day, trying hard to hide my annoyance, I returned to the office and repeated my request to the duty officer. This time I added that I understood I was required to complete a Miscellaneous Applications Form. The officer shook his head gravely. 'No, no, not a Miscellaneous App. You want a Legal Aid App.'

'A Legal Aid App? But I'm not applying for legal aid.'

He looked at me blankly. 'A Legal Aid App doesn't have anything to do with legal aid. It's an application for legal assistance.'

'Oh, I see.'

The officer was already fumbling in a drawer for the necessary paperwork. He retrieved an A4 photocopied sheet, folded it in two producing a sharp crease line, then using the side of the desk as a guide, tore the paper in half, producing a pair of Legal Aid Applications. He handed over one of the halves with a flourish.

'Fill it in with your name, number, hut location and place of work. Then give brief details of why you need to speak to your solicitor. When you've completed the form, return it to the B Wing office before 08.30 tomorrow and I'll get you up in front of the SO.'

'I'm sorry, the SO?'

'The Senior Officer. He'll review your request.'

'Will I be able to make the call then?'

'Oh, no,' he looked at me as though unable to comprehend my ignorance. 'After the SO's reviewed your request, and assuming he agrees it's valid, he'll put you before the Governor.'

Surprised by the complex and protracted process of trying to make a phone call, I hesitated for a moment. 'Why do I need to see the Governor?'

'Standing orders!' The telephone by his side rang and he snatched it from the cradle. I completed the application and handed back the form, not bothering to enquire further into the relevance of the Standing Orders.

Once off the phone, the officer inspected the completed paperwork, and then posted it into a pigeonhole for further processing.

The following morning I received a call up slip to see a senior officer at 09.30. I made my way to the Education Office to collect a movement slip which allowed me to walk the two hundred yards to the B Wing office. I pushed open the door and joined the queue of men waiting in line by the hatch. Ten minutes later I reached the hatch and handed in my call up slip. 'Ah, Middleton, you're late!' He studied his watch. 'It's 09.40, you're supposed to have been here by 09.30. You'll have to wait.'

An hour passed and finally I was called into a tiny room where an officer in a peaked cap sat hunched behind a small desk. 'Right, Middleton, what do you want?' Thinking I was beginning to sound like a tape recording, I repeated my request once again. The officer listened gravely to what I had to say, making notes every so often. 'Right, well I don't have the authority to approve your request but I'll put you before the Governor tomorrow at 10.30. Okay?'

Trying hard to control my frustration, I enquired, 'Will I be able to make the phone call tomorrow?'

He shook his head gravely. 'That's a matter for the Governor.

314

Recommendation 52 of the Woodcock Report only allows phone calls of an urgent nature to be made to legal advisers.'

'But this is urgent. I'm trying to prepare my appeal!'

'Well, these things are always urgent Middleton. You'll have to take it up with the Governor tomorrow.'

The following day I again received a call up slip. I quickly obtained the mandatory movements slip from the Education Department and made my way over to B Wing. It was 10.25 am. 'Right, Middleton, the Governor's not in today but you're going to see the Deputy, Mr Evans. He's tied up at the moment. Take a seat in the hall.' Trying hard to contain my growing exasperation, I slumped down in the hallway and waited.

One and a half hours later I was summoned by Mr Evans, the Duty Governor. He was a heavily overweight man with a corpulent face and a flabby chest resting on a well-developed beer gut.

'Right, I see you've made a request for a legal telephone call.' He opened a red book with podgy fingers and began scribbling an entry. For the officers, paperwork was a way of life, but for me it was a means of frustration and delay. He looked up, blinking several times as he re-focused his view. 'Now, what's the purpose of the call?'

I accept that perhaps I'm not the most patient person in the world but prior to being snared in the quagmire of bureaucracy, I had never before seriously considered violence.

Twenty minutes later, and in a state of shocked disbelief, I left the Duty Governor's office with a signed authority to make a *single* legal telephone call to Piglet. So far it had taken almost a week to reach this point.

That afternoon I collected a fresh movement slip from the Education Department and set off for the Legal Aid Office. Sitting behind the Legal Aid Office desk engrossed in a copy of the *Sun* was the officer that I'd seen a week earlier.

'Middleton. What do you want?'

'I've come to make a phone call to my solicitor.'

The officer studied me gravely. 'I told you last week, you'll have to put in an application to B Wing first.'

'I've already done that. I saw you at the beginning of the week. I've seen SOs, Duty Governors, I've filled in bloody forms! What the hell else am I supposed to do?'

'Don't get on your 'igh 'orse with me son or you won't be

315

phoning anyone!' He put down his copy of the *Sun*. 'I'm far too busy to organise inmate phone calls today. Come back tomorrow at 10.30.'

The following day was a Saturday so both my solicitors and the Legal Aid Office were closed. However, two days later my persistence was finally rewarded with the long-awaited call.

'Hello, this is Will Middleton, I'm phoning from HMP Ford, can I speak to Jonathan Barker?'

'I'm sorry, he's in a meeting at the moment. Can you call back in 15 minutes?'

I placed a hand over the mouthpiece to speak to the officer, who was busily working his way through a mountain of freshly buttered toast. 'Can I call them back in fifteen minutes? My solicitor is tied up in a meeting.' The officer shook his head solemnly, as though he truly felt for my predicament.

'Sorry son, you'll have to put in a fresh application and see the SO tomorrow.'

Another week and three more meetings later, clutching a fresh movement slip, I made my way to the Legal Aid office and resignedly pushed open the door to the sound of angry raised voices.

'I put in a fucking application last fucking week!' It was Jack and he was clearly in a more agitated state than usual. 'Try filing this, you dumb fuck!' Without further warning he forcefully drove his forehead into the bridge of the screw's nose. Something cracked loudly accompanied by a spray of blood. The officer cried out in pain and dropped his buttered toast. Suddenly all hell let loose, tables and chairs overturned. Two more screws appeared from nowhere and sirens sounded.

'Back off and put your hands against the wall!' one yelled.

'Assholes,' Jack replied as further reinforcements arrived.

In a sudden blur of movement Jack was charged by five screws; one kicking his legs from under him as two more spun him around, pounding his forehead down into the concrete floor with a force that would split a watermelon.

He lay there, stunned, pinned senselessly to the floor, legs splayed, gasping for breaths of air between deep feral growls of anger. One of the screws knelt down, cuffing Jack's hands behind his back. The screw with the freshly broken nose strode over and without saying a word, forcefully drove a size twelve boot directly between Jacks splayed legs. Jack gasped in pain, and then faded into unconsciousness. The screw turned to face me, a steady drip of blood still flowing from his nostrils. 'Oh, Middleton, come to make a fresh application?'

Jack was sent to the block and then shipped out to Wandsworth the next day; I would never see him again. It would be at least another couple of years before he'd be given another chance in an open prison.

Over the months that followed, I watched as other inmates ranted and raged against the system, and as the seasons rolled by, the mind games ground on mercilessly. Some inmates lost it like Jack, others caved in and gave up. Occasionally I'd be permitted legal access, usually not, but unlike the other inmates, I conceived a plan. The time had come to play by the rules, their rules.

As the time went by, I recorded each and every application made, along with the times and dates and the names of the officers giving me the run around. For months I just smiled, or responded with nothing more than a hapless shrug as each rejection was handed out. For six months I retained each unused application and held on to every movement slip. Cross-referencing everything to the prison rules, I filed a report to the Prison Ombudsman, with copies to my MP and the Prison Board of Visitors. The report made its way early one evening over the fence and into Beth's bicycle basket, to be safely posted the next day, free from prying eyes. An eight-month external investigation followed, finally upholding my complaint that the Prison Service was, for some reason, systematically delaying the preparation of my application to the Court of Appeal.

Within weeks of the outcome, an official letter of apology was received from Prison Service headquarters. Access would be made immediately to facilities required to prepare my appeal and phone access to my legal representatives would be reinstated. There had been a breakdown in communication, I was told, and Standing Order 16, subsection 7 had been misinterpreted. The entire system would be reviewed. The Prison Service was supposedly grateful that I had brought the matter to their attention.

From that day on I received no recriminations whatsoever by any of the screws and bizarrely most even started chatting to me and referring to me as Will. I had surmounted a major obstacle and, oddly, had somehow earned their respect.

55

The louder they talked of their honour, the faster we counted our spoons.

(Ralph Waldo Emerson, 1803–1882)

HMP Ford (B Wing Office), Littlehampton 26th March 1996, 5.45 pm

The last rays of daylight penetrated the barred window, casting shadows into the tiny office. On the rear wall, two shelves supported a collection of files and on a small table opposite, a computer screen blinked a security message. A light was switched on in the adjoining hallway illuminating the frosted glass of the door. The Governor rose from behind the tiny desk, unable to control his anger any longer.

I had been summoned for placing one of the stickers 'Will Middleton is innocent' on the back of my prison jacket. However, Mr Richards, the Governor had not been entirely convinced of the assertion. The piercing blue eyes regarded me through gold-rimmed frames, the darkness beneath bearing testimony to the rigors of the last two hours of mental chess we had just played.

He was in his mid fifties, five foot eight, and beginning to run to fat. He sported a carefully trimmed greying beard giving him the appearance of the sailor on the famous cigarette pack. 'Where did this sticker come from?' he demanded.

'They're being made up by one of my former sponsors. The company that used to manufacture all the graphics for the race cars. People are apparently sticking them on the backs of their cars,' I replied.

He shook his head, searching for an appropriate response. 'The laws of this land determined that you were to lose your liberty Middleton. I was not party to that decision, my job is simply to incarcerate you. That is my job. We don't have the time, man power or resources to deal with all this. Is that clear?'

319

He studied his watch to indicate that the meeting had come to an end. 'Take this as a warning Middleton. If you continue to ride your little hobby horse at this pace you're likely to come a cropper. Okay?'

I felt like a schoolboy being given a dressing down by the headmaster. I said nothing. My fight against the system was beginning to draw attention, both in Ford and outside, and the system clearly didn't like it.

'You've been under considerable stress; we may have to re-evaluate your suitability for open conditions. Is that clear?'

What was clear was that this was a threat, either shut up and stop rocking the boat or you'll be shipped back to Wandsworth. I would redouble my efforts, of that there was no doubt and he knew it. I'd had the temerity to complain and my approach had finally hit a nerve.

I tried to look behind the face of the man shaking with anger before me. In another setting we'd probably have got on well, may even have been friends, but here he was the governor and I was a convicted prisoner. My complaints had finally reached the top and he clearly considered them a threat to his administration. 'I don't want to hear any more complaints, is that clear?'

I stepped out of the office and wandered back to my room, my mind retracing the meeting. I looked out of the window and across the camp. In the glass the hint of a smile played across my lips. Perhaps I was beginning to break through. Perhaps...

I was summoned to the SO's office, 'Right. Middleton. You've been summoned to appear in the London High Court tomorrow concerning the disposal of certain assets. Some Indy Cars, whatever they are. You will report to the discharge officer immediately to sign your licence. Your solicitor has already been informed.' It was 4.45 pm. I'd been given only fifteen minutes' notice of the following day's hearing.

The Reception Officer went through all the usual formalities prior to placing the licence before me for signature. 'Sign 'ere, 'ere and 'ere,' he indicated with the tip of a biro. I leaned forward to read the document with eyes dull with frustration, close to submission.

'It says I'm to be released at 08.30 tomorrow to catch the 09.15 train from Ford.'

The officer studied me gravely. 'Just sign.'

'But if I'm to catch the 09.15 train I won't get to Victoria until around 11.00. I'm supposed to be at court by 10.30 and I've got to speak to my barrister first.'

He looked at me blankly. 'That's not your problem. Just sign.' Again he tapped the page with his biro.

'It will be my problem if I lose the hearing because I arrive late. It'll be midday before I get to court!'

'That's not your problem. The timing has been set by the prison admin. If it's wrong, it's not your fault, it'll be down to the Governor.'

'But...'

'Do you want to go or not?' He again gestured to the licence.

There was little point in discussing it further. He was after all just a foot soldier, capable of only re-issuing instructions. If I argued, he was more likely to have the licence rescinded altogether. I signed in the sections indicated. 'Right, report for discharge tomorrow at 08.30.'

56

Truth is more of a stranger than fiction.

(Mark Twain, 1835–1910)

An aggressive cloud chased angrily across the sky as I strode meaningfully up the Ford Road in the direction of the little country station. A chill wind swirled empty crisp packets, cola tins and litter into unruly piles. The summer of 96 seemed to have been a non-event; soon it would be turning to autumn.

I boarded the train and it slid gently from the shadows of the station. Several people were still finding their seats or storing their luggage in the overhead racks. A few struggled along the narrow corridor with heavy cases, swaying as the train gathered speed. A disembodied voice announced that we were on board the 09.15 for Victoria and went on to confirm my fears that we would be stopping at just about every station this side of London, before finally arriving in the city at 10.46, a quarter of an hour after I was supposed to be in court.

I sat and watched the Sussex countryside flash past on either side and listened to the normal everyday chatter of the passengers. Suddenly I became acutely aware of a familiar voice a few seats ahead. A dozen thoughts rushed through my brain: *Was it him? Surely not. What a coincidence! Should I talk to him?*

His voice had been raised in convivial banter, but it died away as I stepped forward. 'Good morning Mr Banister,' I said, 'how are you?'

My former osteopath, the man I'd paid thousands of pounds to for treatment following the riding accident, the man who had been due to give important evidence in my defence prior to reading the newspaper coverage of the trial, stared up at me uncomprehendingly. He was clearly embarrassed and did not know quite how to respond. I continued, 'You appreciate that the tabloid coverage was a total fiction?'

322

It was meant as a rhetorical question but he answered anyway. At least he attempted and succeeded in finding some words. 'Oh, yes, well I took no notice of that. How are you these days?'

'Oh, I'm wonderful,' I continued dryly. 'I'm still stuck in Ford as a convicted criminal, but I'm persevering, still trying to prove my innocence.' His colleague appeared shocked. He was in the presence of a convict. A man that was serving time or possibly even worse might have escaped from prison. He embraced his briefcase as though preparing to run at a moment's notice. Mr Banister, on the other hand, appeared to sink deeper into embarrassment.

'Why did you decide against giving evidence at my trial?' I continued. 'What the papers printed amounted to nothing more than a summary of the Prosecution's case. It was total garbage. You simply accepted everything at face value, yet you had treated my injuries since the accident back in 1988. That would have been critical evidence.'

'I told your solicitor I'd still give evidence. I think, er, I think there was just some confusion.' The train juddered to a halt. 'Good heavens, Gatwick!' Banister announced to anyone that could hear, 'We have to get off here. You'll have to excuse me.' He rose and left quickly.

A feeling of anger swept through me as I watched Mr Banister through the carriage window. The wheels began to turn and the train shuffled forward. Clearly uncomfortable from his unexpected encounter, he did not look back. The platform slid slowly past and the train sped on. Forty minutes later we arrived at Victoria.

It had been three years since I'd had a carefree trip to the City. I'd been with Beth then and she'd been like an excited kid, keen to take in all the sights, to feed the pigeons, visit the museum and buy some little nick nack from Harrods that would bring with it the obligatory green bag. That was a lifetime ago, this was today. I checked my watch, it was almost 11.00. I was already half an hour late and I had yet to get across London to the High Court.

I made my way down into the underground, purchased a ticket with all that remained of the three pounds provided by the prison and boarded a carriage. An insurance poster depicting a happy smiling family enquired whether I was well covered. I cursed it silently. I left the underground at Bank, dodging and weaving my way through the heavy jumble of London traffic to the High Court.

Paterson-Smythe was engaged elsewhere on more weighty matters of law, so it was a tall bewigged figure by the name of Jefferson Lumley who stood majestically before the Learned and Honourable Judge Peregrine Fairchild-Brown.

I bowed my head, as I had learned is the custom, as I entered Court Number Eighteen. The court was quite different from that of my trial; smaller, more airy and there was no dock. There was even a large window that appeared to overlook a small courtyard. It was still, however, just another court which seemed to exude gloom. I paused, looking around the room, and considered the events that had been absorbed into the very fabric of the place.

I edged my way along the narrow row of seats. His Honour was seated high on his bench, giving us the full benefit of a rewarding view. He was heavily built with rounded shoulders over which draped his black robes. His head was crested with customary horsehair. His nose was beaky and his jowls hung heavily. He looked down from his high perch like a buzzard surveying its next meal.

I lowered myself into a vacant seat, conscious that I was being studied by this new judge who appeared to pity me for my lack of punctuality. Jefferson Lumley was already on his feet and reciting from a heavy volume. Tigger was seated on the row ahead of me. He turned and beamed a smile of welcome. 'Hello Will!' He spoke in a hushed tone, in keeping with the occasion. 'You're looking very well, must be all that prison food.'

'Yes, I've never felt better,' I replied wryly. 'The damn prison wouldn't let me out any earlier. I've got loads of notes that I need to go through with you.'

'Oh, there's not going to be time for any of that, but don't worry, I think we're really onto a winner this time. I've found a precedent.' Piglet leaned over, smiling and added, 'This judge is very good, very fair. I don't think we've anything to worry about.'

I glanced over Tigger's head at His Honour who was excitedly noting Jefferson Lumley's every word. The learned barrister closed and replaced the volume on the table, before continuing, 'So you see Your Honour, we are most concerned over the Defendant's failure to prepare his appeal in a timely manner, and of course, whilst we wait, the Indy cars are depreciating in value.'

His Honour looked up from his legal pad. 'So you are asking me for an order permitting the Crown to dispose of these,' he scanned his legal pad, 'these *Indy* cars?'

'Yes indeed Your Honour.'

'When is the appeal listed for?'

'I'm not sure that a date has even been set yet Your Honour.'

Peregrine Fairchild-Brown inclined his head hopefully in the direction of Tigger who rose enthusiatically to add a meaningful contribution to the debate. 'Perhaps I could assist Your Honour.' Jefferson Lumley rewound himself into the confines of his bench. 'We are expecting to be listed for the autumn your Honour.'

Fairchild-Brown raised an eyebrow of consternation. 'The autumn! Do you mean to say you do not yet have a firm fixture?'

'I'm afraid not Your Honour. My client has instructed Senior Counsel, Mr Michael Bamforth QC to represent him. My understanding is that Mr Bamforth is fully booked up until the end of October at the earliest.'

'Oh, Mr Bamforth.' His Honour seemed impressed with my choice of new counsel. 'This is still most unsatisfactory. I assume you are objecting to the disposal of these,' the learned judge again studied his legal pad, 'Indy cars?'

'Yes indeed Your Honour.' Tigger pointed out that, far from depreciating, the Indy cars had in fact increased in value, a number of similar examples having just changed hands for more than $100,000 each. Trans-Atlantic had paid little more than $131,000 of the Prize Indemnity proceeds for both cars, which meant that the Lolas had increased in value by over 52 per cent. 'Furthermore Your Honour, the Indy cars will be required as important exhibits, should the appeal be successful and a retrial ordered.' Peregrine Fairchild-Brown made a note. Tigger went on to point out that perhaps another motive might exist for the Crown's sudden interest in disposing of the team's assets.

'Perhaps I could draw your attention to a few documents Your Honour. You will see that until recently the cost of storing the Indy cars, some £4,000 to date, was being met by the insurance companies. Approximately eight weeks ago you will see that they advised they would no longer continue to pay the storage fees. It was only then that the Metropolitan Police, upon whom

325

responsibility fell to store the cars, applied to Your Honour for permission to dispose of the assets.'

Jefferson Lumley unwound himself like some rare breed of silver-crested stick insect and, once on his feet, asserted most sincerely that this detail was purely circumstantial, coincidental and entirely innocuous. The Metropolitan Police were only attempting to act to the benefit of everyone concerned. His Honour seemed happy with this pleasing interpretation of events and made a detailed note of Mr Lumley's proclamation.

I watched in silence as another pantomime was enacted before me. Powerful bewigged men, in long flowing robes. Men who knew nothing of the world of motorsport nodded knowledgeably, with satisfied understanding, as they considered the merits of selling or retaining Trans-Atlantic's assets, their lack of knowledge disguised within a neat package of reasoned logic, logic that was based on incorrect assumptions and distorted facts.

A beam of sunlight filtered in through the tall mullioned window, casting intense rays of light into the gloom of the court. Tiny particles of dust swirled and danced in the beams as the learned men, garbed in their academic robes of office, rose and descended on their judicial seesaw. I remained silent, absorbed in thought as I listened to them discussing my former life; a life before the legal labyrinth had shattered my belief in justice. It all seemed so unreal and yet so familiar, as though my final racing season had ended only a week earlier, every detail of it still so clear in my memory.

Tuscany, northern Italy, June 1993, Mugello International Raceway

The air was still and the sky blue. Sun baked the stationary traffic that backed up for more than four miles. We'd left the hotel at 6 am to travel the short distance to the track for the team's first race. A sea of humanity swarmed into the vast stadium. Thousands of men, women, and children, all fighting to enter the high-octane, high-pressure glamour world. I made my way directly to the paddock, the inner sanctum, the place where the mass would like to be but from which they were banned. A place inhabited by team managers, engineers, sponsors and marketing men; the most expensive camp-site imaginable, filled with exotic machinery, team transporters and motor homes where tactics would be planned and deals struck.

People say racing drivers are mad: why hurtle round and round a track at breakneck speeds? To me, sanity lay in driving racing cars, not with dusty lawyers. Racing was what I did to earn my living, to pay the bills. Perhaps after the police raids and the pending trial, I was not acting rationally. But what the hell, I thought. I have to earn a living – I was no longer eligible for unemployment benefit, WPA had stopped all payments, and the bank had threatened to foreclose. But the new team was ready to go. Maybe with hindsight I shouldn't have, but against medical advice, and in the turmoil of the investigation, I persuaded my doctor to sign my race licence enabling me to take part in the 1993 season. I also needed somewhere to focus my mind and in that respect racing would be therapeutic. It made me feel of some use and for a short time raised my self esteem. I knew it would be more than a year before the Prosecution were ready for trial; if indeed the case ever got to court.

I did not consider for one moment just how a jury of my peers would react, or for that matter how the tabloid press would narrate my actions: *A racing driver fit enough to drive a 240 mph Indy car claimed more than £40,000 from insurance companies for being permanently disabled... Will Middleton swindled insurance companies out of £40,000 by falsely claiming he was too ill to drive after hurting his back... The trial heard he was fit enough to drive a 240 mph Indy car yet claimed more than £48,000 from his insurers.* It had been like having your name misspelt by *Readers Digest*; no matter how often one explained the true sequence of events and the reason I'd returned to racing, the next day another article would appear with the figures inflated even further.

The figures continued to rise like an express elevator, £40,000, £48,000. On the night after sentencing, one full page story had the sums increasing to a staggering £400,000. Humanity is fickle; it seems to derive perverse pleasure in bringing down and causing pain. All I had tried to do was to pay the mortgage and take care of Beth and the children.

The concept of racing Indy cars in Europe was unusual. It wasn't unique, however. Indy cars had last raced in Britain in the late seventies at Brands Hatch, the event being so successful that the 1.2 mile track was renamed 'The Indy Circuit'.

It is generally believed that Indy cars originate from America. In truth, Indy cars, in common with most racing cars, are manufactured in the UK. Despite looking similar to a Formula One car, an Indy car is an entirely different animal. For a start they weigh some 300 lb more. The chassis are manufactured from a combination of carbon fibre and aluminium. The engines are turbocharged and run on pure alcohol rather than petrol which they consume at more than one gallon every two miles. The engines produce around 200 horsepower more on full boost than a current specification Formula One engine and the aerodynamics create sufficient ground effect, at 200 mph, to allow it to run, theoretically, upside down along the roof of the Channel tunnel.

I swallowed a couple more dihydrocodeine and lowered myself carefully into the seat that had been moulded into a precise imprint of my back, twinges of pain reminding me of my GP's warning. I pulled the helmet over my head and the hubbub of the track mixed with the distant buzz of the painkillers.

Simon, the new team manager, wandered over and helped strap me in. 'Now, you're going to find this thing very different to anything else you've ever driven, Will.' I knew what was coming next but the words were drowned out by the prolonged howl of a racing engine strained to the limit.

My adrenalin pump switched to full boost. I grinned. I loved the sounds, the smells, the excitement and anticipation; a million miles from crusty lawyers, police officers, insurance companies and their armies of private detectives. Simon was gesticulating. I nodded in strict approval of whatever his lips were saying, but heard nothing. A blue and white flash blurred past; car number 21, Trans-Atlantic's third entry for the 1993 season. The car driven by Les Heath, Prize Indemnity broker; the entry the judge would prevent the jury from ever knowing existed, the aptly named Scorpion.

Simon stepped to the front of the car and indicated to two mechanics at the back. The engine coughed, fired, then rumbled into life. At low speed an Indy car engine sounds more like a cement mixer than a piece of highly tuned exotica, but lift the revs and a metamorphosis occurs. The sound transforms into a symphony. I selected first gear, raised the revs to 4000, and exited the pit lane leaving 100 yards of Goodyear bubbling on the asphalt.

The purpose of 'first practice' is to set the car up, to 'dial in' the correct settings of which a racing car has an infinite number: springs, ride heights, gear ratios, cambers, roll, dampers, wings and each time one is changed, it influences the others. If the car is not correctly 'dialled in', it will probably not even qualify for the back of the grid.

The track temperature had risen into the mid eighties and the surface danced in a glittering haze of eddies as I eased the Lola onto the four miles of Tuscany tarmac and through the first corner. With rigid suspension designed to contend with up to three tons of downforce, the car felt nervous and the pounding jarred the broken bones in my back. I was thankful for the dihydrocodeine. I snaked the car from side to side, quickly working the Goodyears up to optimum temperature. I completed a lap. Everything was up to working temperature, but the engine wasn't pulling properly and the car still felt nervous; vibrating and pulling badly under braking. I eased the Lola through the sweeping left-hander, up through the gears and into the pit straight, flat out, 10,500 revs, and fifth gear.

Simon held out a black and yellow pit board indicating L4 in white letters (four laps remaining). The surface flashed like granite and the track's features blurred as the massive Garrett turbo kicked in, punching the Lola into hyperdrive, leaving a trail of acrid burnt methanol in my wake. Forty-five inches of boost registered on the turbo gauge. The hundred-metre board flashed past and I exploded onto the brakes. The Goodyears peeled off tarmac; sparks erupted from the skid blocks, my body weight multiplying four fold as the car snaked violently to the left. For a microsecond I fought for control as the car rebelled like a wilful child desperate to go its own way but not knowing quite where that should be. I flicked down two gears, aimed the nose at the apex and floored the throttle. The Buick coughed, died, then refired.

Something was wrong; electrics, fuel, a valve? The Buick motors cost around £35,000 each, and they didn't come with a guarantee. Trans-Atlantic had purchased three engines for the full season and we couldn't afford to kiss one goodbye this early.

I fought my way through the first corner and clicked off two inches of boost, corresponding to a reduction of around 40 horsepower. Gianni Lavaggi flashed past in the Kremer CK7 Spyder, turbulent air boiling from the massive rear wing, the shockwaves of the displaced air hitting my helmet like powerful head blows from a boxer. Miniature explosive blasts trailed like sonic booms as the CK7's turbo waste gates opened to relieve the excess pressure from the Porsche's flat-six engine.

The Buick engine coughed and the Lola bucked violently, the rear wheels kicking with the power of 800 horses. Something was definitely wrong. It coughed again, then cleared, and in less than a second another hundred metres of tarmac blurred beneath me at hyper speed. Again the Buick bucked. This time Rob's Lola dodged past and in the moment's lull before my engine re-fired, it sounded as if his engine was also misfiring.

I eased off the power, coasted into the pits and released my belts. Simon's face appeared in front of me. 'What's wrong?'

I continued easing myself painfully from the cramped cockpit. 'I don't know, but whatever it is, Rob's got the same problem. It could be electrics or fuel, but the actual fuel pressure's registering okay.' I stepped from the cockpit, having completed only three laps, yet my lower back already felt as though it had been worked over by a pneumatic hammer, and again, my right leg had gone to sleep.

Rob coasted into the pits, the only sound from his dead engine the gentle pinging of superheated metal. He released his belts and jumped from the cockpit. 'Misfire?' I enquired casually. The pings subsided like the final clicks of a wind-up toy.

Suddenly and without further warning, there was a searing flash of blue flame followed by a blast of expanding gas, *whummmp!* The sound erupted like a muted thunderclap. There was a moment's shocked hesitation before the commotion ensued. Flames were taking hold of the rear of Rob's Lola. Simon ran to the pit garage, reappearing seconds later followed by two mechanics with extinguishers. The flames were doused and the car saved, but within an hour methanol was also seeping from the underside of my Lola.

Toluene had mysteriously found its way into the 400 gallons of methanol delivered to Italy exclusively for the Trans-Atlantic team. From the moment the first molecules had flown through the system it had began attacking gaskets, fuel lines, ejectors, ravenously consuming the car's rubber fuel cell.

The mechanics backed both cars into the Trans-Atlantic garage. The debut of the Team Lola Buicks was postponed, as Les climbed into the Scorpion's cockpit, preparing to represent the team as its only remaining entry.

Four weeks later on a wet Czechoslovakian circuit south of Prague, the team's Lolas, equipped with new £2000 fuel systems, were fired up in anger but to little effect. Amid the build-up to the trial, strange rumours had started to circulate and sponsors were beginning to withdraw, money was becoming tight. In the race I suffered a heart-stopping wheel rim failure at over a hundred and eighty miles an hour. Rob suffered a high-speed collision with Ralph Goetz's March and ended up in the gravel trap. In the race, despite clutch failure, he went on to finish fifth; I managed a seventh, following the unscheduled pit stop. Les failed to finish.

57

I was brought back to the present by the sound of His Honour Peregrine Fairchild-Brown shuffling his papers, preparing to treat his audience to a little recital. I raised my eyes to the honourable judge as he began to speak.

'I have listened in detail to the submissions of both the Crown and the Defence. The Crown asserts that the Lola Indy cars are depreciating in value, the Defendant has advised the reverse; that the cars are in fact increasing in value and might be required for any retrial. I have seen no evidence from either side to support these submissions. I have however noted that the Metropolitan Police have to store these cars at public expense. I therefore direct that the Lola Indy cars will be sold by a court-appointed receiver and the proceeds placed into a neutral interest-bearing account pending the outcome of any appeal.'

Leaden rain swept the carriage window and for the first thirty minutes of the return journey I remained absorbed in Wilbur Smith's *River God*. A voice came from somewhere above my head. I lowered the book and looked up into the hovering face that had addressed me. A pair of deepset eyes sparkled from beneath a peaked cap. 'Ticket please sir.' I fished in a pocket, located and handed over the travel warrant. The eyes scanned the voucher, sparkling with new intensity. 'Invalid sir.'

'I'm sorry?'

'Invalid,' he repeated curtly and with a notable degree of satisfaction. A few curious noses appeared from behind newsprint. 'This warrant was issued for use two days ago, on the 8th of July. You'll have to buy a fresh ticket.'

'But, I don't have any money!'

'I'm afraid that's not my problem sir. If you've come out without the means to pay you'll have to get off the train.' There followed an uneasy silence whilst I contemplated what to do next.

Earlier that morning, when I'd arrived at Ford station, the ticket office had been closed so the travel warrant went unchecked. Fortunately there hadn't been a check on the outward run to Victoria. Had there been one, clearly I would not have reached the court at all. Could this be just another fluke in a long line of coincidences? The Crown had provided the ticket, how could they have provided a ticket for the wrong date? A date that was two days prior to being informed of the hearing.

I'd pointed out the error in their original timing, but the prison had insisted I follow their instructions and arrive late at court. And the judge, in full knowledge that an appeal was pending, had just sanctioned the disposal of two pieces of key evidence, ensuring there could never be a re-trial. That is, if I ever won the appeal. Was I never intended to get to the hearing? Had it already been decided that there wouldn't be a full appeal?

Dejectedly I left the train at the next stop and wandered aimlessly around waiting for the next one to arrive. Forty-five minutes later the stopping train to Portsmouth pulled in. I made my way to the toilet compartment, where I sat in hiding for the remainder of the journey.

Darkness crept around me like a cloak as I stepped from the warmth of the train and out into the wet greyness of the platform. It was now past six, and a fifteen-minute walk lay between the station and the prison. I had to be back by six at the latest. I turned from the platform onto the Ford road, my mind still alternating between the farce of the courtroom and the seemingly endless bureaucracy of the prison system. 'Bastards!' I cursed out loud.

A heavy lorry rumbled past, throwing up dense clouds of rain and exhaust, the acrid odour of diesel trailing in a plume of spray. Rain pelted against my head, trickled in rivulets down my face and dripped down the back of my neck. The only light came from the headlights of the passing cars, their beams dancing momentarily along the hedgerows lining the road. I lifted the collar of my overcoat and trudged on towards the prison.

Another car passed, its rear lights defusing in a red mist. As it passed, I recognised the silhouette of our old car disappearing into the greyness; it was Beth and the boys, but they hadn't noticed me. The wet, dark, greyness seemed to seep in with such intensity it felt as though it had physical presence. I felt so totally alone, isolated and rejected.

'You're late Middleton!' The officer regarded me sourly. 'You left the court at 14.15 this afternoon, we've checked.' He studied his watch. 'It's now 18.30.' I peeled off my sodden overcoat and fished inside the pocket for the travel warrant. 'You can explain yourself to the Governor tomorrow.'

I decided not to wait for the following day's inquisition and for the next fifteen minutes I outlined every detail of the past ten hours.

'Ah, well okay, I see.' He eyed me with uncertainty. This was the troublemaker, whose complaint to the Prison Ombudsman had just been upheld, triggering an eight-month external investigation. 'Well I'll speak to the Governor on your behalf. It must have been a mix up with admin. I expect you'll receive an apology.'

58

It was Saturday and a long, boring weekend lay ahead. Matthew and I were sitting around a low table on hard orange utilitarian seating, in the so called 'sitting room' of our hut on B Wing. The hut was one of the older prefabs, with a cigarette-burned tiled floor and grimy emulsioned walls that depressed me. 'So, somebody's going to pick up a bargain,' Matthew said as he got up and flicked on the kettle. 'Coffee?'

'Oh, yes please,' I replied, 'and yes, the cars will end up going for a song, and then being resold for their true value by some enterprising sod! The whole thing was a complete farce.'

Matthew opened a fresh pack of ground coffee and placed a filter into a cone, 'How strong do you like it?'

I eyed the foil pack in disbelief, 'Shit, is that real coffee?'

'Naturally, nothing but the best for my clients,' he joked.

'You didn't get that from the prison canteen, did you. I'll have as strong as you can make it; espresso strength.'

Matthew returned to the table with two mugs and a fresh pack of chocolate digestives. 'I get the occasional hamper from the Governor.' He gave me a knowing look, one that said, don't ask. 'Anyway,' he continued, using his best legal voice, 'why do you think they'd do that?'

I frowned. 'The whole thing has been a setup, from day one. The private detectives, the mistaken identity thing, the investigation, the trial, the bias of the trial judge and his "mistakes", the mind games in this fucking place! You know, in the beginning, the police even tried to get me to admit to fraud by suggesting they'd implicate Beth and get the kids put into care if I didn't comply. And what about yesterday's little blunder with the

335

mysteriously mistimed, incorrectly dated discharge licence and that travel warrant. That alone has cost the loss of the Indy cars and pretty much guaranteed that a re-trial will never take place.'

'Look, it's not that I don't believe you,' Matthew said, taking a sip of coffee, 'it's just that there are so many things that don't add up.'

'Such as what?'

'Okay,' he said, playing devil's advocate, 'Let's start with the riding accident. You say it took time for the full extent of the injury to come to light, but then, after you found out, you went back and raced the Indy cars. If you were injured to that extent, who in their right mind would get back into a racing car?'

'If?' I shot back, my voice thick with anger. 'Are you seriously doubting the extent of the injuries?'

'No, but the jury obviously did.' He sat back in his chair and began toying with a gold ring on the index finger of his right hand.

'The judge only allowed the surgeon a few minutes, the court was running late for afternoon tea!'

Matthew looked sceptical.

'Look, I'm not saying I'm different from anyone else,' I went on, 'perhaps just bloody minded. Maybe, being a racing driver, you look at things slightly differently. I didn't have a lot of choice, my insurers had stopped paying and the bank were threatening to foreclose. But the new team was there, set up and ready to go, so I drove. Maybe with hindsight that was a mistake, but it wasn't a crime.'

Outside the weather had begun to change. Wind rattled the ill-fitting windows and rain beat hard against the tin roof. 'Didn't you consider how a jury might react? Or the tabloid press?' Matthew asked.

'No,' I replied, wistfully, 'I seriously thought the case would be dropped. I never thought it would even get to trial, I was just was worried about money, I had to pay the bills, I had commitments, our home, my wife and the kids.'

'And your career?'

I shrugged. 'Yeah, I suppose. It was difficult to come to terms with the idea that it was all over. But how does that affect anything? It doesn't change the fact that the riding accident happened and I broke my back and I was insured. The most you can say was that maybe I was stupid to race again, not criminal.'

'As I said before, maybe they didn't consider the injury was serious.'

'Hell, I broke my back, Matthew! If the judge had allowed the surgeon to give his evidence, he'd have explained. Anyway, I'm seeing the guy soon, I'm going to ask him to do a letter to the Court of Appeal, explaining that he wasn't given time to present his evidence.'

Matthew sipped his coffee, then asked, 'He's coming here, to see you?'

'No, I'm being released to go to hospital for an operation on my spine. The hospital has already done the CAT scans; they've got a nice little picture of my broken vertebrae.'

'You're kidding! Who's paying?'

'It's being done on the National Health.'

Matthew shook his head in disbelief. 'You mean the prison is releasing you, for an operation on an injury that officially isn't supposed to exist?'

I nodded, smiling ruefully, 'Yeah, welcome to my Twilight Zone!'

Matthew's left hand absentmindedly delivered a chocolate digestive to his mouth and he munched silently for a moment. 'That is bizarre, totally bizarre!' Still mulling over what I had just said, he got up and went over to the kettle, refilled it and flicked it on. 'You want some more coffee?'

As the morning drifted towards the afternoon, we went over everything; from the first claim, following the riding accident, to the collapse of Team Capricorn, the Prize Indemnity and the BBC television programme 'Consumer Alert'. Finally, Matthew cleared his throat and leaned forward in his chair, toying again with his ring. 'You know what Sherlock Holmes said – *eliminate the impossible and whatever remains, no matter how improbable, has to be the truth.* I reckon you upset somebody at WPA, somebody with a lot of clout.' He stood up and stepped over to the window. 'I need some air,' he said, 'do you fancy a few laps of the camp?'

I shrugged, 'Whatever.' Glancing up at Matthew, I added, 'So, do you think the police were used?'

Matthew looked sceptical. 'Look, I've got to be honest. Sometimes you might get the odd police officer that is so convinced of someone's guilt that they might close their mind or ignore evidence that could prove innocence. But if that were to happen, it would very quickly be picked up by the trial judge.'

'What if the judge was persuaded to steer the case to a conviction?'

Matthew winced. 'That would never happen, not in this country.'

'Oh yes,' I said, a little too quickly, 'what about the Guildford four, or the Birmingham six or the Bentley case back in the sixties? And the dozens of cases, recent cases, that we now know were manipulated by both the police and the trial judges.'

'Mistakes,' he replied defensively. 'I told you before; it's generally accepted some four per cent of convictions may well be unsafe. That's what the appeals process is for.'

Reaching into my jacket pocket, I removed an envelope and handed it to Matthew. Have a look at this,' I said. 'It's a letter from my former co-driver, Rob Allan. It arrived shortly after I was sent here.'

I watched as Matthew flicked open the envelope and removed a single page of handwritten text and a photograph. He cast me an enquiring glance, and then started to read. The last of the rain pelted down onto the tin roof of the hut. Matthew finished reading and got up. He stepped over to the window. 'It's stopping, I think. We could stroll a few laps of the camp now if you like,' he said, almost absentmindedly, whilst still studying the letter. He remained silent for a few moments, and then returned to his seat.

Still deep in thought, he reached across the table, picked up the coffee pot and refilled our mugs. Finally he asked, 'What does he mean here, *I know what happened between you and Anna?*' Then, before I had time to answer, he added, 'Did you have some sort of affair, or something?'

'Something happened, that shouldn't have,' I said. 'Anna was his partner. But we didn't have an affair, exactly.'

'And this letter was sent to you in here, in prison by the chap that gave Crown evidence against you in your trial?'

'Yes.'

'Did this "non affair" come out in court?'

'No, nothing,' I said. 'What do you make of it?'

He didn't answer immediately, his eyes still alternating between the page and the photo, head shaking in disbelief. Then he looked up, set down the letter onto the table, and said, 'This

Rob Allan chap has worded this letter *very* carefully, but he's clearly telling you why he betrayed you in court. He's in effect saying it's because you betrayed him, with his Anna. The jury should have known about all this. Ignoring everything else you've told me, I think this letter alone is sufficient grounds for an appeal.'

I glanced down at Matthew's right hand. He was still toying with the gold ring on his index finger, slowly, subconsciously twisting the band this way and then that. It was something he tended to do when contemplating deeply. Suddenly with a shock of recognition, I noticed the symbol etched into its black onyx face; a compass and a square, the most revered of all Masonic symbols. 'Oh, yes, Matthew,' I said, 'I could do with a few laps.'

Overhead branches waved in the still high winds. A few broken branches had fallen and leaves lay stacked up in unruly piles where the winds had blown them. Climping beach was less than a mile from the camp and the air was thick with the pungent smell of the sea. 'We'll walk the perimeter, clockwise if you don't mind,' Matthew said. 'Sun wise.'

I'd heard that expression before somewhere, but for the moment it eluded me.

I didn't know how to ask. I couldn't just come straight out with it, so I rehearsed it in my mind, as we strolled around the camp – *So when did you first become a Mason, Matthew? How long have you been a Freemason? How come you ended up in prison if you're a barrister and a Freemason? – Matthew the Mason!* I chuckled to myself.

In the end, it was he that broke the silence. He'd obviously been mulling things over in his mind. 'So how did the toluene get into the methanol at Mugello?' he asked.

'Oh, that! Well, we never found out. We sent samples to a lab in the UK, when we returned. It was the lab that confirmed the methanol samples were loaded with toluene, but the actual suppliers insisted the methanol they'd shipped was 100% pure.'

'But somebody obviously put it in there.'

'Yeah, I suppose.'

'Somebody who knew the engines would run with toluene in

the mix for a time, but not at full power, somebody who wanted to influence the results.'

'We never gave it that much thought. The methanol had been shipped in massive metal barrels from the UK, direct from the supplier. Every barrel was contaminated with the stuff. We just assumed that it had somehow become spoiled. There was so much happening at that time; the investigation, the build up to the trial. I'd just lost my solicitor and had to brief the new guy.'

Matthew stopped, his face grimacing with exaggerated bewilderment. 'Spoiled!' he repeated, 'How could you not give something like that *much thought*! Somebody clearly tried to sabotage the race. Shit, they could have killed you, both of you.'

'I seriously never gave it that much thought. The only conspiracy theory I was following was the investigation and the imminent trial.'

'This toluene stuff, is it readily available? Can anyone get hold of it?'

'Yes, it's just a rubber solvent. Most DIY stores would have stocked it at the time. It's probably been outlawed now because of all the solvent abuse.'

'And the fuel cells were made of rubber?'

'Yes.'

'And this Les chap, the guy that arranged the Prize Indemnity. He *was* present at the Mugello race?'

'Yes, he was racing the third team car, the Scorpion, but the judge wouldn't let us tell the jury that he was part of our team.'

'And I guess the Scorpion *didn't* run on methanol, did it?'

'No, it ran a five-litre Chevrolet engine that used normal high-octane race fuel, supplied by the circuit.'

'Let me guess; Les had provided a Prize Indemnity policy for your team on the Mugello race?'

'Well ... yes. It had been intended we'd run the full season with another Prize Indemnity.' I thought about what Matthew was suggesting for a few seconds – *He tried to kill you, both of you. He contaminated the methanol with toluene, a chemical that would dissolve the rubber fuel cells, and then watched as you were strapped into a pair of 240 mph fire bombs.* I gave him a sceptical look. 'You're quite a conspiracy theorist,' I said, 'for a Freemason.'

He turned to face me. 'Are you on the square?'

'On the what?'

'Forget it. How did you,' he let the words trail away. 'Oh … my father's ring?'

'Your *father's* ring?'

'Yes, my father was a Mason; I kept the ring after he died.'

For a moment we stopped talking. More inmates had ventured out and, like us, were strolling the perimeter in small groups chatting. Others stood around smoking, laughing, larking about, and conspiring. Giving a sideways glance, I said, 'So *you're* not a Freemason then?'

A wry smile flickered across Matthew's face. 'Well, as it happens, yes I am. It's not exactly a secret.'

I thought about it for a moment. 'I thought it *was* supposed to be a secret, at least a secret organisation, a sort of elite brotherhood with some secret knowledge of some kind, information that is not available to us non-masons. Knowledge is power after all … if you had to share that knowledge, you lose the power.'

Matthew didn't reply so I moved on. 'Anyway, how come you're advertising your allegiance on a ring?'

'Well, as I said, the ring was my father's, it has sentimental value, but there's all sorts of Masonic regalia available, ceremonial objects, insignia, cufflinks, tie pins, lapel pins, rings. There are Masonic shops on the high street selling the stuff.' He grinned. 'Everything is in plain view of the average man. We're not a secret society, more like a society with a few secrets. I expect your average officers' mess at the local army camp has its traditions, its initiations, even a few secrets. We're quite open to scrutiny; Masons hide their secrets in plain view.'

'I thought it was all meant to be dodgy stuff, and strange rites, rolled-up trouser legs and bibbed aprons, that sort of thing? An old boys' network.'

Matthew chuckled. 'No, that's the way the general public perceives us. We're just a morally upright, charitable organisation, committed to helping others and assisting with good causes. We raise donations for charities at our lodge dinners, usually from the local business community, that type of thing. We're even in the telephone directory. Not much of a secret society if we're in the phone book!' He gave me a look. 'And before you ask, it's not satanic either. Because of what we stand for, membership tends to attract an honourable type of person, which is why practically all our judges, barristers and Law Lords are members, as well as quite a few police.'

I went quiet for a moment; the word moral certainly didn't seem to fit. Then I asked, 'So, what's the significance in walking clockwise?'

'Sun wise. It's a habit, a lodge thing, humour me, okay.'

'Why would a Wandsworth screw have called out to me to walk sun wise?'

'Oh, is that what he said?' He chuckled. 'Perhaps you didn't look like the typical Wandsworth intake, maybe he was just checking, to see your response.'

'Like asking if I was on the square? If I'd said the right thing, would I have got some decent coffee in Wandsworth?'

Matthew chuckled again but his reply amounted to simply that, just quiet laughter. We continued in silence for a few more minutes, then I asked, 'How come you ended up in here, if you're a Mason? I thought you guys stuck together, helped each other out.'

'I admitted what I'd done. I made a mistake and I'm paying the price.'

'But you do help each other out?'

'Look, Will, I'm what they call a Master Mason, a so-called third degree Mason, fairly low down in the overall hierarchy. There are around three hundred and fifty thousand freemasons in Britain alone. Nobody helped me out, and I didn't ask for help.'

'But it does happen?' I persisted.

'It shouldn't, but I'm not naive, it's rumoured things happen higher up. If you get to the thirty-third degree, you're in the running to become a Bilderberger.' Matthew chuckled. 'They say our MPs and Law Lords are influenced more at Lodge dinners than during any assembly of the Commons or House of Lords.'

'What's a Bilderberger?'

'Bilderbergers are a higher, international and exclusive level of freemasonry. There are only one hundred and forty members of them in the world.'

'I didn't realise there was an elite level.'

'It's more like levels with layers within the levels, but there are two that extend beyond the thirty-third degree. At the top you have the Illuminati, controlled by just thirteen families, then the one hundred and forty Bilderbergers, then we ordinary freemasons but you also have another four thousand Common Purpose "Graduate Leaders". And it's all connected by overlapping memberships that communicate relevant information.' He turned to face me, his eyes locking with mine. 'Will, it's called *the system.*'

I offered a paranoid thought, 'It sounds a lot more than *a charitable organisation, committed to helping others.* It sounds bloody corrupt.'

'I can't believe you're saying this. Do they also practise mass hypnosis?' my words spilt out before I could catch myself. 'Don't you realise what you're saying? This is exactly why people distrust you lot. I mean, if the very people responsible for passing the legislation and creating our laws are being influenced by a secret network, *and* I suspect getting big backhanders along the way, there's no hope; the whole system *is* corrupt, it's poisoned.'

We continued wordlessly for a few moments. Finally, Matthew broke in with, 'We do more good for the world than you'll ever realise, Will. And there are no backhanders.' He grinned. 'There are what's known as "consulting fees". Anyway, that's all rumour and speculation, nothing like that happens at my level. I'd probably be blackballed or thrown out for trying to network.' He paused, 'Look Will, I know what you're leading up to.'

'You do?'

'The police and the trial, the judge; is there a connection, right?'

'Yes, a Masonic connection. I want to find out if somebody with influence was pulling the strings.'

'I can't do that Will. I've taken vows.'

'If you've got a criminal record, how much longer will you be considered morally upright enough to be a member?' I liked Matthew a lot and regretted my sarcastic response as soon as it left my lips.

Matthew looked pained. 'The Metropolitan Police, the judiciary, big city financial institutions; there may be a Masonic connection, it's possible, but it's more likely to be coincidental and shouldn't influence anything, even if some of the key players were members of a lodge and were discussing things behind the scenes. They would all be morally upstanding individuals. At the end of the day, it's the jury that decides.'

'But what if the judge had been persuaded to steer the case

to a conviction, what if the police were trying to cover up a blunder and he was helping?'

'What blunder?'

'The police raid,' I said with exasperation, 'the raid that was triggered by WPA's private detective, the idiot that had been watching the wrong person!' My irritation was palpable.

'But what does it prove? Even if they *were* manipulating things, you're still stuck in here, and you've still got to prove you're innocent, not just point a finger at them and say look they're all part of an old boys' network. I think you have some good grounds for appeal, but you need to concentrate on *them*, not on some conspiracy theory.'

We fell silent for a moment, then I asked, 'You mean like an insurance broker trying to kill us off by putting toluene in our fuel cells!'

He grinned, 'Okay, touché!'

We continued walking silently for a few moments, then he asked, 'So what do you want to do, get out of here, or prove some conspiracy theory?'

I gave him a sideways glance. 'Both. I want to get out of here *and* nail the bastards.'

'And how are you going to do that?'

I thought about it as we continued walking. I had no idea. I did know what I wanted to ask him, but was anxious about his reaction. Before I could say anything he added, 'Did I tell you I'm being released next month, I'm being discharged.'

I turned to face him, 'That's brilliant Matthew, brilliant!'

'It is rather,' he said, smiling. 'Anyway, once I'm out, if there's anything I can do to help out.'

I hesitated, 'Matthew, I know this is a big ask, but with your contacts,' I hesitated again. 'Look, if I gave you the name of the judge and the names and warrant numbers of the police, is there any way that you could find out if they were all Freemasons, possibly even if they were all registered at the same lodge?'

'You need to be very wary of the direction you're going, Will.'

'But could you do it?'

He hesitated for a fraction of a second. 'I do know an official at the Grand Lodge. The member records have only just been computerised on a central database. Before that it would have been almost impossible, everything was on index cards, held at individual lodges. Look Will,' he said, with a resigned sigh, 'I've never seen the data room personally, but I do know it's in the lower level, off one of the old passageways.' He nodded, adding hesitantly, 'Yes, I think I could find out.'

59

Never forget that everything Hitler did in Germany was legal.

(Martin Luther King, Jr.)

The discharge officer appeared slightly perplexed as he studied the licence details. 'Right. You're to be released from prison for a period of seven days, for the purpose of attending St Richard's Hospital at Chichester, to receive surgery to a spinal injury.' He paused for a moment, contemplating what he had just said. The words took a few moments to sink in. *Didn't this prisoner's file state he'd been found guilty of claiming for a non-existent spinal injury?* He eyed me with indecision, but recalling I'd just triggered a major investigation into the prison service, decided it best to continue. 'You will be released from 10.30 on 16th September, until the completion of treatment on 23rd September 1996. You must return to prison immediately on completion of treatment.' He tapped the page with the tip of his biro, 'Sign 'ere, 'ere and 'ere.'

It was a bright sunny day as the local taxi drove me the short journey to Chichester. Elizabeth Ward was a prefab building set in rundown grounds at the back of the main hospital. The ward was reached by a series of covered walkways and passages. It was a mixed ward containing 20 beds, all of which were occupied, with machines bleeping and humming testily. Bottles of fluids hung from stands with tubes snaking into impaled blood vessels and pipes appearing bizarrely from places where previously no natural orifice had existed. I shuddered. I didn't like hospitals!

Later I lay face up, trying to keep calm, covered by a green blanket. Under the blanket I wore a white hospital gown secured by a single tie. A plastic identity band proclaiming me to be patient 375607 had been snapped around my left wrist.

346

Two porters steered the bed down grey-tiled corridors, through swing doors, past the x-ray department, past wards with the hustle and bustle of the daily routine, past nurses, doctors and attendants and finally, to my surprise, into the maternity wing! Despite my anxiety, I felt mildly amused at how Smythe and McGaea might have addressed the matter of my being treated for a supposed phantom spinal injury in a maternity department. Perhaps I was also suffering a phantom pregnancy.

'Hello Mr Middleton, how are you feeling today?' It was Doctor Dolland, presumably preparing for a forceps delivery!

'I'm okay, but I'm not looking forward to this. I thought I was going to be given something to make me drowsy?'

'Oh, you'll be fine,' Dolland replied reassuringly. 'There's nothing to worry about at all. Now we're just going to insert a little needle into the back of your hand, then the anaesthetist will give you a spot of sedation. Okay?'

'I'd like more than a spot, I'm a real coward when it comes to needles.' I tried to maintain some degree of composure whilst looking from my hand to the advancing nurse.

Dolland removed a small electronic unit from a soft nylon pouch. The unit, grey in colour with an electronic display on the fascia, was fitted with a belt to be worn around the waist. It looked more like a Walkman than a medical device. He whipped off the cover and loaded a clear bag of fluid. 'We'll start him with .25 percent Bupivacaine infused at the rate of two millilitres per hour.' A nurse made a note on a chart. Dr Dolland inserted the IV tubing into the bag and allowed fluid to run through until the tube was clear of bubbles before clamping it closed with a blue plastic clip.

A blonde nurse placed a blood pressure cuff around my left arm, and with a stethoscope listened intently to the blood still coursing through the restricted artery. '105 over 70,' she called to another nurse who made a note on a clipboard. The blonde nurse removed the cuff and slapped the back of my hand. Veins stood out like strands of spaghetti. 'You're just going to feel a little prick. Okay?' A sparkle of reflected light glinted from the shaft as she positioned, then inserted the needle into one of the strands. I winced. 'This is a Ventflow. It'll remain in your hand for the week you're in hospital just in case we need to get fluid into you quickly,' she explained.

Dr Dolland tugged on a pair of surgical gloves with a snap. 'I still haven't been put out!' I reminded him, just in case he'd forgotten.

An assistant wheeled the bed the last few feet into the theatre and set it alongside an x-ray table. A visual display monitor was positioned at the foot of the table.

When I'd last been in hospital, just weeks prior to the first police raid, Mr Dolland the orthopaedic surgeon had rectified the damage to my thoracic spine under a general anaesthetic. This time I was feeling distinctly uneasy at still being fully conscious. 'Nothing to worry about Mr Middleton, you'll be fine,' an attractive nurse assured me. 'We just need you to roll across on your tummy.' The nurse peeled back the green blanket. My anxiety level continued to rise as I watched the needle being prepared for insertion into my spine. I did as requested, trying to remain composed.

With gloved hands the doctor prepared my lower back for the epidural. 'You'll just feel something cold. Okay?' The doctor spoke with a practised, reassuring tone.

'Yes, fine, but I still haven't been given any sedation!'

'Nothing to worry about.' He indicated to an assistant at the head of the table who connected a needleless syringe into the Ventflow in the back of my hand. I felt the chill of the anxiolytic course into my vein and immediately, I sensed a gentle disassociation from what was going on around me.

Dolland positioned the needle just above the spondylolithesis in my lumbar spine. 'You're just going to feel some slight pressure Mr Middleton.' How wonderful it was to be called Mister again. Even the pressure of the needle being forced into my spine could not take that away. I was being treated like a human being and, for a week at least, I was going to be both out of pain and out of prison.

With the x-ray machine monitoring every move, the doctor carefully pushed the needle between the vertebrae and through the ligamentous covering of my spinal canal. With practised hands he attached a syringe from the epidural pack and carefully withdrew the plunger to check for pressure; a lack of pressure meant the epidural was correctly positioned in the subarachnoid space.

He connected the catheter to the device resembling a Walkman, and advanced it into the puncture hole in my spine. The small-bore tube would remain there for seven days whilst the pump, attached to my waist by a belt, infused Bupivacaine, a powerful painkiller, into the area directly above the spondylolithesis, the effect being to totally block the nerves and prevent future spasm.

The ward was warm and by the bed opposite, a machine hissed rhythmically like the foaming surf rising and falling over wet sand. I was still feeling the effects of the sedation and my eyelids were heavy. Slowly they dropped and I drifted with the sounds of the ocean into a deep enveloping sleep.

The waters of the Straits flickered invitingly in my dream; shards of silver in a bed of indigo. Their depths, bathed in the rays of the morning sun, stretched far into the horizon. The burning rays scorched my skin. In the background, the waters gently lapped against the coral sand. Just ahead a small group of beach boys were shouting instructions to a bemused client who was swinging precariously beneath the canopy of a bright red parasail. In the distance Beth was playing in the shallow water with the boys. A horse that had lost its rider, was galloping out of control across the sands. I closed my eyes, luxuriating in the glorious warmth of the sun.

'Will,' a gentle voice drifted between the sounds of the waves.

A hand touched my shoulder. 'Will, Will, wake up.' I opened my eyes and turned in the direction of the voice. A beautiful face slowly drifted into focus. A nurse in a green uniform was standing by the bedside. She was probably in her mid twenties, with kind brown eyes. Half dreaming, half awake, I blinked against the bright overhead lights. Consciousness flooded back like a breaking wave. 'Oh, hi. I must have nodded off.' I wondered if she knew she was nursing a convicted felon.

'I've just got to take your temperature and check your blood pressure and pulse.'

I glanced about the ward; no beach, just other patients. A few were sitting up reading; others were resting with their eyes closed. I'd been admitted with two other patients, both were now fitted with their respective epidural pumps with their IV tubes plumbed into their spines. 'That's all fine.' She made a few notes on my record card. 'Er, I wonder,' she sounded uncertain, 'I wonder if I could just have a little look at the puncture site on your back? Would you mind? You see, I'm a student and I've not seen one of these before.'

'Sure. No problem.' I turned onto my stomach. The floral curtains were drawn around the bed isolating us from the rest of the ward. She examined the tube disappearing into my spine. 'Oh, interesting. Does it hurt?'

'No, not at all. In fact for the first time in years there's been no pain at all. This thing in my hand hurts though.' I pointed at the Ventflow. 'It itches like hell. I don't suppose you could pull it out?'

She smiled. 'Sorry. That has to stay in.'

The next few days passed slowly and unlike the other patients, I savoured every moment. Beth and the boys were permitted to visit daily. At my request, Beth brought some files from home so that I could catch up with the mass of legal papers that were still falling foul of the six-inch rule.

It was 8.30 pm on Wednesday 18th September. I lay in the hospital bed studying a large lever arch file filled with correspondence. It dated back to January 1992, the year before the police raid. I flicked absentmindedly through the bundle of documents, quickly checking each page. I was looking for a copy of a letter I had sent to the local planning office regarding the extension to the house.

Suddenly something caught my eye. It hadn't been the content of the letter that had attracted my attention; it was something else, something familiar that I knew I had seen before; a series of irritating little marks that were produced by my photocopier.

I turned to another page. Yes, they were there too. My mind flashed back to the trial and the Crown's forensic report that had referred to 'pick up marks' and Paterson-Smythe's proclamation that I'd 'created' the Trans World invoice on my photocopier.

He'd pointed to some other marks on the bottom of the invoice and announced that they'd been reproduced as a result of me creating a collage from another Trans World document. But it wasn't those markings that I was looking at. It was the others, further up the page on the right-hand side, marks that I now remembered were always produced by my antiquated Xerox machine.

I flicked over a few more pages, carefully checking for documents that had been copied around September 1993, the time of the

Trans World invoice. Yes, there were dozens of them, August, September, October and right through into 1994, and they all had telltale marks.

I'd brought from the prison the only two files I'd been allowed. I quickly found a copy of exhibit 3002, the Trans World invoice. My heartbeat soared. Like the sudden flash of lightning illuminating the night sky, it became clear – exhibit 3002 did not have the telltale marks, but every other document that had ever passed through my photocopier did.

I picked up the file of copied letters Beth had brought over. With my thumb against the edge of the bundle, I quickly flicked through each page in turn. It was like looking at one of those old 'what the butler saw' machines on the end of the pier. As the pages flicked from my thumb, the malformed markings danced like tiny ants; thirty, fifty, a hundred, two hundred pages. Every page had the markings. Every page that is, that had ever passed through my Xerox.

My heartbeat quickened. Keep cool, I told myself, this only affects the Prize Indemnity charges, but I knew in my heart this was significant. It might not be conclusive; after all, the Prosecution were like chameleons, they could change their colours at will – *He must have used someone else's photocopier for this one document then.*

I hadn't and they'd know it, and with a good barrister we should be able to prove it.

60

It was 25th September 1996; I'd been back at Ford for just two days and the transition from patient to prisoner wasn't proving easy. But at least I'd managed to see Governor Richards in record time. Having discovered another flaw in the Crown's case, I needed expert help, a forensic expert, and to get that, I needed the Governor on my side.

He leaned back in his seat behind his organised, utilitarian desk, studying the two pages through his gold-rimmed frames. 'You say the Crown's argument was that you'd forged this exhibit, document 3002, using your Xerox machine,' he placed the copy back on his desk, 'from this document, exhibit 3121,' picking up and studying the second page, 'to create a fake invoice that was used in the Prize Indemnity claim.' He looked up, placing the second page back down. 'Is that correct?'

His eyes remained locked on mine. 'Yes, that's right.' I nodded. 'The charges relating to the Prize Indemnity were all added right at the last minute, and centred around this document 3002, that they said I'd forged. My legal team were all convinced these charges were added because the Crown realised the injury and redundancy charges were weak and likely to fail. The letterheads had been given to us by Mamet Porsche in America, along with the authority to produce any documentation needed for the temporary import and Prize Indemnity. But in court both the American team and my co-driver, Rob Allan, denied it.'

The Governor selected a pen idly from his desk and began

352

rolling it between thumb and forefinger like a cigar. 'The jury obviously believed them,' he said.

'I know, they must have, but what never came out in court was that the team had a grudge against me. They blamed me for the purchase of the Porsche not happening. At the last minute we decided not to buy the Porsche and bought a pair of Indy Cars instead. And the situation with Rob Allan was complicated.'

'Complicated?'

Reaching into my pocket, I removed the letter from Rob Allan. 'Please take a look at this, Mr Richards,' I said, 'It arrived shortly after I was sent here.' I watched as the Governor opened the envelope, removed the single-page letter and began reading.

A few moments passed before he asked, 'What's he suggesting when he says – *I know what happened between you and Anna?* – Who's Anna?'

'I got involved with something, or someone, that I shouldn't have,' I said. 'Anna was his partner.'

'Ah, I see!' He raised an eyebrow. 'And this chap sent you this letter in Ford?' He picked up the envelope, carefully checking the handwriting, address and date.

'Yes, shortly after I was moved from Wandsworth.'

'And this is the chap who gave evidence that you *hadn't* been given the letterheads?'

'That's right, and the Crown concluded that if we hadn't been given them, then I must have forged one.'

'Did your affair with his partner come out in court?'

'No, nothing,' I said, disregarding the 'affair' word, my eyes still watching as his fingers fidgeted with the pen.

The Governor remained silent, head shaking slowly in disbelief. 'I see,' he said, something in his voice softening. 'This Rob Allan chap's chosen his words carefully, but it's almost as if he's implying he stabbed you in the back because you betrayed him with his partner. Are you going to use this in your appeal?'

'Yes, if we're ever granted leave to appeal.'

'Good, I think you should,' he said. 'So, tell me about this new evidence you say you discovered last week in hospital.'

'It's all to do with pick-up marks,' I began, placing two files on the Governor's desk. Over tea and biscuits we went through the papers one by one. Forty-five minutes later I left the Governor's office with the promise of a day release licence and a strong unspoken indication that his door would always be open.

It was now November 1996. Matthew had been discharged the previous month but we still kept in as regular contact as I could afford on my prison pay, using expensive prison phone cards.

I inserted my last card into the slot and punched Matthew's mobile number into the keypad. Somewhere out in the free world Matthew's phone rang. The display on the prison phone registered 2.58 minutes remaining. Matthew answered on the third ring. 'Hi Matthew, it's Will,' I said. 'I've got to be quick; I've only got a few units left.' The display ticked down to 2.39.

'Hi Will, I've been waiting to hear from you. I tried to get through to Beth three times but there was no reply.' The display dropped to 2.29. 'Look, there's definitely no question, both of the police officers, and your Judge McGaea, are all members and they use the same lodge.' 2.10 on the display.

'I knew it!' I said, trying hard to control my composure.

'Detective Barnet,' Matthew went on, 'is serving with the Metropolitan Police and is a third degree Master Mason, Detective Probert is a sergeant with the Metropolitan Police and is in his fourth degree, known as a Secret Master...'

'Secret Master?' 1.48 remaining.

'It's just the level Will,' Matthew went on, 'we all begin as Entered Apprentice then go on to Fellow Craft, and Master Mason. Not many go beyond the third degree Master Mason level, but if you do, you're into the Ineffable Degrees. The first Ineffable Degree is Secret Master and that's what Detective Probert is, a fourth degree Mason.'

'So where does the judge slot in?'

'His full name is George Lampton McGaea and he's a real product of the system; educated at Abbey Grammar School in Cornwell, then Eton, called to the bar in 1969, and he has a reputation for handing down harsh sentences. And from what I've been told there's a long family connection with Freemasonry which might explain how he's risen so quickly to the twelfth degree. Your judge, is very high up.' Matthew paused, 'Look Will, there's something else. Usually this wouldn't leave the lodge.

If I get found out, the *least* that'll happen is I'll be barred for life.' There was something different in his voice, an edge of fear.

'Matthew what is it; who are you afraid of?

'Let's just say there are some people at the top that aren't very nice; powerful, rich, influential and most of all, ruthless. Your judge is known to be associated with one of them and there could be a link.'

'Just give me a name Matthew,' I pleaded as the display clicked down to 0.43.

'I don't want to say any more before I hear back from my contact, but what I will say is that your judge has an equally worrying reputation.'

'Doesn't sound good,' I replied. The display began to blink 0.30.

'It's not! And incidentally, the twelfth degree is known as Grand Master Architect.'

'Sounds appropriate,' I said, 'looks like he designed my trial from the ground up! Look, Matthew, I'm running out of units, I need some sort of documentary proof. Something to prove all this is real, not just paranoia. Is there any way?'

'All that will prove is that they're all Freemasons, and if I get caught...' His voice tailed off.

'It's about to run out, if there's any way,' I begged as the display reached 0.15.

'Will, you *do* realise what you're asking and what you're getting both of us into, don't you?' For a moment there was silence. The display continued to count down, then he spoke. 'Look, I'm seeing my contact next week and he owes me a favour...'

The display reached zero, a solenoid activated with a clunk, ejecting my card from the slot.

61

People say law but they mean money.

(Ralph Waldo Emerson, 1803–1882)

It was two years since my conviction; a hearing date had finally been set by 'The Listing Office'. This time, the Lord Chief Justice of England would personally listen to our grounds for reopening 'The Crown v Middleton'. The Legal Aid Board, however, still refused to provide any support which meant Michael Bamforth QC, the barrister who had taken over the case, somehow had to be funded privately; a challenge that in the outside world might have proven less daunting than to an inmate whose only income amounted to around five pounds a week. The hearing was likely to be scheduled for early 97 and if successful, it was conceivable I'd be released on bail pending a full appeal.

I still had an uphill battle. The Crown had unlimited resources to rebut the challenge, and we were desperately underfunded. Somehow we needed to obtain the official court transcripts of the trial judge's summing up, as well as covering solicitors' fees and also paying for forensic and medical experts to compile reports for the Lord Chief Justice.

Piglet had driven down to the prison. It had been months since I'd spent time with him and it was good to feel that something constructive was happening at last. 'I've been going through your notes and the trial documentation and I think we've gathered together sufficient grounds for the appeal against the conviction,' he announced, handing me a sheath of neatly typed A4 sheets.

I diligently scanned the papers commenting about this and that. The first page gave a brief summary of the conviction and applied formally to appeal out of time based on medical grounds. Page two commenced the list of grounds for appeal; it ran to ten pages. I reached page four and stopped dead. *Mr Giles Adams*

356

was called to the bar in 1981 and whilst he practises solely in criminal work, he had never been involved in a serious fraud case nor has he ever led or been lead barrister in any case.

'It says here Rabbit had never led, or even been lead barrister in a case before. Is that right?'

Piglet's head remained buried deep in his file. I repeated the question. He looked up from his work. 'Yes, that's correct. But he is an excellent barrister. We've used him very successfully in several other cases.'

I had asked Rabbit at the commencement how successful he'd been as a barrister, but the only retort had been, 'I've won more cases than I've lost.' I was shocked more than surprised. Why hadn't he told me this? His experience was clearly limited and doubtless explained why he had been so intimidated by McGaea. I should have been told, particularly when he took over the position of lead counsel.

There were still gaps in the draft and Piglet explained that we had yet to check over the transcript of the judge's summing up, an area where we knew there were dozens of out-and-out howlers.

'Will, we need to file this urgently and we're already very late. The court already refused your appeal against sentence on the grounds that we were out of time, even though you were in hospital with a breakdown and, despite the fact *they* somehow managed to lose two sets of appeal applications.'

I looked up, speechless for a moment. 'They lost my appeal application, twice,' I repeated incredulously, 'and they're blaming *us* for being late?'

'Yes. The first set was sent by conventional post, and they said it never arrived, so we sent a second set by Special Delivery. They admitted that was signed for, but say it somehow got misfiled, so we had to submit a third set which they finally acknowledged.'

I said nothing, my bemusement palpable.

Piglet continued, 'We're going to need the official court transcripts to prove McGaea's misdirection in relation to the various witnesses, but that's going to cost money.'

'Can't we just ask for a photocopy of the relevant sections?' I asked naively, snapping out of my bewilderment.

'It doesn't work that way. All the transcripts are handled by an independent company, DL Sellers, they're the official shorthand writers for the courts, and they charge for everything.'

'But we've all got our own notes from the trial. Both you and Tigger transcribed everything the judge said during his summing up, and I made daily notes on my computer.'

'I know we all made notes, but none of that would be accepted by the Court of Appeal, the only thing they will accept is the official Court record from Sellers. Just the sections relating to Burton and Thompson will probably cost a couple of thousand pounds. For the time being I want you to go through your file along with Tigger's notes of McGaea's summing up. Compare both sets of notes and cross-reference it to what the witnesses actually said.'

I grimaced. '*All* of them?'

'Yes ... I'm afraid so. I know it's laborious and there are *loads* of inaccuracies, but we need to extract the most significant examples and then order the official transcript of that section only from Sellers. Once the Court of Appeal agrees to reopen the case we'll hopefully get legal aid to secure the rest of the transcripts. I'll also need a summary of any additional points that you want to include in the appeal. Take this draft back to your room, read it, decipher it, pull it apart and add anything you can think of to it, then let me have it back as soon as possible. I've still got a number of secondary concerns to explore myself.'

'What about the way the judge mouthed words to the jury and his facial expressions? None of that is provable with transcripts,' I added.

'We'll include it in the appeal but I doubt they will attach a great deal of weight to the way the judge behaved. At the end of the day they know what goes on, but unless there's a lot of public pressure, they'll be reluctant to publicly criticise a brother judge.'

'What about the letter that Rob Allan sent me?' I asked, sliding the letter across the desk. 'Everyone that's seen it, even the Governor, believes it's important.'

Piglet remained silent for several moments as he scanned the letter that he'd read several times before. 'It's inadmissible, and we can't use it,' he said finally.

'Why? He's practically admitting to stitching me up in court because of what happened between me and Anna.'

'I know, but any evidence we present to the Court of Appeal has to be evidence that was not available at the original trial.'

'We didn't have the letter at the time of the trial!' I said with exasperation.

'I know, however we did know about the situation between you and his girlfriend. The problem with his letter is that he's chosen his words very carefully; it's more what's implied between the lines than what he's saying. Anyway, in your trial we decided it best not to bring the matter out in court. If we had, we could have grilled Allan about why he was saying what he was in the witness box, but we all felt it would work against you with the female members of the jury. So we can't use it now; it's inadmissible.'

It had been one of the many things with the judicial process to amaze me. I'd naively assumed that anything that might prove a major miscarriage of justice would be welcomed, if not demanded by the Crown, but that was simply not so. However, I'd also expected the right to appeal would be automatic, and that wasn't true either! A case will only be reopened by the Court of Appeal if it can be proven that a serious misdirection occurred by the trial judge or some striking piece of completely new evidence emerges. The fact was, whilst we did not know the jury's rationale, I had somehow been found guilty and sentenced to serve up to six years in prison. As far as the law was concerned, it was a total irrelevance that x-rays and surgeons could prove my injuries or that accountants could verify my redundancy to have been involuntary.

There were other factors too and they were significant. Details which when discovered had not been entirely unexpected. Some months following the trial, we'd received a number of letters from Crown witnesses, many of whom had been interviewed by the same detectives that had so kindly assisted with the production of both Lee Burton and Margaret Pickup's identical and helpful statements.

A former sponsor of some ten years was one of the first to break the news that the officers involved had been attempting to condition and influence witnesses, during both the production of their statements and immediately prior to giving evidence.

Four Crown witnesses had now come forward and were prepared to testify. On the 10th August one wrote:

All the police officers involved did seem to feel that they had to win their case, because you had to be proved to be guilty. The private detective speaking to the police in the waiting room at the court also put across the image that you were an out and out scoundrel.

Other Crown witnesses added:

In the waiting room, the police were talking to witnesses. They said you were a nasty bit of work and people such as you should be locked up. ... just before I was due to give evidence, the police phoned me but what they were saying was simply untrue ... that you were already guilty regardless of what happens in the trial and had been fiddling your income for years. Apparently the bank had confirmed it; the police said you belonged behind bars but not to mention this phone call to anyone.

On 18th July 1995 a witness for the prosecution sent me a letter:

I remember being astonished at the attitude of the investigating officers, who made it very clear that in their view you were engaged in quite a wide spectrum of fraud and that they had no doubt of your guilt. I felt that it was a lot less objective an attitude than should be expected from somebody investigating possible crime and did wonder at the effect on other people interviewed of this approach! Despite spending several years as a magistrate and therefore not being totally unfamiliar with our justice system, I cannot believe that police officers investigating possible crime should be interviewing in such a manner that very clearly indicates that there is no doubt that the person they are investigating is guilty. There is no doubt in my mind that this conditioning is prejudicial to any statement received and is totally unfair to the subject of their enquiries, who at that point must be viewed as innocent of any crime.

Day blended with day in an unending nightmare of time. Having received permission to make legal calls, I pursued Piglet regularly, sometimes two even three times a week. 'When will

360

the appeal be heard? Is any work being done on the barrister's brief? We need to follow up on the new evidence! We must get the official Court transcripts.'

'It's not as simple as that Will. Without money we're stuck and they won't grant legal aid. I have to work alone, in my spare time. I've got enough work to keep me busy on your case alone for probably two to three months. I just can't do all the work on my own, my practice is suffering, and we need finance.'

'Will, you've got a visit,' Mrs Addington said, handing me the obligatory movement slip.

I made my way over to the SO's office and reported to the screw at the hatch. FJ3866,' I said, 'I have a visitor.'

He studied his clipboard and finding my number on his list, placed a tick by the side. 'Take a seat,' he said. 'You'll be called when your visitor gets to the waiting area.'

Twenty minutes later I was summoned to the visits hall. The usual drug abuse posters adorned the walls as I entered the search area, 'Anything on you that you shouldn't have Will?' a screw enquired.

'No, nothing.' Unlike Wandsworth, there was no fluorescent yellow sash required to identify me as a convict. The screw smiled and waved me on through and into the visits hall. For the past year most of the screws had stopped subjecting me to the humiliating body searches, and a few had even begun calling me by my first name.

Entering the large airy visits hall, I made my way to the officer in charge. 'FJ3866, Will Middleton,' I said. He looked down his list, placed a tick against my name.

'Okay Will, take a seat.' He scrawled something onto a slip and handed it to an assistant, who stepped out into a waiting area to call my visitor. A few moments later Beth appeared at the doorway looking tired and pale.

We hugged and I kissed her. As with each visit, we chatted, and I drank coffee and ate sandwiches and crisps, luxuries I could never afford on my prison pay. Beth sipped her usual mug of hot water.

There was something in her voice today and I could instinctively tell that something was wrong; we'd been together too many

361

years to hide anything from each other. There was clearly something she wanted to tell me but didn't know how to begin.

'Did you speak to Matthew?' I asked.

Beth shook her head. 'I couldn't...' she said, a distinct quaver breaking into her voice that she was trying hard to control.

'What's up?' I said. 'Is there something wrong?'

'I spoke to his wife...' Beth began.

'Oh, good,' I said, 'did she say when he's going to be in touch?'

Beth shook her head. 'She was hysterical!'

'Why, what's up?'

'He's dead!'

I felt the blood drain from my face, my stomach plummeted, as though dropping in an elevator. I swore under my breath.

'He was in London. They're saying it was suicide!' She looked up at me, 'It was in last week's paper.' She slid a cutting across the table. 'I didn't know how to tell you.'

I scanned the brief cutting, with its heading – *Covent Garden suicide chaos.*

For a few moments neither of us said anything. 'I know what you're thinking Will,' Beth eventually said. 'He was doing some kind of research for you, wasn't he?'

I nodded, still stunned. Shaking my head bemusedly, I finally answered, 'Two weeks ago he told me he had proof that the police officers and my trial judge were all Freemasons and they were apparently members of the same lodge in London. He said the trial judge was a high-level twelfth degree Mason. There was someone else as well, somebody very high up, but he seemed very nervous about saying any more. I asked him if he could get me some kind of documentary proof.'

'Did he get it?'

'He said he had some business to do in London, and that he had a contact in the Grand Lodge. That was the last time we spoke. I phoned his mobile several times, but each time it just went to voicemail.'

'But this doesn't prove anything.'

'Yeah, *right*,' I said sarcastically, my mind now racing ahead. 'You know where Covent Garden underground station is don't you?'

'Well, Covent Garden I assume.'

'Yes but it also happens to be a few hundred yards from the

Grand Lodge, in Great Queen Street. Covent Garden is the nearest underground station. He has to have been on his way home.'

She shook her head, 'This just has to be another coincidence.'

'You reckon?' I paused. 'So why go to London to commit suicide ... and why there?'

A klaxon rudely interrupted us. 'Visiting time is now over, all visitors must please leave the visits hall *now*,' an officer bellowed.

We hugged and kissed and I watched as she left the visits room. Turning, I wandered back to the Education Department, Matthew's last words to me echoing hauntingly: 'Will, you *do* realise what you are getting us both into, don't you?'

The prevailing south westerly wind shifted direction, blowing in arctic grey snow clouds, and by December the snow was falling. Christmas came and went, bringing with it little, if any good will. I spent the week in my room, my thoughts at least with Beth and the boys. The Prison Service prohibited visits from family and friends over Christmas. I was held captive by time – time which seemed to have no end.

62

It is easy to go down into hell, night and day the gates of dark death stand wide; but to climb back up again, to retrace one's steps to open air, there lies the problem, the difficult task.

(Virgil, *The Aeneid*)

9.25 am, 19th November 1996, HMP Ford, Littlehampton

The rain pounded against the roof, rattling down like miniature hammer blows. Storm force winds shook the billet and whistled through rotting frames. On the radio, reporters excitedly told of roads blocked by fallen trees and mountainous seas lashing the south coast. More reports detailed the evacuation of the function rooms of Brighton's Grand Hotel as the roof threatened to detach itself in the dramatic gales.

I stepped out onto the concrete path, the ferocity of the winds instantly taking hold, attempting to tug me from my feet. Head down, lashed by the rain, I forced myself forward. Cumulus clouds scurried overhead in turmoiled skies. I lifted the collar of my jacket and pushed on. I was going to be drenched by the time I reached the other side of the camp.

Today was my parole board interview. Theoretically, within a matter of months regardless of any appeal, I could be released on parole. Of course if released, I would then be subject to immediate re-arrest for non-payment of the compensation order, and re-imprisoned for another two years! There was another little problem: to be released, the parole board expected an inmate to have 'shown remorse' for his crimes, to have addressed his 'offending behaviour' and proved that there was little, if any, chance of re-offending, none of which was easily achieved if you hadn't offended in the first place.

I passed the gatehouse and paused by the road that divided the camp. The rain pelted down with even greater intensity. Cars swept past in a mist of spray, their headlights spearing the gloom of the morning. I entered the administration block and made my way to the hatch. 'I have an appointment to see a Mrs Tweed concerning a parole interview.'

The secretary cast me a disparaging glance, 'That's not today, your meeting's on the nineteenth of November.' A light flashed urgently on the telephone switchboard and she directed her attention to the more worthy object before her. I waited until she had completed the call before pointing out that today was the nineteenth. She consulted a calendar on the wall. 'Oh, yes, so it is. Well, she's not in yet.' She studied her watch. 'She's usually late though, so you'd better take a seat.' She pointed to a cluster of chairs in a small reception area.

I sat down, glancing around the reception room. The furnishings were typically utilitarian, the carpeting comprising heavy-duty blue tiles. Display boards exhibited glossy pictures of prisoners working in the various prison industries.

A voice called my name. 'Mr Middleton?' I looked up from my magazine. I'd been waiting for only twenty minutes. Mrs Tweed was very respectably dressed in a smart blue woollen suit over which was draped a tan raincoat. She was probably in her early forties, big boned and with short brown hair. 'I'm Mrs Tweed,' she said in a distinctive Sussex accent, offering a hand. 'Sorry I'm a little late, traffic was terrible. I'll be conducting your parole interview.' She studied me enquiringly as though taking in every detail. 'We'll be going outside to the portacabin, would you like me to order some coffee to take through?'

I declined the offer and we made our way back through the swing doors into the rain and entered the small, damp portacabin. The room was sparsely furnished with a black metal table occupying the centre, surrounded by four matching folding chairs. On one side of the stark white walls was a solitary electric heater.

Mrs Tweed positioned herself next to the heater and unpacked a file of Home Office papers. 'Now Mr Middleton, you're serving four years for fraud, is that correct?' I nodded, resisting the temptation to add the word 'supposedly'. Matthew had spent the last few evenings before his discharge schooling me for this interview. 'If you've got nothing to admit to, you must give them something. If they ask about your crimes, whatever you do, don't say you're not guilty or you can kiss parole goodbye. Just say you appreciate the

365

seriousness of the offences with which you were charged. They'll like that, and it doesn't mean a thing.'

Mrs Tweed sipped her coffee and began by asking a few simple questions; age, home address, children, and any plans I might have if offered early release from prison. Her words were soft, considered, enquiring. She looked up from her papers. 'Perhaps you could run me through the details of your offences?' Her words hung suspended like a web. She smiled invitingly. The eyes were intense beneath carefully plucked brows. They watched as though trying to penetrate my mind.

I began with the riding accident, the collapse of Team Capricorn and my redundancy. 'Mr Middleton,' Mrs Tweed was looking dubious. It was normal for her, under such circumstances, to be dealing with long-term career criminals, drug dealers, child molesters or lifers. 'You're going to have to help me a little. What is it you're supposed to have done to warrant a four-year prison term?'

'Six years,' I corrected her.

'Six years?' The intense eyes flickered and she quickly checked her papers, her puzzlement still reflecting in her face as she looked back up.

'Yes, six years,' I continued. 'When my father died, a deed attached to his will paid money from his estate to build a flat for my mother. She's eighty-three years old.' Mrs Tweed was rapidly scribbling notes. I continued. 'The granny flat was completed in 1992 and is attached to our home. After the trial, the judge decided that because that money was received during the period of my supposed crimes the funds from the will are forfeit.' I couldn't resist using the word 'supposed' and like a cat, Mrs Tweed pounced on the syllables, already digesting their implications. I continued, 'If I don't use those funds, which obviously only exist as bricks and mortar, to compensate WPA I have to serve another two years in prison.'

For the next fifteen minutes I continued to outline the events that led up to my imprisonment. The heater quickly warmed the confined cabin. Condensation ran from the windows. I moved on to the Brands Hatch race and was careful to point out that I knew, with hindsight, that it had been a mistake to drive. 'I shouldn't have competed in the race. But I didn't know the extent of the injuries at that time.'

I had expected the interview to concentrate on the time spent in prison, to weigh up whether I was a risk to the public, to note that I had complied with all the rules, had never missed a day's work, had been recommended for parole by both Prison and Probation Service. I had been mistaken. 'Mr Middleton, are you changing your position concerning admission of guilt?'

'No, certainly not!' Mrs Tweed made a further careful note. 'I agree I made some mistakes,' I repeated, 'silly mistakes. I shouldn't have driven at Brands Hatch. But I did not commit any crime.'

'I see,' said Mrs Tweed, who clearly did not see. 'I'll be compiling my report within the next few weeks. Once it's completed you'll receive a copy and can add any observations of your own.' She rose smiling from her seat and offered a hand once more. The interview was over and so, it seemed, was any likelihood of parole.

I returned to my room. Pausing for a moment, I stared at the wet haggard reflection in the plastic wall mirror; my eyes seemed to have sunk deeper still into their sockets. Uncertainty clouded my mind. What the hell was I supposed to have said! Had I said the right things? Perhaps, for the sake of Beth and the boys, I should have just lied, said what the parole board wanted to hear. *Okay, I was guilty, there wasn't any injury. I made the whole thing up, I created my own redundancy. I'm terribly sorry, I'll never do it again.*

Most long-timers applying for parole spent weeks dreaming up stories of how sorry they were for their former ways and how, whilst in prison, they had discovered enlightenment. At the same time many were already making the most of their new prison-acquired skills, fraud, counterfeiting, drug dealing, mortgage fraud.

I'd told the truth, but was that what she wanted to hear? All at once I realised the insanity of having bothered to apply for parole. All she'd wanted was an admission of guilt. To be able to place a tick in the appropriate box. Guilty. Case proven. The system was right. For almost two years I'd experienced the conditioning – 'the stick' of the prison system. Now it was 'the carrot' of possible early release, and it seemed I'd blown it.

I lay back on the narrow bed and listened to the rain still pounding against the glass. My mind drifted back and again I

367

retraced the nightmare from the first day I'd met DC Barnet and he'd uttered those words:- 'I must warn you that anything you say may be used in evidence...' From that moment I'd been caught up in a mindless mechanical process. We were all puppets in a bizarre show which seemed to have no end, the performance extended for the benefit of our political masters, eagerly absorbed by the deceived public. Mrs Tweed had added to the script and now only time would provide an outcome.

I peered out through the window, the rain continued to lash against the glass. Propping myself up onto my elbows, I checked my watch. The mail room will be open, I thought, maybe there'll be a letter from Beth. I swung my legs round and got up from the hard narrow bed.

I strolled over to the mail office, collected my post from the hatch and returned to my room flicking through the small pile of letters. There were two from Beth. I poked at random through the remaining pile. One caught my attention; it had not been opened, which was unusual as all post was usually opened and checked by curious screws, the only supposed exception being official legal letters.

The letter had been at the back of the pile. I selected it and studied the address in the window envelope. Across the top were typed the words 'Solicitor's Letter – Rule 37A. Mr Will Middleton Prison number FJ3866'. I flicked open the envelope. It was from Toby Jackson, my original solicitor, who'd handled our affairs prior to the honourable judge's insistence that he no longer represent me at the trial. The letter began:

> Dear Will
> Re Car Accident at Chichester, West Sussex on 30th November 1993.
>
> Further to this matter I write to confirm that the driver of the Land Rover that hit you has now admitted liability and we have today received settlement from the defendant's insurers for the damage to the Ford Sierra estate. I have forwarded this to Beth at your home address. The cheque was in the total sum of £2825...

Slowly I replaced the letter in the envelope. It's strange how fate works, I thought, how something unrelated to all that had happened could suddenly reach out from the past to provide what might be our only chance of proving my innocence. Reopening the letter, I reread the figures, *two thousand eight hundred and twenty five pounds*. Three years on from a car crash at Eastergate, more than two years since the trial and only weeks from the hearing before the Lord Chief Justice, I was being handed something. It wasn't a lot, but it might just be sufficient to pay for one or two of the all-important transcripts. The irony was, it was being provided by the insurance industry.

63

I woke excitedly on the 3rd February 1997. Today I was going home. Having served half of the four year sentence, I was being permitted my first home leave. For just seven days I was going to have freedom. Freedom to think for myself, freedom of movement, freedom to go where I wanted and the choice to wear what I liked. I'd also, at last, have the first opportunity to fully study my legal papers, but even more important I'd have the freedom to spend time with my family. Over the phone we had planned in great detail the itinerary of the next seven days.

It was 7.45 am. I knew Beth and the boys had been waiting excitedly outside the main gate for almost an hour. I made my way to the discharge office and joined the queue of waiting inmates. Thirty minutes later I finally reached the head of the queue. 'Ah, Middleton!' My heart sank, it was the bullfrog, one of the most sadistic screws in Ford. 'I suppose you were expecting to be released sometime today?' – the word 'sometime' was emphasised.

'Yes, I'm down for seven days' home leave,' I replied.

The bullfrog couldn't figure out why such a bothersome prisoner had been granted a home leave, but as an Officer of the Prison Service, he knew precisely what was expected of him. He picked up a small swathe of papers, blew out his cheeks and with a long sigh of deliberation slowly and methodically began studying the text. Suddenly something of interest caught his eye. 'Well Middleton, your discharge licence says you've been allotted a release time of 08.30.' He made an elaborate show of studying his watch for the benefit of the other officers. 'It's now 08.20. You're a stickler for details aren't you, and yet you arrive here ten minutes bloody early! You'd better go to the back of the queue, hadn't you?'

I smiled and gave a hapless shrug; there was no point in protesting. After another forty minutes of gamesmanship, the bullfrog could find no further reason to delay my discharge and I was at last unshackled from Her Majesty's care for a full week.

Beth had taken the boys off school for the week and for the next few days I soaked up the blessed joys of freedom; the first day we spent walking in the New Forest with an overjoyed Fudge whose tail wagged uncontrollably as he snuffled and raced his way over the soft moors. The second day we spent at home watching the latest video releases with the boys, the third in London seeing the sights.

The fourth day, Thursday 6th February, I'd set aside to spend time dealing with the appeal papers. I felt rested, refreshed and ready to begin the work which I knew should lead to permanent freedom. I did not relish the loss of even a single day with the family, but I knew this work had to be done. I was likely to be summoned before the Court of Appeal within weeks. I made my way into my former office, lowered myself into the red swivel chair and for a moment studied the debris of files and papers still strewn about the floor.

In front of me on the desk, Beth had already separated out the all-important files. I pulled the pile towards me, opened the first folder and began to work. I worked steadily through the morning and was about to take a break when the phone by my side rang. I hesitated for just a moment, it seemed strange, I hadn't *answered* a telephone in over two years. Eventually I plucked it from the cradle. 'Hello, is that Will?' I heard a voice say.

'Er, yes. Who's this?'

'Where on earth have you been?' It was Mandy, my probation officer. 'Everybody's been going frantic looking for you! Look, I'm not allowed to explain myself but this is in your best interest, you've got to contact the prison immediately.' She sounded excited, happy, as if something good had at last happened.

Hands trembling, I dialled the prison and was immediately put through to a senior officer on B Wing. It seemed bizarre to be speaking to one of the screws on a telephone. 'Ah, Mr Middleton, nice of you to get in touch, we've all been going mad down here trying to find you. I suppose you've heard the good news?'

My mind instinctively flicked to the appeal application, had the court suddenly summoned me, I thought? Perhaps I'd been granted bail! 'No, nobody's told me anything,' I said, voice trembling.

'Oh, well, let me be the first to congratulate you, the Parole Board have sanctioned your immediate release. You've just got to come back for official discharge. It's all been a bit of a cock up really,' he chuckled nervously, 'you should have been told three days ago. You're supposed to have been released by now.'

I was suddenly aware of an involuntary trembling throughout my entire being. Tension seemed to drain from me like pus from a lanced abscess. I replaced the handset slowly, then swivelled the chair towards the window. I could feel the knots in my stomach easing up. I'd been granted parole! A grin spread from one ear to the other. Mrs Tweed had done it after all, she'd bloody well done it!

Wednesday 12th February 1997 – Six days later

Light sliced through the gap in the green curtains. I leapt out of bed and dressed quickly, today I was being released. My release time had been set for 10.00, slightly later than normal because of the mix up. Before then I had to get a form signed by the library, education department, laundry and stores, all confirming that any prison books, clothing, bedding etc. that had been issued to me, had all been returned. Next I had to see the prison doctor, who had to agree that I was free from any medical problems, and finally I had to sign my licence.

I checked my watch, it was 06.45. I wasn't allowed out of the hut until the bell sounded for breakfast at 7.00. Carefully I removed the photos of Beth and the boys from the board and placed them into the prison-issue bag along with a box of her letters and a few personal belongings. Stepping over to the hut window, I gazed up into the bright morning sky. Overhead the first hazy streaks of cirrus were smearing the pale blue. Two years earlier, when I'd arrived at Ford, I'd reflected on the day I'd leave this place. I'd expected it to be sooner than this but at last, today, I was going home.

It was pointless trying to start the process of getting my forms signed before 8.00, as none of the departments would be manned until then. The bell rang sharp at 7.00 and I made my way out of the hut and along the path to A Wing and the dining hall.

As I walked across the camp I was met by a handful of smiling inmates stopping to say goodbye. 'Good morning, Will,' a cheerful voice announced from over my right shoulder. I turned, expecting to see another inmate, but it was Governor Richards. 'I believe you're leaving us today.'

'Yes, three hours and ...' I glanced at my watch, 'thirteen minutes. Just heading over for my last prison breakfast. I'm allowing some extra time today so that I can savour every last morsel.'

He chuckled. 'So what are your plans when you get out?'

'Well, we have the appeal against not being *allowed* to appeal, coming up in the next few weeks.'

He nodded seriously. 'Well, I doubt I'll get a chance to see you before you go, Will, so I'll say goodbye now.' For a moment he hesitated, and then he added, 'I believe your Personal Officer has prepared a letter for the court, acknowledging our part in the unfortunate delays in your appeal preparation. I'd like to extend my good wishes to you and trust you will be successful.' He smiled and offering a hand, added, 'I rarely have cause to say this, but then it's not every day we get somebody in here that shouldn't be. But when you get out, try not to be bitter about what's happened; you've got the rest of your life ahead of you ... okay?' He smiled at me sincerely, like a father.

I nodded thank you, but it took me a few moments to fully process what he'd just said. Not knowing quite how to respond and shocked at what he was implying, I thanked him. His words meant more to me at that moment than I could ever convey; words that would stay with me forever. He patted me on the shoulder, then turned and continued in the direction of A Wing, never looking back.

'Good morning, Middleton,' the bullfrog announced with an unusually cheery face. 'Leaving us so soon! I'm sure we're all going to miss your jolly smile around the camp.'

373

I cast him a sidelong glance. 'I'm sure I'll miss yours too,' I replied with equal sarcasm.

He flicked open a file and removed some papers. 'This is your licence; the conditions of your early release have already been explained to you. 'Sign 'ere and 'ere.'

I signed where he pointed.

Opening a large ledger, he ran a finger down a column of figures. 'You're entitled to £38 discharge allowance, plus you've got £25 remaining in your canteen and a total of £42 in savings, a grand total of £105.' He removed a red cash box from beneath the counter, opened it and counted out ten ten-pound notes and one five-pound note. 'Sign 'ere,' he said, handing over the cash. 'You've got to report to your probation officer at Littlehampton for 2.30 today, is that clear?'

'Yes.'

'Well, in that case I'll say goodbye then, Middleton. I think you know the way out.'

64

If you want a Big Brother, you get all that comes with it.

(Erich Fromm)

I entered the red-brick seventies-style office block and made my way up to the third floor. Ms Mandy Turner, my probation officer, offered me a plastic chair. 'How are you Will?' she asked, flipping open a file.

'A lot better for being out of Ford,' I replied.

'Well my job is to try to ensure you stay out. So let's begin. Now, these meetings will initially be scheduled for every two weeks and will enable us to address any problems you are experiencing, now that you have been released from prison. Is that clear?'

'Yes.'

'Do you have any work lined up?'

'No, I was only released this morning.'

She made a note on her form. 'Do you have any income of any kind?'

'No, but I intend signing on at the Job Centre tomorrow, so hopefully I will be able to find something soon, and with any luck I'll initially be eligible for some benefit.'

Another note was scrawled on her form. 'Have you returned to your former home address...' she studied her file, 'The Old Granary?'

'Yes, I have.'

She ticked a box. 'And you're living with your wife, Beth?'

'Yes, I am.'

Ms Turner made another note. 'And do you intend staying at that address in the immediate future?'

'Yes, I do.'

'I believe your mother is also living at The Old Granary, is that correct?'

375

'Yes, she is.'

'And does that situation work out satisfactorily; are there any family problems?'

I felt like mentioning that my mother had been confined to a wheelchair since the police raid, and that both the bank and the Crown were trying to force us all out onto the street, but I doubted there was an appropriate box to tick on her form. I equally doubted it would help my case, so just replied, 'No, everything's fine.'

'And looking more long term, what are your plans, Will?'

'That will depend largely on the appeal.'

Ms Turner frowned and flicking a few pages of her file said, 'I wasn't aware that you had been granted leave to appeal.'

'I haven't yet, but we have a hearing scheduled for 14th March to argue for a full appeal to be heard out of time, based on medical grounds and the delays caused in prison.'

'I was unaware you were still pursuing this line. I thought you had accepted your conviction and sentence.'

'Absolutely not!' I replied, somewhat indignantly. 'I have always maintained I was innocent. The whole case was bizarre, the injuries were always self-evident and we've got new evidence to present regarding the Prize Indemnity.'

'I see.'

I took a couple of deep breaths, trying to compose myself, then slowly continued, 'The whole thing was a set up.'

Ms Turner shifted uncomfortably in her chair, trying to retain patience with me. Suddenly I realised that it would be wise to shut up.

Completing her notes, she looked up, studying me thoughtfully, considering each word of my outburst and their implications. A few moments passed before she rose from her chair. 'Well, in that case, Will, I think we'll call it a day. I'll see you again in two weeks.' She smiled and offered me a card. 'Please remember, I'm available at any time to offer help and advice, so if you have any problems, just call this number.'

65

'The bank want their money,' Jack, my bank manager, said.

'I'm sure they do,' I replied irritably. I was really annoyed that within days of my release I was being pressurised by the very people who had added extra fuel to the Crown's case.

'It's not me,' insisted Jack, 'it's head office.'

'Tell them I'm working on it,' I said abruptly, replacing the phone with an unsteady hand.

I *was* working on it, but it was always there, waiting in the shadows, like a stalker with unlimited time. I had asked Piglet to see if there was any way out, but he'd just shaken his head. 'They have security. They'll just foreclose and take your home. I'm so sorry Will!'

For the next ten days I pondered what I could do. I read and reread the letters to and from the bank, and studied in minute detail the security document I'd signed so eagerly, all those years earlier, that was now threatening to take away our security, our home. *Where would we go* I thought, *and what about my mother? For her to be made homeless in her eighties* ... it was then that I saw it.

We set off at 8.30 to drive the sixty or so miles to Reading. The meeting was set for 10.30. The fuel tank of our old Audi was showing half empty, something that wouldn't have bothered me a few years ago; but now I wondered whether it was sufficient to do the round trip of some 120 miles. Before the recession, the collapse of the race team and all the legal problems with WPA, I would never have considered the cost of fuel, just pulled into any service station, filled up the 4x4 and paid with my Gold WPA Card. The cards were now cut up and the nice 4x4 a distant memory.

Beth now monitored the finances: seventy-five pounds in state benefits had to feed the four of us and anything left over could go for fuel. She knew the supermarket prices by heart, the cost of everything, milk, bread, economy beans, rice, pasta and basic tomatoes. Only very occasionally the budget might stretch to a cheap chicken.

We had explained what had to be explained to the boys; just the basics. That we had built up a big debt with the bank, mostly interest and extra charges, and the bank now wanted our home, but we would get another one, somehow, somewhere. Both boys had quickly declared that the bank man was a very nasty man.

Beth and I made our way into the impressive smoked black glass and marble head office of the National Charter Bank. I walked over to the reception desk. 'We have an appointment with a Mr Bryan Baggott and a Mr Jack Carter.'

'Mr and Mrs Middleton?'

'Yes, that's correct.'

'Foreclosures and Repossessions are on the third floor. The elevators are at the end of the corridor. Somebody will meet you when you come out.'

We walked over to the lifts, both wondering how the next hour would go. I had to remain calm and businesslike, I told myself; the outcome of this meeting could affect the rest of our lives. We stepped into a lift and were whisked up to the third floor.

The doors swept open and a secretary greeted us. She ushered us down a corridor and into a modern glass and chrome meeting room. Jack was already seated on the far side of a glass table. He jumped up as we entered, offering his hand. 'Good morning Will, please take a seat. Mr Baggott will be back in a few minutes,' he said gravely.

'Would you like some tea or coffee, or perhaps some juice?' the secretary enquired.

'Coffee would be nice, black, no sugar,' I said.

We took our seats on the opposite side of the table and waited. Beth sat nervously to my left. I removed a file from my briefcase. We sat in awkward silence watching the beams of sunlight sifting in through the large plate glass window, radiating warmth into the sterile chill of the room. A few particles of dust danced in the beams as I flicked open my file, preparing for the battle ahead.

Since my discovery, Beth and I had talked non-stop about my idea for a potential lifeline, trying to predict the bank's response; she cast me another glance and smiled reassuringly. A few more minutes passed before the door opened. 'Good morning Mr and Mrs Middleton, my name is Brian Baggott, I am head of repossessions with the bank.' He offered a hand before striding purposefully to the head of the table. 'Well, we all know the background to this unfortunate situation...' he began, flicking open the cover of a blue file, 'so I don't feel it necessary to summarise the known facts.' He spoke with self-confidence, assured of the outcome.

I've been through hell; you don't intimidate me any more! I thought.

'The total due to be repaid to the bank, as at today's date including legal fees is £180,000. This sum originates from a loan provided for the extension to your property, the Old Granary, plus your overdraft, interest, default interest, sundry letters and charges. The bank has formally requested repayment within twenty-eight days.' He inclined his head in my direction, with a hint of a smile. 'The purpose of today's meeting is to hear your proposals for repayment, Mr Middleton.'

'You're aware that the bank wrote to me every two weeks whilst I was in prison, each time adding a £30 charge to our account...' I began.

'The charges imposed are strictly in accordance with our Terms and Conditions.'

'And you realise that the comments the bank made on file...' I turned to Jack, 'about fiddling my income were totally false? That they simply added extra fuel to the Crown's case?'

'Mr Middleton,' Baggott interrupted, already sounding a little exasperated. 'I believe you were found guilty by a jury, and in any event we're not here to discuss comments that the bank may have made in an internal file that was never intended to be seen by any other party. The purpose of this meeting is to hear your proposals for repayment of your commitments to the bank.'

I made a helpless gesture. 'Well, I simply don't have £180,000, so I don't know what you are expecting me to do.'

'Mr Middleton, if that is the case, then the bank holds a first charge over your property,' he studied his papers, 'the Old Granary, and if you are unable to pay and you have no proposals to put forward, you leave the bank with no alternative but to foreclose.'

'So be it…' I said, smiling, 'but you are of course aware of the reason for the original loan, aren't you?'

He glanced at Jack for confirmation, his body language showing signs of increasing impatience, 'Um, I believe it was for the construction of an annexe to your home, the Old Granary.'

'That's correct,' I said. 'An annexe, or more accurately a granny annexe. In fact if you look at the original loan application, you will see it asks for the purposes of the loan, and you will see that I entered, very clearly, that it was for the construction of a granny annexe. I do have copies of the original application, if it would assist. You'll also find a letter in there that accompanied the loan application. Perhaps you could take a look at your copy.' I waited for a moment whilst Mr Baggott flicked through several pages in his file. 'Ah, there it is!' I said happily, pointing to a letter with a set of drawings stapled to it. 'And I see you still have a copy of the architect's drawings,' I added, my voice gradually became more theatrical.

Baggott cleared his throat. 'Mr Middleton, I'm sorry, but is this actually getting us anywhere?'

'Well, *I* think it is, if you could bear with me for a few moments more?'

'So be it, but I do have another meeting to attend in fifteen minutes.'

'That should be quite long enough. I'll just read out the first paragraph of the letter.

Dear Jack,
  Reference Granny Flat
  Re phone call, please find attached completed loan application; reference the construction of the new Granny Flat, also a set of architect's drawings. As you are aware, it is intended that following my father's death, my mother will move into the new granny annexe as soon as the building works are completed. I can confirm that we have now received full planning consent and that my mother

will be paying the balance of £40,000 for the construction of her flat.

'I see you have a copy of the loan application and the guarantee,' I said, wondering if the significance of my words was beginning to sink in. 'Well, if you could just take a look, I think you'll find the bank omitted to obtain my mother's signature on the security documentation and, well, as the legal occupant...' I let my words trail away. 'She does of course have rights to occupancy of her flat.'

'Ah,' Jack muttered under his breath, but his only contribution was loud enough for us all to hear.

'So,' I continued, 'if you decide to foreclose on the Granary and wish to sell it, you will have to explain to any prospective purchaser that the property comes complete with a granny flat with a little old lady as a sitting tenant.'

Baggott didn't answer but continued reading the letter. 'I see,' he said eventually. 'You're not suggesting your mother would stay there if you moved out?' He looked up at me in disbelief.

'Well, she does *hold* legal title to the flat, and no, I don't believe she wants to vacate her property.' I paused for additional effect. 'Perhaps I should also mention that she's already willed the flat to her niece.'

Baggott shifted uncomfortably in his chair as he considered the significance of my words and digested the change of events. He turned to my former manager, who was looking decidedly sheepish. 'Mr Carter, can I have a few words outside?' They both got up, excusing themselves, and headed for the door.

Half an hour later, Beth and I walked hand in hand from the building. Just hours earlier we had been broke, with whatever assets we'd had totally engulfed by the liabilities imposed by the bank. Now, in the space of two hours, it had all changed. We still owed the bank, but the debt was now manageable and the interest frozen. Beth spoke first, 'Did we just save ourselves £100,000?'

I smiled. 'We nailed the bastards! I wonder if I could get it down any further?'

She cast me one of those looks that she reserved for such occasions. 'Don't even *think* about it.'

'Okay. Just joking,' I said. We had won a major victory, the

381

millstone was gone; we could make a fresh start. The fatigue started to lift, I wanted to talk about the future, but now wasn't the time. Maybe after the appeal, when it had all sunk in, and we could get away for a quiet night out and consider our future.

66

It had taken almost three hours to drive from Climping to south London. 'I can't explain it, but I have to do this, Beth ... *with you*,' I said. 'I know it doesn't make any sense but I need to see the place as a free man, and then leave by my own free will.'

We had stopped at a service station to refuel the old Audi, and the place was now close, very close. I could feel it, like a disease infecting me. It was as if it were calling me, watching me, watching both of us. Beth leaned over from the passenger seat and took my hand. She looked deep into my eyes. 'As long as you're ready for this, Will,' she whispered intensely, a look of concern on her face.

I was ready and I was returning, voluntarily, to Wandsworth. Then I'd leave. Of course I would only be able to see the place from the outside this time, but then, maybe, the nightmares would end, or maybe not. But I had to try; I had to try to bury the ghost.

I slowed the car as we approached the huge security gate. A blue and white sign read *HMP Wandsworth*. A security camera swung ominously in our direction and then stopped. Big Brother was watching, waiting. I began to imagine somebody already checking up on us, checking our registration number, cross-referencing.

The image of the place with its razor wire, CCTV and high walls instantly brought back a torrent of terrifying memories, and I almost lost it there and then. I could smell the sickly marijuana fused with the acrid reek of the urine, excrement and sweat.

Beth, sensing my rising apprehension, gently squeezed my

fingers encouragingly as I stared up at the forbidding facade. In my mind I could see the screws, the neverending corridors, gates and passageways, the cockroaches scurrying for cover. Sounds, words, disembodied cries, echoed hauntingly, nauseatingly, through my brain – *Your number's FJ3866, Middleton, remember it! ... Walk clockwise Middleton, sun wise! ... Welcome to Beirut, mate ... Soon get used to it mate...*

'Damn the bastards!' I said out loud. 'How did they manage to get away with all this? *Who* did all this?' I wanted revenge, I wanted to strike out at somebody.

Beth touched my arm gently. 'Will, you're trembling,' she said, 'are you okay?' She leaned over, hugging me tightly.

Suddenly, in a moment of terror I looked up to see a police officer approaching in the rear view mirror. The events of the past had changed everything that I had ever believed in or trusted – *Believe no one. Trust nobody. Question everything* – except for Beth. That was my new maxim.

Trying to not look suspicious, I nonchalantly edged the Audi away from the kerb. 'Let's go round the back,' I said.

We made our way around the outer edge, along the perimeter road to the rear of the twelve-acre site. Above the high walls I could clearly make out the central hub with the different wings, each with their four landings. I pulled over again and wound down the window, pointing. 'I think that must be B Wing,' I said, trying to orientate the place in my mind. 'I was on the second landing, cell 18. They called it Beirut!' I counted the number of barred windows from the end of what I believed to be my wing. 'That must have been my cell,' I said.

We sat for more than ten minutes, as I tried to control my feelings. 'Okay,' I said finally, still struggling to slow my breathing, 'that's enough. This place is just too creepy. Let's get out of here and find a nice little restaurant and get some lunch. Somewhere without bars.'

I started the car and drove away, in search of our happy-ever-after ending, but couldn't resist a last fleeting look back at the image in the rear view mirror.

67

All truth passes through three stages.
First, it is ridiculed.
Second, it is violently opposed.
Third, it is accepted as being self-evident.

(Arthur Schopenhauer, 1788–1860)

Court of Appeal, London, 14th March 1997 (four weeks later)

Loaded with files, we made our way up the spiral stone staircase
and along the corridor to Court Eighteen. Piglet held open the
heavy mahogany doors and we eased our way into the body of
the court. This time, having served what the system considered
an appropriate sentence for my acts of villainy, I was considered
safe to sit, unguarded, with my legal team.

Strangely, bearing in mind the staggering amount of public
money spent on bringing the original trial to court, the Prosecution
had decided not to attend the hearing. Perhaps it was due to
the court already having decreed it would only today be resolving
whether or not to allow an appeal to be heard 'out of time'.
Or perhaps it was for another reason, perhaps the Prosecution
already knew something that we didn't.

I looked up at the embellished ceiling and the tall mullioned
windows. To the left of the court an ornate clock ticked tirelessly.
Directly ahead, raised high on their judicial thrones, the three
appeal court judges sat impassively; on the left Her Honour
Justice Catherine Symes; next in line with wig set stylishly askew
like a crocheted beret, His Honour Justice Carruthers; and to
the extreme right, observing fair play through half-moon spectacles,
the bearded and Honourable Judge Tourne. Before each inquisitor
a microphone hung, suspended like a tantalising tropical fruit,
and above each noble brow, soft, ornate lamps bathed their
honours with a celestial glow. *The three wise monkeys*, I thought

385

cynically; *hear no evil, see no evil, and speak no evil, unless of course one is the defendant.*

Michael Bamforth QC, my new senior barrister, was already on his feet explaining how, whilst the original case had in its essence been simple, the Prosecution had thrown up such a dust storm of slurs and accusations that the true facts had become lost. 'This was a case that clearly warranted leading counsel.' Bamforth asserted.

Justice Carruthers regarded my new advocate with a glint in his eye. 'Are you saying the trial judge was wrong to have denied leading counsel?' The learned judge spoke intently. 'I seem to recall a case some years ago in which I had the pleasure of opposing you, and you, as junior counsel at that time, did rather well.' Bamforth smiled, and nodded an acknowledgement. I felt like adding that, had I had the pleasure of Mr Bamforth, even in his junior days, I might have done quite nicely myself, but I knew my place.

For more than an hour my new advocate continued to argue for a full appeal to be allowed out of time. 'Clearly my client was incapable of dealing with the appeal within twenty-eight days of the trial as he was in hospital at that time having suffered a breakdown.'

Judge Tourne, who doubtless had been cogitating very deeply, surveyed my advocate through his half-moon spectacles. 'Whilst your client may not have been well during the twenty-eight days immediately following the trial, his condition clearly improved some time after this.'

Bamforth went on to explain the difficulties of preparing the appeal without legal aid whilst in prison. He also pointed out that there was clear evidence that a number of witnesses had an interest to serve in perhaps holding back elements of their testimony. Justice Carruthers leaned back in his chair. 'Are you suggesting this was a *Brock* type case?'

I listened uncomprehendingly while the learned judiciary discussed the text from a previous historical trial. 'I think pages 16 to 17 of Archbould contains the relevant passages,' added Her Honour Justice Catherine Symes, helpfully.

I cast a glance at Piglet on the bench in front, who along with the gentleman of the press was vehemently transcribing the scholarly words that flowed from the judicial lips. I shrugged mentally; this was *not* what I'd expected.

'If you would refer to volume two of the summing-up transcript,' Bamforth continued, 'you will note that the trial judge implied that Mr Middleton did not experience any problems with his back at Brands Hatch. The court stenographer recorded the witness, a Mr Thompson, as telling the court that Mr Middleton was in some pain with his back. He then went on to say that Mr Middleton had not wanted to drive in the second heat.'

'My understanding,' interrupted the Honourable Catherine Symes, 'was that the learned trial judge simply advised the jury,' she opened a notebook and flicked through the leaves, 'that the Defendant had made "no big thing" of his back problem, whilst at Brands Hatch. Judge McGaea didn't say that the witness had advised there was no problem at all.'

It had been decided by my legal team that we would not raise the matter of Judge McGaea's 'facial gestures', as to do so might displease the honourable bench, but for the next half hour my barrister continued to outline the need for the case to be reopened. He explained about the discrepancy in Mr Burton's evidence, the difficulty of addressing the general slur that I'd somehow orchestrated the collapse of Team Capricorn. 'This is all very well Mr Bamforth,' interrupted Justice Carruthers, 'but we don't have any transcripts to support these submissions.'

'You do in respect of Mr Burton, Your Honours,' insisted my QC, 'and you could in respect of everyone else as well, if legal aid was reinstated to cover the cost of the required transcripts.'

Following a short recess for lunch the court reconvened and Justice Carruthers, with wig now firmly clipped in place, produced a small swathe of pre-prepared text from which he began to read. For the benefit of the court stenographer and press, he outlined the original charges and explained that, having served over two years in prison, I'd been released on parole. He went on to summarise the grounds that had been submitted for appeal and pointed out that the first judge had refused leave to appeal the sentence back in May 1995.

I leaned forward to speak to Piglet, who was busily transcribing the judge's words. 'Jonathan, I don't think they're going to allow us to appeal, he's reading all this from a pre-prepared, typed script, the whole things been decided in advance.'

His Honour continued to point out that the court was being asked to rule upon whether to allow an appeal to be heard outside the authorised time limit of twenty-eight days. 'One of the difficulties the court has had to contend with, is the lack of official transcripts,' Carruthers continued, as though covering himself, should the corpse they were burying ever rise again from its grave and point a skeletal digit in their direction. 'Mr Middleton has made available transcripts in relation to Mr Thompson and Mr Burton, and it is clear from this evidence that the trial judge did misdirect the jury in these areas. However, we find it inconceivable that this misdirection alone would have affected the minds of the jury. We therefore find that there are no grounds to allow an appeal to be heard out of time. We do however have some misgivings over the compensation order and in order to assess this matter fully, a transcript of this section of the trial will be ordered at Crown cost.'

The court usher requested that we all stand as Their Honours departed. I helped to stack together the last cases of files and walked from the court. Michael Bamforth picked up his briefcase and followed on behind.

A thin mist of rain greeted us as we left the court. 'So that was it?' I said with frustration. 'No appeal. They won't even allow us to present our case.'

Bamforth was standing next to Beth. He turned, looking at me intently. 'Will, the facts are self-evident. You *should* have been granted an appeal, but then it's also obvious that this case should never have gone to trial. The trouble is, this isn't a high-profile case...' he paused, 'and there's little if any media attention, so unless you've got the resources to fight, you'll never get anywhere. You heard what they said about the compensation order; it's my opinion that they know something was very wrong with the trial. I suspect they're planning to do something with the order in the hope that you'll give up and go away a happy man.'

Piglet appeared from the swing doors and walked over to join us. 'I'm sorry, Will,' he began, shaking his head. 'Despite everything that's happened, I just didn't expect that. It was as if they'd already decided the judgement.' He turned to Bamforth. 'Did you see how the ruling was read from a *prepared* statement?'

Bamforth shook his head. 'I've seen it too many times before,' he admitted. Turning to face me, he went on, 'Will, our legal system is a war zone, a battleground.' He gave me a resigned smile. 'You were fortunate to come out of this as well as you have. In a war, there are plenty who never make it home at all.'

Bamforth and Piglet continued to talk. My mind began to wander and my gaze drifted up through the rain towards a statue perched high on the roof, the goddess of justice, law and order. The figure that symbolised the British legal system: Justitia – Lady Justice, the icon that adorns courts and courtrooms all around the world. Justitia, the combination of two goddesses, intended to embody impartiality by blending the Roman blindfolded Fortuna (luck), showing justice is meted out objectively, with the Hellenistic Greek (fate), and sword-carrying Nemesis (vengeance).

In that moment something caught my eye. Irrational, I thought, but in the same instant, powerful words spoken to me in Ford flooded back, underpinning the notion. *Masons hide their secrets in plain view*, Matthew had told me. His words had seemed strange at the time, but now, staring up at a gilded bronze statue that had for almost a century symbolised our legal system, they brought new meaning. *In plain view of the average man* Matthew's ghost whispered into a dark corner of my mind. I shivered as icy needles prickled down my spine.

In that moment the revelation hit me. How many famous miscarriages of justice had occurred from *pre-prepared* rulings I wondered, cases that would never have been overturned, had it not been for public pressure? Again Matthew's words drifted across my mind: *The generally accepted figure is 4%, Will, that's around 3200 people locked up that shouldn't be.*

Beth had followed my gaze up through the rain to the roof and was looking puzzled, 'What are you staring at, Will?'

I looked into her soft brown eyes. I saw the little girl I loved, but in her face I could also see the pain that she'd carried throughout the trial, and it had all returned. I pulled her close and held her tightly to me. 'Something intriguing…' I stopped mid-sentence.

I turned to Bamforth. 'Who designed the statue?'

Bamforth shrugged, then following my gaze, replied, 'Oh,' his face flickered into an enigmatic smile, 'Lady Justice?'

I nodded.

'Frederick Pomeroy,' said Piglet with his cutomary flourish.

'He was a prominent stone mason and a member of the Royal Institute of British Sculptors. Why do you ask?'

'Was he by any chance a famous member of the Masons as well?' I asked.

'From the little I know,' Piglet replied, 'Frederick Pomeroy was both a Royal Academician and a prominent Mason. He was awarded vast numbers of commissions by the establishment, for some of the most iconic statues through the United Kingdom. Why are you asking? He died almost a hundred years ago.'

'If you were to ask most people...' I went on, still staring through the rain at Lady Justice, 'most would able to describe it, don't you think?'

Both Bamforth and Piglet exchanged uncertain looks. 'I suppose so,' Bamforth answered with a shrug, 'a blindfolded lady holding the scales of justice in her left hand and a double-edged sword in her right hand.'

'Precisely! So *where's* the *blindfold*?' I asked.

'You've lost me,' Bamforth replied, turning sharply back to the roof.

There was a short silence. Expressions changed to frowns as everyone realised what I was alluding to: a justice system that in *truth* was anything *but* impartial. A system controlled by powerful individuals with agendas that most could never remotely envisage. Piglet's mouth was open. 'Good heavens,' he finally mumbled, his head cocked, staring up at the statue. 'It's true, she has no blindfold!'

'Rather appropriate, don't you think?' I said. 'The blindfold is removed when joining the brotherhood and entering into the First Degree. I believe Masons describe that part of the ceremony as *awakening* or *enlightenment* – seeing the light.'

A flicker of unease crossed Bamforth's face. For a few moments all our thoughts hung unspoken, then he turned back to face me. 'The big question Will is, where do you go from here?' He glanced at his gold Rolex. 'Look, I've got to go; I've got a conference to chair in half an hour.' Then with a warm smile he added, 'Just let me know what you want to do.'

I thanked him and Piglet for all their help, a show of appreciation which seemed a little inadequate given the amount of time Piglet in particular had personally put into the case. A few moments later they were both off, disappearing into the hubbub of the London traffic.

Beth bent down and picked up one of the boxes of files. 'Well, it's been an interesting day.'

'I wouldn't call it interesting,' I remarked. 'I think tragic would be a more appropriate word.' I looked out into the London traffic. I suppose I knew at that moment that our days of fighting were over, we'd been through too much. Without legal aid we could do nothing and the past four years had aged us both.

Right from a child I'd always been a fighter but as we become older it gets more difficult to just keep going. It's not that you don't *want* to fight, it's just that there's a realisation that there's no real point. The system will, at the end of the day, do whatever it wants. The only hope for change is by public pressure. Things will happen in your life that you can't stop, but that's no reason to switch off from the rest of your life. There was Beth and the boys to consider; the investigation and trial had ruled more than half of Jonathan's young life and George was now a teenager.

Beth yawned. She looked tired. 'This has all been so unbelievable, like a never-ending nightmare. I think we should talk to the press, we have to do something.'

For several seconds I didn't speak. 'They're not interested in real news, only tabloid fodder,' I finally answered. 'How do we know what kind of spin the media would put on all of this? It's easier for them to produce a story about a dishonest racing driver than to research hard news. They can say what they like about me; remember I'm the proven felon so they're unlikely to be sued. Anyway, what real proof of collusion do we have?'

'You could push on to the House of Lords and even the European Courts,' she insisted.

I shook my head. 'I've lost too much faith in the system,' I replied, as Matthew's ghost whispered again – *practically all our judges, barristers and Law Lords are members.*

I glanced again at Beth. Sometimes, I thought, it's important to remember what you still have. When you determine to follow your life's dreams it can be that the dream itself, quite wrongly, becomes life. Yet we all know that we're meant to wake from our dreams, and that is when we're supposed to live our life. I'd been naively chasing *my* personal dream, my big prize, for so long that I hadn't appreciated I'd already found it. For more

391

than fifteen years she'd been there, loyally by my side. So, what did I need to prove? With Beth I already had unconditional love, and a happy ending.

'More men in bloody wigs,' I continued, 'men whose only qualification to sit in judgement over others, is being born.' Again I stared up at the famous statue, perched high on the roof, the goddess of justice and law, the figure that symbolised the British legal system.

I stood for a few more moments, lost in thought; the events of the past four years once more flooding back. Over those years a part of me had died. My belief in justice had died much earlier during both the investigation and the trial, but in prison my belief in our system had died as well. I'd become old, the little boy that was the fighter just didn't want to fight any longer. I didn't want to lose any more faith. 'No, I don't think so darling... I don't think so.'

Beth tilted her head, a puzzled look on her face. 'But I've never known you not to fight. Are you sure you can just walk away from this? They've labelled you a criminal, Will. They've given you a criminal record.'

A smile spread across my face. I'd always been a bit of a rebel, but from now on, I thought, I'll be a *rebel with a cause*. 'It is the *only* blemish on an otherwise untarnished life,' I replied jokingly.

'*Untarnished?*' she gave me one of her looks. 'Hardly *untarnished*!' Shaking her head she added, 'Look, this is serious; you'll have to live with that official record for life.'

I thought about it. 'We all love to label people,' I said, 'good, bad, guilty or not guilty. Usually we never know the full facts.' I knew that now. It happens every day, each time someone picks up a newspaper they make judgements over the lives of others they've never met and on things that may be totally untrue. I looked at her, 'I don't know, maybe we should just go away somewhere, somewhere warm, a long way away from here, a sanctuary from this mad, crazy world. I always liked Thailand; what do you think?'

She grinned, 'I don't think so; did you ever read *Bangkok Hilton*!'

I smiled, 'Well, I think we should go off somewhere, what about Sri Lanka?'

She thought about it for a moment, 'Too many Tamil Tigers

there, but we do know some people in Madagascar,' she said quietly, running with the idea.

'Where's Madagascar?' I asked absentmindedly, as my eyes again drifted up through the drizzle to the impassive statue.

A comforting hand rested on my shoulder. Beth followed my gaze up to the unblindfolded figure. In the statue's left hand were the balanced scales of British justice, in her right hand a three-foot double-edged sword, signifying the power of those making judgement, a power that can be wielded for or against even the innocent.

'Darling,' Beth whispered, a sudden mischievous tone in her voice. 'There might be a way of turning all this around.'

'Oh?'

'Have you ever heard the expression: *The pen is mightier than the sword?*'

Postscript

Do not adjust your mind, there is a fault in reality!

(R.D. Lang)

It happens less often now, but I still have the odd sleepless night when I think about what happened, and try to make sense of it all. Of course my legal team knew how it happened, and we were pretty sure we knew why and also who the key players were that influenced the outcome. But simply put, we just didn't have the resources to fight it.

More than sixteen years on from the events portrayed in these pages, the thing I've found most difficult to accept has been the hypocrisy of our justice system. A system that is infected, that not only failed to see beyond the narrow scope of its own prejudice, but was in the opinion of many complicit in ensuring that a flawed, unsafe conviction would stand. I've been told the practice has a name, and that it's been around forever. It's called Noble cause corruption; put simply, it's where the end supposedly justifies the means. It's where 'the system' or powerful individuals working within it, convinced of a person's guilt and with the limitless resources of the state, set about securing a conviction whilst ignoring or even stage-managing any evidence that might stand in the way.

The process survives to this day because, in general, the public's belief is that our system of justice stands for everything that is good, honourable and true. Any alternative belief would be simply too frightening to consider. It is a view validated by a self-serving media and endorsed by ministers eager for our votes and so, in a world cynically manipulated by financial institutions, press and politics, society simply tolerates the greed and corruption. Whilst busying itself with its various daily concerns, it has no time to reflect on the architecture of injustice they call the best legal system in the world... so it survives. This fact has been exposed repeatedly through British legal history from the simplest to the most complex and high-profile cases.

So, as powerful multinationals and government ministers enrich themselves on the back of the everyday populace, we simply stay on our treadmills. It is my inability to accept this system that led me to spend the last 13 years writing Chequered Justice.

But before I conclude, I'm obliged to remind you of what I said in my opening note: that what you have read, whilst inspired by true events, is fictional. After all, financial institutions such as banks and insurance corporations are, as we all know, run by totally honourable people, and our system and The Metropolitan Police have only our best interests at heart. None of the corporations or individuals depicted, the lawyers, the racing drivers, police, judges or race teams etc. actually exist, as far as I am aware. I made them all up, figments of my overactive imagination.

The key policies featured in Chequered Justice are known as 'Payment Protection' or 'PPI' policies. Incidentally, in 2011, following a judicial review and after more than a decade of legal wrangling, the banks and insurance industry were finally forced to set aside multi-billion pound funds to compensate former PPI policy holders. The industry was however spared the cost and humiliation of compensating any that had purchased such policies as far back as the 1980's! Also in 2011, changes were implemented to the 'Sick Note' system issued by GP's. In future 'Fit Notes' are to be issued in their place, differentiating between sickness or injury and advising what the individual can in fact do.

Anyway, almost a decade on from my riding accident we did make it to our tropical island, but if you're interested in that piece of fiction, you'll have to wait for Mary's, or should I call it Beth's, account of our journey: No Battery Hens, Three Travel Journals, Two Curious Boys & a Golden Retriever called Fudge! With Chequered Justice now published in hardback, paperback and eBook, we expect Mary's follow-on to be completed within a year or so.

I suppose that despite never being able to formally prove my innocence, we did secure a few major victories along the way, and as a family we're all still together and are much stronger for the experience.

As for the others, following the events portrayed in Chequered Justice, 'Paterson-Smythe' was appointed Queen's Counsel and a few years later 'Rabbit' became a part-time Recorder, a type of judge that sits with the power of a Circuit Judge. 'Les Heath' the teams 3rd driver and agent who brokered the Prize Indemnity Policy, left 'Track Star' faster than a speeding bullet, immediately following the trial! 'David Mamet' still runs his Porsche team over in sunny Florida. Rob Alan's racing career petered out by the mid 90's, having failed to become a houshould name. We remain good friends with 'Piglet' who ultimately decided to leave the world of criminal defence and now works as the head of global litigation for a major corporation.

As for me, nowadays I switch on the TV and watch as other men fight to fulfil their dreams, resting my back in the comfort of my old leather recliner, in the safety of our new home, but occasionally 'Beth' catches me fantasizing, remembering the thrill of those glory days and dreaming of doing it all again.

www.chequeredjustice.com
www.AmazingJourneys.co.uk
Twitter@ChequeredJ

John Bartlett left school at 15, with an undistinguished academic record, a dream of becoming a racing driver and his headmaster's last salvo: 'You will never amount to anything' ringing in his ears. At 18 he set up his first business, an electronics company, in a shed on an industrial estate and within 2 years was employing 25 people and driving his first classic Aston Martin. In 1979 he turned his back on security to focus on his childhood dream. From little backing, he rapidly secured major sponsorships propelling him into the World Championship. In 1985 he set up his own World Championship Le Mans team and qualified as a helicopter pilot John, now a Master Instructor, trains Scuba divers near his home in Maidstone, Kent.

Synopsis

Will Middleton lives for motor racing. More than just a sport, more than a hobby, it's his first love, his livelihood, and the centre of all his dreams. Thatcher's Britain is in meltdown, yet despite the deepening recession, Will's new team, Trans-Atlantic Racing, has just pulled off a major coup, sponsors are queuing up, nothing can go wrong now, surely.

The police raid comes out of the blue. Will is questioned under caution and charged with fraud, and finds himself in a Kafkaesque world where his guilt appears to have been decided in advance. How could a riding accident, an insurance claim, a bounced cheque and a brief moment of temptation all converge into such a nightmare? Even as his legal team fights for his acquittal, Will knows in his heart that there is a conspiracy, and the roots of it lie deep in the ancient secret society of the Masons. Trans-Atlantic becomes a distant memory as Will encounters a much darker side of life and leaves the glamorous world of motor racing far behind.

397